There's Always SOMEDAY

D1495655

HARLOE RAE

Editor: Infinite Well
Cover designer: Book Cover Kingdom
Photographer: Rafa G. Catalá
Model: Alex
Interior design: Champagne Book Design

novels by
HARLOE RAE

For my son, who is the little boy version of Tallulah.
Thank you for bringing hilarious inspiration, pure joy, and
endless love into my life.

And to all the hopeless romantics ready to
become more hopeful.

playlist

If You Love Her by Forest Blakk and Meghan Trainer

Only Love Can Hurt Like This by Paloma Faith

Lonely by Justin Bieber (with Benny Blanco)

Drunk by Elle King and Miranda Lambert

No Sad Songs by Niko Moon

Don't Give Up On Me by Andy Grammar

If The World Was Ending by JP Saxe and Julia Michaels

Earned It by The Weekend

Love On The Brain by Rhianna

Like No One Does by Jake Scott

If I Didn't Have You by Banners

I Guess I'm In Love by Clinton Kane

"Give your heart to a man worthy of the claim."
That's been his constant excuse for keeping distance between us.
Little does he know that I'm his for the taking.
If only he'd have me.

Nolan Jasper has been my broody neighbor for almost six years.
I've been hopelessly infatuated with him just as long.
The bond I have with his little girl only serves to strengthen that hold.

Since they moved in that stormy night, I've been trying to restore what was lost.
I would do just about anything for those two.
Acting as Nolan's reliable doormat is getting old, though.
Especially when he seems incapable of accepting love.

I'm finally willing to admit that man is a lost cause.
Too broken.
Jaded.
Withdrawn.

Nolan Jasper has pushed me away for the last time.
If only he realized it before I'm already gone.

There's Always
SOMEDAY

prologue

Clea

POUNDING RAIN SPLATTERS AGAINST THE WINDOW THAT I'M sitting in front of. The surface that was spotless ten minutes ago is now streaked with erratic patterns. I abandon the book in my hands when a bolt of lightning flashes across the black sky. Seconds later, a gasp escapes me as rumbling thunder rattles my bones. This storm is gaining momentum with each passing moment.

Flowing rivulets are sluicing down the glass in earnest when bright headlights cut into the darkness. A sting pierces my eyes and I squint against the glare. Our quiet street rarely gets traffic this late at night. The torrential downpour is already making me edgy. This odd appearance raises my hackles higher.

I sit forward to get a better view as a truck pulls into the driveway next door. A large trailer is hitched behind the vehicle, clueing me in to the purpose behind this unexpected presence. The 'sold' sign has been displayed for weeks, but I have yet to catch sight of the owners.

Kody strides over and peers over my shoulder. "Looks like our new neighbors have arrived."

I glance at my brother. "Pretty poor timing, huh? Jeez, to unpack in this weather would be even shittier than usual."

"Maybe we should offer them a hand."

An exhale sputters from me as I stare at the havoc being wreaked just beyond our walls. The wind is howling, blowing the rain nearly horizontal. "That would be the welcoming thing to do," I admit.

His chuckle fogs the cool glass. "Scared to get wet?"

"No," I protest. "It's just… late."

"Mom and Dad aren't around to scold you."

The reminder still makes me pause, even weeks later. "I can't believe they took off for Florida. The ink on my diploma is barely dry."

"Can you blame them?" He gestures at the sloppy disaster in our yard.

"Not at all. If only we could go with them. Instead, I'm stuck with you."

Kody grunts. "Wow, thanks for that."

I nudge him with my elbow. "No offense, big bro. It's weird to be on our own, I guess."

"You can always transfer down there."

"Oh, sure, let me apply real quick. It shouldn't be an issue that I haven't started college yet."

"That makes the switch easier."

"With only months to spare. Why didn't I think of this sooner?" Sarcasm drips from my tone. He's well aware that my ass would be down in sunny Florida if I wanted to be.

"It's never too late to change your destiny."

"Quit trying to get rid of me. I'm not leaving you alone." Despite my earlier comment, I'm perfectly content to have the house to ourselves for the foreseeable future. I just refuse to waste an opportunity to needle him a bit.

He ruffles my hair, earning a glare in return. "I appreciate the company, but quit stalling. We should go over there."

I return my gaze to the storm and the truck parked next door. Whoever's inside hasn't gotten out. "Maybe they're waiting for things to clear up."

He strides to the foyer. "Then we'll just introduce ourselves. The rain isn't letting up anytime soon."

I leave the comfort of my reading nook to search for an

umbrella. Two just happen to be hanging in the hall closet. I pass one to Kody as he hands me my raincoat. After he opens the door, we step onto the porch. The overhang gives us a delayed reprieve, allowing us to get situated. I rub my arms, preparing to get drenched regardless of my protection against the elements.

But that turns out to be unnecessary.

The rain comes to an abrupt halt just as we're about to step off the stairs. It's like I snapped my fingers to turn off the water spigot. I squint up at the dark sky, expecting another pregnant cloud to start gushing, but nothing happens. The night returns to the quiet calm of early summer.

"That's strange," I note.

My brother shrugs and tromps into the wet grass. "Meh, it was random to begin with."

An earthy punch assaults the crisp air, chasing off all traces of warm sunshine and blooming flowers. Dusk attacked with overbearing stealth this evening. It's almost as if the shadows are warning us away. No matter, though. We could follow this path blindfolded.

As we approach the line of grass separating our adjoining properties, the door of the truck pops open. The interior light reveals the silhouette of a lone man behind the wheel. He unfolds himself from the vehicle and goes to retrieve something from the backseat. When he straightens, a pink bundle is wiggling in his hold. It's not just him after all. He's cradling what I assume is a baby, mostly covered in a fuzzy blanket.

The guy moves from the vehicle's shadow and turns back around—only to gasp, startled as he sees us cutting a path toward him. "Oh, hey. I didn't notice you there."

My brother waves. "Didn't mean to sneak up on you. We just wanted to say hello."

This is probably the point where I'm expected to join in the conversation, but I'm struck speechless. The man is handsome—dare I say, gorgeous. My naïve heart takes off in a punishing sprint. The rapid rhythm sounds foolish, even to my own ears.

But those doubts can't stop this hopeless reaction from thrumming through me.

The ground quakes as I suck in a shallow breath. My lungs refuse to expand further than a quick inhale allows. For a moment, I believe the storm has found a second wind and is attempting to knock me sideways. But my feet are steady.

I attempt to clear the fog with several measured blinks. That does little to dissipate the immediate trance he's put me in. I always thought that meeting the man of my dreams would be a special occasion. An elegant gala or a fancy dinner party seems more appropriate. But here I am, standing in the mud, and it's all I can do to stop my jaw from falling open in shock and admiration.

From what I can see in the pitch black, he's extremely attractive. Strikingly so. He's tall, with a strong jawline and hair that's somehow both unruly and perfectly styled. His eyes, even in the dark, have a soulful hue. It's as if he's already seen too much and his inner spark took the brunt. I almost recoil from that haunting gleam, but I stand firm. Mama didn't raise me to shy away from the tough stuff.

A closer inspection reveals that his neutral expression is forced and brittle. His lips are drooped in a solemn frown. Creases and shadows linger around his eyes. Harsh lines across his forehead scream of strain. There's a noticeable hunch in his broad shoulders. The weight of something extremely heavy appears to be crushing him. He seems to be running on empty, seconds from collapse under some unknown pressure. The energy surrounding him is dull, with a listless quality. I can't stop myself from wondering what brought this stranger so close to being drained dry.

But none of that interferes with his appeal. If anything, he's more attractive in spite of it all.

He's young, probably early twenties if I had to guess. Thick stubble covers his square jaw. His features are sharp and sculpted. The artist hidden within me discovers a muse in this statuesque man. Rugged angles that threaten to leave a mark, either on the surface or far more permanent. Probably both. I get the impression he's complicated with countless protective layers. The image of a beautiful rose cocooned in thorns appears in my mind. That's too ridiculous and I gulp against the tickle in my throat. Laughter won't be appreciated in this instance.

Rather than getting lost in the flutters he spontaneously creates, I find myself heading straight into a bleak abyss. It's obvious that this guy is the furthest thing from emotionally available.

A tiny wail cracks into the silence. That's when I remember he's clutching a baby against his chest. I can't imagine having a child at my age, and he can't be much older than me. To further remind us of her existence, a tiny fist thrusts into the air and swats at the air blindly.

I've never felt such a powerful urge to capture the moment behind my lens. My index finger twitches with the desire to click the shot. The picture they create deserves to be displayed.

He begins to shush her while bouncing in place. "Uh, sorry. It's past her bedtime. We've been on the road for hours."

His words finally break me free from my mesmerized bubble. I start talking without conscious thought. "Oh I don't mind. Ha ha. She's adorable, by the way. Long drives can be really hard even for grown-ups." I internally scream at myself to get it together, but my mouth is moving too fast for my brain to catch up. "Hi, um, I'm Clea, we live here—not like 'we' as a couple. That would be super weird since this is my brother. We live right over there. Sorry, I already told you that. Where did you come from?"

Kody gives me an elbow to the ribs to shut me up. "What my nosy sister means to say is that we're glad to have new neighbors. This house stood vacant for too long. I'm Kody."

Fire singes my cheeks. I find myself grateful that it's dark out, or this handsome stranger would see me turning redder than a beet.

"Nolan," he offers. "It's nice to meet you both. Oh, and we're from Madison."

It's safe to assume he's referring to the city in Wisconsin. "What brings you to Minnesota? It's the lakes, right?"

Kody pins me with a glare. I almost wither into the soaking lawn. The last thing I want is to chase him away with an insulting inquisition, but Nolan squashes any concern that I've potentially overstepped. "A fresh start. That's the plan, at least."

I wait for him to say more, biting my tongue to get ahold of myself before I invade his privacy any further. When only the crickets answer, I decide it's safe to proceed. With caution, of course. "Well, you really picked a great place to live. Excellent choice."

Face meet palm. I'm beginning to sound like a welcome wagon on too much sugar and caffeine.

The harsh lines exposing his sorrow lighten just a touch when he glances at me. "I really needed to hear that ringing endorsement. It's a good thing you stopped by."

Whether he's being sarcastic or not isn't important. I'm not ashamed to admit that the hint of a smile on his face sends me reeling all over again.

"Can we help with anything?" I paste on what's meant to be an encouraging smile.

Nolan wears defeat like a familiar cloak. His glassy eyes lift to mine. The man looks close to tears. "Could you hold her for me?"

My tongue sticks to the roof of my mouth. I have zero experience with kids, but that doesn't mean I'm not intrigued by the little pink bundle snuggled against his chest. Denying him, especially in his current state, is impossible. "Umm, sure."

Nolan deposits the squirming bundle into my outstretched arms. My movements feel wooden and odd. The corner of his lips hitch, just the slightest bit, and only briefly. "You'll get the hang of it."

I nod, believing his words deep in my gut. "What's her name?"

"Tallulah." The word is choked from him. "We call her Tally for short."

I stroke a finger down her satin cheek. "She's absolutely beautiful. Aren't you, precious girl?"

"She gets that from her mother." A single tear rolls down his cheek with that broken statement. A tight knot dips in his throat as he swallows. "If only she were here to appreciate the similarities. It's just us now. Tally's mom isn't… in the picture."

The urge to ask tickles my tongue. There's clearly a story there. I'm curious enough to tug at the thread, but guilt would instantly gnaw at me. This isn't the moment to pry. For now, I'll give him the comfort of holding his little girl while he unpacks.

"I'm just going to grab a few sleeping essentials, if you don't mind keeping her occupied." He hitches a thumb toward the trailer.

A disgruntled noise squeaks past my pursed lips. "Not at all. Take your time."

"I'll help carry stuff inside." Kody's features are screwed up into a tight pinch. My brother rarely frowns, but this entire evening is dragging us into unfamiliar territory.

"Thank you." Nolan sniffs and wipes at his face. "You have no idea how much I appreciate this."

"That's what neighbors do. You'll see." I send him another comforting grin to pair with my sentiment.

He yanks at his shaggy hair. I find myself wondering if he's let the length go astray on purpose. "Yeah, okay. You might need to be careful, or I'll take advantage of that kindness."

"Oh, whatever," I scoff. "If you need me, just give a holler. I'll be right over."

His rigid posture eases at the edges. "Don't say I didn't warn you."

"I wouldn't dream of it." The reflex to wink flutters my lashes, but I hold off at the last second.

My brother nods his agreement before following Nolan behind the truck. Then it's just me and the baby. Soft coos and gurgles fill the quiet enveloping us. Good thing my mom isn't nearby to catch sight of this. It might be enough to speed up her grandmotherly instincts.

As I stand there with Tally in my arms, the fog finally lifts as clarity returns. A solid mass settles in my belly soon after. But this sinking sensation isn't laced with dread. It feels more like divine intervention. Just thinking of some magical forces at play makes me giggle. That storm must've put something goofy in the atmosphere.

Yet I can't ignore my sneaking suspicion. It would take very little effort on my part to fall for this man and his little girl. There's no doubt that I'm about to find out just how easy the tumble will be.

chapter one

Clea

A TELLTALE CREAK SIGNALS THE FRONT DOOR OPENING. WITHIN seconds, Rory and Rufus dart toward the entryway to give our guest a proper greeting, their tails whipping with unleashed excitement. My dogs only go bananas like this for a select few, giving me a decent hint of who's making an unexpected appearance.

The patter from small footsteps skips across my foyer, aiming directly at me. "Clea?"

"In the living room," I call.

Tallulah's angelic face appears around the corner moments later. The gap in her bottom teeth is on display as she smiles wide. "Hey!"

I lift my lips in a beaming grin. It's been a dull twelve hours since I last saw my pint-size neighbor. "Hi, Lulah. What's shakin' with your bacon?"

She propels herself forward with dramatic flair. Her limbs seem to go in every direction as she collapses onto the couch beside me. "I'm bored."

A laugh bubbles from me. "By all means, take a seat. It's always nice to see you, kiddo."

"I'm almost seven, you know."

"And already so full of sass."

"Dad says that's 'cause of you."

I twist my lips to one side. "He's probably right."

Her mouth droops into a frown. "My dad is too busy for me."

"Is he working?" I put my laptop aside. Tally takes that as an invitation and immediately flops into my personal space. Not that I have any, where she's concerned.

Tally nuzzles closer, plopping her head onto my thighs. "Uh-huh."

That explains her disheveled appearance. Her long hair is a blanket of tangles. Dirt smudges decorate her freckled cheeks. It's obvious she dressed herself, if the clashing colors and patterns are anything to go from. I'm pretty sure her shirt is a swimsuit. This kid is resourceful, not to mention resilient.

I stroke a palm down her arm. A sticky residue clings to her skin in several places. Is that gum, or pure sugar? Not that it matters. She's a mess. An adorable one, without a single doubt, but a germaphobe's worst nightmare all the same.

"Did you ask him to hang out?"

Her huff is forceful enough to give me a whiff of her breath. Someone forgot to brush this morning. "I tried talking to him, but he didn't listen. He just did that stupid grunting noise and waved me away."

My stomach sinks with a load I'm all too familiar with. We've been having similar versions of this conversation ever since Tally could speak in full sentences. That's going on four years at this point. I'm still holding out hope that Nolan pulls out of this rut and becomes more present. So far, no luck.

I frequently reflect on how much my life changed the instant Nolan and Tally crashed into it. I met this little girl when she was only nine months old—so tiny and fragile. Since then, I've done everything in my power to become a strong female role model for her.

The truth of what happened to her mother remains a mystery. That's not really surprising, considering Nolan is anything but forthcoming. All I'm certain of is that she died, and rather tragically, based on his extreme reactions to certain situations.

I've never pushed for more details than he's willing to give. The story is his to tell, and he will if we're ever going to become more than this. But Nolan hasn't been ready, or willing, to cross that line.

Six years is a long damn time to be infatuated with someone who doesn't reciprocate. The itch is becoming more insistent. I'm usually more than capable of avoiding messy predicaments. He just happens to be my weakness. I'll have to make a decision soon. That thought brings a chill and I almost shiver. Not today. For now, I'm more than content to be in this cutie pie's presence.

I boop her nose. "I'll talk to him, okay?"

Tally's gaze skitters off me. "You don't have to."

A protective quake erupts in my veins. "I want to. He needs to do better."

Her slim shoulders rise and fall with a defeated exhale. "Why doesn't he then?"

The ache in my chest threatens to crack bone. That's an impossible question for me to answer. Nolan is trapped in his jaded misery more often than not. Regardless of my attempts to prove otherwise, that man has some vendetta against himself. For what or why, I'm still not sure. It's obvious the suffering stems from whatever happened to Tally's mother. If only he'd trust me enough to confide in.

"Your dad has a very important job. He has to concentrate really hard on all those numbers or something will get screwed up," I attempt. The lie tastes bitter on my tongue.

Based on the sour expression Tally shoots me, it isn't fooling her. "He just works on computer stuff. It's not rocket science."

It might as well be, for all I know about it. Nolan is a tech genius with some fancy gig that pays him the big bucks—and with that generous compensation comes too much responsibility. He's used that over the years as a convenient crutch to submerge himself in work. For all his brains, he fails to realize that fatherhood should always come first.

"Didn't he just get assigned to a new project? The deadline

is soon. Then he will have more free time." Why I'm bothering to defend him is beyond me.

"He'll just start another one. It never changes," Tally replies bitterly. Her doubt isn't misplaced, and my heart breaks for her. She's far too young to already lose faith in men. The fact that her dad is the reason for this lack of trust makes it so much worse.

"It'll be different soon. I promise, okay?" One way or another, something has to break. This horrible habit of his can't continue.

"He cares more about his job than me." Her bottom lip trembles.

"That's not true, Lulah." I haul her in for a tight hug. "You mean everything to him. He loves you so much."

"It doesn't feel that way." Her soft murmur wobbles with emotion.

My nose burns as I blink the heat from my eyes and fight the overwhelming urge to stomp next door this instant. Nolan is due for a solid scolding if he's ignoring Tally more than usual. My knees jerk in preparation, but I remain glued to the sofa. Interfering when he's in the zone won't accomplish anything major. That doesn't mean I'll quit trying. He can wait, though. This moment is about Tally.

I begin picking at one of the larger snarls in her hair. "Well, guess what?"

She winces and bats my hand away. "Chicken butt."

"Clever girl," I laugh. "You're in luck. I started work extra early today, which means I'm already done."

Her gasp ricochets between us. "Really?"

"Yep. I'm already done, so we can have all the fun."

"Hey, that rhymes." Her giggle is the ultimate mood booster.

"Good catch. You're so smart."

"And you're the bestest." She loops her arms around me, resting her face against my torso.

My heart squeezes at her easy affection. Nolan is such an idiot. "Whatever you want to do. Just name it."

"Can we play Barbies? Have a modeling shoot? Will you take me to the park? Or the swimming pool? Oh, oh! How about a walk with the dogs?" She wriggles excitedly, scooting closer to the edge of the cushion with each suggestion.

"All of those are great ideas." I tap my lips, pausing for dramatic effect. "But I think a bath comes first."

I keep a bag of her belongings in the spare bedroom for occasions precisely like these. I learned that lesson the hard way. Spare clothes are a necessity when it comes to kids.

Her green eyes sparkle. "In your big tub with extra bubbles?"

I scoff. "As if there's another choice."

"Yippeeee!" Tally bounces off the couch, her butt landing on the carpet with a muted thud. The collision does little to slow her down, though. She's on her feet and zipping toward the stairs before I can blink. "Race you to the bathroom!"

"That's not fair, Lulah! You cheated!" I laugh.

A peal of laughter from the landing confirms she's extending her lead. "Like you could beat me anyway."

There's no argument from me. I heft myself off the couch with slightly less enthusiasm. "You'll always win with me, kiddo. No matter what."

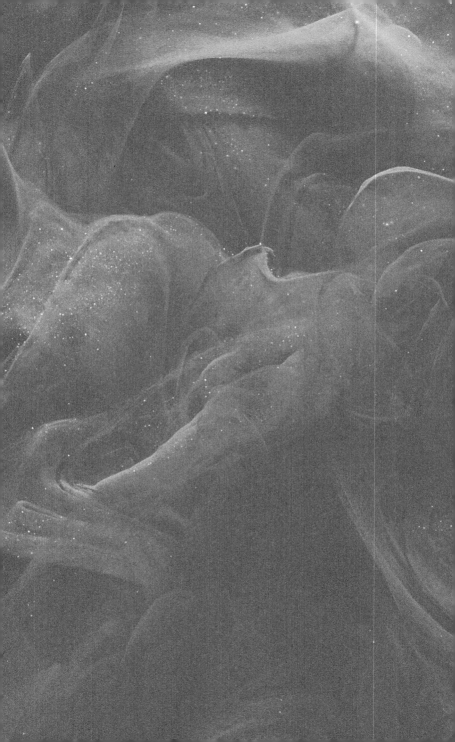

chapter two

Nolan

M Y FIRST WARNING IS HER DETERMINED STOMP ACROSS THE floorboards above me. Dust particles float from the ceiling with her sure stride. Her tread is confident and quick, without any attempt to remain undetected. Clea wants her presence announced loud and clear. Message received.

Next comes the groan from the wooden stairs as she makes her descent into my den. I drag in a deep breath and slam my eyes shut, preparing myself to resist mauling her like the savage beast these baser desires turn me into. My pulse is already spiking. These demands are becoming more insistent. I often wonder what will happen when my restraint finally snaps.

I try not to reveal my inner turmoil from her close proximity. My feelings must remain on a tight leash, or I risk ruining the somewhat comfortable balance we have. I can't afford that. Tally would be devastated without her.

In truth, Clea Montague is my obsession. She's fantasy, possibility, and reality blended into one alluring bundle. Six years is a long damn time to stew in my feverish lust. Just knowing she's close gets me hard.

She approaches my desk, demanding to be acknowledged as she taps her shoe on the concrete floor. This woman means business. "Are you serious right now?"

The jig is up. I can no longer avoid her, not when she's standing only a few feet from me. I lift my gaze and regret immediately slams into me. My mouth goes dry at the sight of her. I cough to cover the reaction. "Hello, Patra."

Clea scoffs, crossing her arms in a defensive pose. "Don't you 'Patra' me. Cutesy nicknames won't get you out of this one."

"No? It seems to do the trick well enough." Once I made the mistake of comparing her with Cleopatra, I couldn't undo it. Now she's stuck with the reminder. But that's a nonissue right now.

She shakes her head. "Not anymore. What's so urgent that you can't pay attention to Tally?"

"Not sure what you mean." The lie is blatant enough to be a neon sign hanging over my head. I'm damn good at developing security software. Being a father? Not so much.

"Don't play this game. I don't have the patience for this."

I glance at my watch, squinting at the bright display. "Why are you here so late? Shouldn't you be in bed?"

She parks a hand on one of her seductive hips. "It's barely ten o'clock on a Friday night. I'm going out with my friends."

That comment derails my thoughts and I sputter. Then I take notice of her outfit. Her brown hair is styled in sleek curls that cascade over her shoulders. She's wearing a skirt short enough to stop traffic. The neckline of her glittery shirt shows off way too much cleavage. I can't even look at her high heels without picturing them thrust into the air over my shoulders. Heat rushes to my cock once the image enters my mind. The last thing I need to do right now is pop wood.

She's bound to meet someone—and looking like that, she will. I curl my hands into fists. Dammit, I want her as mine. Call me a selfish prick and I'll agree.

"Where are you going?"

She quirks a knowing brow. "To a bar."

"Don't be coy with me, Clea."

Her eyes roll skyward. "Oh, that's real rich coming from you. And my evening plans are beside the point."

I stroke my jaw, which reminds me that my overgrown stubble is due for a trim. "And what is the point of this intrusion?"

She thrusts an arm out to the side in frustration. "Tally needs you!"

I stumble to my feet, sending the chair toppling behind me. "Is she hurt? Sick?"

"Neglected," Clea corrects.

I drop my head with a slow shake. "Not this again."

"There's such a thing as emotional neglect."

"Thanks for the psychology lesson. That one course in college must've been top-notch."

Clea clacks her teeth, likely imagining biting my head off. "You're not an asshole, so don't act like one."

"Fuck." I drag a hand through my hair. I never meant to disrespect her. "You're right, and I'm sorry. That was uncalled for."

"It's all right." Her hand rests on my shoulder, offering a gentle squeeze.

It takes all my strength not to groan and shudder from the sheer pleasure rushing through my veins. This woman doesn't touch me nearly often enough. It isn't helpful that I'm starved of human contact in general.

My sanity is constantly in question when it comes to Clea. She pushes me beyond feasible reason. There's no telling where the line is—or if one even exists anymore. I've lost my good sense. Hell, that's been gone long enough I can't recall what it's like to be logical. All I want is to claim her the old-fashioned way, which I highly doubt would be well received.

She's unaware that I'm struggling to compose myself. Her palm remains rooted in place, burning into me with branding force. "I don't mind helping with Tally, Nolan. You know that I'll always be here for her. There should be limits, though. Some days, I feel like the word 'doormat' should be stamped across my forehead."

Pressure clamps around my throat until I'm gasping for breath. "Shit, Patra. That's the last thing I want you to feel. I warned you that I'd take advantage. You always step in to help—"

"This is more than that," she cuts me off. "I'm not helping—I'm doing it practically by myself. You're not present at all. Snap out of it, Nolan. That little girl needs you."

Clea has every reason to scold me like the ignorant fool I am. I've been more withdrawn than ever since she graduated from college and moved home last spring, and I've only succeeded in driving a larger wedge between us over the last eighteen months. Tally starting kindergarten last fall certainly didn't improve matters.

Working with computers is easy. It's almost more natural than breathing at this point. I've allowed the simple tasks to take precedence, ignoring the more challenging parts of my life. I've been a coward, content to shuffle off my responsibilities to others instead of shouldering the weight that's mine to carry.

The edge of my vision turns dark. I fear the worst is approaching—Clea is finally reaching her breaking point.

"Do you resent me?" I ask. I'm not sure what I'll do if she confirms my suspicions.

After fleeing Madison in a desperate attempt to start over, this woman has been a short call away with reassuring words and open arms. The latter she reserves mostly for Tally, but that's my fault.

"No." Clea shuffles backward, her fingers ghosting along my sleeve before dropping away entirely. "Not yet, at least."

I miss her touch immediately. A visceral pain slashes across my abdomen at the loss. "But I'm leaning on you too hard."

She nods, giving me the confirmation I already feel in my gut. "Are you aware that Tally snuck over to my house thirty minutes ago because she had a nightmare? She chose to wander next door rather than come downstairs to you."

I flinch at her implication. "That's not surprising. You provide nurturing comfort."

"But you're her father. She's practically screaming for your attention. Did you see her outfit today?"

I'm ashamed to admit the truth. The sour churning in my gut says it all. "I've been busier than normal with work."

"What else is new," she mutters.

"This project is stressful, and my fuse is shorter because of it. I figured that keeping myself more isolated would be best for everyone."

She sighs. "I understand that you have an important job, but Tally should be your first priority."

"She is. Always." The conviction in my voice falls flat. I'm well aware that I'm failing my daughter—and the woman in front of me.

"Then prove it, Nolan. Even free-range parenting has limits."

I furrow my brow. She's not speaking a language I'm fluent in. That's further proof of my shortcomings. "You're right. Again. I'll fix this, just tell me what to do."

Clea tucks some dark hair behind her ear. "Be a parent."

"I am." The defensive edge clangs from my tone. I'll never win father of the year, but I'm not completely incompetent.

"Do better."

"I've gotten better." Or Tally has become more capable. She's six, going on seventeen.

"Barely. She's at my place more than anywhere."

"Are you complaining about that? I thought you liked having her around."

A knob in her throat wobbles with her thick swallow. "I do. That's not what this is about."

"Then what's the problem?"

She averts her gaze. "You're never around. It would be great if this were more of a team effort."

That's a loaded statement if I've ever heard one. It's eerie how often our minds sync. My gut clenches at the impact. That's part of the pipe dream.

Clea used to look at me with interest and desire—but lately, that desire has given way to glaring disappointment.

"I don't know how to raise a little girl." The flimsy reasoning falls on deaf ears, mine included.

"And you think I do?"

"Without a doubt. You're a natural, Clea. Tally has been drawn to you from the beginning." Their effortless bond made it that much easier for me to fade into the background. I curse under my breath. There I go again, finding another escape from feeling guilty.

I realize belatedly that Clea has been quiet too long. She's staring at me with a glassy sheen reflecting in her gaze. "But that responsibility isn't mine. She's not mine, Nolan."

I jolt at her words. She could be. I want her to officially be tied to Tally and me. But that's not possible. Continuing down this path will only lead to disappointment.

My posture deflates faster than a leaky balloon. "No, you're not."

"You can talk to me," she offers.

She's referring to the secrets I keep hidden about Tally's mother. "You don't understand."

A shallow scoff streams from her. "Whose fault is that? You don't tell me anything unless it involves Tally. I know your security codes. I have a key to your house. But I don't know what haunts your dreams. Why you get spooked whenever anyone gets close enough to pry. I can tell there's a hollow gleam in your eyes, but I have no clue what put it there."

"I'm not ready." It's a pitiful excuse I've been regurgitating more often than not lately.

Clea's blue eyes bore into mine like open waters beckoning me into the tide with gentle waves. I'm so damn close to drowning in her. "Well, I'm ready to listen, if you'd give me a chance."

"I can't. Yet," I tack on as a compromise. "I just need to finish this job and things will get better."

Her exhale is heavy. That sound reveals her waning faith in me. It's worse than a knife to the heart, yet I do nothing to mend what's tattering. Quite the opposite. "That's what you always say."

"I mean it this time." There's a formidable force bearing down on me. A warning I should heed. If I let Tally—and Clea—down again, I might not ever earn their forgiveness, nor deserve it.

"All right." She points an unwavering finger at me. "I'm holding you to it."

"I hope you do." The distance between us is slight, but those mere feet might as well be miles. A sharp longing pierces me. *What would it feel like to hold her in my arms for more than a friendly hug?*

The fight vanishes from her rigid stance and she slumps against the wall. She loops a finger around a glossy curl by her temple, staring off at an unseen point. "I never thought I'd be a nag, especially at the ripe age of twenty-four."

"You're not." I'm three years older, yet she's far wiser.

Clea flicks her gaze to me. "I certainly feel like it. We've had this conversation so many times."

"One more reason for me to apologize." Our connection has never felt so strained. I need to fix this before it's too late.

"I've had enough apologies from you. Actions would be better. What can I do to drag you from the shadows?" She gestures at the dark corners and dim lighting.

"Nothing." My tone is wooden. "I've been working too much. That's going to stop."

"That little girl needs you."

"I know, Patra."

"Do you?"

"Of course." A plan is already solidifying in my mind.

"Okay, good. I'll leave you to it." She sighs and turns away from me. Before reaching the stairs, she peeks at me over her shoulder. "I refuse to let you be a deadbeat. Just do better. For Tally. She deserves at least that much."

Then she disappears from sight.

The urge to chase her is a primal drive. A staccato beat drums in my ears, demanding to be heard.

I don't want her to go. I never do.

But I let her walk out all the same.

chapter three

Clea

Vannah's hand smacks the table between us. "All right, listen."

I purse my lips at the snarky redhead sitting across from me. "Are you about to call me Linda?"

"Very funny," she deadpans with a roll of her eyes, sarcasm grating from her tone. "Enough of the gloom and doom, Clea. We're here to have fun. Just spit it out so we can offer advice and solve this problem."

"It's not that simple." I shift my gaze off hers, focusing on the bartender who's juggling three liquor bottles to entertain a very captivated audience. The three girls are practically drooling into their beers.

Vannah's growl yanks my attention back to her. "Fucking Nolan. I should've known he was responsible. What did he do now?"

I stare at my best friend, reminded of a similar conversation we had not long ago. She was in the hot seat then. The tables sure turn at a rapid rate.

My other two besties sit on standby. Audria is leaning forward in her seat, ready to pounce on the latest gossip. Not that I blame her. She's been holed up in Tiny Town, Iowa for two years. A disappointed scoff—aimed solely at myself—escapes me. I can admit that my bitter attitude is fueled by envy. Bampton Valley is rather lovely, and so is her husband.

Meanwhile, Presley is all smiles while she happily listens

to us bicker. The woman shits rainbows on the worst days. If I had her optimistic outlook, my situation with Nolan would be an entirely different story.

The four of us don't get together nearly as often since graduation. That's why we're parked in a rickety booth at The Library. This place was our stomping ground in college. Just sitting on this unforgiving wooden seat is a comforting balm against our adulthood woes, welcoming us into a soothing embrace with open arms. Yet somehow, I'm still managing to ruin our evening by being a downer.

Fuck Nolan indeed.

I shove the toxic vibes away with a silent curse. It's only been thirty minutes. The night is far from over.

The scent of buttery popcorn, loose inhibitions, and nostalgia wafts through the air. I inhale a big whiff, letting the memories wash over me. After studying for hours, we'd hole up here to take a load off. Whether it was playing pool or shaking our butts on the dance floor, this bar always came through for us. An image of Tally and Nolan twirling around their living room sweeps into my mind. I can almost hear the nonstop giggles as he lifts her high while spinning extra fast, making them dizzy enough to crash on the floor. He used to be more involved, the way a parent should be. That changed once I moved home. Maybe I should've stayed gone, only visiting on weekends.

"And we've lost her again."

I shake off the memory at Presley's whimsical voice. Dammit. That man always manages to wiggle into my thoughts, especially when he doesn't belong.

Vannah takes a long sip from her drink. "My worse half is stuck in Chicago. Distract me so I don't call him like the whipped wife he's turning me into. I can't cave, Clea. Perk this party up."

I cock my head at her. "Isn't it better half?"

Her entire body shakes with a throaty laugh. "Not in our case."

"Humble as always," I mutter.

Vannah sobers, all traces of humor evaporating into the stale air. "Okay, quit. I'm trying to be ridiculous and hilarious, but even that is falling flat with you. Spill your troubles, lady. I want to hear all the word vomit."

Presley and Audria nod in agreement. The secretive glance they share isn't getting past anyone, least of all me. They're probably thinking I'm a lost cause. I wouldn't be hard-pressed to agree.

"Get the negativity out of your system so we can move on to something way more entertaining."

"And what's that?" I raise an eyebrow.

"Matchmaking." Audria hitches a thumb at Presley.

"Sounds like a great plan to me. I'm kid-free and want to take advantage. My honey pot hasn't been properly dipped into since I got knocked up." Presley makes fake binoculars out of her hands and scours our surroundings.

"Um, hello? I'm single too." Is my tone a tad petulant? Maybe. After my earlier conversation with Nolan, I'm allowed some leeway.

Vannah snorts into her cocktail. "No, you most certainly are not."

Well, that's news to me. "Do I have a mystery boyfriend that even I don't know about?"

"Oh, please. You're attached without being officially off the market."

"She's right, Clea. That broody single dad has owned your ass since he moved in next door. Don't pretend." Audria shrugs in what appears to be a half-hearted apology.

"Nolan doesn't have a hold on me." Is it hot in here? Suddenly my pants feel like fire. I fan my face, which only spreads the sting across my cheeks.

"Yeah, and Audria doesn't love to deliver glitter bombs." Vannah tilts her chin at a haughty angle.

"I actually have some." She begins digging in her purse.

"That's not necessary." I huff hard enough to send hair flying off my sticky forehead.

"Neither is you denying the truth." Audria's quiet pitch hammers against my skull.

Presley abandons her man hunt. "We're not accomplishing anything."

I laugh when she reveals a pout that rivals the one Tally uses to get ice cream. "Is that a problem?"

Her midnight tresses gleam navy under the overhead lights. "Yes. We'll never get out of this slump if we keep digging a deeper hole. Let's get back on track so we can check 'Bashing Nolan' off our list."

A sour taste hits the back of my throat. "I don't want to bash him."

Vannah smacks her lips. "Don't lie. You're allowed to be honest and vent. That's what we're here for."

There's no stopping my frown. "What about drowning our sorrows and having fun?"

Presley places a delicate hand on my shoulder. "You're not ready for that yet, which means we need to address this."

Vannah winks at her, then pins me with an unflinching stare. "I know lately these outings have turned into pity parties. We need an uplifting boost. When was the last time you went on a date? Admit it, Nolan's got you wrapped around his finger."

"Asshole," I grumble.

"It's okay to be hooked on a guy. I just wish he treated you better." Audria's calm teacher tone has little impact on the ache spearing my chest.

I trace a water ring on the table, avoiding their burning gazes. "I'm feeling very ganged-up on."

Vannah inspects her French manicure. "Not so fun when you're the one in the spotlight, huh?"

"We've been there." Audria motions between her and Vannah.

Presley flutters a palm to her chest. "And I've been busy raising a human. The hot seat will find my rump soon enough."

I crumble under the pressure, hunching low in my seat. "Am I stupid for still pining after him?"

"Not stupid. Too forgiving and gullible would be more accurate," says Vannah—and then promptly yelps when Audria elbows her in the ribs.

"What she means is that you care about him. We all know too well that love makes us do very foolish things."

"Such as provide him free daycare. That shit is expensive, let me tell you. He owes you thousands in retro pay." Presley rubs her fingers together, signaling all the cash money.

Her comment only serves to remind me of that pint-sized princess. "It's not just about Nolan. I have to think about Tally too."

"That little girl is the cutest," Presley agrees.

"She needs me. I can't leave her," I argue.

Vannah covers my hand with hers. "No one said you have to, babe. You can still be there for her while finding a man who's capable of appreciating you. How else is he going to learn, Clea? You've been his reliable safety net."

She's right. That doesn't make the truth any easier to gulp down. "It's my fault too. I allowed this to happen."

"But Mr. Sad Eyes didn't have to take advantage of your kindness."

"Or your crush on him," Audria adds.

I toss some popcorn in my mouth. The loud crunch is barely audible over the crowd's growing volume. "I made it easy for him."

Vannah points at me. "Quit giving him excuses. That guy is too much trouble. What do you even see in him?"

My smile is automatic, even when I try to tug it down. "Is it cliché if I say everything?"

"Extremely," she retorts.

"I can't help it. He caught me from those first moments. His soulful gaze spoke to me."

Presley's sigh is full of whimsy. "Wow, I want that."

My nose stings and I sniff at the emotional threat. "I don't have him. It's been six years with little to show other than my unrequited feelings. That's pathetic."

They're silent for several beats. I use the reprieve to reinforce my defenses. Vannah is the one to speak up, gesturing to my empty glass. "You're going to need something a lot stronger than shandy to get over him."

I never had the chance to be under him either. Sadly, I no longer possess the faith to believe there's another alternative.

Earlier, while driving to The Library, I made the decision that my situation with Nolan needed to change. My infatuation with him has only brought me pain. The sharp twinge cramping my stomach is the latest ailment. I blow out a slow exhale, trying to ease the discomfort. Sticking to my resolve will be the biggest challenge.

"It's gonna be a bumpy road. He just promised to do better with Tally. I'll be less involved now." I'm proud of keeping my voice level.

Presley twists in the booth to face me. "Do you believe him?"

"Sure," I say, when in reality I'm the furthest thing from that. In his defense, Nolan hasn't broken a promise. Just about every other type of commitment, though.

"And what happens if he doesn't change?"

A strobe lamp from the dancefloor flashes in my eyes. It gives me an excuse to avert my gaze. "I don't want to think about that."

Audria fiddles with the popcorn bowl. "What do you want to think about?"

"How many girls that bartender is bringing home."

They all look to where I'm pointing. The man in question is twirling two bottles in one hand while intermittently pouring booze in an awaiting mouth. He looks like a papa bird offering worms to his babies.

"All of them." Presley sighs. "Is it bad that I'm almost desperate enough to join the fray?"

We stare at her with matching expressions of shock. My eyes feel ready to pop from their sockets. Audria chokes on the kernel. Vannah, of course, is wearing a smug grin.

"Go get him, mama. The riffraff will run off once you enter the arena."

The raven-haired beauty seems to contemplate it, tapping her chin to a rhythmic beat. "I prefer to be chased, not the other way around."

That gives me pause. Maybe I've been doing this wrong. My dry spell is proof enough—not that I can really consider it as one to begin with. I can't miss something I've never had.

A curl twitches my upper lip. Talk about cringe-worthy. My friends are right. I've allowed my feelings for Nolan to trap me.

It's about damn time I take the hint. I've been saving myself for a man who doesn't really want me.

chapter four

Nolan

SUNLIGHT STREAKS ACROSS MY VISION THROUGH THE OPEN curtains. The rays paint a shimmering reflection on the beige carpet as I cross into the hallway. I feel like my mind is awake, but it's taking my body a while to catch up. My legs feel leaden and packed with concrete. There's a noticeable twinge in my muscles whenever I move, and the churning in my gut won't quit. I'm exhausted and weary, but struck with a healthy dose of motivation.

The conversation I had with Clea last night has been playing on repeat. Visions of Tally being taken from me plagued my dreams, making me toss and turn for hours without reprieve. That possibility is too real. But I deserve far worse for slacking on my most vital role. It's a disgraceful offense, one I plan to correct immediately.

Tallulah is bouncing on her bed when I enter the room. Sleep-rumpled or not, she's already running at full speed. "Hi, Daddy!"

"Rise and shine, fun fans! It's a great morning to be good," I announce brightly in my best over-the-top gameshow host impression.

"You're silly." Her giggle is stronger than a double shot of espresso. "Watch how high I can go."

The mattress squeaks in protest when she doubles her efforts. A smile automatically stretches my lips at her overflowing exuberance, regardless of the early hour. If only adults still had access to that bottomless energy. "You belong in the Olympics, Little Lou."

Her tumbling routine comes to a grinding halt. Tally's glare is fierce enough to make my steps falter. "I'm not little anymore."

I frown at the sudden change in her demeanor. "Yes, you are."

She slams a fist on her hip, giving me a terrifying preview into the teenage years. "Am not!"

I hold up my palms in surrender. The last thing I want to kick off my parenting renovation is to get in a battle I'll never win. "All right, fine. You're a big girl. Little Lou is just your nickname."

Now she stomps her foot. The sound is minimal, but her meaning is deafening. "But I don't like that."

A painful pinch attacks my chest. I should've known she no longer liked to be little. "Since when? I've been calling you my Little Lou for years."

"Clea told me I'm a young lady. That's way cooler than being little."

"But..." I let that word dangle while trying to decide how to proceed.

There's no denying that Clea has a better understanding of my daughter's current preferences. She's been playing a more primary role for over a year, while I've faded into the shadows. At this point, I might as well be trapped in the dark. That doesn't make the bitter pill of betrayal any easier to choke down. But the only traitor is me. I'm well aware that all fault rests heavily on my shoulders.

That doesn't change the fact that she's already growing up too fast.

I clear the grit from my throat. "How about Lou? Is that okay still?"

Tally scrunches her face while mulling that over. "Yep, that'll do."

"Do you still like pink?"

"Uhm, duh. It's only my favorite color." She points to her jammies.

"I see the sassy attitude is getting stronger," I grin, feeling relief that not all has been lost. "How about milkshakes with extra sprinkles?"

"Don't forget the whipped cream and cherries."

"Glad that's settled." I almost wipe my brow.

She drops on her butt, rolls to the edge of the bed, dismounts, and sticks a landing in one seemingly smooth motion. A standing ovation from her adoring audience, complete with whistles and cheers, shortly follows. She bows while waving her arms. I make a mental note to search for gymnastics classes.

Tally twirls over to where I remain rooted in place. "Is Clea coming over? Or am I going to her house?"

"We're spending the day together," I correct her with a grin.

"With Clea?"

I tap her nose. "No Clea. Just you and me."

Her jaw goes slack as she stares at me. "Huh?"

There's no stopping the wide smile from stretching my lips at the sound of her disbelief. "We have a lot of catching up to do."

"Like buying a pony?" Tally hops up and down while crossing her fingers.

That's rather extreme. "Not quite."

"Oh." The excitement flees her flailing limbs. "But I really want a pony."

I scratch my head while digging for a compromise. "How about a stuffed one? Extra big and fluffy."

Her spirits brighten with a squeal. "Yay! What else are we gonna do?"

"Let's start by getting dressed." I stride to her closet and swing open the door. Every single hanger is empty. The drawers in her dresser suffer the same fate. "Where are your clothes, Litt—uh, Lou?"

My daughter—pouting about my little slip—points to her

hamper that's overflowing with dirty laundry. "I don't know how to wash them."

My lungs seize and breathing becomes a chore. The choppy exhale I manage to release does little to extinguish the searing guilt threatening to incinerate me. It's not even eight o'clock in the morning and shame has stabbed me no less than a dozen times. "You shouldn't have to, baby girl. That's my job."

A disgruntled huff explodes into the silence. "I'm not a baby, Dad."

I hang my head. "Right. Of course not. How about a princess?"

She rolls her eyes. "Duh, always."

This shouldn't be such a challenge. It's been nearly seven years, taking care of her should be second nature by now. I wouldn't feel the need to curse myself at every turn had I just done my fatherly duties as expected. But no, I chose to disconnect for no reason other than selfish insecurities. I deserve the sharp agony ripping at my skin. If I had been paying attention rather than hiding in the basement for months, none of this would be happening.

Good Christ, I'm a fool. I've let my daughter grow without me. Precious moments have been wasted, forfeited for no reason other than cowardice. Those are memories I'll never be privy to, or have the chance to earn. All I can do is make sure this distance never gets shoved between us again.

"Do you need a hug?" Her soft voice breaks apart the putrid fog I'm trapped in.

"I really do, Lou." Then I kneel and open my arms.

There's no hesitation from her. She flings herself at me with an easy comfort as if none of my blatant neglect fazed her one bit. Summer flowers, warm laughter, and soothing memories envelop me. I'll never forgive myself for ignoring the one person who depends on me. Blistering heat attacks my eyes and I blink at the pooling moisture. Tally is my daughter, and I'm failing her.

That losing streak ends now.

I pry us apart with a sigh, sitting back on my heels. A fresh wave of emotion cascades over me as her green eyes sear into mine with unwavering devotion. In truth, I don't deserve her unconditional love. But she's given it to me anyway. Now I have to dedicate my life to the process of earning it.

I brush a thumb along her cheek. "I'm really sorry, Lou."

She tips her head to the side. "For what?"

I puff my cheeks with the endless wrongs I've committed. "Everything. Not being around lately."

"But you're gonna fix that, right?"

"Right." I give a nod for additional conviction.

She mirrors my affirmation. "We can do everything together again. Just like before you got really sad."

"You're too forgiving." Just like her mother. Except at the end. I wince at that, running from the ominous storm those memories brew.

"Clea told me that being mad at people isn't good for you. Unless the person does something super bad. She called it... holding a gudge?"

I chuckle at her mispronounced word. "A grudge. She's very wise," I reply.

Our neighbor is also too forgiving—and I can't leave out patient, kind, compassionate... beautiful. That genuine personality is what makes her too damn endearing and irresistible.

"She's really fun, too," Tally adds. It's a blessing that she's taken to Clea so much. Truly, I don't know what I'd do without her.

"What do you say, kiddo? Have I earned another chance to be the best dad ever?"

"Yeah!"

"You won't regret it." I clutch the space over my heart in a solemn vow.

"Nope, never." Her smile shows off three missing teeth, reminding me of the nights I almost forgot to be the Tooth Fairy. Clea saved my ass in that regard too.

"All right, let's get rolling." I stand and grab an armful of assorted colors to bring downstairs. "Go potty and brush your teeth while I dump this in the washer. Then we can eat."

"I need help with my hair." She lifts a matted clump near her scalp.

"How'd that happen?"

A tiny shoulder lifts. "I dunno. Clea says I must be a wild sleeper."

One more thing I missed in my absence. "No problem, Princess Lou. I'll be back in sixty seconds to handle that mess."

"I'm gonna time you." She sings the threat, which makes it far less intimidating.

I do a quick stretching lunge for optimal presentation. "The pressure is on."

"Go!" Her giggle chases me as I descend the stairs at maximum speed.

Tally is sitting on the closed toilet seat when I walk into the bathroom less than a minute later. Not that I was counting or anything. My labored breathing speaks for itself. "How'd I do?"

"Fifty-three." She passes me a fancy comb and tips forward to give me better access.

I punch the air. "It's a new record."

Her eyes sparkle with humor. "Too simple. That was just a warm-up. You need to get my tangles out."

"Challenge accepted." With the finesse of King Kong, I begin attacking the largest patch.

"Ouch." She yanks her head away. "That hurts."

I wince on her behalf. "I'm sorry, Litt—uh, Lou. Your hair is really snarled."

She points to a bottle on the counter. "Clea bought that for me. It gets rid of tangles."

Sounds too promising to be true, but what the hell do I know. I grab the spray and squirt on a generous amount. The comb skates through her knots without a hitch. "Talk about a miracle cure."

Tally relaxes against the counter. "Clea is so smart. Isn't she pretty, Daddy?"

That's a trap I won't be able to talk my way out of. Instead, I glance at our reflections in the mirror. My hair is unruly and overgrown. One more thing I've been neglecting. "Maybe we should cut our—"

"No way, Dad!" With a pitchy shriek, she dodges out of my reach. Then she cradles her long tresses like they are priceless treasures. "I want to be Rapunzel. She never cuts her hair. Not until the end, but she didn't really have a choice. Eugene did it. He loves her. *Tangled* is so romantic. We should totally watch it tonight. Maybe Clea can snuggle on the couch with us. I'll even share my popcorn."

My daughter's rambling makes me smile. The pressure in my chest eases ever so slightly. "Okay, got it. No trim for you. Movie later. How about food now?"

On cue, her stomach lets out a loud grumble. "Yes, please."

With a forward sweep toward the hall, I set us off to do the next task. "I'm making your favorite for breakfast, with extra bananas in the pancakes."

She follows me into the kitchen, wearing a sour expression. "Ewwww, gross. I don't like those anymore."

I let my mouth pop open. "Since when?"

Tally shuffles her foot across the tile floor. "I dunno? A super long time."

It takes great effort not to let my disappointment show. We used to bond over flipping flapjacks on the skillet. "Okay, Princess Lou. What do you like to eat?"

"Skittles."

I scoff. "Not for breakfast. Nice try, though."

Tally sticks out her bottom lip. "Ugh, you're no fun."

"I care about your health. And teeth. How about waffles? Or… toast?"

"Lame." Then her eyes brighten. "Can we have cinnamon rolls like Clea makes?"

"Sure. Do we have a roll of them?" I open the fridge and begin searching for a blue canister.

She pokes her head in beside me. "Huh?"

"You know, like the tube you pop open." I make gestures with my hands—explosion and all.

All I get in return is a bland stare. "Clea always puts together a bunch of ingredients. I help her stir everything in the mixer thingy."

I rest a palm on my clammy forehead. "She makes them from scratch?"

Tally squints at me. "Uh, yeah?"

Is there anything that woman can't do? It's official. I'm competing with Mary freaking Poppins. But no, Clea is the furthest thing from my adversary.

"I don't have the recipe." Not that it would be hard to find one. But master chef I am not. Pancakes are above my expertise as it is.

"We could ask Clea." She scoots in the direction of our front door.

The entire point is to avoid asking for her help. I crack my knuckles and begin digging out supplies. "Nope, I got this."

Fifty minutes pass, proving the opposite. The monstrosities meant to be our breakfast resemble sugary blobs, even after several attempts at fine-tuning the mixture. I increased the temperature and let them rest in the oven. Nothing.

My pride takes another hit as I scan the room. Our kitchen looks like a bakery exploded. Flour and batter cling to most surfaces. Dirty dishes clutter the rest. It's a shock that icing isn't dripping from the ceiling. This is a total disaster.

"I'll just have cereal." My daughter slumps her shoulders and trudges to the messy table.

My own stance takes a hit as I stoop under the weight of yet another failure. I pour two heaping portions and slide one over to her. "I'm sorry the cinnamon rolls didn't turn out."

Tally swirls the fruity flakes with her spoon. "It's okay. Why couldn't we call Clea? She would've known what to do."

There's little doubt she would have. This is my ultimate reality check—in big, bold letters. I'm fucking up at every turn, but I can't constantly rely on Clea to save the day. She's already swooped in and fixed too many of my problems. "We shouldn't bother her so much."

"Why not?"

"She has other stuff to worry about. This is about you and me. We should be able to handle any problem on our own. I'll be the one you come to for everything again. There's no reason for us to involve Clea."

Her eyes track my finger as I motion between us. "But she's part of our family."

I choke on my recent bite. After dabbing the milk splatter from my mouth, I paste on a grin. "Not really, Lou. She's our neighbor and friend. That's it."

She peeks up at me from under a curtain of golden locks. "What if she wants to be my mom?"

Another tortured wheeze rattles from me. The scar tissue encasing my heart burns. I press a hand against the ache, but the pain only spreads. Tally has asked Clea to be her mother on countless occasions. I've been present for several of those instances. The glaring truth never loses its shine.

I settle for a pitiful excuse. "That's not possible."

A stubborn line firms her lips. "Yes, it is. You can get married and she can live with us."

"Tally," I sigh. "Clea and I don't like each other that way. We're just friends."

That's all we'll ever be. I can't offer more.

She crosses her arms with a huff. "I don't believe you."

"I'm very sorry to hear that."

My daughter isn't the type to back down. "Clea wants to be your girlfriend."

I shake my head. "I don't think so, Lou. Even if she does, that won't change anything. She's my friend. That's it. Period."

Her eyes narrow on me before darting away. "Whatever."

At this rate, I won't return to her good graces until I'm old and gray. The chance—regardless how slim—to salvage our day pushes me onward. I find myself once again wondering how I allowed this disconnect to happen. If I had a dollar for every shred of doubt, I'd be a billionaire. And we've only been at this for a few hours.

"What should we do next?" *What else am I willing to attempt?*

"I dunno."

"What's wrong?"

She offers a limp shrug. "Nothing."

This feels like another premonition of her teenage years. "Just tell me, Lou."

"I'm fine."

That's a red flag statement. *Where's my damn rulebook for raising a daughter when I need it?* I comb through my hair, tugging at the roots. "How about a tea party? Or we could practice our dance moves. Do you want to go shopping?"

Her nose wrinkles, dismissing my ideas. "We could have a Barbie pool party."

I rub the back of my neck. "If that's what you want to do, I'm game."

"Sure, I guess." Her tone reveals her lingering disappointment.

"All right." I clap and stand from my seat. "You gather the toys and I'll get a load of dishes going. Meet in the backyard?"

Tally pauses in her retreat to gape at me. "Not the bathtub?"

I furrow my brow. "Why would we stay inside for a pool party? It's sunny and warm out. We can fill up on vitamin D."

The somber shadows disappear from her features, replaced by a giddy smile. "Okay, cool. I'll find a bucket!"

We're reunited fifteen minutes later. I barely made a dent in cleaning, but leaving Tally for longer than that didn't sit well with me. The kitchen could use a serious scrub, but that's not a priority right now.

I tug open the sliding door and step onto the patio. Tally has her entire Barbie collection laying down in the grass. Seven of the eight dolls are girls. Ken is one lucky dude. She found a clear tub to fill with water from the hose. This is clearly not her first rodeo. The scene is all set and ready for us to unfold.

My daughter pats the lawn beside her. "Sit by me, Daddy."

Those are the sweetest words. I don't hesitate, parking my ass on the ground. "This looks great, Lou. How do I play?"

She laughs—loud and carefree. "You're so funny. Here."

I take Ken from her outstretched hand. His trunks are very snug. The deep grooves that define his sculpted abs are a bit too embellished. Not to mention completely unnecessary for a child's toy. "He looks… nice."

"Uh-huh." Tally is occupied brushing a brunette's pigtails. When she's satisfied with the glossy texture, her attention switches to the doll's outfit.

I watch her for another minute. Pressure to perform settles on my shoulders. "What does this guy like to do?"

She gives me a wicked side-eye. "That's for you to choose."

My imagination isn't what it used to be. Interaction is a solid choice. With the swagger of a stick figure, I walk him over to her girl. I lower my voice to be extra gruff. "Hey, Barbie."

Tally scoffs, flipping the doll's hair. "I'm not Barbie. My name is Louise."

I cringe. "Whoops. Sorry about that. Hi, Louise."

"Hello, Kenny." She waves the thin arm.

Ah, he's not a simple Ken. Good to know. "I like your, uh, swimsuit."

Her giggle makes all my stumbling worth it. "Thanks."

Now what? I think about the cheesy heroes from her favorite Disney movies. "Do you come here often?"

"Well, yeah. This is where we live."

"Right, duh." I cough and slip into a macho persona. "High-five!"

"Uh, okay." She slaps her doll's hand against mine.

"Want to squeeze my biceps?" *Want to squeeze my biceps?* I move the doll's legs, pretending to strut his stuff.

Tally quirks a brow, not looking impressed. "Why would I want to do that?"

Fair question. "To prove that I'm really strong. The better to protect you with and all that."

Her skeptical expression doesn't lift. "Don't act weird, Dad."

Okay. I'll do what comes naturally. My decision is cemented with a glance at our makeshift pool. "Cannonball!"

Kenny makes a big splash, sending water in every direction. Tally shrieks when she gets wet. To be fair, she's sitting in the danger zone.

"Daddy! What'd you do that for?" She flicks droplets from her fingers.

"It's fun, Lou. The entire point of a pool party is to swim. That's what he's doing."

She shakes her head hard enough to send blond hair flying in a whipping arc. "Ugh, no. That's not how we play. Our dolls like to lounge and sunbathe."

I frown. "Well, maybe my guy wants to change the rules."

"No."

"But—"

"I like how Clea taught me. Just be normal."

"I don't know what that means." I'm so far out of my depth. There are certain things this little girl will need a female influence for—I'm man enough to admit that fashion and menstrual cycles are beyond my limits—but pool parties? Apparently, playing with dolls is another weakness I'll need to overcome.

"Dad." She drags out that one word with an exasperated tone. "You're just not doing it right."

I seem to be finding out just how out of tune I truly am this morning. I've let this go too far. Shame washes over me in a scalding wave. I haul her against my chest for a tight hug. "I'm so sorry, Tally."

She pulls away and eyes me with a quizzical expression. "For what now?"

"For not already knowing the right way to do all these things. I should be the one explaining how to do it, not the other way around."

"That would be super hard for you, Daddy. She's really good at everything."

I flop flat onto the grass with a groan. This is one more harsh reminder that my neglectful actions have dire consequences. My daughter would rather be with Clea, not that I can fault her wishes. That doesn't make her blatant favoritism any easier to swallow. I've brought this onto myself.

Heat stings my eyes and I rub at the threat of tears. Getting emotional will do nothing except upset Tally further. "I'm not Clea. I know she's your favorite, but I'm going to be around a lot more now. You'll have to get used to me messing things up."

She cuddles into my side. "Don't be sad, Daddy. I love you."

I don't shy away from her affections. I bury my nose in her hair, inhaling the forgiveness and healing acceptance she gives me. "I love you so much, Princess."

"No duh." Then she wrinkles her nose. "Can we just see if Clea can play with us?"

My chuckle jostles her against me. "We shouldn't bug her so much, Lou. Let's have lunch and see how we feel after that."

Tally straightens and pins me with her clever gaze. "I want grilled cheese and Clea's version always tastes the best."

I pinch the bridge of my nose. "Why am I not surprised?"

"Can we go ask her?" She folds her hands together. "Please, please, please?"

My resolve crumbles under the pressure of her begging. I'm a weak man. Raising a white flag after a single morning is low, even for me. But a short visit won't bruise my ego too much.

Of course, it doesn't hurt that I'm desperate to see Clea

myself. That woman is my addiction and I'm overdue for a fix. I check my watch. It's almost one o'clock on a Saturday afternoon. She's probably home.

I stand, grab Kenny from the pool, and tuck him in my pocket. "I'm bringing reinforcements to improve my chances. He might earn me some brownie points too."

Tally squints at the doll. "You're gonna need more than that, Dad."

chapter five

Nolan

CLEA COMES INTO VIEW THE MOMENT WE REACH THE FRONT yard. Sunlight filters through the trees and glints off her dark hair. Even with the length of our lawns separating us, her seductive figure fills my vision. I clench my empty hands and slow my pace to appreciate the sight.

Her body is voluptuous in every sense of the word. Those generous curves would fill my large hands. She complains often enough about her weight that even I've overheard. Each muttered insult she slings at herself slices at me with the intensity of a serrated blade. The desperation to prove her wrong has been building inside me since we met. Eventually, that defiance will rise to the surface whether I hear the confession or not.

It takes every piece of my fraying control to concentrate on the task before me. She's standing on her driveway, facing the street with her back toward us. That gives us the element of surprise. Her position also allows me to see who she's talking to.

Pete fucking Harris.

The cocky architect has a major hard-on for Clea—and doesn't bother hiding his interest. His advances have become more direct in the months since he moved into our neighborhood. I can practically smell his putrid eagerness ruining the air quality. To my knowledge, she hasn't encouraged or reciprocated his attraction. That does little to dissuade him, though. He's currently shirtless, sweaty, and crowding her personal space. She's busy ogling him like a juicy steak. *Is he suddenly allergic to cotton?*

A low growl escapes my throat. Not fucking happening.

I have no right to be jealous. That doesn't stop the fire from engulfing my veins. While warring with my primal instincts, I catch movement near their legs. Rufus and Rory—Clea's dogs—are circling the pair like helicopter parents waiting for the opportune second to split them apart. Apparently, I'm not the only one concerned about this situation. Those mutts make great wingmen.

As if hearing my thoughts, the lab mixes halt in their tracks and swivel to discover me creeping just across the property line. The duo launches in my direction in a competitive sprint. I crouch in anticipation of their approach. They almost plow me over in their haste to greet me. Rory butts his head against my chin while Rufus climbs onto my lap, both fighting for the same goal: wrestling their way into the prime spot to receive the best pats. It's practically a gold medal to these two.

I give them extra scratches behind the ears. "Such good boys."

Spoiling them with more attention will have to wait. There's an intruder in our midst that needs a reminder of where he doesn't belong. I straighten and prowl toward Clea at a fast clip. She appears unaware of my presence—or is choosing to ignore me. More likely the latter. That's when I realize Tally has beaten me to the punch. She's already hovering at Clea's side, beaming up at her with the innocence of a toddler who just ransacked the snack drawer.

My daughter skirts around to Clea's front, effectively cutting off Pete's inappropriately close proximity. "Hi, Mama!"

Clea's wince is visible from my vantage point. Meanwhile, I whack my chest to reset the erratic beat that's pummeling me. "Hey, Lulah. Didn't we talk about you calling me that?"

"Uh-huh."

"And?" She taps Tally on the nose with a trembling finger.

"It's just a nickname." The little troublemaker blinks at her with adoration potent enough to make hardened criminals beg for mercy.

Clea hesitates under the impact. "I think we can find something more suitable for me."

Tally peeks over her shoulder at the man who's still standing too close. Pete's gaze bounces between the girls. He's probably trying to assess the authenticity of Tally's claim. My daughter smiles at him, then returns her focus to Clea.

"But you're gonna marry my dad." It's safe to conclude that she's the best interference I could ask for.

The brunette bombshell laughs, but the sound is awkward. "Um, well, I don't—"

"He really wants to see you." She blindly points in my general direction.

That's when Clea and Pete notice me listening in from the sidelines. I offer a quick wave while striding over to their mismatched huddle. Rory and Rufus trot alongside me, loyal soldiers ready for battle. "Hey, everyone."

"Nice doll." Pete tacks on a sarcastic snort, as if I need the extra assurance that he's fucking with me.

Clea whips him with a narrow gaze. I know all too well how it feels to be on the receiving end of her wrath. It's unpleasant at best. "Are you making fun of him for playing Barbie with his child?"

"Uh, no?" Dude-bro is bound to shoot himself in the foot. I won't have to say a word against him.

Tally shoots him with a glare of her own. "It's not nice to tease people. Grown-ups are supposed to behave better."

Pete scrubs over his mouth, properly chastised by a six-year-old. "I was just messing around. We're all friends here. Right, Nolan?"

I jut my chin at him. "Sure, man."

"Well, I should probably get going. These muscles aren't going to condition themselves." He flexes his pecs, alternating from left to right. Such a douchebag.

"Thanks for stopping by." Clea's grin is brittle.

"The pleasure is all mine, babe. I'll be seeing you soon. Maybe we can have dinner sometime." Then he winks at her.

Tally growls. I'm nearly giddy to hear what she spews next. She doesn't disappoint. "She's busy. We're watching *Tangled* tonight."

Rufus and Rory flank her like twin pillars of strength not to be tussled with, a clear warning in their menacing stares.

Pete lifts a brow, looking to Clea for confirmation. "I guess we'll try for another day."

"Probably not," Tally snips.

Clea clucks her tongue and ruffles my daughter's hair. "All right, feisty pants. Let's not be rude."

She flares her nostrils, huffing out a harsh breath. "But—"

"Don't worry about it right now." Clea gives a subtle shake of her head. Then she mouths something only Tally comprehends.

Her rigid posture relaxes, and she grins. "That's what I thought."

Any lingering tension bleeds from my system. It's so magical to watch them interact. I feel honored to experience it.

Clea rocks on her heels. "I guess we'll see you around, Pete."

I almost forgot about him standing there. "Yeah, thanks for keeping our girl company while we were preoccupied."

My daughter giggles when Clea rolls her eyes.

Pete nods, holding up a palm. "Okay, fine. I can take a hint. Enjoy your happy family, Clea."

She steps forward. "We're actually not—"

I reach for her hip. That subtle touch simmers with possessive energy. "Just let him leave already."

The look she skewers me with warns of a severe tongue-lashing. I'll gladly welcome whatever she has in store, so long as she ditches this clown. Tally plasters herself to Clea's side, cinching her skinny arms around her waist. In this locked position, we do appear like a cohesive unit. The suggestion that vision offers is too much. Too… tempting.

I avert my gaze and cough into a closed fist, using the opportunity to split myself from them. "This weather is great, huh?"

My predictable attempt at a distraction stems from truth. We've been having a tolerable summer so far. Late June can be really nasty in Minnesota. I berate myself with an internal curse. Here I am, digressing about heat and humidity. How fucking lame.

Clea's glare reignites, proving just how transparent I'm acting. "Was that really necessary?"

I scan the cloudless sky. "Not interested in discussing the mild climate?"

She scoffs. "No. I want to know why you thought stomping over here like a crazed caveman was a good idea. My brother exudes enough overly protective fumes as it is."

"I highly disagree. The message isn't getting through if Pete is still sniffing around." Something about that guy just rubs me the wrong way.

Clea relents with a sigh, an adorable wrinkle forming above her lip. "You might as well just pee on me."

Tally makes a gagging sound. "Yuck, Lele. That's super gross."

Clea startles. "Whoops. That wasn't meant for your ears, kiddo."

"Do you actually want my dad to go potty on you?"

Her complexion leeches enough rosy color to reveal the answer. "Nope, you're right. That's super gross."

Tally wipes a hand across her brow. "Thank goodness. Being a grown-up is weird."

"No kidding," Clea mumbles.

"I'm gonna chase the dogs while you yell at my daddy. Maybe you should take his favorite toys away to teach him a lesson." Her giggle floats along the breeze as she skips off to throw a ball for Rory and Rufus.

Once she's out of earshot, Clea spins to face me. "What do you have to say for yourself?"

The sizzle in her scolding tone sends a blast of heat through me. Is it bad that I'm getting turned on? I widen my stance to hide any evidence. "What did I do?"

"Don't pretend to be innocent."

"Patra," I start.

"Oh, no you don't." She holds up a finger and shakes her head. "You're not getting out of this with a few purred words."

That makes me sound rather animalistic. I kind of appreciate the notion in this context. "Tally did most of the talking. I can't control what comes out of her mouth."

"You're really going to let her take the fall?"

A grunt puffs from my flattened lips. "Of course not."

"Then you knew exactly what would happen by coming over here while I was talking to Pete." Clea raises her eyebrows, practically begging me to prove her wrong.

"Are you actually interested in him?" That possibility is a crack against my stubborn pride.

"That's not the point."

"It sure as shit is. Your answer determines how I interrupt his next social visit." I squint against the rays streaming through the leafy canopy above us.

Clea nibbles on her bottom lip. "He's nice to… look at."

A hot poker stabs into my gut. "Should I take off my shirt so you can ogle me?"

"I was hardly ogling him," she huffs indignantly

"Bullshit." I move forward, towering over her shorter frame. "I'll give you something to fantasize about."

"That's not—" She trails off, swallowing in an audible gulp.

I tease my hunger, brushing stray hairs from her forehead. The brown strands are silken under my thumb. "What's wrong? Already have plenty of material?"

She studies me with that soulful gaze. Her blue sea dares

me to plunge under those inviting depths. "What're you doing, Nolan?"

Her question douses me with frigid water, extinguishing the growing flames. I exhale the fiery desire from my lungs. That single motion cools the lust from my blood and allows me to remember my place. This is very dangerous territory.

With a measured retreat, I shove several feet of needed space between us. "I, uh... shouldn't have done that. Sorry."

"Right, that's what I thought." Clea avoids my gaze and focuses her attention on some random spot. "So, what brings you by?"

"Do I need a reason?"

"Yes."

Damn, she's not letting me off the hook. "My mission to get Tally back on Team Dad has been bumpy so far."

"Oh?"

Her feigned nonchalance drags a smirk from me. "I bit off a tad more than I could chew, to say the least. Tally made that perfectly clear."

In return, her pouty lips smooth into a firm line. "It's been less than twenty-four hours. I'm certain you can survive longer without running to me for help."

"I tried. Tally wasn't having it. You know how she is. Rome wasn't built in a day, Patra. We all start somewhere."

"You started six years ago," she points out.

"That's true." I raise my hands in acknowledgment of her point.

"I'll admit, she *is* very opinionated and strong-willed," she adds.

"Thanks to you nurturing those traits, no doubt."

Clea hums. "Buttering me up?"

"Asking for advice," I clarify. When she doesn't immediately agree, I toss in an extra incentive. "Tally insists you're the expert in all things. I couldn't agree more. Teach me your ways and put me out of my misery."

"You're being dramatic." Her gaze sparkles with hidden knowledge. She's hoarding a freaking fortune that needs to be equally distributed.

"You would be too after the morning we had. The final straw was our pool party. I don't know how to play with these." I jostle the Ken doll in my grip.

Clea's twinkling amusement is a tune to treasure. "Ah, yes. I can see why you struggled. Throwing the perfect Barbie pool party requires a certain expertise."

"But it comes so naturally to you. It's like I've been wearing training wheels since she was born and am still not ready to handle the ride."

"I've had a lot of practice, especially lately."

A familiar pressure tries to shove me down. She's not being condescending. That's just my perspective assuming the worst. Lack of opportunity has never been the issue—I've just wasted each one. There's no reason for me to be lacking. "I've failed her."

"But you're trying to repair that. Just keep going. Your confidence will soon follow."

"If only I shared your faith in me. I won't lose sight of who and what is most important. She deserves all I have to give, plus an abundance I have yet to discover." Clea is part of that equation, but there's no sense in revealing my inner demands.

"And I'm very happy, for Tally's sake." She blasts me with the full force of her stare. "Now, tell me what this has to do with you acting like a jealous lover and chasing Pete off?"

A resounding bang slams down the wall to my insecurities. I lower my gaze from the collision. "You don't understand."

"That excuse again? Maybe you don't know, but I'm very well versed in the art of listening." Clea cups her ear in demonstration.

"And I'll let you prove it one day."

"Just not yet." The gears are spinning behind her guarded gaze. She's already been more than patient with me.

Tally saves my hide by sidling up beside me. "Miss me?"

"More than you know, Princess." I ruffle her unruly mop of hair. Somehow, she's managed to tangle her golden tresses again.

"Did you tell Clea about our fun?"

"No." And I can only imagine the doom of my dignity that she'll divulge.

My daughter proceeds to recount every moment, not missing a single detail. What gives me pause is that she sheds a positive light on each moment of our morning. Where I stumbled, she describes a successful execution. It's as if my missteps were figments of my imagination. I can hardly believe what I'm hearing because nothing matches my version of the story.

"You should've seen him run to the laundry room, Clea. He's so fast." She bounces on her toes while polishing off the final embellishments.

"He's also standing right here." She's not wrong in that respect, though. I blow off my fingertips as if they're smoking barrels.

"See?" Clea smiles at me. "You're her hero, like Superman."

Tally scoffs. "No way. Daddy is way cooler. He might even be better than Flynn Ryder."

Clea gasps. "What? I don't believe it. He's your favorite."

"But I love my dad more." She blinks at me with bottomless green eyes that reflect the humble pride in mine.

An ache blooms in my chest, but this burn isn't brought on from shame or sorrow. With Tally's words, I find a value in myself that's been long lost. Maybe we can pull this off—together—after all.

chapter six

Clea

THE CLOSING CREDITS ROLL ACROSS THE SCREEN AS TALLY mumbles incoherently and snuggles into my side. Her head started lolling halfway through *Frozen*. It's after nine o'clock now and she's lost in dreamland. This was the final film in our lineup. We already watched *Tangled* and *Raya*. A Disney marathon has become somewhat of a weekly tradition in the last few months. Her father's attendance is hit or miss, though.

Tally is wedged between Nolan and me, keeping us planted on the couch until one of us decides it's time to call it quits. I've sat in a similar position with them before, but this feels different. Nolan has been abnormally silent. Other than offering to get me an adult beverage once Tally dozed off, he's barely acknowledged my presence. I've been too afraid to voice my suspicions. The temptation to sneak out has been poking at me since the little princess fell asleep.

Nolan stands with her cradled to his chest like the precious merchandise she is. He gestures for me to remain seated, and I'm curious enough to follow his command. Even if I wanted to flee, he's back within minutes. Any escape plans are officially thwarted by his swift return. He had no intention of dawdling upstairs.

As if I'd actually leave.

Pathetic.

I fidget with the pillow on my lap. "Is she asleep?"

He nods. "All tucked in. She didn't stir—totally conked."

"Turned out to be an eventful day, huh?"

Nolan settles onto the sofa, choosing to erase much of the Tally-sized gap that had been separating us. "Thanks to you."

Heat tingles my cheeks. To avoid his stare, I drain what's left in my wine glass. "You don't have to give me all the credit."

"Care for a refill?"

"I should probably get going."

"Other plans?"

"No, but we don't really do this." That odd sensation niggles at me again.

His shrug brushes along my arm. "I thought we could talk for a while."

"About?"

"Does it matter?" His aloof demeanor only serves to veer me further off course.

He's giving me an open window to leap through. This opportunity rarely happens, and might never again. Depending on how this goes, we may no longer be on speaking terms.

"All right, I'll stay."

"Good. I think we need this." The relief sags his broad shoulders into the cushions.

It fuels the voice that's pestering me to pry. I've managed to silence that nosy hound for six years. The gag order has reached its limits.

"Can I ask you a question?" I mentally cross my fingers in hopes that he won't get offended or use it as an excuse to withdraw. We had a moment earlier—an electrified connection. The sparks are still sizzling on my skin. I'd very much like to explore our potential further.

Nolan squints at me. "Sure."

"Do you ever imagine getting past the grief of losing Tally's mother?"

Am I the worst ever for even suggesting such a thing?

But the man must have urges. It's only natural to assume.

I'm considering this due diligence for the female population. Not to mention the last shred of hope I'm clinging to that my obsession with him isn't a total loss.

"What do you mean?" A shadow crosses his face from the soft glow in the room.

"I never hear you talk about moving on… romantically, or even just physically. You haven't been on a single date that I'm aware of. Six years is a long time—not that I can pretend to understand what it's like to lose my special someone." I've never had a serious relationship to mourn in the first place.

He cuts his focus from me with a grunt. "Meeting other women is the last thing on my mind. The idea isn't appealing to me."

I study his sharp profile. Nolan is only twenty-seven. It's hard to imagine him being alone for the rest of his life. That's my selfish desire talking. I berate my inner hussy. This man will never be mine.

The regret in my throat triples in size. "Right, of course. How insensitive of me. I'm sure she was an incredible person. You don't just get past the love from someone that special."

"Where is this coming from?" Nolan's eyes return to mine.

"Stupid curiosity. Forget I asked." I'm so fucking awkward. The modest neckline on my dress is suddenly suffocating.

"Be honest with me, Patra." His raspy tone is difficult to deny.

I let the calm in his green gaze wash over me. The color is such a stark contrast to his dark hair. He's the standard I hold every man to—very unfairly. That's probably why I find myself rooted to this couch rather than cuddled up with a guy who's actually available. I let out a shuddering, heavy exhale.

"It's no secret that you're attractive. Anyone with functional eyeballs could see that. It just gets me wondering if you'll ever accept—and return—a girl's advances." I hold up a hand when a scowl twists his lips. "But I realize how horrible it is for me to question the circumstances as to why you're single."

"You think I'm stuck because of Tally's mother?"

"Well, yeah. What other explanation is there?"

"You."

I choke on my saliva. "Me?"

"Yes, you. There's overwhelming guilt about Rachel, of course. But you're the one I can't escape."

I blink at him while my pulse surges to a gallop. "What's that supposed to mean?"

Nolan scrubs over his face with a tortured groan. "We were too fucking young. I was shallow and only cared about sex. Rachel showed up on my doorstep months after our one-night stand. I was prepared to become a father and take care of Tally. That didn't include being Rachel's husband. She wanted to be a family, but I pushed her away. That was unacceptable for her. Until her dying day, she was trying to bring us together."

I'm almost afraid to respond. This is the most he's revealed about her, and the pain holding him hostage. "What does this have to do with me?"

The unguarded glimmer in his eyes disappears under my watchful gaze. Nolan tucks that temporary vulnerability behind a stoic mask. "Never mind. It's late, and I'm not making sense."

I consider letting him off the hook. This conversation can easily take a catastrophic turn. But I've come too far to shy away now. I can feel the tension brewing in my stomach. The pressure is insistent, refusing to be ignored. We're going to hash this out.

Because just as easily, this exchange could end on a high note.

We tiptoe around one another. Dismiss the smoldering chemistry intoxicating us. Overlook the glances full of unresolved need. Those desires will never be fulfilled if I don't make a move. I take a breath—and my chance.

"What's your deal? Why do you insist on brushing me off?" I'm not sure where this bold attitude is coming from, but I lean into the shift.

Headlights from the street reflect through the front window, illuminating his frown. "I shouldn't have said anything."

I scoff and cross my arms. "Don't pretend that you haven't thought about exploring more between us. I see the lingering stares. Those subtle touches that last far longer than friendly brushes. I won't wait for you much longer."

He averts his glare to a spot on the floor. "I never expected you to."

"Then why are you sabotaging my love life? Pete is a nice enough guy, but you ran him off. Is that you marking your territory?" I couldn't care less about Pete and his pushy tactics, but the principle remains.

"Do you want me to?"

"No."

His smirk calls me on my bullshit. "You don't need his kind of trouble."

"But I need yours?"

"Be careful with what you're implying."

There's no diverting the roll I'm on. "Why?"

"Because you can't take it back."

"Maybe I don't want to."

Nolan straightens, shoving frigid distance between us. "We can't cross this line."

That's the moment I snap. A haze flickers across my vision as I swivel to face him. "Am I fucking invisible?"

He recoils at my harsh tone. "No."

"Then why have you been looking through me for six years?"

His expression morphs, cracking under the pressure. In the next instant, his mouth is slamming against mine. I jolt from the sudden onslaught. Nolan tunnels his fingers in my hair, locking me in place against him. The shock vanishes when he groans against me.

Blistering passion explodes from where we're connected. I part my lips and grant him entry, heat flooding me instantly. His need pumps in my bloodstream with every swipe of his tongue against mine. The fist in my hair guides me to the position he wishes. His demand for control only stokes the fire rushing under my skin. I shiver from the burn. He hauls me closer, and I seek solace in his warmth.

Screw going slow for a mere taste. This man is devouring me.

I've longed for this moment for years. My mind has tormented me with the unfulfilled desire to kiss Nolan since the day I met him. The reality far exceeds my pathetic fantasies. He's hard in all the right places, a wall of steel against my soft curves. His broad chest and thick arms create a cage I never want to leave. He makes me feel small and delicate. That's a rare gift for a busty girl who struggles with body image.

The tangle we form makes me ravenous. I shove forward and tilt to pull him deeper, swallowing his gravelly moan of approval. His teeth tug at my bottom lip as I claw at his shoulders. We strike with starved fervor claiming our motions. We're trapped in a bubble of our own lust, flooded in long-awaited desperation. I had no idea how deprived I was until he swooped in. Nolan is sating far more than my drought with this kiss. I clutch his shirt in my fist and drag him further into this craze.

Bubbling need rushes to the surface in a crushing burst that's desperate to escape. The force of his lips against mine is our only outlet. There's nothing gentle about this impulsive collision. Enthusiasm and fracturing resistance scent the room. We're ruled by this driving pressure to get closer. Our hurried pace rips at any remaining protest or argument that we're not meant for each other. After this, there's no way he can deny our chemistry.

Maybe I'm a glutton for being cast aside. Nothing has ever filled me with so much wanton desire. Satisfaction should be thrumming through my veins, but the opposite is true. My unsatiable need only grows with each passing moment. I'm hot and eager, ready to beg for more. Just as I'm contemplating straddling his lap, he rips his mouth from mine.

"We can't do this."

I lunge at him, lost to the seduction from his caress. "Yes, we can."

"No, Patra." His touch turns to abrasive stone as he breaks us apart. "This is a mistake."

The denial is like slamming into a brick wall. The hammering in my heart plummets and I suck in a gasp. "No. You're wrong."

"I'm not. You know nothing can happen between us."

"How can you say that?" Resentment invades the bliss I've been high on.

"You deserve far better than what I can offer."

He should know it doesn't get better than him. I rest a palm against my shredding chest. "What if that's all I want?"

"Don't settle for less."

"Isn't that for me to decide?" I'm already pissed at him for pushing me away, and now he wants to steal my choice? I'm livid.

"You're blinded by me mauling you. I can't stand the thought of you with anyone else, but that's not fair to you."

I glare at the vaulted ceiling. "So, what? You just let me walk into another man's arms?"

A muscle pops in his jaw. "That's shitty, Patra."

"What do you expect?"

"Nothing. Not from you." His thumb traces the apple of my cheek. "I've taken too much from you already."

"You have, but that's my fault. I shouldn't have made myself so available for you." My tone slices with a bitter edge.

Nolan hangs his head. "I'm a selfish prick."

"Then let me go." I'm not strong enough to sever ties with him on my own. That truth makes my eyes water. The first tear is the hardest. I can't let him see me cry.

"I won't. I can't. Not truly. You're already buried too deep." He clutches my face in his trembling palms. "I feel so fucking guilty. These feelings I have for you... they're wrong. I'm betraying her memory by crossing this line with you."

"How?" My voice cracks. I hate that he's witnessing this weakness.

He clenches his eyes shut, lost to an unseen memory. "I never gave Rachel a chance, regardless of how much she begged. She should strike me down for the depraved fantasies I have about you. It's not right."

I almost startle at her name intruding into this moment, which immediately sends a pang into my belly. She owns a piece of his past. Her spirit deserves to be with him always. I stand from the couch. "Okay, I get it. This was a mistake."

The words are acid on my tongue.

"Fuck." He thrusts his head back with the curse. "This is so fucked up."

I shuffle my feet. "Maybe I should go."

"Not like this."

"What's going to change?" My breathing is far from steady. There's little doubt he can see the rapid rise and fall of my chest.

"Your closure. I want everything with you, Patra." For a split second, I'm foolish enough to believe he's about to confess his undying love for me. Then he shakes his head. "But I can never be the man who deserves you. Give your heart to a man worthy of the claim."

That statement is too familiar, and I barely mask a wince. He's uttered that excuse every time I've been brave enough to expose the tiniest hint of interest in him. Brutal honesty is painful to hear. Nolan is serving me a hefty dose. It's about damn time I listen.

We're just spinning our wheels, going absolutely nowhere. This routine is staler than the tap beer at a frat party. Nothing is happening between us. He won't accept more from me than a free nanny service. If I don't break this cycle, we'll just keep going in circles until one of us finally falls off. Change is long overdue.

Acknowledging the correct path doesn't make the initial steps any easier to take. I need to accept that he's incapable of giving me what I've been chasing. He's stuck in the past with noble intentions, but that doesn't mean I need to stick around for the downfall.

This is the end for us, yet we never truly had a start to begin with.

With that reminder leading the charge, I spin on my heel and stride for the door. His pursuit pounds on the floor behind me. Nolan grips my elbow and stalls my retreat.

"Where are you going?"

I keep my gaze locked on the dark foyer. "Home."

"You can't leave like this." His breath ghosts across the exposed skin on my shoulders.

"Watch me," I seethe between clenched teeth. He's prodding at my festering wound without remorse.

"Don't, Clea." His hold on me tightens, a shackle to the prison of my own making.

Irritation melts away while I sniff at the burn in my nose. "If I stay, we'll make it worse."

He moves further into my space. "You don't know that."

Just the feel of his body against mine is agonizing. "I know how much I care about you, and that's devasting."

The rumble he releases mirrors the hollow beat of my heart. "Why am I getting the feeling you're saying goodbye forever? I'm afraid to let you go."

"That's a risk you've already decided to take."

Nolan turns me to face him. The heat of him warms me; his woodsy cologne and ripe hesitation envelop me as he pulls me into his chest. I give myself permission to savor this final pleasure from him. Hot streaks race down my face, dripping off my jaw. Our last hug might as well be the one to destroy me.

With a slow exhale, I steel my composure. Crying over this man—yet again—sends a prickling awareness over me. A fiery thump clogs my throat, which delivers an angry stream to pour over me. I spend thirty seconds going through an emotional gauntlet while silently berating the injustice. A soothing numb follows.

I wiggle free from the comfort of his embrace. "Do me a favor? Please handle your parenting troubles without involving me. I don't want this to be any harder than it already is."

The space I wedged between us doesn't stop him from resting his forehead against mine. "What's already hard?"

"Getting over you."

Nolan stills against me. "No, Patra."

"You say that like there's another choice."

"Tally needs you. You can't stay away. Think about how that will crush her."

"Don't drag her into this. She's not a pawn to use whenever you need a shield against me."

His upper lip curls. "I would never treat her like that. That's not what I'm doing."

"Sure sounds like it to me."

"I'm just asking you to consider Tally's feelings in this."

The urge to throttle him twitches my hands. "She's the only reason I'm still standing here."

He smooths his features and I brace for the impact. "Don't act like this, Clea."

"Don't you dare shame me for being emotional." If only my finger didn't tremble when I point at him.

"You can't punish her for my shortcomings."

I shake my head. The jerky motion is in tune with my heart breaking. "No, Nolan. You need to get over yourself. She needs her father. I'm done being your safety blanket."

His eyes blaze. "That's not fair."

"But it's completely acceptable for me to raise her?"

"You're crossing a line!"

"There isn't one left because you decimated it!" I fling an arm blindly toward the sofa.

He exhales hard enough to flare his nostrils. "This isn't accomplishing anything. I don't want to fight with you. We can talk more tomorrow."

Little does he know, that won't be happening.

I've been treading water for years. It's high time I improve my stroke and actually swim. But where will I go? How can I leave? The conflict bubbles inside of me as it does so often when this subject stabs at me.

That uncertainty will soon fade, or I'll adjust. All directions lead to the same destination: whatever distance is enough to forget Nolan Jasper.

chapter seven

Nolan

THE SEVERITY OF CLEA'S RETREAT BASHES AGAINST MY SKULL, even twelve hours later. I chug what's left of my coffee and grab the pot for a refill. As the dark roast fills my mug, I compare the rich color to Clea's long hair. My fingers were buried in those glossy strands as I breathed her in. A deep inhale grants me a lungful of the espresso blend, but my nostrils are clogged with vanilla and the elimination of boundaries.

There's no escaping her.

The last thirty-six hours have provided more drama than the past three years. That's telling on its own. Sleep has eluded me for the second night in a row. I gave up trying by two o'clock. Our entire exchange has been playing through my mind on a constant loop. Thick exhaustion is bearing down on me, which only fuels the repetitive cycle. I don't have enough strength on reserve—or willpower—to muster anything else into my brain right now.

Our conversation, her melodic voice, plays on repeat. The misunderstandings, impulses, and resulting downward spiral plague me. I should've talked more and reacted less. Maybe vice versa. Alternative scenarios and outcomes assault me, each error I made highlighted in sharp relief. All the things I could've said and should've done are discarded in a useless clump. Images of her pinned beneath me, writhing from pleasure, flood my already jumbled imagination. That euphoric anticipation building and cresting the instant I thrust and join us as one. Fuck, I can almost feel her clenching around me. The exhale from her relief bathing my skin. Blood rushes in a downward wave while I try to steer away from the fantasy.

It had felt too comfortable having Clea in my house. Doing something so simple as watching movies shouldn't fill me with that much satisfaction. I can see us decades down the road in the same position, just content being together. But I want far more than neighborly friendship.

I always figured my feelings were unrequited. *Why would she want me?* Imagine my surprise when she proved the opposite to be true. If I'm being completely honest, the shock from Clea's blatant desire hasn't worn off. I find it hard to believe that she returned my hunger with such visceral ferocity. Her interest goes beyond superficial attraction. I'm willing to bet Clea would volunteer to end my strike against dating, and avoidance of the opposite sex in general.

A frown crosses my lips. Well, not anymore.

That chance went up in flames along with everything else. I pushed her away much like I did with Rachel. The circumstances are completely different, yet tied to each other. That connection is one more fault topping an already teetering pile. I'm sabotaging my future by allowing the past to dictate my decisions.

The gravity of our situation hammers into me. I'm repeating the same mistakes but on a much grander scale. What I aim to lose with Clea far outweighs any significance I had with Rachel. Tally's mother was never more than just that to me. I didn't pretend otherwise, much to her bitter resentment. The accident was her own doing. Her erratic behavior wasn't my responsibility. I couldn't control her reckless choices. The guilt clings to me all the same—but why? That question, and resulting blame, has crippled me all these years. I know the only way to regain my sanity is to break free from these restraints.

When I peer outside, only the dreary gray clouds greet me. There are no blinding rays streaking through the windows this morning. Go fucking figure. This weather fits my mood and impending destruction. To say I'm frustrated is putting it mildly. Something has got to give, and I'll be damned if what does is yet another sacrifice to my happiness.

Other than my absolute devotion to Tally, I've shut myself off from getting attached. It's my factory setting. The influential roots from my childhood are still very much intact. I was raised by a single mom who busted her ass to cover our basic needs. My dad was never in the picture. When I think of Clea comparing me to a deadbeat, every inch of me rebels. I'm better than this, dammit.

A groan rips from my throat and I hang my head. My normal is scrambled. That's probably the best gift she could give me. I'm running on fumes and caffeine and the motivation to find a solution. It all meshes into a blur as my obsessive thoughts continue to churn.

The heated words. Her tears. My stupidity. Our kiss. That last one hogs the most brainpower. I can't help getting stuck on the pleasure that consumed me when her body pressed against mine. She seduced me with her enthusiasm. All it takes is one glance from her to get me hard. The memory of her hunger feeding mine drives me to madness. I'm a bastard for leading her on, but that didn't stop me. Touching her should be forbidden for all the sense I lose.

For five agonizing minutes, Clea was mine to hold. Then reality crashed in, and I ruined the possibility of us. That's my greatest regret right now.

Sending away my only source of distraction probably wasn't a great idea either.

I gave Tallulah permission to go next door and visit the target of my fascination. Alone. It seemed like a better idea than forcing Clea to face me before she's ready. The punishing silence is making me regret not joining her. I'm no stranger to solitude, but the stillness is suddenly staggering.

The memory of the door clicking shut from Clea's retreat only solidifies the stifling feeling. With that exit, my forced indifference flipped on its axis. That slight sound might as well have been a snare drum ricocheting off my sternum and pounding against my ribs. I should've chased after her and apologized. Then what? She wants more than I can give. Yet that gives me pause. Why can't we be together? There's no reason beyond my own hesitation. These walls are mine alone.

But it was late, and she needed to cool off. Lord knows I took advantage of a cold shower.

Now, nothing but static air greets me. It's too fucking quiet. I'm not the man for her, but that doesn't mean I don't want to be. The possibility of meeting any other woman to share my life with isn't plausible. That's not a secret. The only one I want is right under my nose. After that kiss, I'm ruined for all others.

Son of a bitch. Even my own psyche won't let me escape this toxic ride for a minute. I need a break. Or more coffee.

A resounding bang shatters my frozen isolation. Thundering footsteps immediately follow. With a blubbering wail, Tally crashes straight into my legs.

"Clea isn't there!"

I kneel and hug her tight while assessing the situation. Maybe my unstable mental state is rubbing off on her. "I'm sure she'll be home soon."

"No," she cries. "Kody said she won't be back."

Clea's brother isn't one to keep close tabs on her unless the circumstances involve men. "He probably just meant until this afternoon," I offer.

"That's not what he told me." Her tone is nearing hysterical levels.

I rub a soothing palm down her back. "Okay, calm down."

She pulls away, her wet eyes a punch to the gut. "I can't! Clea left me."

"Just for a little bit," I insist.

Tally collapses into a heap against me again. Her small frame shudders with wracking sobs. "She's staying at her friend's house."

I press a kiss to her hair. "See? That's fine. She'll be home tomorrow."

Tears spill down her splotched cheeks. "No, Kody said she's moving out."

"What?" I almost fall flat on my ass. "That can't be true. He's just teasing you."

"That rhymes, but I don't even care." Her bottom lip trembles while her voice quakes in outrage.

I shush her with a soft coo. "We can't overreact, Lou. Clea won't disappear. She loves you too much."

She sniffs and wipes at her face. "What about you?"

"What about me?"

"Lele loves you too, Daddy."

Not this again. I cough into a closed fist. "She's my friend, yes."

Tally's emotional outburst suddenly sobers. A twinkle sparks in her gaze. "Kody also said you're in the doghouse. Is that where friends go together?"

"Not exactly." Not on purpose at least.

"Then what's that mean?"

"Nothing good," I mutter. "It's just a joke."

"I don't get it."

"Grown-up humor."

Any lingering sadness vanishes with an exaggerated yawn. "Boring."

I nudge her chin. "Glad you're feeling better."

"Can we call her?" She bounces on her toes, clasping her tiny hands together.

The suggestion bathes me in warmth. But her reception would douse the flames. "Maybe later."

"That means no."

My exhale is harsh. "Clea is busy, Princess. That's why she's gone."

She groans and stomps her foot. "But I miss her."

"You'll see her tomorrow." I stand and retrieve my cold coffee. The bitter edge jolts me.

"That's too long." Petulance vibrates in her voice.

"It's a lesson in patience." One I'm still learning from.

She whips her head, sending blond hair flying. "Nah-uh, it's mean. I can't wait like that."

Clea has always been readily available whenever Tally seeks her out. The issue with that instant gratification is currently presenting itself. "How about we do something extra fun today? Just you and me."

She sends me a sidelong glance. "Like what?"

"The zoo? Or... the mall?" That second one makes me cringe. I need to prepare myself, though. Her craving for shopping will only get worse, or so I hear.

"I wanna go to the movies," she murmurs. "But I want Clea to come with us."

"Next time."

"But why can't—"

I tap her nose. "Don't worry, okay? She'll come back."

"What if she doesn't?"

That thought is inconceivable. "We'll find her."

chapter eight

Clea

THREE DAYS.

That's how long it's been since I've heard Tally's infectious giggle, or felt her rowdy charm ground me. She's the best balm to soothe my stress. I've gotten far too attached. Being apart from her, even for a short stint, is shredding my spirit.

If only I had an actual claim to her.

That thought reminds me of the only person who does.

Seventy-two hours isn't nearly long enough to forget the glory that is Nolan's stupid-sexy face. He's such an asshole for being such an... asshole.

How creative.

"Earth to Clea." Fingers snap in front of my nose. "Hello? Are you listening to me blab about the latest alien smut?"

I blink my surroundings into focus. The park is a buzzing hive of activity for a midweek afternoon. Rory and Rufus are tuckered out after an hour chasing each other in the off-leash section. Archer—Presley's toddler—is engrossed in his rainbow selection of toys. It's a sight that should make me smile. Instead, I'm staring at Presley's frown.

A quick rub to my temples does little to alleviate the fog. "I'm sorry, can you repeat all that?"

Her mouth slopes lower. "We're supposed to be using the scenery to our advantage."

I follow her blind gesture toward two guys standing nearby on a flat patch of field. They're tossing a football back and forth, the muscles in their arms and legs bulging from the effort. That visual should definitely get a rise out of me. I barely feel a spark. "You need to get laid."

Presley huffs at my deflection. "Like you're one to talk."

"Not helpful."

She twists her lips to one side. "Do you want to call him?"

"Yes," I blurt. Then I reel in my insistent impulse to cave. "But that won't accomplish anything. I need to get used to this separation."

"Do you really?" She sounds less convinced than the gullible romantic hogging real estate in my heart.

I'm nodding, but the motion is jerky. "It's not healthy for any party involved. I don't want Tally to be dependent on me. Eventually, Nolan will find a woman to penetrate his jaded stubbornness. That will destroy me more than his recent rejection."

Presley kicks off a peek-a-boo contest with her son. Archer takes a turn, beaming up at his mom from the blanket spread across the lawn. She hides again while seamlessly maintaining our conversation. "I wasn't aware that we're discussing things that are never going to happen."

I watch their exchange with a slice of envy, which is totally ridiculous. *Is it so bad to wish Tally were mine?* I shake the longing away. That line of thinking will lead to my ultimate demise. "There's just no bright spin in our situation."

"Only if you block the sunshine."

"That's my default when it comes to Nolan." I chew on my thumb nail. "Am I a horrible person for being jealous of a dead lady?"

"Morbid, maybe. Delusional, definitely." Her eyes narrow at me. "He told you they were never an actual couple. She wanted him, but he didn't feel the same. Why are you jealous of that?"

I glare at the gray sky, bland with a dreary overcast. "Because she has a child with him. Whatever else they shared is strong enough to continue hindering his love life—or lack thereof. It's one hell of an aversion. He's been critically warped. And yeah, you don't need to answer. I'm terrible."

She swats my arm. "You are not. I think that's his guilt talking. We don't know the entire story. Tally's mother might've been a stage-five clinger with zero boundaries, may she rest in peace."

I'm about to deny that implication, but the retort stalls on my tongue.

"Holy shit." Vannah appears from nowhere and drops onto the bench beside me. She belatedly realizes what just came out of her mouth, clapping a palm over the offending orifice. "Crap, sorry. Is Archie old enough to repeat stuff yet?"

"Not quite. Maybe once he's two. Isn't that right, buddy? We're still working on words in general." Based on Presley's soothing pitch and loose posture, our friend's bad language is already forgotten.

Rory and Rufus stretch their necks to reach Vannah's hand. After they take turns greeting her with licks, their heads returned to the ground. A laugh escapes me at their resistance to move a single inch more than necessary. I did a decent job depleting their seemingly endless supply of energy.

With a nudge to her side, I address our tardy bestie. "Why the hold-up, Van?"

She tucks a lock of red hair behind her ear. "My boss is a real bitch. She made me stay at the office late."

Another giggle squeezes past my lips. "You work for yourself."

"I know. She sucks, right? My partner tests that theory at every turn. Lannie demanded we take an extended lunch for, well… you know." Vannah's overt wink makes me laugh.

"No need to brag," Presley grumbles. Sex talk is proving to be an effective method of dulling her optimism.

"The celibacy is getting to her." I stage-whisper the words from the corner of my mouth.

"You have a man." Vannah juts her chin at Archie.

"Very funny," snarks Presley, but her expression practically glows at her son.

"What about those two? They look friendly." Vannah motions toward the football guys.

"That's what I said!" Presley tosses her arms in the air with an exasperated huff. "But this one only has an appetite for a certain broody dick. I'd be more offended if he didn't have the body of Thor. His tattoos only support your solitary diet."

There's nothing I can say without getting defensive. That will only prove her point.

When my phone pings, not a single ounce of surprise pinches me. I've been building a theory that Nolan has some sort of sixth sense when it comes to intruding precisely at the wrong moment. I dig in my purse to check the message against my better judgment. Call me obsessed, or just that desperate for an update on Tally. It has nothing to do with Nolan. Not even a little bit. The piercing ache in my chest threatens to call my bluff. So does the flurry in my pulse when I see his name on the screen, accompanied by another ping.

Nolan: I'm trying not to use Tally against you, but...
Nolan: *image attached*

A sheen of blistering heat immediately attacks my eyes. I groan and fan my face as the picture loads.

Tally is grinning at the camera, holding up a drawing. Three blobby figures are scribbled in a row. Each has a name above their head. Mine is listed as Lele/Mama. I wonder if Nolan bothered to correct her in this instance.

Another message comes through as I attempt to gulp around the lump in my throat.

Nolan: She misses you. I do too. We need to talk. When will you be home?

Presumptuous of him to assume I'm coming home at all.

Vannah peeks over my shoulder. "What is it?"

Presley joins from my other side. "Oh, he's stooping to dirt levels. You okay?"

I sniff and wipe under my eyes. "I'm fine."

"Strike him back." Vannah pounds a fist against her open palm.

I'm almost positive she isn't about to suggest physical harm—almost. She is a bit of a loose cannon. "How?"

"We could go to the beach. I'll take a picture of you in that hot pink bikini we saw at Target."

Bile rises in my churning stomach. The thought of my excess flab being enhanced and squished from tight strings—in addition to being on full display—isn't pleasant. It might be effective in dissuading him from pestering me, but my pride would pay the consequences. Presley and Vannah don't need to hear me complaining about my weight, though. "That will only encourage him. Not to mention giving him the wrong idea."

Vannah paws at the air. "Not if we pretend that he received it by mistake."

That sounds worse than me in a skimpy two-piece. "I don't want to play games with him."

She pins me with her signature no-nonsense stare—quirked brow and all. "And what do you call him sending adorable pictures of Tally?"

Just one more fact I can't argue with. "I need to move on. Period."

"That's so sad," Presley groans. "It's the end of an era. You've been hooked on Nolan since we met."

"Thanks for providing further evidence to how pathetic I am."

She rests a palm on my arm. "Don't be like that. It's endearing. Most girls we went to school with were too busy mattress-hopping to catch a single feeling. If you ever want to feel better, think about what happened with me and Chad."

The mention of her baby daddy makes me smile. I trap the humor behind squished lips. "That's different. You didn't have a one-night stand with just anyone."

"What I did is worse. Plus, we have incriminating evidence." She hooks a thumb at Archer.

"As if you can regret it."

"Not even for a fraction of a second."

"That's what I thought." Does my tone have a cranky edge? Perhaps.

Presley has a beautiful son from that drunken debacle. I don't have a single sexual experience to share. All I get for pining after Nolan all these years is a bruised ego. His little girl that I can easily pretend is mine adds more insult to injury. A misplaced bitterness seeps under my skin, sending a flush to burn my cheeks.

Yes, because our situations belong in the same sentence.

I bite my tongue to kill the snarky retort. Presley is a dainty gazelle prancing all about without a care for her size. Meanwhile, I'm the chubby panda who can't lose weight regardless of how much I exercise. I've fought hard to feel comfortable in my skin. It's an ongoing battle that is far from over. My full figure is proportionate with the confidence I've struggled to gain. I tip my chin, letting the familiar acceptance wash over me. My body will never be a twig. I've learned to embrace that. Many are envious of the curves I've been blessed with. Men certainly seem drawn to my generous boobs, hips, and ass. Not that I've actually proven the theory. I never let a guy close enough to penetrate my Nolan haze.

The result is my perpetual singleton status—and virginity.

I paste on a smile, but the edges feel brittle. "Is Archie with Chad this weekend?"

Presley sighs, her bottomless sparkle losing a little luster. "Yep."

"We should go on the hunt." That suggestion feels foreign, but I refuse to shy away.

Her enthusiasm rebounds with a squeal. "Heck yes, roomie!"

Vannah pouts. "No fair. You two are reliving our college days and leaving me out."

Since being shacked up with my best friend rather than an insatiable husband is something to covet. I shake my head with a laugh. "Can you manage a night away from the hubby and join us? You can be our buffer."

She blows some red strands from her forehead. "Well, yeah. It's not like we're attached at the hip."

"No, just your genitals." I make a circle with my thumb and forefinger, driving my other pointer through the hole.

Vannah smacks her lips at my gesture. "I'll make sure to take care of him before I leave."

"Do you do anything together other than have sex?"

"No," she scoffs. "We're still super married. The nympho craze will fade soon enough."

"Doubt it."

She inspects her manicure. "I'd be fine with that too."

"Anywho," Presley sings. "It's a date. Friday night. Extra hot."

"Fingers crossed I packed appropriate bar attire." I mentally catalog the clothes already at Presley's house.

She brushes that off with a wave. "If not, we can go shopping."

"Or I can just stop by my house."

Her gasp is comical. "And risk a confrontation?"

"You make it sound like a hazard to my health."

"Emotional, yes." Her deadpan tone makes it seem like a no-brainer.

A single shoulder hikes at her concern. "I'll be fine. It's not like I can avoid him forever. Not seeing Tally is what's hurting me the most right now."

Presley considers for a moment, then her eyes grow wide and she starts bouncing on the metal seat. "Brand-new, fantastic, must-do idea."

This conversation has gone off in too many directions to follow. If nothing else, these two provide enough entertainment to keep me preoccupied. "Okay, let's hear it."

"Oh my gosh, this is brilliant." Presley sits forward and pauses for dramatic effect. "We can meet for kiddie dates. Now that Archie is old enough to comprehend the fine art of sitting in one spot for longer than five seconds, we can bring them here to use the playground. Tally loves acting like a big sister. She can push him on the swings, or they can dig in the sandbox."

"But Tally isn't my kid."

"Might as well be," Vannah cuts in. "I doubt Nolan would mind, especially if it means he gets to see you."

Presley bumps me with her elbow. "And you'd be helping me fulfill this odd desire to bond with other mothers."

"I'll think about it? That seems kinda weird to me with our current standing." The uncertainty in my voice matches the bubbling doubt that's festering inside of me. "Finding my own place should take priority."

I've never been more thankful to have a job that allows me to be remote. I stumbled into digital marketing by accident. My communications degree is broad enough for me to choose from countless paths. For now, I'm happy to manage social media accounts for my clients while having the flexibility to pursue photography on the side. A few of the accounts I run have purchased pictures from me. Talk about a win-win.

One day, I hope to turn my hobby into a career.

And I'm officially getting way ahead of myself.

Presley yanks me down from the clouds. "You're free to stay with me however long you'd like."

The sweet scent of freshly mowed grass tickles my nostrils as I smile at her. "Thanks, Pres. Your spare room has made this much easier on me. I'm sure Kody enjoys having the house to himself."

"With his social calendar? Absolutely." Vannah blows on her nails, dusting them off on her shirt.

"I can't believe you were almost one of the harem." My gag is involuntary.

She wrinkles her nose. "Naïve mistake. I've learned a lot since freshman year. Also, my door is open to you whenever. Just say the word."

I wave my arms in front of me. "With the newlyweds? No, thanks."

"Amen to that." Presley holds up an open palm for me to slap.

"Jealous spinsters," Vannah spits. The twinkle in her eye betrays any false sense of upset.

"Duh," Presley groans. "Do you see my green complexion?"

Rufus and Rory rouse from their stupor. I toss them the rawhide bones from my bag. Those will buy me another ten minutes before they'll get restless for supper. A topic worth ending on sparks in my brain. "Speaking of noticeable features, I want to make a statement. Something drastic."

Vannah makes a husky noise. "A tattoo?"

"No. I'm saving that for good vibes." The rose and heart I planned are for a special occasion. The likelihood that the design will ever stain my skin is slim.

"You can get something pierced." Presley winks with her suggestion.

Vannah leans in. "I highly recommend getting your—"

I press a finger against her painted lips. "If you're going to suggest a certain region below my waist, I will kindly decline."

"Your loss," she mutters.

"Vannah?" Presley looks scandalized with a slack jaw and stalled exhale.

"Don't be a prude. It was Landon's idea." She wags her brows.

I don't know if I should be envious or concerned. "No wonder you have long lunches."

She goes quiet while staring off into the distance. "My man loves to chow down and savor his meals."

"Okay, wow. This isn't what I had in mind." My cheeks feel hot enough to start a fire.

Vannah shakes off whatever reverie she was caught in. "Right, sorry. Drastic change. I can't wait to see what you decide on."

We exchange a curious glance while the possibilities swarm in. "Me either."

chapter nine

Nolan

"DUDE, YOU FUCKED UP."

That's the greeting I get from Kody upon opening the door. He stomps inside, uninvited but not necessarily unwelcome. It's been too damn quiet since Tally started summer camp on Monday. I've been so restless I could crawl out of my skin. These are the uncomfortable instances when having my office at home further proves how reclusive I've become.

My friend's brash tone warns me that this isn't a random social visit to stave off my loneliness. Not that I'm clueless enough to pretend otherwise.

"Please come in," I offer belatedly.

"Yeah, thanks," he throws over his shoulder while striding down the hall. "You got any beer?"

I furrow my brows and follow his path. "It's eleven o'clock in the morning."

"You're right." Kody pauses and rocks on his heels. Then he studies me with a narrow gaze. "We need something stronger. Whiskey?"

A dry chuckle rolls from me. "I'll get you a healthy pour, but none for me."

He just shakes his head. "You'll change your tune after hearing what I have to say. Bet you won't last ten minutes before diving into the strong stuff."

I walk to the kitchen and fetch him a drink. Kody usually

prefers his bourbon on the rocks, but I refuse to dilute the expensive liquor I'm treating him to. Serves him right for demanding booze so damn early.

I find him in my three-season porch, sprawled like a king on the couch. "Sip on that."

He grabs the proffered glass, taking a long whiff. "Oh, this is the good shit."

I drop onto a chair. "Did you expect rubbing alcohol?"

"Nah, you're too much of a label snob to buy cheap bottles." His lips smack after a slow swallow.

"Oh, fuck off. I refuse to drink swill. Quality taste speaks for itself." My liquor collection is a source of shallow pride. On the rare occasion I indulge in hard liquor, I want it to be worth savoring.

"And I'm reaping the benefits." He raises his glass in a salute.

"At least someone is," I mutter.

"I'll add that to your list of faults." His mouth tilts into a smirk.

"Oh, here we go." I recline against the soft cushions, but the pillows resemble concrete blocks.

"All right, listen. I'm gonna shoot you straight," Kody drawls. "Clea is pissed as shit at you. Not sure what you did, but the girl is crushed. If you weren't my friend, we'd be having an entirely different conversation."

A knot instantly yanks taut in my gut. He has every right to call me out, much like his sister did for the way I'd been slacking on parenting with Tally. While I've made huge gains with my daughter, the situation with Clea remains painfully complicated. The crossroads we've reached has left me spinning my wheels while she vanished from sight.

I tip my face to the ceiling, avoiding his gaze. "She won't return my calls."

Except when Tally leaves a message. The only peace I get lately is knowing their bond is still intact. Hell, it's probably stronger than ever through this experience.

Kody takes another swig from his drink. "Can you blame her?"

"No."

He scowls at my curt reply. That doesn't dissuade him from trying again. "Why would she even give you the time of day after putting in this much effort to get away?"

"How else am I supposed to explain myself? She needs to hear me out." I should probably inject more confidence into my response, but I don't have much left when it comes to her.

"What do you plan to say?" Kody spins his wrist, urging me on.

I cradle my throbbing temples. His question is one that's been hounding me since Tally told me Clea was gone. It's been over a week. All I have is radio silence to show for my incessant mulling.

"Well, I need to apologize."

He kicks his feet up onto my coffee table, crossing at the ankles. The third degree is only kicking off. "No shit, but for what?"

I try to imitate his relaxed pose, but the strain in my muscles refuses to ease. "The last two years, for starters."

"Try six."

"Why ask if you're just going to correct me?"

His smile is too wide for our topic of discussion. "That's part of my brotherly duty."

"I wasn't aware that role entailed being a condescending prick." But what do I know? I'm an only child.

"Hey!" He points a steady finger at me. "Believe it or not, I'm here to help you."

I blink at his hostile tone. "Could've fooled me."

Kody sits upright, all traces of his aloof demeanor vanishing in a second. "What, do you need me to coddle you? Consider yourself lucky that I'm over here at all. I'm caught between my little sister and the joker who's supposed to be my best friend. You need to fix this."

A shrill note rings in my ears at the generic advice. "Don't you think I know that?"

"Yet you're sitting here doing nothing." He waves a sloppy hand in my direction.

"Clea won't talk to me." The dull ache in my chest spreads with each reminder.

"How hard have you tried?"

"I call her daily. I've texted her at least five or ten times a day. She's probably filing a restraining order as we speak."

"And you haven't heard shit from her?" His voice carries a hint of outrage in my defense.

I dig my phone from my pocket just to satisfy the prodding urge brewing inside me. It also corrals the glimmer of hope somehow managing to peek through my clouds of doubt. With a sigh, I turn the blank screen toward him. "Not unless Tally reaches out to her."

He drags in a noisy breath between his teeth. "Well, I'm not surprised. Clea has been staying with Presley for this last week. Remember her?"

A vision of eternal optimism with black hair comes to mind. "I think so."

Kody nods along with the recognition on my face. "That tribe is fierce and protective, especially if Vannah is involved. My balls quiver just thinking about that man-eater. I don't even want to imagine what righteous bullshit they're feeding her. I mean, you deserve their wrath, but it's still vicious."

That draws out a barking laugh from me. "You think?"

"Look, I know these girls. They're not going to tell her to make amends and forget this ever happened. They'll tell her to go on the war path."

"Great. Another thing to look forward to when she comes back."

"You don't get it, man, if it's up to them—absent a divine intervention—she's not coming back."

I almost double over from that punch to the gut. "She has to. This is her home."

His frown fuels the fear stabbing me. "It's not like she's planning to live with me forever. Eventually, she would find her own place. I just didn't think it would be happening yet."

"How are you so calm about this?"

"She's an adult. I can't lock her in the basement."

"This isn't happening," I grumble.

Kody shrugs and collapses against the sofa. "Sorry to burst your bubble, but it is."

I feel the veins in my throat bulge, the muscles flexing under pressure. "She can't be gone for good. It's impossible."

What's more probable is me staggering under the weight of this colossal mistake. I've been blind for years, content to lounge in the companionship she so freely gave me. Memories assault me on a whizzing reel. My stomach growls, sending even more moments flooding through my memory.

Clea would normally pop by to check on me during lunch. More often than not, she would whip up something for me to eat. Such a fucking schmuck. I comb my fingers through my hair, yanking on the overgrown length. Those impromptu meals meant more to me than I could properly express. Choosing to say nothing instead was a grave mistake.

I took her for granted. Now that I've consciously realized that, I can't handle the thought that I'd do that to her. She finally met her threshold for dealing with my ignorant ass. No one can blame her, least of all me. That doesn't mean I'm accepting defeat.

My defenses rattle and more stolen moments clobber me. The bated breaths. Static in the air. Thinly veiled desire. Forced indifference. Wasted opportunities.

This isn't how our story fizzles to an end. We are the furthest thing from finished, dammit.

After letting me stew in silence for several minutes, my friend exhales his frustration. "You're not the only one upset,

Jasp. Take my feelings into account for a minute. She's not just my sister. We've been roommates since my parents moved to Florida. I appreciate an empty house to do whoever I please whenever I want, but the mortgage is too steep for me to survive on my own. I rely on her half of the money. Mom and Dad quit the financial support once she graduated college. Don't even get me started on her cooking."

I pin him with a hard glare. "You better be fucking joking."

He leans over and slaps my back. "Of course I'm messing with you. Lighten up, man."

"Forgive me if I'm not in the mood right now."

"Yikes, tough crowd. Well, since I have your attention, how about that drink?" He jostles the remaining liquor in his glass.

My clarity is impaired enough with the torrent of emotions running through my head. The last thing I need now is liquid assistance. "No, thanks. I'm fine without."

"Sure." His easy grin slips when I shoot him a severe scowl. "You're going to win her over. I have faith in you two. Just don't plan on me putting in a good word. I tried to plead your case, but that got me the cold shoulder. She ignored me for two days."

"Sounds familiar." I rub my palms together, suddenly wishing for a tall mug to occupy me, but to have alcohol right now would be a terrible idea. "What should I do?"

Kody chokes on his whiskey. "What are you asking me for? Are you that desperate?"

"Do you think I'm capable of handling this myself?"

He snorts in response. "We know the answer to that."

"Fuck." I hang my head with a groan. "I'm never going to win her back."

His noncommittal shrug doesn't improve my sinking spirits. "Not with that attitude."

"Are you planning on offering any useful suggestions or just here to gloat?"

"I'm not sure what my sister sees in you." That's the first promising thing he's said.

The spark in my veins is premature. That doesn't stop me from adding a little kindling. "Not past tense?"

He rolls his eyes. "She's been stupid obsessed with you since the night we met six years ago. She's not just going to move on after a week. You need to strike before she comes to her senses, though."

"Helpful," I deadpan.

"Change your tune, brother. What's your deal? No bullshit."

"Want to be more specific?"

"My sister is obviously crazy about you. Based on this conversation alone, you feel the same. What's holding you back?"

I gulp at the suffocating pressure ballooning in my throat. "When Tally's mom died, I made a vow to stay away from women. Rachel wanted love between us. I refused to give her a commitment beyond caring for our daughter. It only seemed fair that no one else got that part of me either."

Kody rears back. "Says who?"

"Me. Rachel screwed with me once Tally was born."

"How so?" He scrutinizes me with a squint.

Ice seeps beneath my skin as I get lost in those unpredictable months.

"Manipulation tactics, mostly. She couldn't use my daughter against me thanks to our court order. That didn't stop her from trying to get my attention. If I didn't want her, she would find someone who did. She was bound and fucking determined to prove me wrong. I should've stopped her before she spiraled. Her behavior became too destructive. When the cops came to deliver the news, I was already numb." Her bruised and battered body—cold and lifeless—still haunts me. Guilt twines around my neck, tugging tight enough to choke.

"It's not your fault, Jasp." The message isn't new, but the meaning is finally sinking in. Kody's solemn tone loosens my burden ever so slightly.

The scars will never disappear, but I'm learning to heal in

spite of them. "I realize now that it might have been a bit rash and extreme to cut myself off forever."

His broad frame bounces with a humorless chuckle. "No shit."

"You don't understand," I protest for what feels like the millionth time. The familiar phrase bashes against my skull. I've used that excuse to keep Clea at arm's length for years. And for what purpose? All I've accomplished with that distance is create more pain.

"Then let me tell you what to do." He freezes me in place with the promise of pain in his gaze. "Learn from your mistakes. Cut Clea loose or make a move. Pick one. I honestly don't care, but this back-and-forth is just miserable—and I mean for me. I didn't have to deal with this when she was gone for college, but now I have to witness the spillover. And now I'm emotionally invested."

"I love her," I admit.

"And I believe you do. She doesn't, though."

Once again, I can't blame her for doubting me. All I've done is reject her. "How do I prove myself?"

"Grovel your ass off." He makes that sound so easy. "Be sentimental and shit. Clea is hurting and needs to feel appreciated. Beg for mercy if you have to. I'm talking about grand gestures worthy of romance flicks. Go big, then go bigger."

I scratch at my stubble while my mind goes blank. "Uh, okay."

Kody mumbles a string of expletives under his breath. "Clea has been going out more than usual with her friends. Most of them are single and on the prowl. It's only a matter of time until some guy comes along and gives her what she's been wishing for from you. She's done waiting for you."

That gets my synapses firing. "You were doing such a great job reassuring me. Why'd you have to ruin it?"

"Look, this is on you. You fucked up, you've gotta fix it. I'm not about to offer you ice cream and sappy movies. That's for chicks, man. If you don't go get her, someone else will. And then I'll laugh about it."

"Fuck you."

"Don't get pissed because I'm right."

My knee bounces to an erratic pace on its own beat. I'm getting jittery. Nothing I do is good enough. Kody is making that quite clear. Tally wails every other hour about how I forced Clea to go away. Her sureness that this is my fault is almost frightening. It must be some underlying girl-power gene I don't possess. My daughter will never forgive me if I don't bring Clea back to us. More than that, I won't forgive myself. Not for this.

I stand from my seat while clapping in rapid succession. "Okay, I'm pumped. This is going to work."

Kody follows suit, unfolding himself from the couch. "You've got this, no problem. Clea keeps to a pretty predictable time. She goes to her favorite coffee shop and the park during daylight. Then she meets the girls at one of the local bars after dark when the mood strikes. All within walking distance of Presley's house. If you happen to see her out, that's great. If not, try harder." He ticks off her frequent locations on his fingers.

This so-called foolproof scheme resembles a hunter stalking his prey. I can't believe her brother is encouraging such extreme methods. "Wait a hot fucking second. Let me get this straight. You're recommending that I corner her? Confront her by any means necessary?"

I can almost picture Clea backed against a wall, spitting mad, and cursing my existence. Kody's advice is proving to be pretty terrible.

"It's creepy when you put it that way." He slices a palm through the air. "Just trust me."

We'll see about that. My faith in him is debatable at best. "And if this goes south?"

"It won't. Not with our secret weapon." He's referring to Tally.

I refuse to acknowledge that strategy. She doesn't need to be involved in my mess. "One last question."

A confident grin stretches his lips. "Shoot."

"Will you be joining me on this excursion?"

He slaps a hand to my shoulder, giving me a shake. "Hell to the yes, buddy. Now we're speaking the same language."

I'll be ditching at the first sign of trouble. "Then let the disaster begin."

chapter ten

Clea

ALOUD, INFECTIOUS POP SONG BOOMS FROM THE SPEAKERS overhead as I slurp at the fruity concoction through my straw. The catchy beat tempts me to get off my butt and shake what my mama gave me—that would certainly catch a few stares. I force the antsy twitch in my muscles to release and remain plastered to the vinyl cushion. The grumble in my belly won't be satisfied by leers from strangers.

"This is a great spot," says Aspen, fellow dog mom and hot guy enthusiast, as she studies the thick logs stacked along each wall. The decor resembles a traditional cabin interior.

My stool wobbles beneath me when I lean forward to rest an elbow on the glossy rail. "I've only been here twice. They have yummy cocktails."

"Leave off the tail for me. Our seats are in the optimal location for catching eye candy." She uses two fingers to motion from her eyes to the abundance of patrons surrounding us. One glance confirms that the large majority are guys.

"Oh, that too." But I barely notice any features beyond towering heights and bulky frames.

"Maybe we'll lasso a trio of lumberjacks." Presley wiggles her brows.

"Just a pair will do," I mumble under my breath.

"This was your idea." Presley's hearing is too sharp. Must be all that selective listening with Archie. "No more moping, remember?"

"Yeah, yeah." I've been regretting that decision ever since our first attempt last Friday. It took less than fifteen minutes to determine I'm not ready to flirt with other men. Stupid Nolan and his sexy face. No matter how much physical distance I put between us, he finds a way to invade my mind.

"We're in this together," Aspen chides with an elbow to my side.

"In an open market," Presley adds with a purr matching the clawing gesture she makes with her hand.

I roll my shoulders, infusing enthusiasm into the motion and willing a smile into being on my lips. "Right. You're right. It's hunting season."

Presley pumps her fist. "That's the spirit!"

It's only fitting considering the establishment. The vibe in this place is homey with a rustic spear on the side. I could almost pretend we're in a vintage lodge up north. The unique style is what puts Buck Trap on downtown's trendy scale. A snort escapes me. With a name like that, the customers probably come running.

Stale sweat and desperation hang heavy in the air, but not enough to overpower the ripe tang of possibility. I've had just enough alcohol to drown my sorrows while still clinging to my wits. There's a noticeable warmth spreading through my limbs as I savor another sip. Even with the sticky heat from too many bodies, I'm floating in a comfortable bubble. Nothing can bring me down.

Aspen is parked to my right while Presley surveys the crowd from my left. Pickle in the middle. I'm buzzed just enough to giggle at that. Our extended leave of absence from sexual activity is what unites us. That reminder feeds my purpose.

"I'm ready for action." I polish off what remains in my glass with extra suction, guzzling every drop.

Aspen's rapt focus latches onto me. "You'll have no problem keeping a man happy with those skills."

More liquid courage sizzles in my veins. "I should test that theory."

Presley's blue shirt highlights her sparkling gaze when she smiles. "Glad to see you're back in the game."

"I don't want to be stuck on him." A long sigh curves me into a saggy lump. "My heart is stubborn."

"Emotions can be a real pain in the ass." Aspen is speaking from experience. From what she's told me, her ex is the lowest scum. Over a year later and her trust in the opposite sex is still bruised.

"Amen, sister." Presley raises her drink. She's no stranger to complicated relationships.

I'm in damn good company. If nothing else, we're having an excellent bonding session. "Thanks for listening to me complain so much lately. I love my ladies."

"Aww, group hug." Presley loops an arm over my shoulder.

Aspen leans in, resting her head on mine. "This is quality soul food."

"Absolutely." I close my eyes and soak in our combined strength.

Presley fidgets with her straw while giving me a slow once over. "I still can't get over your hair."

With all our idle chatter, I'd almost forgotten about the daring cut and color I had done earlier. I smooth a palm over my snipped locks. The choppy bob will take some adjusting to. "Do you really like it?"

She flips a platinum strand that tickles my chin. "Umm, yes. Totally obsessed. A perfect score on the drastic scale."

Aspen hums in agreement and ogles my new do. "If only I had the nerve to dye mine. I've always wanted to try pink."

"You should do it!"

She purses her lips. "You've definitely inspired me."

"When you're ready, I found the best stylist."

"Well, I have the best friends. Let's take a picture." Aspen passes her phone to me. "Do the honors, since you're the photographer."

I preen at the title while switching the camera app to selfie mode. "Cheese big and say blowjobs."

"*Blowjobs!*" we recite in unison.

It's not my imagination when a hush falls over the noisy room. We erupt in a fit of giggles at the flaring interest zeroing in on us. Practically every man in the room holds their gazes at us, continuing the semi-silence for another pregnant pause before the room returns to its rowdy norm.

Presley's grin still shines like a megawatt bulb. "Why don't we do this more often?"

"Adult problems." I signal for another round when the bartender stops by.

"Growing up sucks." Aspen groans her displeasure to the wide beams bisecting the ceiling.

"It will only get worse. Just wait until you have kids." Presley makes grabby hands at her fresh margarita.

Most days, I could convince myself that the honor of raising a child was already mine. Not anymore, though. A shallow pang reverberates against my ribs. I'd been foolish to ever feed that fantasy a morsel. In the wake of that crushing truth, my newfound bravado cracks and I wince.

I fiddle with a stray coaster. The flimsy cardboard is emblazoned with a thunderous cloud with a torrential downpour streaming from underneath. Whenever I hear the rain, my mind trails to Nolan. I give an internal eye roll. Pretending won't grant me any favors. A storm isn't necessary for my thoughts to immediately travel to him. I want to bang my head on the bar for being so weak. It's a habit I desperately need to break.

And it's not just him I need to get over.

Invisible priorities crash in my lap with a whoosh. I shouldn't be wasting my time splashing in a testosterone-infested pond. There are more important things that deserve my concentration. Well, mostly one person. Tally has made sticking to this upheaval nearly impossible. I'll never abandon her, but our attachment hit a dependent point. This separation has taught me that with an unrelenting ache. Her father is jabbing at that painful wound with every text and voicemail.

The latest batch of unread messages is burning a hole in my pocket. I need to move on. He has to let me. Then we can have a civilized conversation.

Honestly, I didn't expect Nolan to pursue me with such ferocity. A few days, sure. It's been almost two weeks with constant attempts to get ahold of me. Too bad he didn't display this voracious intensity sooner. There's no telling how long his chase will last. Until I give in? Then what? We fall back into the routine until I snap again?

Why can't I shove that ache aside and remove the shackles tying me to responsibilities that aren't even mine? I'm young and free. Don't I have the right to take advantage of my youth?

Presley has a toddler and is having no trouble detaching from reality for the night. She's already shimmying her hips to the sultry rhythm.

"Oh, no," Aspen wails. "We're losing her again. Code Frown! Call for reinforcements."

I laugh at her antics. "I'm good. No need to bring in the calvary."

"If only I believed you." Presley shoots me a sidelong glance.

It's no wonder she's losing faith in my resolve. Some fun sponge I've become. I'm going to appreciate those who are present and willing to stand—or sit—by me. Forget Nolan and his mixed signals. If he wants to be friends, we'll need real boundaries. That news probably won't be well received.

A throbbing begins in my temples. The alert warns me to quit overthinking. Or maybe I should drink faster. There's a cure for that within reach.

I chug my blackberry mojito. A frosty sensation attacks the burn in my chest, encouraging me to finish the rest. The ice rattles in my glass and I grin at the small victory.

"Yes, girl!" Aspen hoots from beside me. "Now you're catching on."

"Let's keep the momentum flowing." Presley lifts her hand and motions for three refills.

The tension in my posture fades and I exhale in relief. This is more like it. I twirl a section of my hair while scouring the growing swarm. "Who's looking good?"

Aspen tilts her head. "Do you mean good-looking?"

I wave off her correction, my movements feeling sluggish. "Either way."

When I chance another peek at the nameless options, there's a group hovering nearby. A noticeable lack of distance separates us from them. If that wasn't enough, the overt staring would clue me in. It's only a matter of moments until they find the balls to approach us.

"Okay, I got this." Presley shakes out her hands and sucks in a deep breath. "Back to business."

"Work your magic." I rub my palms together. The rapid motion sucks me into a trance.

"How about that one?" Presley lifts her chin toward a blond man.

I swivel my head and get clobbered with a dizzy spell. Not worth the effort. "Eh."

Her flawless features pinch into a scowl. "You're not even trying."

My shrug is sloppy. "I'm not going to force it."

She rolls her eyes and sways from the exertion. "All right, fine. There's another fine specimen over there."

I quirk a brow. "He's smiling too wide."

Presley dips her chin with a groan. "You're impossible to please."

"Oh, my." Aspen perks up from her silent stupor. "Who's that prime slab of male hunkiness? I bet he could do some damage to my dry spell."

I straighten on my stool to spy the fortunate target of

her objectifying. Bile rises in my throat. "Eww, no. That's my brother."

She smacks her lips. "Really? He's all sorts of delicious."

I slap a palm over my mouth. "Yuck. I'm gonna barf."

"It's not like you have to watch." She gives me a playful nudge.

"Please stop." The two cocktails in my stomach are churning into an angry punch.

In a synchronized motion, Presley and Aspen shift their gazes to the left. Whoever they find causes a mutual gasp to reach my ears.

"It seems that our entertainment for the evening has arrived." Presley's expression lights up brighter than the fireworks finale over Lake Minnetonka.

I search the crowd for the source. When my scan lands on a familiar face, I almost fall off my stool. "No, this is bad. No, no, no."

"Yes, yes, yes. This is happening." Aspen is nodding too fast for me to follow.

I suck in a sharp breath. The sight of Nolan is sobering, to say the least. A bucket of freezing water getting dumped over my head would've been less shocking.

The impulse to hide has me launching off my seat. That knee-jerk reaction sends my stool toppling backward. Even enveloped in the ruckus, the resulting crash echoes like a gong. Nolan's head snaps in my direction. He doesn't temper his reaction, exposing the span of emotions with bold confidence. His expression morphs from disbelief to primal satisfaction without blinking. That smolder reveals what I'd been trying to avoid.

I'm totally busted.

chapter eleven

Nolan

SOMETHING HEAVY SMASHES INTO AN UNFORGIVING SURFACE. That resounding crack splinters across the wide space and diverts my attention to the right. What I find is a blonde bombshell buried in a sea of dicks, gawking at me like she can't believe who's staring back.

I do a double-take. The woman filling my vision is Clea, but her hair is shorter and very light. She's always been a brunette with glossy waves flowing past her supple breasts. Now, the longest layer kisses her jawline and frames her exquisite beauty in shiny platinum. Maybe she's wearing a wig. Or she decided to make a major change to her appearance. I'm mesmerized either way.

Clea has always been a knockout. But this? Just looking at her gets me hard. The throbbing pulse behind my zipper twitches with approval. My damn pants strain to the point of discomfort. I try to adjust without being obvious.

She's as petrified as a deer caught in my headlights, waiting for the inevitable crash. Her baby blues shimmer under the dim lights. Those honest depths whisper the inevitable while every other roar tries to drown her out. Her radiant beauty is the only thing that registers. I've got her now.

"Well, damn." Kody claps me on the shoulder. "Clea looks ready to bolt. Better make your move."

He doesn't need to tell me twice—or once, for that matter. The actions are pure instinct. My feet carry me toward her while I fight to get the rest of me up to speed. I'm still recovering from actually seeing her in the flesh. The crowd parts for me while I stalk forward at a fast clip, blood pounding louder in my ears with every step. Clea watches me approach through frozen features.

Before I realize it, I've erased the distance separating me from the girl responsible for my unraveling sanity.

Nothing else exists at this moment. Not our feud, or the unspoken words. I suddenly forget about being ghosted for nearly two weeks. Our differences don't matter. Just this undeniable attraction that's hauling me into her orbit. I couldn't rip my eyes away if an earthquake threatened to decimate this place.

Her jaw goes slack when I pause mere feet away. Two women flank her on each side—Presley and Aspen, I assume. They twist on their seats to catch the drama unfolding. I don't let our audience stop me from solving this overblown clusterfuck once and for all.

There's so much I need to say, yet the words stick to my tongue. What trips from my lips is far from noteworthy. "Wow, your hair is different."

She blinks at me. I almost expect her to scrub her eyes to make sure she's seeing me. Her stunned state finally thaws, releasing her tongue so she can communicate. "It's a bit drastic." She tucks some bleached sections behind her ear. "I'm still getting used to the cropped length."

"I love it. You look beautiful. But that's nothing new." And the word vomit is just getting started.

Not the smoothest introduction I could scrounge up, especially with grit in my tone. That's the effect this forced separation has on me.

"Buttering me up for a reason, Nolan?"

A furrow tugs the skin between my brows. "Am I not allowed to compliment you?"

Her gaze shimmers. "You've lost that privilege, I'm afraid. It got tossed out the window with my heart."

I finch at the naked hurt in her voice. "Clea, I never meant—"

She holds up a hand to stop me. "No. We've already hashed it out. What're you doing here?"

The question doesn't penetrate. "There's plenty more to say."

Clea sniffs and does her own stubborn pivot. "I wasn't sure you'd recognize me."

"Change whatever you want. I'll always spot you in a crowd."

She seems to recall something, her stance going ramrod. "I suppose you managed to find me. Now what?"

"You've been avoiding me, Patra."

"Um, duh?"

"That's all I get?" I ask. I've been an unreliable loser. I don't deserve forgiveness, but I want to beg her to consider anyway.

"Consider it a gift." Her tone is cutting with a blurry edge.

I eliminate another foot between us. "Hearing your voice certainly is."

It takes every ounce of my fraying control to hold off from touching her. My muscles flex against the struggle.

A breathy sigh from the blonde friend attempts to distract me. Then I realize her attention is solely reserved for Kody. He lingers behind me like a teammate waiting to be tagged in. Since his advice has been stellar so far.

Kody's creative and aggressive methods proved to be unsuccessful. I left a note with flowers on her car. A handmade, glass-blown frame—which included a photo of the three of us that Clea snapped—received no response. Her favorite meals were delivered for lunch and dinner, with plenty to share. Nothing in return. My desperation is reaching critical levels. I'm ashamed to admit that camping out on her friend's front lawn has crossed my mind.

This was the next logical step.

Clea's accelerated breathing and ferocious glare reveal the error in my thinking. It's too late to turn back. Then I'm granted a small reprieve. Her friend saves me from the firing squad—happy accident or not.

The blonde slinks off her seat and bends to whisper in Clea's ear. "I'm gonna tell your brother to climb me like a tree. You know, because I'm Aspen."

"Gross." The fury washes away with a gagging choke. Clea's flushed complexion loses some luster, taking on a slightly green hue.

"You'll thank me when we're sisters." Then Aspen slinks around me and out of sight. From my periphery, I notice Presley sneak off in the opposite direction. Good riddance.

"That's a disturbing visual." Clea gives her body a shudder, forcing her limbs to cooperate. Her somewhat bleary gaze lands back on me. "What were we talking about?"

"You dodging me." The reminder is painful to admit.

"Oh, right." Her suspicion returns with pinched lips. "Are you following me?"

She's not letting this reunion pass as a coincidence. Go figure.

"No," I hedge.

She parks a hand on her cocked hip. "You just so happen to choose this bar on the same night?"

I'd never choose this sausage fest from the lineup, but she doesn't need to know that. "I had to see you. My options are limited."

"Maybe you should've thought of that before you had your way with my lips. It was you who made that smooth move. Why'd you do that, huh? Kissing is super intimate. I don't just agree to play tonsil hockey with anyone. You made me think something more could happen, then bam! It was all a big mistake."

The rambling onslaught is hard to follow, but I get the gist. Her brazen tone and flashing eyes threaten to incinerate me. This isn't the sweet girl I've fallen for. It seems her hair isn't the only update. Clea has never been a timid wallflower, but the snarky attitude has reached new extremes.

Her jaded demeanor suggests that she's already done with me for good. I'd assumed that outcome but wanted more than anything to be proved wrong. She's already given me too many chances, but that won't stop me from being a selfish bastard and pleading for one more.

"I reacted poorly, Patra. Please hear me out. I'm so fucking sorry."

"Uh-huh, sure. I see you brought Kody for support. Where's Tally?" She looks behind me as if expecting to find my daughter hovering there. Her motions are listless, making me wonder just how much she's had to drink.

"You think so little of me that I'd bring a child to the bar?"

She snorts, then hiccups. With wide eyes, she smacks a palm over her lips. "Oh, yeah. That would be sil-silly," she hiccups again, handing over confirmation that she's guzzled more than a few drinks.

"And irresponsible. Not to mention illegal, since there's an age requirement to get in."

"What if she's your sober cab?"

Sure sounds like she needs one. "How much have you had to drink?"

"Not enough, now that you're here."

"That's not an answer."

Clea rolls her eyes with an exaggerated huff. "No, I'm fine. Unfortunately. I'll need to have a few more to black this out."

Her combative mood shoots another fiery blast into my already raging gut.

"Why do you hate me, Patra?"

She dips her gaze to my throat. "That's the opposite of what I feel for you, stupid sexy face."

"What'd you call me?"

She gestures at me with a sloppy finger. "You have a stupid sexy face. It makes me do dumb crap."

Her lips are loose from the booze. Call me an asshole, but I'm taking advantage of this truth serum.

I take a measured step forward. Only a slim foot remains wedged between us. "Such as?"

Clea's expression turns steely with blatant determination, but still shines with a sultry undercurrent. "When I'm feeling extra horny, I like to part my curtains and watch your shadowy outline in the shower."

I blink, shocked by the admission. Of all the things I thought she'd say, that certainly wasn't in the top fifty. I allow my hunger to feed on a slow perusal of her body. It's only fair after that baited hook she dropped. I probably resemble a starving lion licking his chops as dinner is served just beyond reach. But damn, she's so fucking sexy. My mouth waters and I swipe a palm there to catch any drool.

Shiny green fabric conceals her luscious curves—just barely. An iridescent sheen makes the material look like liquid whenever she moves. Her tits are nearly spilling out. I want to bury my face in her cleavage while palming her lush ass. Then I imagine most of the guys in this joint have a similar fantasy. None of these bastards are worthy of an eyeful—me included. That doesn't stop me from soundlessly reciting a filthy vow to offer pleasure. We need to escape the throng and find privacy. If she could hear my inner dialogue, she'd promptly slap me across the face—but I'd gladly accept the punishment just to get her hands on me.

Sweat dots my forehead, which has nothing to do with the oppressive heat in this pressure cooker. I'm not sure what the fuck has gotten into me, but I know for damn sure staying away from Clea for nearly two weeks has been hazardous to my health. The lewd fantasies are nothing compared to the bone-deep longing just to be near her. If falling to my knees and begging her to listen will ease this torture, I'm ready to bow down.

An undeniable—and relatively safe—truth climbs to the surface. "Are you trying to get a rise out of me?"

"If you're offering." She bites her lower lip.

How easy it would be to slam her against me so she can feel my arousal. But I'd never do that when her sobriety is in question. I'm mindless with want, but the desire to earn her forgiveness drives me.

"We need to talk, but not like this," I insist.

Clea highlights her blonde statement with a bold fling, her golden strands arcing like a halo. A defiant laugh mocks me further. "Oh, for a second there I thought you were apologizing."

The thrum of failure smashes into my skull. Frustration bursts out of me with a snarl. "It's too damn loud in here."

She crosses her arms, shoving another tease onto the platter. "Take that as a hint. We should talk about this later when I'm not trying to have fun."

"Oh, so you can just keep ignoring me?" I'm finding it difficult to keep my eyes level with hers—instead of looking down into delicious temptation.

"I'll consider answering next time you call."

"No, we're taking care of this right now."

"What?" She cups her ear. "I can't hear you. All this noise is drowning out your sorry excuses."

I spot a dark hallway along the far wall. "Don't make me toss you over my shoulder."

Clea goes visibly stiff. "You wouldn't dare."

"I guess you don't realize just how serious I am."

She pauses to study me. Her flaring nostrils pull in a lungful of my potent intent. "That won't be necessary."

Hoisting her onto me would be a rare prize, but I won't steal her from the scene by force. "Sure about that? You'd get a great view of my ass."

A dopey grin tilts her lips, the ire from mere moments ago wiped away. The dreamy glint in her gaze reflects the liquor in her system. She's never gawked at me with such open admiration.

If we were alone, I'd do a thorough investigation. Her

permission—or lack thereof—plays a huge role, though. "Why are you just staring at me?"

Her exhale is heady, curling a fist around my demanding girth. The smell of wanton decadence stirs. "You're... really nice to look at. Very pleasing on the eyeballs."

I raise an eyebrow. She must be more intoxicated than I originally thought. "What, like Pete?"

She scrunches up her face. "God, no. You're way, way nicer to look at."

I smooth a palm down my plain T-shirt. No one told me I can't entice her. "Want to see what's underneath?"

Her gaze follows the slow path down my abs. With a jolt, her eyes snap to mine. "Oh, shit. I'm supposed to be mad at you."

I want to smack my forehead. This conversation is going nowhere. My chuckle is dry, yet genuine. "Do you need a ride home?"

She shakes her head. "Not from you."

"I hope you're not expecting me to leave you in this cesspool unattended."

"My friends are here, thank you very much. More importantly"—she stabs my chest with her finger—"you're not my keeper."

Not officially, but that won't stop me from hanging around to ensure she gets home safely. I doubt Kody would willingly leave her behind. A glance to my right proves that he has his hands full of Aspen. The other chick is nowhere to be seen. It works wonders in my favor if they're occupied.

And if nothing else, this loopy exchange has been enlightening. Clea wants the real deal with me. I plan on convincing her to feast until all that's left is our entangled future. Redeeming myself is an uphill battle, and I'm ready to climb.

From the corner of my eye, I spy an empty pool table. Her competitive side is a convenient distraction. I jut my chin in the direction of our neutral ground. "How about a game?"

chapter Twelve

Clea

A THICK GURGLE RICOCHETS OFF THE SLOPED TUB WALLS AS water circles the drain. I lift my foot onto the porcelain edge and slather moisturizer along my freshly shaved leg. Terry cloth swaddles me while the lasting calm settles any wayward unease.

The whirring fan drones from above, spreading my relaxing lull. I stopped at my house for a deluxe bubble bath and more clothes. It's been over three hours. Am I delaying? Without a doubt.

What am I hoping to accomplish? I refuse to acknowledge the reason, masking it with a disgruntled grumble to reinforce my stubborn pride. It's only a matter of seconds before the inevitable wiggles his way into my thoughts.

Just because Nolan showed up at Buck Trap doesn't mean he's going to randomly stop over to see if I'm here. It wouldn't take much effort to determine my whereabouts. One glance out the window would reveal my car in the driveway. Assuming, of course, he's observant enough to notice or cares enough to look. He's probably quit checking at this point.

Another low sound escapes me. Our latest confrontation is still haunting me days later. Between the confidence granted by my impulse new 'do and the buzz of alcohol, I was a teetering mess. Our mini pool tournament was the final peg in a rather eventful evening. I rub a lotion glob across my thigh while re-calling the finer details. The stakes were steep, but I agreed to his terms. Nolan requested a date with me. I wanted to be left in peace. A longer-than-necessary shake sealed the deal. My freaking palm tingles at the reminder.

I'm convinced he let me win, which defeats his entire purpose. That fact needles at me like a thorn I can't remove. I pump more moisturizer into my hand and blindly slop the load on my exposed chest. Nolan must have some ulterior motive.

Vanilla salts and lavender soap perfume the small space. The overly sweet combo has me wishing for woodsy pine with a side of masculine scruff. I'm lost in those thoughts when the bathroom door swings open. The breath stalls in my lungs and I instinctively hunch inward to close up my robe. My heart leaps up to my throat as I spin to face the door, panicked terror flooding through me.

The intruder bursts in merrily, encrusted in neon pink and extra sprinkles. She showers me with a gap-toothed smile. "You're home!"

She barges in and bounces toward me. So much for privacy. I catch my breath in relief and immediately smother that thought. Screw boundaries. They don't belong between us.

After the initial robe-clutching wears off, my heart rate slows back down to normal. I crumble to my knees with open arms. "Oh, Lulah. It's so good to see you."

At my welcome, she runs toward me at full speed. Her little body leaps across the remaining distance and into my waiting embrace.

Two weeks apart is barely a blink in the expanse of our relationship. That doesn't mean I haven't missed her with every fiber of my being. We've spoken nearly every day I've been gone, but it wasn't enough.

"Why are you creaming yourself?" Her wobbly voice is further muffled against my shoulder.

I choke on my saliva. There's no chance I heard that correctly. "What?"

"You're so creamy. There's white stuff all over your hands."

She doesn't release her grip from around my neck. If anything, she tightens her hold.

"Oh, it's lotion." The notion is hilarious, albeit horrifically inappropriate considering my current company.

"But there's so much. Why is it so thick?"

I snort and immediately bury the noise in her shirt. Her curiosity can be misconstrued in the worst possible ways. The punchlines are endless—or I just have a dirty mind. That's probably more plausible.

A reasonable explanation sits on my tongue. I can only release the trapped amusement clogging my throat. It squeaks out undetected. "This is a normal amount. You'll find out when you're older."

She shoves upright from our hug and stares at me. "I don't wanna wait. Can you cream me that much too? Right now?"

I squint at the ceiling and beg the giddy tickle to subside. Why is she so hilarious? I squeeze my eyes shut to avoid the corner crinkles giving me away.

If I expose the humor behind what she asked, I'll be in big trouble. She'll be asking everyone in town if they cream themselves. Even worse, she'll tell them I creamed her.

Nope, not going to happen again. The selfie incident from last summer taught me a valuable lesson. I almost peed my pants after Tally exclaimed that she flashed herself with the bright light. Nolan wasn't impressed when she repeated that phrase whenever silence stretched for longer than ten seconds.

Remember when I flashed myself?

All these months later and I could still roll on the floor in a fit. I squish my lips into a sealed vault. I dare not laugh. I can't let a single hint slip. It's not funny. A giggle brews in my belly. No, dammit.

I wrack my brain to find a more appropriate subject. A dull throb in my knee reminds me that I'm still crouching on the tile floor. I shift my weight and the towel slips off my head from the disjointed motion. Tally gasps, her eyes blown wide.

"Lele! Oh my gosh, we match!" She holds a section of her untamed golden locks against mine. "Our hair is the same color. Did this happen because you're gonna be my mommy now?"

Oh, what a magical fairy tale land that would be.

I almost smack my sternum to get my cracking heart pumping again. "Ah, no. I'm sorry, kiddo. This doesn't mean I'm your mom. I just needed a change. I thought blonde looked good on me."

"But we match." She stomps her foot, letting me know this similarity is a deciding factor in her mind.

"We sure do. Isn't that fun?" I should've considered this outcome while picking the dye.

Tally tugs on my damp tresses. "I guess. It'd be cooler if you were my mom."

I cup her soft cheek, my smile wobbling at the edges. "I know, Lulah. Sometimes it really feels like I should be since we're together a lot."

"And you love my dad. Then I'd have two parents." She blinks at me, those green depths pleading for me to surrender.

Sidestepping is the coward's escape, but this is a slippery slope I can't tumble down.

"It's hard not having a mama, huh?" I've always swooped in as that vital role whenever necessary. That's how we got into our current predicament.

"Eh, not really." She shrugs and her expression brightens. "I don't need a regular one. You're way better. All my friends want you as their fake mom too."

There goes that cramp in my chest again. This girl is killing me today. I press a kiss to her balmy forehead. "That's quite an honor. I'm happy to fill that role for you."

She gives me a sharp nod. "Good. Not like you had another choice."

"Ah, there's my sassy princess." I grin and rock back on my heels to stand.

"Whatcha doing today?"

"First, I need to get out of this robe."

The mirror is still foggy and useless, so I guide us into my room. After grabbing some clothes, I walk to the room divider set up in the corner. I bought this outdated relic at a yard sale for moments exactly like this. It's impossible to get space or ask Tally to step into the hall. She's as stubborn as they come, and even more curious. Modesty has no place in our relationship. Our compromise is her sitting on the bed and promising not to peek behind the curtain. That method isn't foolproof, of course. I slip on my bra, panties, and dress in a hurry just in case her patience is extra thin this morning.

The troublemaker is inching her way to my hiding spot when I step out from behind the panels. With a squeak, she backpedals and flops onto my mattress. Tally slaps a tiny palm over her eyes. "I wasn't gonna look."

"You're a little turkey." I give her a pass since we haven't seen each other lately.

"I'm not little." She flings herself upright with a pout.

"Whoops, I forgot since you were going to break our rule. Big girls listen, right?"

"You look super pretty." She rests her folded hands under her chin.

Her flattery is an obvious distraction technique. Not that I planned a serious teaching moment or anything. There's no scolding this cutie.

I pat my wet head. "Compliments will always grant you favors."

"Does that mean you have to do what I want?" She bounces off the bed and shadows my stride across the room.

"That depends." I sit at my vanity bench to put on makeup.

"What if I call you beautiful? Like way prettier than a model, or Barbie." Tally hovers behind me, giving me a direct view of her beaming smile in the cosmetic mirror. There's clearly a secret agenda brewing behind that seemingly innocent expression.

I hang my head with a laugh. "What's up, Lulah?"

"Uncle Kody is going to keep an eye on me while you talk to my dad." If that's not a regurgitated statement, I don't know what is.

"He's your uncle now?" I deadpan her.

"Yeah!" she cheers.

"How convenient," I mumble while dabbing concealer under my eyes.

She scrunches her brow. "What's covenant mean?"

"Convenient," I repeat as I dust glittery powder across my lids. "Like something just falls into place too easily."

Pure sugar and too much energy filters into the air when she shakes her head. "But we've been thinking about doing this for a super long time. It wasn't that easy."

And the plot is revealed. I add a few swipes of mascara to my lashes. "Oh, Lulah. How am I supposed to tell you no?"

"You don't." Her tone brooks no argument.

I giggle at her no-nonsense stance. "Those guys shouldn't involve you in their scheme."

"What's a sheeme?" The mispronunciation hisses through the gap in her teeth.

I've been hanging around adults too much. "It's like a plan."

"They didn't do the sheeming." She scoffs and screws her lips into an upwards twist. "I get the credit. This is my idea!"

"Okay, okay." I hold up my palms. "You're the brains of this operation."

"That's right, I am. I want you and my daddy to be happy again. When you're sad, he's sad. And guess what? I'm sad too. Don't go away again."

I'm not sure how to drop the relocation news. Probably best to just rip the band-aid. "Tally, I'm probably moving to a different house."

She ticks her jaw forward. "Nah-uh."

"Tallulah," I warn.

"Oh, no." She wags a finger at my reflection. "Don't use the mom-voice if you're not gonna be my mama. No more pretending if you're just faking it."

I drop the blush brush and rub at the painful stab searing into my stomach. "What do you want me to do?"

"Stay!" She points to the floor.

"I don't think that's possible." The sting in my nose has me averting my gaze.

Tally fiddles with the strap crossing my shoulder blade. There's never any hesitation to just reach out and touch me. That natural liberty I've always allowed shreds any walls I might've tried to build between us. "Give me one reason why."

Admitting the truth is too raw, and probably too much for her young ears. "It's time for me to get my own place. I can't live with my brother forever."

"But he'll be lonely."

I snort. "Not a chance. He's rarely home."

"Not Uncle Kody. I meant my dad." This girl would make an excellent attorney. She might as well start law school now.

"Oh." There's no masking my wince.

Something flickers across her expression. It's the subtle narrowing of her eyes that warns me Tally isn't going to back down. "I've been going to camp, you know."

My nod is slow while I search for a red lipstick. Once I find the ruby shade for me, I pass her the cherry gloss I have stashed in my bag. Another compromise. "Are you swimming a lot?"

"Uh-huh, and crafting." She makes fish lips at the mirror while digging in her shorts pocket. "I made this for you. It's been a secret forever since you weren't home. But I've been keeping it safe."

The rainbow necklace she holds up takes my breath away. It's more beautiful than the finest jewelry of solid gold—and more valuable too. Moisture blurs my vision and I blink at the heat. "Oh, I love it so much."

"Will you wear it?"

"Yes." I make grabby hands toward the precious gift.

"On a date with my dad." She slips that in with a casual flick. Serves me right for interrupting. "He's already waiting downstairs."

I squint at her while she slips the beaded treasure over my head. "Of course he is."

She claps at me. "I'm so excited."

"I haven't agreed to go yet."

"But you will." She's going to convince me by any means necessary.

"My hair is still wet." Grasping at straws is my specialty. I study the semi-finished application project that my face has become. He's seen worse.

"Should I blow you?"

And that settles it. I burst out laughing, my filter blown into smithereens. My tears are for an entirely different reason as the humor leaks down my cheeks. "All right, you win. Take pity on me."

She wiggles her eyebrows. "Did I make a funny joke?"

"Yes, but it's private. Just between girls." I wink at her.

Her gaze sparkles. "Oh, those are my favorite."

"Mine too, and we have quite a few."

"You made a rhyme! This is a great day." Tally shimmies her hips.

"I'm glad you came over to see me," I say, and mean it.

Nolan, on the other hand, is a different story. I blow out a thick exhale, regaining my composure. "I'll talk to your dad, but this doesn't mean anything serious."

"Uh, yeah. It totally does. You'll see. My sheeming is super good."

I don't bother correcting her. At least this way, I can pretend she isn't plotting against me. But if I let my foolish heart have a vote, we're on the same side.

chapter thirteen

Nolan

THUNDERING FOOTSTEPS POUND ON THE STAIRS, SIGNALING Tally's hurried descent. No matter how confident I pretend to be, not one bit of me assumes that Clea actually has decided to see me. That knowledge is just one more slash across my gut. My breath hitches from the nervousness. I have to believe for both of us.

There's always someday, dammit.

"Daddy, Daddy, Daddy!" My daughter's squeal hits a higher octave with each step. "I did so good."

I momentarily forget the pain while concentrating on her bubbling glee. "Yeah, Princess?"

Her nod is a blur with bountiful enthusiasm as she comes into view. "Uh-huh. You'll be super happy."

"Well, that's easy. I already am." And that's the truth. It's impossible not to get a boost from her infectious excitement, and knowing that Clea is upstairs only cranks up that zing an extra notch.

An *oomph* escapes me when Tally launches herself at my legs. I stumble backward into a crumpled kneel. She adjusts her grip and climbs into my lap, latching onto my neck as if her arms are freaking pythons.

"No, like *really* super happy." She wiggles to get free and begins hopping in place. "Clea changed her hair. Did you see it? She's a Goldilocks like me."

The reminder spreads my smile. I had a hunch that Tally would love that similarity. "Yes, she's very pretty."

"Yep." She pops her lips. "And you're gonna make her stay with us, right? I don't wanna see her cry ever again."

That's another thing we agree on.

"We better start slower than that, Lou. Is Clea coming down?" The anxious energy tingling along my spine returns.

"Well, duh. Aren't you listening? I just said I did so good. Now I'm gonna go tell Kody. He better not be playing marriage party without me." Then she zooms away, leaving a cloud of eager dust for me to choke on.

I'm still folded on the floor, dazing off in the direction Tally dashed off to, when a throat clears beside me. My neck snaps toward the noise on pure reflexive instinct. Who I find has my mouth going dry, then immediately pooling with lava.

"Kneeling at my feet?" Clea's melodic tone sends a molten shudder through my limbs.

Any semblance of a response fizzles on my tongue. Instead, I take full advantage of the slumped position I'm in. Fuck, she's a sight that shrines are created for. If my eyesight fails tomorrow, I'll be comforted by this image plastered to memory.

Her dress hits mid-thigh, treating me to a delectable eyeful of toned legs. Her skin is smooth and begging to be caressed. It's never been so challenging to look and not touch. Lucious curves, silky lines, and soft edges fill my vision. From down here, I could easily slide up her hem and see what else she's hiding from view.

It's no secret I desire her. I just saw her on Friday, but I'm finding distance has made my heart more desperate. The sheer proximity practically sets me ablaze. The barest hint of her vanilla scent is enough to wreck me for all others. We're close physically, but the gap separating us might as well be a cavern. I could cross that expanse. Hell, she might even let me, if the glimmer in her eyes is any indication.

Her sunny waves are wilder than they were at the bar. The style is a ringing endorsement for Tally's case—as if she needed another. My daughter has been relentless in her pursuit to get Clea home. It's my job to convince her that she should stay put. That task might seem daunting, but it's giving me purpose. Joining forces with Tally toward a common goal isn't too shabby either.

That intrinsic motivation spurs me on. I want to haul Clea against me and never let go. Common sense holds me back. A simple hug wouldn't be well received. I can't even entertain the idea of another kiss. My muscles bunch against the resistance.

But there's so much more than carnal need thrumming through my veins. I need to prove she's the end-all for me, however long that might take. It's already been so many years. Patience is my trusted companion. But the wait is finally over. Now to withstand the power of her endurance against me.

Chemistry has never been an issue for us. I have faith in our connection, but reassuring her is vital. The resentment she's built against me—for good reason—will be what ruins us. I need to wipe the doubt away before adding more layers.

"That's fine, just keep staring." Those words might suggest annoyance, but the hint of amusement in her tone betrays the truth.

"Can you blame me? You're a fucking vision, Patra. If you're trying to make me realize what I've been missing by showing it all off, it's—well—it's working."

Clea crosses her arms but says nothing.

"Do you want me to beg? I'm ready." I motion to my bent knees.

Clea tilts her head. "Is this why you sent Tally to fetch me? Not going to lie, I had higher expectations."

"Ah, don't worry. This is just an awkward start."

She quirks a brow, not appearing convinced. "Feel free to give it another go. I can hardly contain myself."

"Really? You don't look very pleased to see my… what was it you said? My 'stupid sexy face'." I aim for nonchalance, but the gravel in my tone gives me away.

She snorts and rolls her eyes to the ceiling. "You're losing points at a record pace. The clock is ticking. Chop-chop, Nolan."

"Putting on the pressure, eh?" I tug at my collar.

"This is your doing. Be thankful I'm entertaining it." She waves a floppy hand at me.

The credit belongs to Tally, not that I need to mention that right now. She wants to claim Clea as ours. I've determined that my best course of action is to follow Tally's lead. It might be a dick move, but this woman can't deny my daughter anything. She's never been able to, and I highly doubt that's going to change.

I drag a hand through my hair. "Maybe we should try this again."

Clea pinches the bridge of her noise. "Will you please get off the floor?"

It's only then I realize that I'm still worshipping the ground at her feet. I have no problem parking my ass on this carpet so long as she's standing within reach. Best not to press my luck, though. With a groan, I rise to face the consequences waiting for me.

"We need to talk." This conversation is long overdue.

"Okay, well, here I am."

"Where should we go?"

"Oh, you actually want to leave?" Her hesitation crawls under my skin.

I frown at her. "Well, yeah. That's the entire point. I want to take you out."

She falters, knotting her fingers into a tangle. "Just the two of us?"

That's when it hits me. We rarely go anywhere alone. Tally is always glued to Clea if given the choice. My daughter must really trust me to fix this if she's willingly surrendering precious time with her favorite person.

More weight drops on my shoulders. I try not to hunch from the force. "Do I make you uncomfortable, Patra?"

She shakes her head with a sigh, then walks to the hall closet. "No, of course not. Do you want to let Kody and Tally know we're going somewhere?"

"They already know."

"I should have figured as much, considering you're all behind this little operation." Her soft grin lightens the mood. "I guess we can walk to Cuppa Steam. Rory and Rufus can join us."

"You need a buffer?" A slither of unease snakes around my throat.

Her shrug is slight as she peeks back at me. "Just in case this goes south. I can always use them as an excuse to leave you in the trenches."

Her voice carries an amused tune that deflates the strain in my lungs. "You wound me."

"The feeling is mutual." That lob smacks me straight. She's not ready to joke with me. Yet.

I mentally berate myself. The rebound is automatic and fluid. Until a brutal reminder punches me. This isn't the Clea I'm accustomed to dealing with. She's guarded and wary after I drove a wedge between us.

She lifts her fingers to her mouth and lets out a shrill whistle. The dogs bound toward us in a heap of wiggling butts and excited yips. Her rigid posture relaxes while she gathers up the proper supplies for our chaperones. Clea clips a leash to each collar and passes me one. The vibe shifts for the umpteenth time, but I shake off the familiarity. I need to quit assuming we'll fall back into a regular routine.

Rufus immediately wraps the nylon cord around my legs as he runs in circles. His owner laughs at my trapped predicament but makes no move to offer assistance. Sunlight pours in as she opens the door. Then she flounces onto the porch without a backward glance. Rory trots dutifully beside her while my companion tightens his restraints. After a protracted struggle to get free, I exit the door and meet her on the driveway.

We set off at a brisk pace, thanks to the pups insisting they sniff every surface at record speed—and immediately mark their territory. I match her stride, aligning us as a synchronized pair. Our stilted state eases with the natural flow. I could almost pretend this is a regular routine. Perhaps it will be, someday.

Summer sprawls in each direction as we stroll along the sidewalk. Leafy branches from above cast dancing shadows on the concrete. The intermittent shade grants us a reprieve while still allowing us to bask in the warmth. August is polite compared to July, allowing us to be outside without sweating our asses off.

Clea inhales until her chest expands wide, devouring sugary pollen and toasty afternoon delights. A delicate breeze kicks up the cropped blond brushing her jaw. I'm content with the lull, but there's much to be said. Those tattered seams bear down on me. Just as I dredge up the nerve, her voice cuts in.

"So, how's work been treating you?"

My scoff is hollow. "Seriously?"

A dent carves at the smooth skin between her brows. "What?"

"Are we really doing this?" If we're going to fill the silence, it can't be mundane chit-chat. Not with so much on my mind.

"Doing what?"

"Talking about… work?"

She tugs on the leash after Rory tries to chase a squirrel. "I was using a strategy from your suggestion box. You tend to bring up the weather when the silence grows long enough to sprout flowers."

I'm caught in my own web. "Touché."

"Fine." Clea rolls her neck until a joint pops. "Will you tell me about Rachel?"

I don't stumble at hearing her name. My inner defenses get a nod in gratitude for keeping up appearances. After how we left things, I knew to expect this question. Even so, there's no preparing for the onslaught of guilt as the past crashes into me. That sinking sensation is as familiar as an old buddy—but this friend is one I'm more than ready to break ties with. Maybe finally revealing the truth will help. I already planned to spill the details to Clea. The secrets between us are plaguing our future. We need to purge the toxins keeping our relationship poisoned, once and for all.

"For the record, she's one of the topics I wanted to address today," I start, peering at her from the corner of my eye.

She nods, but the motion is jerky. "Wow, okay. Honestly, I figured you'd deflect as usual."

"No, not anymore. Things will be different now, Patra." The words are meant to prepare her. No more fucking off and ignoring who's waiting right in front of me.

"We'll see about that."

I ignore her doubt. I'm done delaying, and I'll prove it to her. "Tally's mother died in an accident, which you might've guessed by now. I'm overly cautious about driving at night and cars in general because of that."

A sympathetic shadow crosses Clea's face, but she nods at me to continue.

"The person behind the wheel was intoxicated. Witnesses reported that the vehicle was speeding and swerving. It was a disaster in the making. They smashed head-on into a guardrail, killing them instantly."

"Oh," she whispers. "I'm sorry."

"I've... learned to live with it. In my own way," I tell her.

Another silence falls between us, but I don't let it linger. I've only told her half the story so far.

"Honestly... part of me always thought it was only a matter of time. I wish I could say for certain that Rachel wouldn't be willing to get into an unsafe situation like that. Based on her destructive behavior, she might've done it on purpose."

Clea chokes and slaps a palm to her chest. "What? Oh my gosh. Why would she do that? She had a baby depending on her."

I squint against a patch of bright rays streaking through the trees. "I've asked myself that question enough that it's permanently dented into my skull. There isn't an answer I can give that will ever absolve her, or me."

"It's not your fault. You weren't there, right?"

I shake my head. "But her negligence became my own."

Creases line her forehead. "How?"

"I could've stopped her. She wanted to be a family. I didn't. She wanted to marry me, but we didn't love each other. Maybe if I—"

"That's not fair to you, though," she cuts me off.

"Well, I kept her at a platonic distance, refusing to even entertain the possibility. If I'd given that to her, she wouldn't have spiraled out of control."

"You don't know that. She might've had a dangerous personality and spun out of control regardless."

"It's the unknown that's fucked with me the most."

Her fingers flit to my forearm, gripping with purpose. "You can't take responsibility for her actions. That blame will wreck you, and for what? Rachel's decisions were her own. She chose to be reckless."

My acceptance is a slow exhale. "I've come to terms with that. Between you and Tally, I'm convinced there wasn't much more I could do without sacrificing myself. That wouldn't have been fair to her either. Eventually, she would've realized my commitment was forced. I don't imagine that going over well with anyone."

"No, not at all."

More confessions bubble to the surface. "It's obvious that I'm withdrawn and jaded, but this is why. The fear of history repeating itself crippled me. I stayed far away from women. If I never got close enough to form an attachment, she wouldn't hurt herself because of me. Shit, does that sound narcissistic or what?"

Clea holds up a sliver of space between her thumb and forefinger. "Maybe a bit. I don't blame you for being careful.

Although, I should probably be offended you didn't see me as a threat to this theory."

"You're not a risk for me to take, Patra. From that first moment, I should've recognized you as the one. My cure in plain sight. I just wasn't willing to believe in chance. That level of devotion was foreign to me. My mother and Rachel don't count as examples, but they're pretty much all I had until you. It took you leaving to wake me up. Truly, I have to thank you for releasing me from the toxic cycle. Only you and Tally have the power to truly reach me. Believe it or not, you already have." Regardless of the severity, a calm sweeps over me.

Then I dart my gaze toward the approaching intersection. Soon we'll be engulfed in the bustling throng. The best is still left unsaid. I find my stride shortening to prolong our privacy. If Clea notices my stalling tactics, she doesn't comment.

"You're not a risk," I repeat. "You're the one who proves love is selfless and pure and… possible. That's the love worth depending on. To lose yourself in. Find the faith to believe again. The kind that inspires and makes us stronger together. A never-ending embrace. Not worrying about being vulnerable since that person will always support you. Free of judgment and ridicule. There's no fear of what might happen when you're consumed with the present. Every moment is a blessing and is treated as such. It's the most sincere exchange you can share with another. One day with that compassion is better than a lifetime without. That's what we have, and I'm ready to prove it."

About halfway through my admission, Clea halted in her tracks to gawk at me. Now, she's sniffing and turning her head away from me. I catch the movement as she wipes beneath her eyes. "Damn you, Nolan Jasper. That's a really stellar speech. I wasn't aware that you had all that charm hiding," she whispers in a laugh. "Should really warn a girl before you make her swoon."

"You don't need a shield against me, Patra. I didn't spew all that just to sway you. It comes from inside here"—I slap my chest—"and you deserve to hear how I feel. Maybe it will help my case. Even if you couldn't care less, the impact you've made on me needs to be celebrated. I'd still be cowering in the basement if it wasn't for you. Think about all I'd be missing."

She scrubs a hand over her damp cheeks, still avoiding my gaze. "Jeez, dude. Give me a chance to recover before you drizzle on more romance."

I chuckle at her mock outrage. "You don't have to forgive me. I wouldn't expect you to so quickly. This is just me being honest."

"Yeah, good. I'm not that easy." A flush paints her cheeks once she's done speaking.

"I don't want easy. I just want you."

"Pretty, pretty words. We'll see how you reinforce them."

"Does that mean you'll give me a chance?"

Clea snorts. "Take it easy, big talker. I probably wouldn't be here if Tally hadn't convinced me."

I don't bother hiding my wince. "Kick a man while he's down and exposed."

She glares at the swaying branches above us. "Don't act butthurt. This is more than you deserve."

"But you don't hate me?" I phrase it as a question and give voice to my growing doubt.

Her narrowed eyes shift onto me. "Why are you asking me that again? Do you require constant reassurance?"

"When it comes to your feelings toward me? Absolutely. I'm not arrogant enough to spout false bravado where you're concerned. Not brave enough to even pretend. You scare the shit out of me, Patra."

To her credit, she doesn't react other than a slow lump bobbing in her throat. It's my fault that the light no longer shines quite as brightly in her eyes. I did that to her. She shouldn't settle for me, with all the burdens I've placed on her. A slicing pain follows my realization. The baggage I carry is overwhelming and stubborn and discouraging. But dammit, I'm a selfish bastard. It's not just me I need to worry about. If Clea vanishes from my life, she won't see Tally nearly as often. If ever. That's a steep consequence. I can't let her go without a fight.

The chance is mine for the taking. I'm determined to keep her talking. Plucking at a sentimental chord has bridged the gap in my favor before. "Remember when Tally was younger?"

"Of course. Do you?" Her flat affect isn't lost on me.

"Ouch." Maybe this is a bad idea.

Clea flails an arm to the side. "Don't ask ridiculous questions if you can't handle the backlash."

"That's fair." And it is. That doesn't mean I have to approve. "It's just that we were a team then. I have such good memories from those earlier years. She was such a cute baby. That toddler phase, though," I cringe. "Talk about a test of willpower."

"Are you trying to remind me of your more recent disappearing act?"

"Hardly," I grunt. "I hate the distance I've put between us. That choice will always haunt me. If only I had the courage to face my demon sooner. It really fucking sucks. But I'm going to fix us."

"I don't know about that." She mutters the doubt under her breath, but the quiet ferocity clangs against my own.

"Are you done with me?"

She bites her bottom lip and exhales through flared nostrils. "I want to say yes."

Hope flares and fans a spark of confidence. "But?"

"I can't." She pauses for an extended beat while focusing on her dogs. Rory and Rufus have been obliging our social hour, but they're beginning to get restless. "We should probably haul ass or head back. There's packing to be done."

"Are you going on a trip?"

Her laugh is dull and sharp. "Ah, no. I'm moving. Guess you didn't hear."

A ripple of shock so large it's tangible invades my system. It begins with a prickling scalp and reverberates down my face like a slow-motion reel. I feel my eyes blow wide in disbelief while my jaw goes slack. My body remains motionless otherwise. Her brother mentioned something along these lines, but I figured he was just trying to ignite a fire under my ass.

The breath whispers from me with a quiet hiss. "What? Where? When? How did this happen?"

"Yeah, it's a recent decision. I decided it was high time to find my own space. Kody doesn't need me cramping his style. Not sure exactly when or where yet. Once I find an affordable place where these two knuckleheads are welcome. Until then, Presley is letting me stay with her."

I'm shaking my head before she's done talking. The denial I've been submerged in is deep. I'd tricked myself into believing these past two weeks were about gaining some perspective and temporary space. How fucking blind I've been. "This is because of me."

She tilts her chin with a laugh. "Careful, or I might assume you're actually a narcissist."

"I'm being serious, Patra." I drag rough fingers through my hair. "Please reconsider."

"You're having a more adverse reaction than Tally." Clea massages her temple.

"Are you surprised? We don't want you to go." The thought is catastrophic, ripping at the scabbed crater in my chest.

Her cheeks puff with pent-up air that she releases in a whoosh. "I can't keep doing this. Not that there's ever been a this with us."

"Oh, we're definitely a this."

"Don't be cute. I refuse to be strung along. It's embarrassing how long I've hung on to the idea of us." She sounds extremely disappointed in herself.

In turn, acidic bile burns in my gut. "And I never meant to be a worthless asshole to you in the first place."

"I appreciate that, Nolan. Truly. I'm even leaning toward the accepting side. Although, it's crazy to hear you waxing poetic about love. That's still sinking in. You've given me a lot to think about, but that doesn't change our immediate situation. There's so much to repair before I'd consider… whatever it is you're offering." She motions for me to fill in the blanks.

Based on the direction of this conversation, I'm afraid to freak her out with my intentions. "Just don't move yet, okay? Give me a week or two. I need a chance to prove we belong together, Patra. I want to be the man who gets the privilege to walk beside you. Toward our future. I don't expect today. Or tomorrow. Not even the day after that. Just promise me someday. Soon would be preferable. But I won't push it."

"You hurt me, Nolan. For so long. I refuse to put myself back in that position." Her blue eyes shine with conviction.

My knees tremble with the instinct to buckle and beg. "Let me fix this. Prove I can be the man you want. I'll stumble and fuck up, but I won't stop trying to make you mine. Ours."

"Dragging Tally into your business again?"

"It's a package deal." I don't relent when it appears she's about to interrupt with another rebuttal. "We'll go at your pace. Just friends or more, it's completely up to you. I'll follow your lead. Just give me a chance."

I have every intention of chasing her. Clea will feel desired every waking moment if I have any stake in this game. I'll reach her in slumber too. That's when the best fantasies take shape.

Clea straightens from her slouching pose. "I'll think about it. Maybe."

"That's better than not at all." I stretch my arm toward hers, threading our fingers together for a gentle squeeze. "Can we start with coffee?"

She stares at our clasped palms. Her thumb ghosts over mine before she tugs free from the gentle embrace. The loss is instant. My skin pebbles from cold after thriving on the heat from hers. But she let me hold her hand for a moment. I'm not going to obsess over the negative.

"Okay," she assents with a small—albeit visible—grin.

The gift of her smile showers me with comfort. Her

expression is a kindness I don't deserve. She's always been too generous with her attention. Why did I ever take her for granted? Never again.

The emotion swells in my throat. "Yeah?"

"I'm still standing here talking to you, aren't I?" She gestures to the path.

With that, we resume our trek. The hum of activity from engines and fellow pedestrians greets us as we leave our neighborhood and turn onto the main drag. Our town—Greenbury—is a decent size without being too crowded. There's somewhat of a downtown area less than two miles away. Clea's favorite coffee shop is bundled among the commercial blocks.

There are small tables lined up in front on their small patio. I spy a few empty spots. "Why don't you grab us seats while I get the drinks?"

She gapes at me as I stride toward the entrance. "Do you need my order?"

"Nah, I got it." I tap my temple.

"How can you be so sure?"

I shoot her a wink, feeling revitalized after weeks in the dark. "Wanna bet?"

chapter fourteen

Clea

THE POOCHES ARE LOUNGING ON THE CONCRETE BY MY FEET, idly patrolling the scene with waning interest. My focus, on the other hand, is rapt and narrowed in on a specific target. I track Nolan as he struts inside Cuppa Steam like a seasoned alpha male who gives zero fucks about the peons bowing at his feet. Between the confident swagger and a playful smirk, he reeks of multiple orgasms delivered by a dirty mouth. He's more efficient at lowering my inhibitions than a fishbowl margarita.

I mean, the man has his freaking dimples on full display. He's obviously trying to decimate my control—and any other women with functioning eyeballs. My jaw hasn't resumed its locked position, still hanging slack after his slew of revelations.

It's an internal battle to rip my gaze off him. This effing guy. I've only been in love with him for six years. He barely acknowledged my existence for most of them. What a cruel joke. How badly I want to walk away without giving him the chance he finally wants to take. But that hopeful, naïve girl buried beneath the scar tissue is pleading.

Another silent curse slips from my lips. Damn him and his sweet sentiments. I need to be careful. If this unrequited love taught me anything, it's to be open-minded, yet vigilant.

I'm not caving. Yet. I earn a mental slap for that. I still need to guard my heart.

The line is long enough to buy me an express pep-talk. I dig out my phone and scroll to a reliable ball-buster.

"Hey, babes. This is a fun surprise in my boring schedule." Vannah's chirpy tone puts me on alert.

I squint at a random spot in the distance. "You're not in the middle of riding a certain something, right?"

She growls a string of expletives under her breath. "I answer the phone while having sex one time and never live it down."

"It was a traumatizing experience." A shudder wracks my limbs at the salacious reminder.

Her responding hum makes the unwanted recollection worse. "We had a good laugh."

"You and that other exhibitionist, maybe. The perceived visual still disturbs me." I gag loud enough for her to hear. "So, you're not having a bit of afternoon delight? I need verbal confirmation."

Disappointment leaks through the line. "No, Prudette. I'm at the office, fully dressed. Hubs isn't even in town. And besides, it's morning."

"Okay, good. I need your advice. Quickly."

A creak sounds. She's most likely tipping forward in her chair to hear me better. "Oh, this is so much better than reviewing inspection reports. Give me the scoop."

"All right," I exhale. "I'm alone with Nolan at the moment."

"Naked?"

I hang my head at her blurted question. "No. What's wrong with you?"

"Me? I'm concerned about your vagina. The poor girl needs some action."

"This was a mistake," I mutter.

Vannah cackles at a pitch that makes my dogs wince. "Oh, shut up. I'm fucking around. Quit taking me so seriously. Please continue. I promise to behave."

That'll be the day. But my options are limited. "Long story short, he confessed that he... loves me? Maybe? Strong feelings, for sure. There were all these ultra-romantic lines, but he was raw and genuine. The apologies were nonstop. He's been super flirty and sincere, but I'm mad at him. I need to reinforce my resolve. That's why I called you. Tell me how to be strong."

She clucks her tongue. "You want my honest opinion?"

"Yes, obviously." Annoyance bleeds into my tone, but she deserves it for questioning otherwise.

"I say you go for it. Start fresh. Forget the past."

"Wait, what?" I pull the phone from my ear to check the screen. Vannah's name is displayed in bold pride. "Who are you and what have you done with my brazen pessimist?"

She groans. "I've been listening to you blabber on about an obvious decision for years. Literally. Now that the truth is revealed and the air is cleared, you two can be together. That's what you really want. You don't need me to discourage you. No matter what I say, you're going to forgive him. This is Nolan and Tally we're talking about."

"Tally is innocent." That's the only piece I care to address at this moment.

"But she's a package deal."

I grunt in frustration. "That's exactly what he said."

Vannah clucks her tongue. "So?"

I scowl at the glaring truth standing in line just beyond the window. Rory and Rufus set their heads on my lap with a mutual whimper, as though my distress is theirs. "Why do you make so much sense?"

"Been there, done that."

"Yeah, right. You'd never cling to a man this long if he didn't show interest."

"Maybe if I met him at eighteen. Those are impressionable times. I envy you, babes."

The air gets trapped in my lungs. I nearly crack a rib in the coughing fit that follows. "Now I know you're fucking with me."

"Oh, ye of little faith. I'm trying to give a heartfelt speech. The snarky bitch route only goes so far. It's not fun as a lifetime gig.

We can recall all that stellar advice you gave me about Landon." She snorts. "Thanks for that."

The delectable scent of freshly baked bread distracts me momentarily. I suck in the mouthwatering aroma. Maybe Nolan will get a sandwich for us to split. That thought is sobering. "I can't believe what I'm hearing, Van."

"Okay, let me be more clear. Please, for all our sakes, fuck the man already."

"You don't have to be so crude."

"And you don't have to marry the guy. Just let him pop your cherry and see where that leads." She clears her throat and continues in a whisper. "But we all know it's straight to the alter."

"Your mind must be a terrifying place."

Vannah cracks up, the amusing sound full of pride. "You mispronounced 'thrilling'."

"Ever consider being a motivational speaker? You should consider a career change."

"That's a good idea," she muses.

I catch sight of Nolan paying at the register. "Well, this has been enlightening. I'm on my own, apparently."

"You're welcome."

"Talk soon, horndog."

She's still laughing as I end the call. I'm still grumbling about good-for-nothing friends when Nolan approaches the table with two to-go cups. He passes me the one with my name scrawled across the orange cardboard sleeve. I wrap my hands around the warm cup and take a long whiff. "Is this what I think it is?"

He sits in the chair beside me, ignoring typical etiquette that would strongly suggest the one across from me. His dark hair shines like melted chocolate under the afternoon sun. "Just try a sip. Then you can dole out my winnings."

Ah, yes. He attempted to raise the stakes. I quirk a brow at his candor. "We never agreed to any terms."

"Eh, talking with me is reward enough."

I could get lost in that lofty statement. Without further delay,

I try a swig of the mysterious coffee. A familiar—and very appealing—flavor combination bursts across my tongue. The Get 'Er Done. It's a signature choice from Cuppa Steam. Vanilla-Mocha Macchiato, extra shot of espresso, three sugar-free caramel pumps, and extra whip with a caramel drizzle. Freaking yum.

It's a horrific indulgence that I treat myself to every now and then. I usually just order a large hazelnut blend with skim milk. Apparently, this is the beverage Nolan seared to memory. It's complicated enough to be impressive.

There's no stopping the pleasure from dripping off my lips. "Oh my gosh, this is so good. It's been months since I've ordered one."

That gives him pause. "Did I get it right?"

I find myself nodding. "Yes, but this doesn't mean anything."

"You're right. It proves everything." He settles deeper into the metal chair, wafting his irresistible hotness at me. Just the effortless position he's sprawling in screams sultry overload. He's not even trying, and I want to come-hither.

I steel myself as best I can. No way am I stepping in that landmine until safer avenues are exhausted. I avoid his heated stare and lift my cup. "Thanks for this. What'd you get?"

"Just a dark roast." He swallows a gulp as though it's vital.

I'm hypnotized by his Adam's apple as he chugs another mouthful. That stubbled notch is mesmerizing. "Plain and simple."

"That's me." He seems to be in his element, which is odd since this isn't one of his typical haunts. "I haven't been on a date since—"

"This isn't a date."

His chuckle has the perfect amount of grit to curl my toes. "Yeah, it is. I won't let you slip through my fingers after finally getting you out with me."

That's a stretch of the imagination. "You lost the bet from our pool game."

"But did I really lose?"

"Don't make me regret agreeing to this little outing."

"We definitely can't have that." A low sound rumbles from him. "Tell me I'm not too late, Patra."

I flick the plastic lid on my cup. "For what?"

Nolan licks a tantalizing trail along his bottom lip. "Are you playing coy on purpose?"

My blink is heavy and slow. "Um, no? It was a legitimate question. You still haven't revealed the ulterior motive behind this friendly chat."

"How far in the future do you want me to reveal? I'd hate to spoil the surprise."

I'm sure my expression is blank to match my brain short-circuiting. "Huh?"

He drifts a finger down my arm, eliciting a trail of goosebumps. "Immediately, I don't want you to move. After that, I'll gladly—and enthusiastically—devour whatever scraps you're willing to toss me. Just know that I won't stop trying for more until you're in my bed every night."

I have a sneaking suspicion that he'll be relentless in his pursuit. That should scare me more than it does. Deflection is my only hope. "Are you adding suave cockiness to your profile too?"

"Would that please you?"

"Good grief, Nolan. What's gotten into you?" A noticeable fire has erupted across my cheeks.

"This is me, Patra. I've just been in hibernation. Thanks for rousing me."

"I feel like there's an innuendo beneath the surface."

He nods at his lap before hiking a wicked brow at me. "Want to find out?"

Coffee burns my throat as I choke. "Excuse me?"

His extremely forward suggestion is going to incinerate me. Then he straightens and the molten lust vanishes from his gaze. "You're it for me, Angel."

The nickname has me coming up short, along with every word prior. "Angel?"

"You swoop in and save me when I need you most."

A muffled moan squeaks past my squished lips. I must resist launching into his arms. But the temptation is coiling me tighter than a spiral perm. It takes Wonder Woman effort to yank my stupefied gaze off him. "Wow, that's, uh, really... wow. It's what I've been waiting to hear since we met. It's no secret I like you, Nolan. More than like you, honestly. But that's gotten me nowhere. Now, suddenly, you've had an epiphany and I'm supposed to cheer? I can't hop into familiar ruts because they're comfortable. Excuse me for being skeptical."

The emerald hue in his eyes darkens. "I'd be worried if you weren't. This is fast, but also long overdue. Still, I don't blame you for being suspicious."

That settles the jarring nerves pinging in my belly. "I don't want to seem ungrateful, or bleak. It's just hard to digest. I'm not hopelessly falling for your stupid sexy face more than I already have."

A twitch wiggles the corner of his mouth. "All I'm hearing is that you find me insanely attractive."

"You've got the insane part right. I'm not sure what's gotten into you."

"Logic. I've finally found reason and good sense." He leans forward, propping a muscular forearm on the table. A hint of the tattoo on his bicep winks at me. "I'm looking right at her."

And I'm dizzy from his abrupt flip. This is a man who rarely shows emotion, and suddenly he's a dynamic connoisseur of the feels? I pinch myself to make sure I can actually believe what I'm seeing. To make matters more confusing, he's choosing to use all that newfound heartthrobbiness on me. I'm not equipped to defend myself against this seductive flood.

I wipe my brow with a sigh. "All right, Casanova. You're spreading the mush on pretty damn thick."

Nolan frowns. "Is that bad?"

My head shakes without hesitation. "Not at all. It's just weird coming from you. This is so... extreme."

He pounds a fist against his sternum. "It's been building

inside me. The blockage finally burst. I'm crazy about you, Patra. No more hiding."

"Okay, whoa." I cradle my head in an open palm. "This is just a lot to take in all at once."

"But I'm not pressuring you, right? It just feels so liberating to get these feelings off my chest."

And who am I to deny this divine intervention? "I'm really happy for you, Nolan. It's great to see you smile without restraint."

On cue, he provides me with another dazzling grin. Those panty-melting dimples threaten to pull me under. "If nothing else, you've set me free."

The earnestness in his tone threatens to crumble what remains of my resolve. Just as I'm about to pepper him with a spicy retort, movement from my right stops me. A server pauses at our table with two plates.

"I have a chicken club, cut in half to split." She smiles in my direction, then at the man not bothering to look up.

"That's us," Nolan replies, without taking his rapt focus off me.

"What's this?" I zero in on the unexpected delivery while my stomach groans in approval. Rory and Rufus—who I almost forgot about since they've been so quiet—perk up at the savory smell of grilled meat. I do, too. My mouth is already watering from the toasty aroma of sourdough.

He shrugs. "I thought you might want a snack. Their bread is hot from the oven, right?"

Well, that settles any lingering frustrations. I stare at yet another peace offering while trying to absorb the emotion stinging my eyes. It might seem small, but the meaning is momentous.

"You don't have to eat it." The uncertainty clipping his tone makes me flinch.

I hate that I'm making him doubt his very considerate gesture. "This is my favorite sandwich. It's very thoughtful of you. There was a passing moment earlier where I imaged us sharing one."

His expression brightens. "So, I did well?"

"Very. For a man who rarely dates—"

"Never," he cuts in.

"What?"

"I never date."

"Oh, okay." I pause to shake my head. "Not sure that makes a huge difference."

"It does to me."

"Fine," I huff at his insistence. "You seem very capable of spoiling the ladies rotten with all these lavish displays of affection."

I don't even know what to call them. My description stream has run dry. He's turning me into a puddle.

"Just for you. I wouldn't do this for anyone else."

"That's easy to say when I'm sitting next to you."

"Trust me. I wouldn't be out with anyone else."

There's only so much my resolve can withstand before crumbling under the sugary swoon. I blink to clear the stars from my vision. This stud muffin is barreling forward at full tilt. How long can I actually hold out? Do I really want to? Damn him and his gentlemanly qualities. He has one major breakthrough, and I'm ready to straddle his lap.

Maybe Vannah is right. Admitting that stings, but it's only my stubborn pride. I'm all out of reasons to shove distance between us. It was a valiant effort. Not nearly enough, but that's beside the point.

"I surrender, okay?" He perks up to respond, but I hold up one finger to silence him. "Just about moving. I'll pause my search—until further notice."

Nolan's brilliant gaze sparkles under the afternoon sun. "That's plenty for now."

"Why do I sense a 'but'?"

His chuckle does delicious things to the excess warmth collecting in my lower belly. "Don't worry, Patra. I have big plans."

That's exactly what scares me the most.

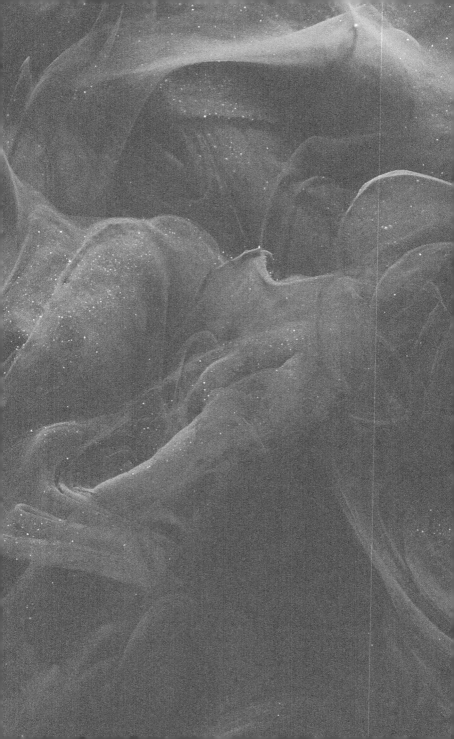

chapter fifteen

Nolan

TALLY GIGGLES AS WE LAND ON THE FINAL STEP. I PRESS A FINGER to my lips, and she slaps a palm over her mouth to muffle the sound. A squeaky floorboard announces our arrival to the second floor as we shuffle across the carpet. Not sure why we're trying so hard to be quiet. Kody is making a ruckus downstairs.

This impulsive—and risky—maneuver can easily backfire. Tally insists that Clea won't be upset if we wake her. That might very well be the case where my daughter is concerned. Not sure that leeway extends to me. My damn ass is sweating just considering her less-than-thrilled reactions.

I raise a fist to knock on Clea's closed bedroom door. Tally's manners need some fine-tuning. She turns the knob without warning, the wood barrier disappearing before my hand can make contact. All concerns flee my brain at the sight that's revealed before us. There's no space for regret. Only a tiny flicker to thank my little girl for being a genius.

Clea is awake—barely. She's in a rumpled state that I've never had the privilege to witness. All groggy and soft, no armor in sight. The shirt she's wearing is crooked, exposing just enough of her perky breasts to border on scandalous. If my daughter wasn't present, I'd already be pleading for her to dip the fabric lower. I chase that fantasy away with an internal growl and force my focus elsewhere.

Those lush lips are slightly parted in a lazy pout. Her blond hair is in disarray. The golden mess only adds more fuel to the burning need inside me. She's laying down under the covers, propped up on her side by a bent elbow. Her bleary eyes are squinting at the phone in her hand. Those lazy lids pop wide as we cross the threshold.

Tally doesn't waste a second for decorum or permission. She dashes to the bed, hurtling her body onto Clea's blankets. "Morning, Lele!"

Clea scrubs at the creases denting her cheeks. She inches upright and rests against the headboard. Her fingers automatically clutch at the scooping neckline, righting the material with a harsh yank. With careful movements, she tucks the comforter against her sides. "Uh, hello. I wasn't aware you two were stopping by so early."

"It's after eight o'clock, sleepyhead!"

"But it's the weekend." Her protest falls on deaf ears.

"I don't really know how time works." Tally's reminder is better than any excuse I could muster.

Sunlight streaks through the blinds as I lean against the wall. I'm content to stand and watch them interact. It's such a natural exchange. Any awkwardness at our abrupt—and unexpected—visit doesn't hinder their effortless flow. A slow exhale sags my posture. I find myself completely at ease in this scenario.

But the feeling isn't mutual. My intrusion is no secret, based on the frequent side-glare Clea is shooting me. Leering on the sidelines like a creep isn't going to grant me any favors.

I straighten and dip my chin in greeting. "Are you decent?"

"Sorta." Her lips hitch at the corner. "Just don't peek under the duvet."

If only that were an actual invitation. "Do you want me to go?"

She absently toys with Tally's unruly curls. "That depends on why you're here to begin with."

"We brought you breakfast." I lift the mostly forgotten bag.

Her gaze latches onto the offering in my grip. "Did you cook?"

"No way! My dad burns toast. I don't want you to get poisoned, Lele." Tally flips over with a giggle. Her feet kick at the air in wild arches.

I scrub the back of my neck. "Thanks a lot, Lou."

"She's not wrong," Clea laughs with a wink.

Humoring her at my expense is just fine. "Thanks for the rave review, but we ordered from Muddy Pig."

Her lashes flutter. "Do you have potato pancakes hiding in there?"

I make a sound in agreement. "With your name on them. Extra bacon and applesauce on the side."

"Oh, you're not playing fair. This is cheating." But she beckons me toward her with a grabby motion.

Like a puppet on a string, I move forward without conscious thought. Clea's vanilla scent hangs heavy in the air. The aroma envelops me in heady bliss. I inhale deep pulls as if starved for oxygen. My lungs ache in protest, but that doesn't stop me from dragging in another breath.

I put the bag on her nightstand, then return to the hallway. Clea's jaw drops when I go about setting up the tray table over her lap. I unpack the containers and utensils, arranging them so the girls can eat together.

"Wow, you're really prepared for this. I've never been served in bed." She watches me with rapt focus.

"It bodes well for me that this impresses you, since I can't cook for crap."

Tally halts the one-sided conversation she'd been having with her imaginary friend. "Eww, Dad! That's potty talk."

I cringe. "Right, sorry."

Clea cups a palm around her mouth to secretly mumble, "Don't let her pretend she's innocent. I catch her saying that all the time."

"It's not my fault the boys at school are poopy heads."

"See?" Her gaze is still on me as she waves at my daughter. Then she pins Tally with a stare. "Don't be the potty talk police if you're not going to follow the rules too."

Her little shoulders slump at being called out. "Okay, fine."

I grab the remaining to-go box and survey the scene. The seating options are limited. Clea might not appreciate my ass parked on her mattress. This truce between us is fragile at best. I snag the chair from her desk to be safe.

The woman misses nothing. She tracks my movements with a shrewd gaze. Her eyes skip to Tally, who's polishing off a blueberry muffin. Crumbs litter her mouth as she happily chows down. Clea takes a meaningful look at her supplies.

"Lulah, will you get napkins from the kitchen? Maybe some juice too."

My daughter glances from Clea to me, mulling over the request. "M'kay. But no talking about super fun stuff without me. I don't like being left out."

Clea nods. "Got it. Just boring adult things."

Tally skids to a halt near the door. "Like how my dad is in the doghouse?"

Bottomless baby blues dance with mirth as Clea looks to me for confirmation. "What?"

"Nothing," I grumble.

But Tally doesn't take the hint, of course. "Uncle Kody said you put my dad in the doghouse. I still haven't found it. Do Rory and Rufus sleep there? He also told me that Daddy needs to kiss your butt. That's super gross, right?"

Clea's eyes are now bulging at me. "It sure is."

"I have no control over what comes from your brother's mouth."

"You could discourage him from using that language around your child," she deadpans while glaring at me.

"That would probably be wise." I tap my chin.

My daughter gasps. "You can't get more mad at us. We have lotsa 'pologizing to do. Daddy told me that we're gonna do lots of special stuff for you. Then you'll forgive us and won't move away."

"Tallulah." I really need to be careful what I say around her.

She wrinkles her nose. "Uh-oh, now I'm in trouble."

Clea's entire body is trembling with laughter. "You're perfect, Lulah. I could never be mad at you."

"See, Grumpy Gus?" Tally gives me a pointed look. "She totally loves us. We did it!"

A croak comes from Clea. There's no doubt the hollow noise is aimed at me. I raise my palms in defeat. This is spiraling out of control. "Lou, how about those napkins?"

"Oh, duh! Be back soon." Then she disappears from sight with a squeal and stampeding footsteps.

With Tally noticeably absent, I brace myself for Clea's tirade. There's a reason she sent my daughter on an errand. Waves crash in my ears as I wait for the inevitable. Deliberation. She was generous with her affections yesterday. I deserve her wrath for taking that kindness for granted again.

"Well, this is new." She gestures at the spread on her tray.

The grunt I give in response falls flat. "It's barely a blip in the grand scheme."

Her hum is suspicious. "I didn't agree to stay at home so you could invade my privacy at all hours."

"Is this crossing a line?"

"What do you think?" A slim brow cocks in offense.

"Tally mentioned that you've always wanted breakfast in bed. You call it ultra-romantic in all the movies." I shrug while regurgitating my daughter's words. "I figured she could be trusted for the juicy intel, and wouldn't steer me wrong."

Clea huffs. "That little stinker is a double agent."

I chuckle at her mock outrage. "We already knew that. She has a lofty agenda of her own."

"No kidding." With that, Clea gives my hunched form a slow once-over. Her brazen perusal strokes my ego.

The instinct to stand and stretch for her ogling jostles my

muscles. "Maybe someday you won't mind me being here bright and early. Or I'll still be snug against you from the night before."

Fiery red blooms across her throat, carving a flushed path upward. "I see your bold attitude hasn't cooled from yesterday."

"It's only getting hotter." If she tells me to fuck off, I'll be forced to rely on less daring strategies. Until then, I'm taking the liberties and chances she might've allowed all along.

She tugs at her tank top. "The power balance of our current predicament is becoming glaringly obvious."

I rear back. "What's that supposed to mean?"

Clea stares at her lower half hidden from view. "I don't have pants on, or a bra for that matter."

The primal urge to rip off her blankets ripples through me. I spread my legs wider to hide any growing evidence from that visual. "Should I, uh, leave? Are you uncomfortable?"

"No, it's fine. This just isn't what I had in mind while picturing you in my room with me mostly naked."

"You've thought about it?"

"Well, yeah." Her tone makes that answer seem obvious. "I told you as much at the bar."

"Nah, I remember quite clearly. You were peeking through the curtains to see me while I showered."

Her laugh is sultry to the extreme. The sound gives me the fucking chills while setting my blood to a boil. "That's just what I admitted out loud."

"I'm back! Did you miss me?" Tally runs into the room with a carton of juice and a paper towel roll. Kody is clearly responsible for gathering the items. Or maybe not.

It feels like she was only gone for thirty seconds. That's what Clea does to me. I could easily lose myself in her for days on end without skipping a beat.

My own shock is mirrored in the woman responsible. She fidgets and swallows nervously. There's a healthy amount of guilt mixed in too. What would happen if we had another five minutes alone? It's best not to tempt my desires with those impossibilities. I recover first, coughing into my fist.

"We always miss you, Lou. Did you grab everything Clea asked for?" I could probably send her back downstairs for cups. All that will accomplish is dumping more aggravation on my already blistering lust.

"Duh, Daddy. I'm good with directions." She passes her bundle to Clea, who's busy shoveling food into her mouth.

She gives Tally a sealed-lip smile, forking another bite. "So yummy."

"Glad you're enjoying it." The omelet I ordered tastes bland and seriously lacking. My appetite is concentrated elsewhere.

Tally begins twirling in circles. "Can we go to the park soon? Oh, oh! How about the zoo? Or that one playground with the huge slide. I love that place. We could stop at the pet shop first and visit all the puppies."

Clea rubs her temples with a groan. "I need coffee. An entire bucket. And a shower. Then I can participate in activity planning."

I stand from the chair, brushing imaginary crumbs from my jeans. "All right, we'll get out of your business."

My daughter stops spinning with a screech. "What? No. We just got here. You told me Clea has to spend the entire day with us."

The chuckle rumbling from me is forced. "That's not quite what I said."

A snort comes from the lady still in bed. "I don't know. Sounds familiar to me."

My sweet little girl looks stricken as she stares at her idol. "Oh, no. Don't be mad at him, Lele. My dad is really sorry for not treating you like a queen. He told me so. Once you get married, he'll be the king and buy you the biggest crown ever. Then I'll be a princess for real. Won't that be so fun?"

Clea resumes rubbing her forehead, wiggling a bit more than before. "I can't... Ummm, sure?"

Tally claps. "Yay! I knew you'd agree. He goofed up, I guess. But not on purpose. So, you're taking him from the doghouse?"

"I guess?" The woman of my dreams shoots me a pleading stare.

"Clea needs some privacy, Lou."

"She can use that." Tally waves at the paneled divider in the corner.

"I need to do more than get dressed, Lulah. It won't take long." She nods toward the bathroom.

"Promise?" She holds out a pinky, which Clea wraps with her own.

"Yep. I'll be over in less than an hour."

Tally groans. "That's like forever. I can't wait super long without getting bored."

I scoop up the impatient princess. "We'll play a game to stay busy. Your choice."

She quits struggling in my grip. "Ooooh, okay. I wanna do Uno. No, Trouble. Oh, how about Operation?"

I stride to the door with her dangling over my shoulder. "All right, you think about it on the walk home. Say bye to Clea."

Tally pushes upright against me. "Bye, Clea!"

She waves from her safety under the comforter. "See you soon."

"Don't dawdle, Patra." I nip at the air, enticing her to hurry.

Clea nibbles on her bottom lip. "Wouldn't dream of it, King Nolan. And save that cheese to snack on with some wine later."

My daughter bursts into a fit of giggles as I begin our descent. "She totally loves you."

chapter sixteen

Clea

BOUNCE MY KNEE IN TEMPO WITH THE THUMPING TIRES. WE'VE BEEN on the road for a solid thirty minutes. The droning beat of rubber hitting pavement keeps me from obsessing about the man beside me. Or it just makes me think about a different kind of rhythmic pounding. Yeah, I'm not fooling anyone. It's definitely the latter.

Nolan is behind the wheel, looking sixty-nine shades of sexy. I treat myself to another sneaky peek at him from beneath my lashes. His forearm is draped over the center console, knees splayed wide. This guy could sell a dozen of these trucks to girls who have no business driving one. He steers with a loose grip, not a strained tendon in his body. Why is he so damn hot? The answer requires far more gawking.

I've never seen him this carefree. Ever since our big chat, he's been carrying a noticeably lighter load. It's about freaking time. But there's no sense dwelling on the past. Fresh start and all that.

"You're not being very covert." Nolan's raspy tone snaps me from my reverie.

I scratch my eyebrow. "Am I supposed to be?"

He rolls his neck against the headrest to glance at me. "Do you realize what having your undivided attention does to me?"

"I could take a guess."

"Or you'll let me show you."

I twist my lips to one side. There's nothing to actually ponder, but I can't be putty in his palm yet. "Perhaps."

A throaty sound rips from him. "Careful, Patra. I might get the wrong idea."

"Or the right one."

Am I flirting? Absolutely. He deserves a little schmoozing after breakfast this morning and Cuppa Steam yesterday. Maybe I'll get to watch him squirm while in a precarious position.

"You're trouble," he groans.

I wiggle my brows at him, letting the saucy vibe off-leash. "This is what you get."

"Come a little closer. I won't bite."

"Don't forget who's in the backseat." I lean in for nothing more than an extra tease.

Nolan's focus shifts to the rearview mirror. "That princess couldn't care less about us right now. I haven't heard a peep from her since we left. Screen time is precious. She won't waste a second."

A snort streams from me. "Those nosy ears are always listening."

And I don't blame her one bit. This family-style outing feels so normal. We're in our element.

I've decided to just live in the moment. Nolan and Tally are extremely important to me. Spending time with them isn't a chore. What's the harm in sticking around to see how this pans out? The worst that happens is my relocation plans get derailed. I'm choosing to be optimistic and giving him this chance. He better take advantage, proving those rental searches to be unnecessary.

There's a limit, though. I can't lose my heart again. Sharing this small space with him, even for less than an hour, is brutal on my determination. It would be a mere reflex to sag against him while fiddling with the radio. There's no escape from the impulse in these enclosed quarters. His woodsy scent is ingrained in the freaking leather. We need to change the subject before I get carried away too far.

"I totally forgot about the Belvine County Festival."

Nolan chokes in mock horror. "How could you? There's a fair or something along those lines every summer weekend in Minnesota."

"I've been distracted lately." I let the corner of my lips curl at the suggestion.

His chuckle is gooier than warm caramel. "Work and the mild weather are keeping you occupied."

I snort at his antics. "Yes, my clients have been more demanding lately. How are your current projects going?"

"Just finished another major software update. I'll be receiving a hefty bonus for my efficient efforts."

"Thrilling," I murmur.

"You two are so cuuuuuute."

The chirp from our eavesdropper marks a win in my column. Nolan earns a quirked brow from me. When I turn to look at Tally, she's beaming so wide. I return her smile and add a finger wave for good measure. "But you're still the cutest, Lulah."

"I'll be even cuter as the flower girl in your wedding." She flutters her lashes at me.

This girl is going for the jugular. She's never been so relentless. One sly glance to my left explains the culprit. If only he hadn't built a wall between us in the first place. Maybe we'd be married by now.

I nearly swallow my tongue. Where in the actual fuck did that come from? Pipe dreams like that will only lead to further pain. I focus on my leg that's jostling to an erratic pulse.

"You okay, Patra?"

I use a flat palm to shield my wide eyes. With my gaze firmly pinned out the window, I offer a disjointed nod. "Yep, just peachy. Perfect, really. You?"

His posture turns rigid in my periphery. "What just happened?"

"Nothing." I avoid the intense focus that's burning a hole into me.

Nolan's fingers tap on the cup holder. "Shouldn't we be honest with each other?"

"That's not even a question." There's no masking my indignant tone.

"So?"

I'm already shaking my head. "Nope. You don't get a backstage pass to all the nonsense I conjure at random. I'm allowed to omit details that will embarrass me. Ask me again in a year."

He's quiet for long enough that I relax against my seat. "You expect me to forget, but I won't."

I bite my lip to stop a silly grin from growing. "Good luck with that."

"Oh, oh!" Tally's excitement spreads in a giddy cascade, crashing over my momentary blip. "I see the Ferris wheel. Does that mean we're almost there?"

"Good observation skills, kiddo." My chipper tune betrays the pesky fantasy still taunting me. It's not a huge deal. He should be flattered that I've considered it once or twice.

Nolan flicks on the blinker. "This isn't over."

"I already forgot whatever it was." A mental scoff calls my bluff. Fat chance of that happening.

"What should we do first?" Tally is practically vibrating the truck with her eagerness.

I take a moment to ponder the highlights. "How about the big slide?"

Her dad furrows his brow in contemplation. "Or a pony ride?"

She groans at our suggestions. "No, we're getting cotton candy. Like three bags."

I laugh. "Then why didn't you just say that?"

Her answering squeak drips with admonishment. "I was giving you two the chance to be right. But guess what? You're both wrong."

"We better hurry or you might have to settle for a snow cone."

"Don't tease me, Daddy. Nobody ever runs outta sugar."

Nolan finds an open spot to park in the grassy field. "I've wished that our neighbor would. Then she'd have to ask us for a cup."

"Huh?"

I peer at Tally over my shoulder to see her expression matching mine. "Yeah, what she said."

"That's something you can ask me about later." Then he winks and gets out.

I scrabble with my handle, almost breaking the freaking lever off. "Oh, you're going to play like that? I didn't hide anything on purpose."

"You still started it," he chuckles while popping the door open for Tally.

The pint-size instigator begins marching to the entrance. "Less talking, more walking. I have cotton candy to eat."

"She doesn't like to joke about the precious," I whisper-shout under my breath.

"Clearly," Nolan drawls. The smile he dons allows those sinful dimples to poke through the surface.

I want to stroke one, but that would be inappropriate. Instead, my hungry eyes study his profile with blatant interest. There's no point trying to pretend he doesn't do it for me. "I forgot to comment on your shave earlier."

He scrubs a palm along his jaw. "Almost to the skin. I couldn't pull the trigger on going completely bald. It would make me feel naked."

Maybe he'll discover that I don't hold my excess body hair to the same standard. A tingle zips along my spine at the mere implication. There's always someday. In the meantime, I clear my throat.

"I like the stubble. It's been years since I've seen you with less than a thick layer of scruff." I hum in approval. That coarse trim would offer delicious friction in certain areas. Thankfully, those musings don't get a chance to prosper as we reach the ticket booth. I'm bound to get myself in trouble eventually.

Nolan waves me off as I start digging in my purse. "Don't even think about it."

I pop my lips. "Oh, really?"

His exhale ghosts across my temple when he towers over me. "Second date."

My tremble is unavoidable. The rumbling noise he emits tickles along my heated flesh. I'm totally busted. "You're pretty optimistic with the phrasing."

Those soulful green depths sear into me. "Better believe it, Patra. Feel free to use whatever term makes you feel most comfortable about this."

Oh, there's that illusive *this* again. "I'm not shying away."

"You're wary, though."

"And for good reason. I'm still here, aren't I?"

"Right where you belong."

Good grief, he's cranking up the heat and it's barely noon. I'm yanked—quite literally—from the swoon haze when Tally snags my arm. Without further delay, she hauls me toward the one stand that matters most. Nolan lengthens his stride to match our hurried pace. She's lucky there's a scrap of space wide enough for us to fit through.

We step through the gate from the grassy lot, entering into the midst of chaos. The grounds are overrun by children on sugar rushes and their frazzled parents. Laughter tumbles down from the top of the Ferris wheel and the other rides. The warm scent of fried dough permeates the air. Belvine County Festival isn't a huge event, but it still offers the classics.

The atmosphere is saturated with deep-fried fun and family bonding. And I'm among them with two of my favorite people. Once again, a soul-deep rightness settles over me.

Tally slams to a halt in front of the cotton candy vendor, cooing at the pink fluff being spun through the small window. Her skinny fingers twitch in anticipation of getting sticky. The guy tries to pass the massive blob to Nolan, who nudges his head in Tally's direction.

She snatches the proffered treasure with a hum. "Thank you, sir."

"Oh, she's polite when there's cotton candy involved." Nolan gets a snicker from me for that line.

"Darn skippy," she toots.

I shield my eyes and survey the crowded scene. "Now what, Lulah?"

Her face is mostly buried in the pink cloud. "You choose."

"Games?" That will occupy Nolan and me while she eats her beloved sweets.

"Ooooh, yes!" Tally stops munching long enough to agree.

We set our aim toward the colorful alley bursting with crooked odds and steep fares. The usual gimmicks are ready to lure us in. I spy beanbag tosses, strongman games, water gun races, and whack-a-mole tables. Several attendants are spouting off nonsense about how lucky we can get with one swing. Every girl knows it takes more than that.

Nolan nods at the stand to our right. "Milk jugs?"

"No way. They're rigged the worst."

"Ring toss?"

"How about darts?" I lift my chin at the rows of balloons waiting to be popped.

"Perfect." He rubs his hands together.

Tally smacks her sugar-coated lips. "This will be easy peasy, lemon squeezy."

Nolan strides forward to the attendant. "Pick out the prize you want, Princess. Daddy is going to win big."

A bubble of humor giggles up, lifting my shoulder. "Cocky much?"

He grunts. "I've totally got this."

Forty dollars later proves the opposite. Although to be fair, Tally is now the proud owner of an enormous stuffed dog. The thing is larger than her, and I'm not exaggerating. She's calling him Rupert to match Rufus and Rory. We would've moved on, but she insists I need a puppy too. Nolan has been all too happy to oblige and show off his throwing skills. I'm not sure how his wallet feels about this drastic diet.

Finally, after I've lost track of time, Nolan spears the balloon that lands me a massive pooch. The dart shark is practically glowing while accepting his reward like it's a priceless painting. His jovial mood is infectious, especially when it's been so rare in the past. I can't help smiling in return.

"You just spent a small fortune."

He swats my concern away with a flick of his wrist. "I have some to spare thanks to my reclusive lifestyle."

"This was a tad excessive. We could've just gone to Target."

"Where's the adventure in that? Look how happy she is." His eyes gleam as he watches Tally speak with her new friends.

My heart threatens to burst. "You're so good with her."

"That didn't always seem like the case. I couldn't do this without you, Patra."

I dispute his theory with a harsh scoff. "You can."

"But I don't want to."

"Ah, there's the difference." I wag a finger at him.

Nolan bends toward my naysaying digit and gnashes his teeth. "Can you blame me?"

Not even a little bit. It's been my freaking fantasy since I was eighteen. I offer a noncommittal shrug. "It's no secret that caring for a child is easier with a partner."

"I want far more than that."

A flutter erupts in my belly. "You're beginning to convince me."

"I'm glad you gave me another shot. This could be us all the time. Our daily routine." The honesty in his gaze threatens to incinerate me.

There's too much weight in this moment. I could easily let it pull me under. The bait he's dangling is almost painful to resist.

I drop my gaze, focusing on the oversized loot in our posses-
sion. "Well, now we have to lug two of these bad boys around."

"I'll take them to the truck once the shine wears off." Nolan
lowers the dog in his grip so Tally can give it a pat.

"What're you gonna name her, Lele?"

"Oh, it's a girl?"

"Well, duh. The boys need a sister."

"Right, of course." I hold the comically large mutt out in
front of me. "Umm, how about Ramona?"

"That's super pretty. Rupert and Ramona are going to love
their new home. I'm gonna sleep with them in my bed tonight.
They can meet their brothers tomorrow." She gives the stuffed
giants another scratch before turning her sights to more lively
attractions. "Can we visit the petting zoo?"

Nolan raises his brows at me in question. "Want to manage
that while I ditch the twins?"

I'm all too eager to regain the use of my arms. "Fair deal,
partner. Just don't leave me hanging for too long."

His wide smile snuffs out proper brain functioning as he begins a backward retreat. "Nah, you're stuck with me."

The hours pass in a blur. It seems like we've visited every
corner of the fairgrounds at least twice. My shins are screaming. Tally's curls are one degree away from being a frizzy nest.
Nolan is just soaking it all in. He hasn't muttered a single complaint. Even when his daughter started whining about being
tired—during her most recent sugar-crash—he just smiled and
scooped her into his very capable arms. The visual of him cradling her snoring form is ridiculously attractive. It seems he can
do no wrong today. But the night is still young.

He shifts Tally so she's sprawled across his left side. In that
position, he can hold her with one arm. Don't get me started
on the bulging veins in his forearms. The sexy single dad angle
is doing him a lot of favors. He's catching more than a few interested stares for providing the mommy porn.

I force my gaze away with a muttered curse. "You're just flexing on purpose. Such a show-off."

Nolan smirks. "She's not too heavy. Nothing more than a sack of potatoes."

I glance at their tangled snuggle. "Isn't that a cute comparison?"

"Want to take a load off? I can carry you too." He beckons me in with his open arm.

My laugh is sharp and maniacal. Then I realize he's not joining in on the amusement. "Um, that's impossible."

"Why?"

"I weigh a lot more than a sack of potatoes." Try a barrel of sand. The flare at my waist accentuates that point.

His gaze is liquid fire scorching a path across every inch he peruses. The implication that stare translates to gets my pulse skittering. "Thank fuck for that, Patra. I'd hate to worry about breaking you in half. Your body is meant for me to satisfy. Very thoroughly."

I stumble in a ghost hole, nearly crashing to my knees. "Wow, that took an unexpected turn."

"Too much?" He licks his bottom lip and I nearly faint from the lack of oxygen to my brain. "I'd love nothing more than to have both of my girls clutched against me. Safe, protected, and mine."

Sweet and spicy is a dynamite combination, especially when this man is serving up the goods. There's no missing the claim he just put on me. That's not what I'm gaping at. It's just him. The entire package. Literally begging for a chance with me. How is this real?

"That's a solid argument. Maybe we can test your limits in private before exposing them to the public." I'm confident in my curves, dammit. There's just no reason to push the issue and amplify my figure.

"Never doubt your appeal, Angel."

The fuck-hot look he's scalding me with is proof enough.

Suddenly, my generous hips don't feel wide enough to fit all that's he's apparently planning to give. I'm getting very hot and bothered. Sweat prickles my hairline and I swear there's a permanent flush staining my cheeks.

"Noted," I mumble dumbly.

Nolan's hip bumps into mine for what feels like the umpteenth time. I'm beginning to realize the subtle move is very intentional. His excuses for touching me are becoming more obvious. That doesn't mean I'm going to tell him to stop. Then his hand nudges mine, confirming my suspicions. A gentle twitch from his pinky. The rotation of his wrist as he tests the boundaries. Every subtle move is magnified under the darkening sky. I nearly swallow my tongue when he slides his palm against mine, interlocking our fingers. He dips down to my ear, his breath shooting off a thousand tingles across my skin.

"Is this okay?" He rubs my inner wrist with his thumb.

It's silly that my heart is pounding simply because we're holding hands. I exhale a sputter in a failed attempt to calm my nerves. "I'll allow it."

He tightens his grip on me, notching us in an unbreakable seal. A slight squeeze and I'm swaying toward him. That's our chemistry. Freaking magnetic.

I feel his lips against my hair. "I'd waste a lot more money on rickety games with crappy odds just to see you two smile. It always feels special with you near."

"What can I say? I have a knack for brightening the occasion."

"This is a day to celebrate, just like tomorrow and the next. Wherever we go and whatever is waiting there can be ours. You elevate even the most mundane experiences. Before you argue that, just look around. This was your find. Tally is passed out in blissful wonderland thanks to you. That leaves us with a little time of our own."

I suddenly find it very difficult to draw in a full breath. "And you have a fancy way with words."

"I've been saving for this moment, and there's an abundance in storage."

"So, I should expect the pit to fill soon?" I don't want to be a woman scorned. That bitterness only spreads a numb ache. Still, there's some part that won't allow me to completely believe in him.

He lifts our clasped palms, dusting my knuckles with soft kisses. "I can see your fight, understand it even. But there's no reason for your guard to be up against me. I'm here and ready. You're it for me, Patra."

This isn't the first time he's confessed that. A bit more resistance melts off my weak armor. Silence clogs my windpipe. Faint buzzers and clangs break the tension pressing down on me. Those repetitive noises remind me that we've been lapping the carnival section. I absently wonder if he realizes we're going in aimless circles.

An upward glance finds his gaze locked solely on me. He doesn't have a clue, and I'm a goner. "How am I supposed to resist you?"

"Maybe you shouldn't."

"I'm scared," I admit in a whisper.

With a soft tug, he brings us to a stop. "I won't hurt you, Patra. Never again. I'm here, and I promise to never abandon you again. Please find enough faith to believe that. You rejuvenate me. Tally binds us closer. Together we can have the love people envy. The three of us."

His earnest tone resonates deep within my soul. There's no escaping this man. If I'm being honest, I've never truly wanted to.

Nolan searches my gaze, the green in his eyes vibrant against the harsh fluorescent bulbs flashing at us. "Can I kiss you?"

I wet my lips on instinct. If Tally wasn't snoring and limp as a cooked noodle, I'd never consider his request. "Since when do you ask permission?"

He inches closer, his shoe bumping mine. "Just taking what I wanted didn't work so well for me before."

"And now?" An accordion is collapsing and expanding in my stomach from this wild ride.

"No more holding back."

At my nod, he erases the remaining distance. The brush from his lips against mine is chaste, but the powerful thrum between us is more potent than if we were full-fledged making out. We barely need to touch for sparks to ignite.

With that slight touch, I feel static energy pump into me. This is the strength Nolan fuels me with. I'm recharged and flipped upside down. Or maybe shoved onto the correct course.

He pulls away before my lashes finish fluttering shut. I'm tempted to go back for seconds, but there'll be time for that later. His hitched breath breezes across my parted mouth.

We're frozen in the moment, lost to one another. There's a nonstop buzz swirling in the background, but it doesn't register. Our intimate exchange is protected by a soundless bubble.

My mind flits to the image we create, standing in this tight-knit embrace. Most wouldn't spare us a glance. But to me, this tender display means everything.

He twirls a section of blond around his finger. "I love what you did with your hair."

I take a second to watch his left dimple appear as he smirks. "Yeah?"

Nolan is studying my platinum locks. "Insanely sexy."

Well, that's a level of crazy I'm willing to succumb to. "I'm glad I went through with it. The dramatic change for a fresh start was just what I needed."

"What else?"

I squint at the horizon, painted in purple and orange from the setting sun. "Moving, I guess. A certain someone derailed that."

"It was too extreme."

"And what do you call this?" I motion between our lips, which are still within kissing range.

He ghosts the tip of his nose across my fiery cheek. "Destiny."

It takes great effort not to sag into him. "That's some romance hero charm, Nolan."

"Figured you'd like that."

"It's definitely scoring you extra brownie points."

"We're going to be so good together, Angel." His forehead rests against mine.

There isn't a single part of me willing to disagree.

chapter seventeen

Nolan

TALLY POKES HER HEAD FROM THE DOORWAY OF CLEA'S HOME office. Those golden curls are wilder than usual, much like her personality. Her small hand is spinning fast enough to blur as she demands that I hurry up. A jerky nod from me appeases her while she watches us approach with measured steps.

I guide Clea across the hall with my palms firmly pressed over her eyes. She huffs, but otherwise allows me to blindly lead her where I see fit.

"Is this really necessary?" Her protest falls on deaf ears.

"It will be worth it."

"Worth it?"

"For the shock factor."

"Should I be concerned?"

"Maybe for your heart. That precious gem will belong to me shortly."

Clea's body trembles with her laugh. "Your confidence is so humbling."

I bring her to a halt over the threshold. "Ready?"

Her closed lids twitch. She's definitely rolling her eyes at me. "Well, yeah."

"All right, open up." I pull my hands away.

Clea's palms immediately lift to cup her cheeks as she stumbles into the room. I stand back to appreciate our handiwork while she digests the sight. The space she uses as a studio is now covered with photographs of us. Glossy and matte prints are plastered across every available surface. Some are featured in color. Others were more suited for a black and white filter. This extremely talented woman—currently gawking at the scene—taught me that much.

The assortment highlights the past six years. It's a combination of Tally with Clea, Tally and me, and even some of the three of us together. A slow scan along the decorated walls betrays a severe shortage of pictures featuring just the two of us. Clea and me. A stab of guilt slices into my gut. We're definitely lacking in the couple department. I'll have to remedy that. Soon.

"What…?" Clea croaks. "How…?"

"Kody kept you occupied for a reason. I owe him a few."

She's still in a trance. "What's all this?"

I move to stand beside her. "It's us. This is our foundation."

"What're you trying to do to me?" She sniffs while shuffling further into the room. Moisture pools in her eyes, glistening the vibrant blue into iridescent pools.

My feet follow automatically. "I wasn't trying to make you cry."

She peeks up at me through wet lashes. "These are happy tears. Very happy."

"I'm trying to prove myself. I still have a lot of things to apologize for. I can't fix those mistakes, but I promise to be the man you deserve from this point forward. You've captured our memories. It's my turn to show how much—and deeply—I care about you. These are snapshots of the best we've shared. I'm hopeful that you'll be encouraged to make many more with us." Just in a different capacity, with her living closer than next door. She has to forgive me before I even consider suggesting that.

Clea ghosts a hand over an image of us at the beach two summers ago. "I took all these?"

"Most, and this is only a small fraction." I focus on a picture of Tally and Clea making snow angels after a blizzard. There's a snowflake falling right on Tally's nose and her tongue is stuck out in an attempt to eat it. Clea's head is thrown back in wild laughter.

That was a good day.

"Where did you find them all?" She traces over the history with an imaginary touch.

I hitch a thumb at my daughter, who's been abnormally quiet. "She knew where to look. You've given me a few flash drives too."

From afternoons at the zoo to movie nights on the couch, it's all documented for us to reminisce about.

"This is incredible." She strokes a thumb over the nearest print. Tally is hoisted onto my shoulders while we traipse through the corn maze at the Twin Cities Harvest Festival.

Clea takes a leisurely lap, sparing a tearful glance at each captured moment. Days at the park. Messy breakfast experiments. Playing tag in the backyard. Birthday celebrations. The gondola ride at the Minnesota State Fair. Dance parties in the living room. Spaghetti dinner—one of the few dishes I'm capable of cooking. On and on the memories flow. All printed out for her to see. The final one she finds is a selfie of us I snapped just last week after our peck at the carnival.

"I just… wow. There aren't words meaningful enough to describe what's happening in here." She pats her chest.

I'm willing to bet it's exactly like the soothing comfort spreading through mine. It's a balm I didn't realize existed. This woman cures my every ache. "You're already part of us. Just look around."

She does another sweep, a wobbly grin melting the last of her reluctance. "It seems that way."

"We did good, Lou."

Tally slaps the palm I have stretched in her direction. "Told you she would cry."

I wince, but a chuckle escapes regardless. "That wasn't my goal."

Clea wipes under her eyes. "You made an impact, either way.

This might be the greatest gift ever, except for the necklace Tally made for me. That's tough to beat."

My daughter glows under the praise. "We've done lots of stuff, huh?"

Clea shakes her head in presumed disbelief. "It's surreal looking back at all these. I never considered it because I was always behind the lens. It's crazy to see our memories spread out like this."

"I asked before if you remember when Tally was a baby. The real purpose was to venture back to our beginning. That's where we started." I point to an image of my little girl swaddled against Clea's chest. "I wanted to remind you of everything we've already been through together."

"Mission complete," she sniffles. "As if I could forget."

"You might've wished to once or twice. Especially the last year or so." The warmth pumping through me takes a hit, cooling slightly at the edges. But we're on the road to repair.

Then she rekindles my flames with the fire in her stare. "No, not really. You two have brought so much joy into my life. I've hidden my feelings from you, but it's probably clear now."

"Very much, and likewise." I reach forward and thread her fingers with mine.

"Oh my gosh," Tally whispers under her breath. "It's actually happening."

I cock my head at her. "What's that, Princess?"

She slaps a palm over her mouth, eyes wide. "Nothing! I'm not interrupting."

Her enthusiasm stokes my certainty that Clea is meant to be ours. It helps that Clea doesn't pull away from my gaze. If anything, she leans in a little closer.

"You're a vital part of the team, Lou. I couldn't have done this without you," I say.

My not-so-little girl huffs. "Well, duh. I'm super smart with the sheeming."

I should probably correct her, but the odd word is growing on me. "And what else do you have?"

She starts digging in her pocket. "I almost forgot."

"No," Clea protests, blinking rapidly. "There's only so much I can handle."

I dust a kiss along her forehead while my daughter is distracted. "It fits with the theme."

Tally whips out the small box. "I didn't make this, but it's still pretty cool."

Clea accepts the gift with a trembling palm. She lifts the lid, a garbled breath wheezing from her in the next beat. Her shaking finger pets the shiny contents as if the metal will fall apart in her hands.

The silver chain has six charms—one for every year we've known each other. Clea removes the bracelet from the padding, her movements delicate and careful. "I'm afraid to touch it. That's how perfect it is."

I'm beaming broader than a Mega-Millions lotto winner. "It's fairly durable. Tally tested it out."

That seems to appease her, and she holds the bracelet up with more confidence. Each plastic disc is lasered with an image. I was skeptical about the picture quality based on the size, but the clarity is better than expected.

"Tally chose which photos to include."

"You picked very well, Lulah. I love these the most."

"Want me to unhook the clip thingy so you can put it on?" Tally appears ready to burst. This has been an eventful day and it's only two o'clock in the afternoon.

"Yes." Clea thrusts her arm forward and we secure the clasp. The pieces click together when she twists her wrist. "I'm obsessed. This... everything... it's perfect. You're both incredible."

Tally clutches her folded hands to her chest. "Now you'll always think about us."

"I already do." Clea sidles closer and bumps me with her hip. "Tell the truth. Was this your idea?"

A slight shrug shifts her against me. "Tally can take the credit. Again."

"So, she's the owner of my heart then."

Tally's eyes light up and she gasps. "Really? But don't you need it, Lele?"

"You'll keep it safe. I trust you." She boops her on the nose.

Tally puffs out her cheeks. "That's such a big a-sponsibly."

Clea chuckles at the mispronounced word. "Good thing you're a big girl. You know how to be a-sponsible."

"Uh-huh, yep." Then something sparkly catches her focus and she dashes to the corner.

I realize Clea has gone still beside me. "What's on your mind?"

"It's just overwhelming, in the best possible way. As lovely as these copies look plastered all over my walls, I'll need a better spot to store them. Eventually." She pauses, seeming to contemplate the decision further. "Maybe in a month or two."

"Well, Tally volunteered to put them in a scrapbook. She already picked a few out. Most are family-style." I peer at her from the corner of my eye while speaking.

"That's really sweet. I'm touched that you did this for me. It's truly special."

"Grand gesture worthy?"

Clea laughs, the twinkling sound striking a match to my blood. "Without a doubt. This is huge."

I pump my fist. "Take that, Kody."

"Oh, gosh. I can only imagine what he suggested."

"Stalking you at the bar, obviously."

"That didn't turn out too bad." She teeters her hand back and forth.

"Maybe I should've tried sneaking into your bedroom while you were sleeping."

She snorts. "That definitely sounds like my brother. I still wonder what happened between him and Aspen. Maybe I should call her."

"It's probably best if we leave that alone. That's not something I want to think about."

Her expression turns sour. "Yeah, good thinking."

Tally returns to her spot in front of us in all her twirling glory. "Can we take more pictures now?"

Clea's gaze bounces between us. "Oh?"

"That was part of the plan if you approved. I haven't seen you in action lately."

"You like watching me shoot?"

"When we're the subjects, sure. This made me appreciate the art all the more." I gesture at our photos.

Tally bounces on the balls of her feet. "Oh, we can have a modeling contest?"

"That's one option," Clea replies with a wink at me.

"I was thinking that it would be nice to document our new beginning. And how our relationship status has changed." I hold my breath, every muscle growing taut.

Both of my girls smile at me. Clea is the first to respond. "I can't think of a better way to celebrate our evolving dynamic. There are a lot more memories to make today."

"And tonight?"

She loops her arms through mine, earning another squeak from Tally. "I won't discourage you."

chapter eighteen

Clea

FINISH THE FINAL CURL AND SET MY IRON DOWN. "WHAT COULD Nolan possibly have planned now? The man is a bottomless pit of romance. How didn't I realize this sooner?"

"He's good at hiding it?" Presley's voice blares from the speaker setting and echoes off the tile walls.

A frown gets aimed at my phone. "Why can't we video chat? This feels so impersonal."

She hums. "I'm not dressed. Boob out and all that."

Shameless to a fault, this one.

I furrow my brow. "Why? I thought you weren't breastfeeding anymore."

Her disapproving huff rattles down the line. "Can't a girl just let the ladies fly? This is supposed to be a no-judgment zone."

I'm nodding, but the background racket gives me pause. "Why is it so loud at your house? Wait, are you pulling a Vannah and getting busy while talking to me?"

That would explain her so-called nakedness.

Presley serves me another disgruntled noise. "Yeah, because that's plausible. I'm binging *Bachelor Pad*. You really get the rowdy factor when it's cranked to the max."

That's definitely a feasible explanation coming from her. I stare at my reflection, giving the completed look a thorough appraisal. "Um, okay. But—"

A resounding smack bangs against my ear. She hisses, as though in pain. "Will you quit fussing at me? You just made me slap my leg for no good reason. Worry about getting ready."

"What's the rush?" But I'm walking to my room to pack a purse.

"Nolan is waiting for you," she scolds. Then clears her throat. "I mean, probably. Don't leave him hanging."

"I wish he'd be a bit more demanding in that department," I muse while dropping a red gloss into my clutch. I consider for a second, then toss in another tube for good measure.

She chokes. "Uh, okay. Have you talked to him?"

It sounds like she's power-walking through a beach bonanza. The episode she's watching must be really intense. Without overthinking, I stride to the stairs. "I'm afraid to ruin what we have going."

"Maybe he feels the same. I'm positive he wants you."

"Yeah, he's made a few comments." I bite my lip. The flip in my stomach is impossible to ignore.

She sighs. "Nolan is the ultimate man. He's all harsh growls and smoldering glares. No-nonsense, alpha hottie. But to a select few—ahem, you and Tally—he's all gooey goodness with a side of chocolate sauce."

"Awww, that's a cute notion to imagine." And not far-fetched. Nolan has done a total one-eighty where I'm concerned.

Presley sounds her agreement. "It's true."

"He's been groveling his ass off, Pres. Just yesterday, I caught him and Tally coloring my driveway with chalk art. The designs are crazy adorable. I'll send you a picture."

Her cooing response is exaggerated. "Cue the swoon. The man is a total grump without you around, though. Does he ever smile?"

"You make it sound like he's next to you or something." I laugh while opening the front door.

"What?" Her tone goes a bit shrill.

My footsteps halt on the porch as I listen to her hushed voice murmuring to someone. "Are you okay, Pres?"

Her giggle is forced. "Yeah, totally. Just almost… singed my nipple off."

Why are my friends so ridiculous? It's a question I ask myself daily. "I'm not going to ask."

She blows out a whistling exhale. "Thank the good Lord for that. Anywho, what's taking you so long? Shouldn't you be hustling next door to discover his latest secret?"

"I'm beginning to believe you're in on this secret."

"Don't be silly. I'm just invested in your happily ever after. It's about damn time, you know?"

"It is." Suspicion darkens my agreement as I cross the lawn onto Nolan's property. That's when I hear the ruckus coming from his backyard. I strain my neck to peer over the tall fence blocking my view, but still can't see much. I do hear several voices engaged in low conversation, though, only popping up a giant question mark above my head. "What the fu—"

"She's here!" Then Presley ends our call with a click.

The gate suddenly springs wide, revealing Nolan in all his handsome glory. I stumble to a stop just to gawk. He walks toward me with a confident swagger that accentuates his broad frame. Freaking drool.

His arms loop around me, enveloping us in a cozy hug. "Hey, Angel. It's about time you arrived."

"What did you do?" The curiosity is muffled against his chest that I'm all too willingly pressed against.

"We're having a party."

I rest my chin on his sternum, gazing up at the pristine wonder that is Nolan Jasper. "For?"

"Us!" Tally pops up beside me from out of thin air. "You took forever, Lele. I've been fighting with my patience. Do you know how hard that is?"

I untangle myself from Nolan and haul her against me. "Well, to be fair, I had no idea that you were scheming again."

"Really?" She straightens from my hold to squint at me. "My dad didn't spill the beans?"

"Not a single one."

Tally raises her flat palm to him. "Nice job, Pops."

He gives her a high-five, but his expression is pinched. "Pops?"

"Uh, duh. It's way cooler than 'Dad'." She rolls her eyes, landing on a spot somewhere behind him. The sass is coming out strong for this occasion.

"That makes me sound old," he grumbles.

"Oh, I found him!" Tally dashes off without another word.

I watch her dip and weave until she disappears in the throng. "All right, Pops. Should we follow her lead?"

"Very funny. She's chasing a boy." Nolan's gritty timbre holds an edge as he glares in the direction she just went.

"Hate to break this to you, but it's only going to get worse."

He scowls at the crowd before dragging his attention onto me. All that cloudy frustration melts from his features as he gives me a lazy once-over. His mouth crooks into a semblance of a smirk. Those dimples are bound and determined to destroy me. "Hey, you."

Being the object of his sole focus is something to cherish. It doesn't matter that I've been showered with his unabashed desires for almost three weeks. My cheeks still heat with a fiery blush as I dip my chin. "Hi."

Nolan snakes an arm around my waist and pulls me against him. His upturned lips find mine in the next beat. I part my mouth on a sigh, and he takes full advantage. Warmth floods under my skin as his tongue coaxes the fire to grow. On a breathy exhale, I glide my tongue against his and let the heat swallow us. He tugs me closer, splaying a wide palm on my ass. That possessive streak makes me dizzy. I sway into him while delving deeper into the flames.

The slight shift brings us that much closer, eliciting a rumble from his throat. That vibration makes me gasp and nearly lose my footing. I lift onto the tips of my sandals to wrap my arms around his shoulders. My anchor against the storm brewing inside me. Nolan's woodsy musk cocoons me as he tightens his grip. With a nip of my bottom lip, he stokes the inferno to dangerous levels.

I still have a hard time believing that this is real life. This is not just some dream or fantasy I've constructed in my mind. I lose myself in the moment. This kiss extends even longer than the six agonizing years I waited.

And as far as I'm concerned, I could stay here forever.

"Yo, love birds. You have an audience, and several have impressionable minds." My brother's announcement isn't welcome, but a necessary reminder all the same.

We break apart with a groan. Nolan drops his forehead against mine. "Fuck, you make me ache. And that was just an appetizer."

I let my jaw go slack when he presses hard proof against me. "Heya, big boy. When can I expect the next course?"

"Hungry for more?"

"Starving." I toy with the ends of his shaggy hair.

"Just how I like you." He gives my butt a final squeeze, then releases me.

"Do you, uh, need a minute?" I glance—somewhat discreetly—at the bulge behind his zipper.

Nolan tips his face skyward with a rough exhale. "Guinea pigs, my grandma, burly Irishmen, glitter crafts, Kody in a speedo."

I remain silent while he chants. A shudder wracks his limbs soon enough. "All good?"

"Yep. Are you ready?" He motions toward the flock of guests gathering in his backyard.

"For what, exactly?"

"Just a fun gathering. I wanted to get our people together as one cohesive unit. Blend and mingle and coexist."

I peek over at him. "Is this a couple reveal party?"

A dent creases his brow. "Is that a thing?"

"Probably. There's a title for every event."

Nolan leans in, his lips brushing my ear. "Is this you asking me to make it official?"

Telltale flutters do a jig in my belly. "I feel like you're doing that by hosting this shindig."

"My intention was to celebrate summer while it's still in swing. Others were eager to join for a carefree evening. No ulterior motives. I just want to see you smile, relax, and enjoy yourself. If the fact we're dating happens to get put on display, so be it." His pointed look doesn't go unnoticed.

I fiddle with the hem of his shirt. "You seem to be making a massive statement."

"Is that bad?" He murmurs the question against my temple.

"Not even a little bit."

With his fingers threaded with mine, he guides me forward. I catch sight of Presley near the makeshift bar in the corner. She wiggles her manicured nails at me, tossing a flirty wink into the mix. Two guys flank her. They seem to be competing for her interest, if their cocky posturing is anything to go by. Vannah and Landon are beside them, too busy eye-fucking each other to notice me. I wave to a few neighbors, my local clients, and some girls who share my passion for photography.

Aspen and Kody are locked in a heated exchange. Either a quarrel or verbal foreplay. I yank my gaze off them before their spat reaches indecent heights.

"Wow, everyone is here. Except my parents, but that's obvious." My offhand comment is met with a chuckle.

"I invited your friends, of course."

"But Presley—"

"Was a decoy."

I nudge him with my elbow. "You think of everything. I'm not very observant lately."

Nolan juts his chin at someone I haven't met yet. "I take it as a compliment that your head's in the clouds."

"Must be," I muse. "You're pulling off all this stuff behind my back without me noticing."

As we're passing the snack table, another familiar face materializes from the outskirts. I stiffen as Pete tromps toward us. His presence is a tad shocking, since Nolan has never been a fan. The man currently attached to my hip doesn't waste an opportunity to let his opinion be known. This could go south rather quickly.

Nolan's gaze is already zeroed in on our intruder when I glance at him. "Did you—?"

"No." He spits the retort through clenched teeth.

Oh, shit. We're already circling the drain. "I'm sure he's just swinging over to say hello."

He widens his stance. Spine straight and muscles flexed. "He will use any excuse to paw at you. Not at my house."

"Or mine." I chew on my response as Pete wedges his way into our twosome bubble.

He claps Nolan on the shoulder. His posture is loose and causal, but I'm not buying the nonchalant act. "I must've missed my invite, man. This looks like a great party."

Nolan is glaring mortal wounds into the other man's face. "It's for friends only."

"Are you trying to hurt my feelings?" Pete is laughing, but there's no humor in his tone.

Their awkward greeting is already bumming me out. A pungent odor punches into the air. Bitter acid burns my tongue. That doesn't mean I'm going to interrupt, though. I'm all too happy to remain quiet on the sidelines while this caveman charade plays out.

Nolan scrubs over his mouth, hiding the smirk brewing there. "Was there something you needed, bro?"

"I'm not your fucking bro." Pete curls his upper lip.

"No?" He tilts his head to study him. "Then why are you here?"

These two peacocks are ruffling their feathers with comic flair. I'm thankful Tally isn't nearby to hear this nonsense.

Pete takes a strategic step forward. "The gate is open. Figured it was a free-for-all."

"You shouldn't assume shit. It can get you in trouble." Nolan notches a palm into the small of my back.

Pete gapes at him. "You trying to stake a claim on my girl with that smooth move, Jasper?"

Nolan leans in, towering over his shorter stature. "She's her own person. Not yours or mine, unless she's willing to grant us the privilege."

He's not deterred. "Oh, I see. You're a tough guy swooping in on a mighty steed. Please, drop the noble shit. No one believes that."

My silent streak cracks as I sputter at his audacity. My tolerance for misogynistic bullshit is extremely narrow. Mostly nonexistent. The possessive alpha shit only works for Nolan. Call me a hypocrite and I'll own it—a girl has the right to be picky with preferences. But from this nincompoop? I'd rather leap into an active volcano.

Nolan's jaw is locked, molars grinding behind dark stubble. He's prepared to defend my honor, and do so without making me seem insignificant. That might make me appear weak or biased, but I love that he's territorial. It allows me to be comfortable returning the favor if the occasion arises.

Pete isn't fortunate enough to have the leniency that I offer Nolan, for countless reasons. Whatever old-fashioned rock he crawled out from under doesn't suit my progressive taste. That's a job for whatever woman decides to date him. This dude has always been too pushy for me.

But escalating this into a testosterone-fueled battle won't accomplish anything other than souring the mood. The men are already exchanging glares fit for fighting words. This could go in two vastly different directions. I don't want a sullen, jealous cloud to dilute the thoughtfulness behind this gathering. We're supposed to be celebrating.

I shake the offending coil from my fists. "All right, boys. This ego-boasting session is thrilling and all, but I'm beginning to feel like a trophy to be won."

Nolan recoils as if slapped. "Did I go too far?"

I give a limp shrug. "Maybe, but it's not just you."

Pete rubs at his nape, gripping the skin until redness blooms. "I wasn't trying to make a scene."

"Could've fooled me," Nolan grumbles.

"Hey," I poke him in the chest. "That's not helping."

He frowns at my finger, a deep wrinkle scoring his forehead. An apology is swirling in his eyes when he pins those green pools on me. "Are you mad at me?"

"No," I insist. "The possessive alpha stuff just isn't necessary."

Pete holds his palms out. "Yeah, fine. I get it. Let's calm down. We don't need to stir the shit pot."

The hurt in Nolan's expression morphs to indifference when he glances at Pete. "Isn't that a pleasant visual." It's a statement, not a question.

His chuckle sounds genuine. "It's my contribution to the party."

"You can dump it over there with the other crap." He blindly gestures to the side.

"What Nolan is trying to say is that we're doing just fine. Thanks for asking." I tuck a stray curl behind my ear. The movement causes the bracelet on my wrist to sparkle in the sun.

Pete notices the gleam. "Oh, it's like that?"

Nolan grunts but doesn't speak on my behalf. I paste

on a tight-lipped grin. "Yep. There are plenty of single ladies around. I'm just not one of them."

"Well, damn. I missed my chance?" He never had one to begin with, but there's no need for me to dump salt in the wound.

I dig my foot into the grassy lawn. "Seems that way."

"Lucky asshole," he mumbles under his breath.

"Weren't you heading somewhere, bro?" Nolan's hint wins a giggle from me.

Pete is less than impressed based on his flat features. "You gonna make me leave?"

Nolan's laugh is a punch of mockery. "That wouldn't be very neighborly. Feel free to continue crashing, if that's your style."

"Ah, nice burn. Good luck with that, Clea." But there's no malice in his tone. "In all honesty, I should've seen this from miles away."

"Ah, shucks. I guess the mystery is solved. Real glad you cracked the case." Nolan earns a playful pinch to his bicep from me. His resulting scowl is entirely for Pete's benefit. He appears to rein it in, biting his tongue for good measure. "Stay and hang out. You're already here. Might as well take advantage."

Pete cocks a brow. "Truce?"

Nolan glances at me from the corner of his eye. "Sure. If that blows your skirt up."

"Thanks, man. I'll stay outta your hair." He slaps Nolan on the shoulder again.

"It was great seeing you, Pete." I'm ready to shoo him if necessary.

"Likewise. Congrats to the happy couple." He lifts a cupped hand in an imaginary toast and begins backing away.

Once Pete saunters off to initiate his newfound prowl, Nolan peers down at me. His expression is guarded. That wary mask is one I'm all too familiar with. I hate the uncertainty that's resurfacing from such an insignificant incident.

Nolan scrubs a palm over his face. "Fuck, that dude bothers me. I don't even know why. He's not a real threat. I'm aware of that much."

I turn toward him, my lips in a twist. "Are you?"

"Yes?" The fact that he's questioning it is telling. A slight cringe pinches his features. "Am I about to get the wrath?"

My mouth droops into a frown. "For what?"

"Marking my territory." He regurgitates the accusation from me in a robotic tone. "This isn't the first time. I can't promise it will be the last either."

"You were definitely making a statement with all that." I wave in the direction Pete vanished off to.

He pins a fierce glare on the ground. "I can't help it, Patra. This possessive urge drives me to act like a crazed fool."

"How appealing," I drawl.

"That didn't come out right." He hangs his head with a muttered curse. "It's hard for me to control everything I feel for you. There's too much happening, but also not enough. This is all so new to me."

"It is for me too. Don't forget that." I reach for him, lacing our fingers together.

His stare shifts to our entwined hands. "I couldn't, regardless of what you might think. You're all I think about. Well, in addition to Tally."

I trace his palm with my thumb. "That's the same for me, which is why you have nothing to worry about."

Nolan lifts his gaze to mine. "I'm confident in us. It's everything else that causes complications. Especially other men who like to parade around you without a shirt on."

"He did that once."

"Which is once too many."

I roll my eyes. "Kody is a bad influence on you. It's not a battle you need to win."

He flinches. "Shit, I can't believe I'm ruining this."

I place my other palm on his straining forearm. "Nolan, you already have me. I'm not going anywhere."

"Yeah?" The lingering doubt wafting from him hurts my heart.

"Yeah." I provide plenty of conviction for both of us. But for added reassurance, I tip my chin and press our lips together. Nolan responds instantly, turning the peck into something much deeper with a swipe of his tongue.

The sliding glass door behind us opens with a whoosh and I'm reminded—once again—about our audience. I pull away from him with a sigh. The noise reminds me of Tally running too fast. I'm sure that's exactly what she's doing now. She must be having a blast with that boy Nolan tagged as an enemy.

"Nolan, your house is just lovely."

My breathing stalls, then exits in a rush as I spin on my heel. Standing on the deck—as if none the wiser—are my parents. I haven't seen them since Christmas, and wasn't planning to for at least another month. It takes several moments for my brain to process their appearance. This is too much. Again.

I slap a palm to my forehead. "What is happening?"

My mother trots forward and smothers me in a hug. "My Clea. It's wonderful to see you."

I'm a soggy sack of disbelief in her grip. "How is this possible? My brain is spinning."

She pushes me away, squishing my cheeks in her palms. "You landed a good one, sweetie."

I peek at Nolan, who's busy talking to my dad. "He did this?"

"Sure did. That gentleman of yours even insisted on paying for our flight."

That gentleman of mine is going to be made explicitly aware of just how much I appreciate this. Very soon. In the meantime, my gratitude spills from my eyes. "I don't even know what to say."

"Well, I'm certainly glad to see you in capable hands." My mom's smile is toasty and warm and makes me go all squishy on the inside.

That comforting expression also reverts me into a bumbling mess.

"You're so tan. The retirement bronze is beautiful," I wail.

"Florida is very good for the skin, dear." She bops my head.

"What's with the screeching?" My dad strides over, followed by Nolan.

I soak in the attention like a dehydrated sponge. This entire day collapses on me all at once and the waterworks flow. "I'm so emotional."

Nolan's expression is positively stricken. He glances between my parents, who wave off his concern. My mother *tsks*. "She's fine, honey. This just means she cares."

He bobs his head. "Okay, I can handle that."

She pats his cheek. "You already are."

Watching them interact through blurry vision sends fresh tears to pour down. "Gah, please stop being so wonderful."

"Which one of us?" My father chuckles, elbowing Nolan in the side.

I massage at the pressure building in my temples. "How long are you guys here? Or in town, I guess."

My mom wipes at an errant droplet streaking along my skin. "Nolan asked if we would come for a visit. We'll be watching Tally for an extended weekend."

"What? Why?" My watery gaze lifts to the man responsible.

Nolan's green gaze is open and honest. The affection searing into me puts a dopey grin on my face. "We're going on a trip."

"You and me?" I motion between us.

He tugs on my belt loop. "Yeah, Angel. I thought we could use some time alone. Uninterrupted."

"Oh, wow." The whimsy in my tone might embarrass most.

"Ah, to be young again." My father drapes an arm around my mom, tugging her close for a hug.

We all share a laugh. I can already envision us as a little pod during the holidays. What a glorious sight. The image kicks my pulse into a staccato. I'm officially getting ahead of myself. Not that anyone can really blame me.

"You kids have fun. We're going to mingle." My mother blows me a kiss. She sets her sights on Kody still arguing with Aspen, and drags my dad in their direction.

I turn to Nolan, gripping a fistful of his shirt. "You."

"Me?"

"Yes. You're getting so lucky." I pull until he's bending to my level. "This weekend, apparently."

"You're in an awful frisky mood."

"Just wait until later."

His eyebrows hike upward. "Are you planning something of your own?"

I walk my fingers up his chest. "That depends."

Nolan's gulp is audible. "On?"

"If you stick to the usual nightly routine."

A naughty gleam enters his gaze, and he smirks. "Oh, you can count on me delivering."

chapter nineteen

Nolan

ANTICIPATION THRUMS THROUGH MY VEINS ALONG WITH A sanity-altering dose of carnal longing. The air is cool, but I'm overheating. Sweat clings to my skin for no apparent reason. There's a simmer in my gut that's set to boil. If anyone were to stumble upon me, they'd assume I'm losing my shit.

That assumption would be correct.

I stride across my bedroom with purpose, leaving a trail of conquered hurdles behind. Clea savored the unexpected time with her parents. Tally played tag with that boy until they ran out of steam and fell asleep under a tree. Everyone has gone home. The moon and stars are the only witnesses to what comes next.

This part of the night has stolen my concentration more often than I could count. Since Clea dished out that haughty tease, I haven't been able to focus on much else. That woman drives me to distraction and I fucking love it.

Black and white tiles beckon me forward as I flip the switch. The lights are brighter than usual, casting a glare across the blue walls. I squint while scouring the simple space. My bathroom in itself is lackluster at best. But one glance at the curtained window plunges fire into my bloodstream. The arousal is instant and potent. This spot won't hold a neutral quality ever again.

I palm my steely girth with a squeeze, more than ready to ditch the restrictive boxer briefs. This side of my house faces Clea's bedroom. Just across our yards, the woman from my fantasies is preparing to reenact one of her own. My mind is still tripping over her hushed request.

She didn't provide me with many instructions. Her most recent text merely hinted that we should start soon. Part of the experience is remaining authentic. She doesn't want this to be too staged. I'm more than eager to oblige her every whim.

As it turns out, my girl is kinky. She wants to watch me fuck my fist to the mere idea of her spying on me. The plan is for us to get off on one another. Mostly the illusion of it. Shadows and perspectives and imagination. The demand for more, but forced to remain apart. Without more than a teasing stroke, I'm already drawn tight and nearing the edge.

A low buzz knocks me from my reveries, yet fuels the fire in the same beat. I grab my phone off the counter. Her message is as predicted, yet still unscripted.

> *Patra: I just got home.*
> *Me: From where?*
> *Patra: Drinks with the girls. I'm kinda tipsy.*

Role play getting thrown into the mix only heightens my blinding lust. Fuck, just thinking about her makes me dizzy.

> *Me: Sounds like trouble.*
> *Patra: You have no idea.*

I smirk at her coy act, not hesitating to play along.

> *Me: Why don't you tell me?*
> *Patra: I'll show you instead.*

An image appears on the screen. She's biting her bottom lip. Her blond hair is mussed. Those mouthwatering tits squished between the cage of her arms. I bite my tongue to stave off a growl. We haven't started, but my mind is already spinning at the projected scene. The impact only succeeds in cranking my desire to blistering levels.

> *Me: You're so fucking sexy, Patra.*
> *Patra: If only you were here to tell me in person.*
> *Me: I could be.*
> *Patra: You are in my mind.*
> *Me: Such a tease.*
> *Patra: Speaking of, I'm going to bed now.*
> *Me: Alone?*
> *Patra: Unfortunately. Are you suggesting a slumber party?*
> *Me: I'd never say no.*
> *Patra: Soon.*
> *Me: Tomorrow.*
> *Patra: Until then.*

The three dots appear, signaling that she's typing more. I pause with my fingers hovering over the screen.

> *Patra: Oh, shoot. I can't seem to find my pajamas. Hopefully no one peeks into my window.*
> *Me: That sounds like an invitation.*
> *Patra: Only if you accept it.*

And that's my cue. No further prompting—or delaying—is required. My cock is throbbing from holding off. Another minute and I might lose all sense of composure.

I set my phone on the counter, grab the lotion bottle, and prowl forward. The shades taunt me, just one more barrier that stands in my path to her. A thin sheet of fabric is no match for me.

In one fluid motion, I shuck my boxers. My dick is solid, the head slapping against my lower abs with a smack. The sensation barely registers. I part the drapes with a steady hand. The gap is just wide enough to give her a peek without being obscene. A primal urge demands that I wrench the curtains off the pole altogether. Fuck hiding. But this is for Clea.

And there she is.

My gaze immediately latches onto her silhouette in the shrouded room. Her curtains are drawn but sheer, giving me a tantalizing outline of her figure on the bed. She's getting warmed up, smoothing a palm across her torso. I can feel her heat even with the walls and lawns separating us. That distance isn't more than a football field, yet it suddenly feels like uncharted territory I can't cross. In the same beat, it provides a direct tunnel to offer Clea the fantasy she's been envisioning.

I prop myself against the wall with my palms, framing the window in front of me. My muscles bulge and flex for her perusal as she turns to look in my direction. All the hours spent working out my frustrations are paying off if she appreciates the view.

With a blind sweep, I grab for the lotion and squeeze a blob onto my palm. I flinch as the cool cream makes contact with my sizzling flesh.

"Holy shit," I wheeze.

But my slight discomfort is instantly forgotten when Clea's hand drifts down. I slather my length with a tight grip while gawking like a creep. If she wasn't aware of me standing here, this would be a horrific violation. I've never done anything like this. That doesn't mean I haven't thought about her in this same position on a constant loop. It's similar to many nights I've spent alone, imagining Clea naked and wanting. I just never believed those dreams could be reality. My imagination didn't do her justice. Those images pale in comparison.

I begin stroking myself with even pulls. The yearning chomps at me, desperate for an outlet. Patience is a virtue that has no voice here. The woman across from me must feel the same haste. Clea arches her back, an arm arrowed between her bent thighs. Fuck, the visual she gives could make me come. This is erotic foreplay like I've never experienced. I'm blown away, and about to be even more so.

Her sexual appetite might rival mine. For a reason I can't fathom, she was truly made for me. Never in my filthiest fantasies did I predict this could happen. I look forward to discovering what else turns her on. This bold, adventurous side is a surprise. Better yet, she's comfortable enough to share it with me. Exploring our deepest desires together gets my blood rushing even hotter.

It's torture seeing her out of my reach. The solution melds with Clea's squirming hips. I'm not actually touching her, yet I can see her beneath me. The rigid length in my palm becomes satin curves. I picture that she's vocal during sex. Her mouth is parted with breathy moans. She begs for more. Spurring me on with dirty commands. I'm all too eager to follow, stroking my cock faster. She cries my name while clenching around me. Her thighs cage my hips, squeezing tighter as I thrust deep. She's tight, almost painfully so. The pressure has me ready to bust as I slam into the hilt again. I pump my hips, getting lost in the perceived motions.

A thin beam of moonlight streams into her room. That gleam showcases her writhing form in the throes of passionate self-love. My gaze is fastened on her arching spine, her trembling lips, her stiff nipples pointing at the ceiling. She palms her breast with one hand and pinches the peak. I'm enraptured, hypnotized by this woman's pleasure.

Clea bucks her pelvis into the air. It seems as though she's chasing the orgasm that's taunting her. Through heavy-lidded eyes, I catch the tremble in her legs. She's almost there. I'm a man possessed, jerking myself faster to reach her. Sweat beads on my skin. The rhythmic jacking is muffled by my labored breathing. My mind grows hazy with need. She's all I see through this lustful fog. Her pitchy moans are almost loud enough to pierce my ears.

My dick is hidden from her vantage point, but she can

see my arm pumping furiously. It's no secret what I'm doing. Sweat and musk perfume the room. I drag in a greedy breath, ravenous for her to consume me. A rough growl scrapes from my dry throat. It's too much, but not nearly enough.

I seethe in painful pleasure. My shaft is swollen and aching, an angry purple hue shading the tip. Then her limbs lock with tension as she finds release. She tosses her head back, her neck straining. The quiver in her body shoots through me. Corded muscles strain under the force and I increase my tempo.

After the spasms calm, Clea turns onto her side and faces the window. I can't see her eyes, but there's no doubt she's watching me.

My turn.

Thank fuck. I can't hold off any longer. The need is too strong. I stumble to the shower—one aspect Clea was fairly firm on. There's something about me under the spray that gets her going. I'm not about to let her down.

With a crank, I turn on the stream. I don't bother waiting for the water to warm. My burning lust is plenty to heat me. I fist my cock and resume the brutal pace. It only takes three strokes before the telltale signs resurface. Chills erupt across my lower back. My legs threaten to buckle. I nearly lose consciousness from the intensity.

A fiery rush races up my back. I choke on a curse as the fire rages out of control. Tingles spread through me in a hot flood.

"Fuck," I bark.

Thick spurts coat the tiles as I find relief. I continue jerking until every drop is expelled. The white burst clears from my vision within seconds. Hunger still claws at my stomach. That barely took the edge off. No pleasure by my own hand will satisfy me.

I rest my forehead against the cool wall while attempting

to get my breathing under control. But there's no reprieve. The sated state is temporary—maybe thirty seconds, at most.

Images assault me from behind my closed lids. Clea's bee-stung lips pouting at me with a plea for more. Those endless curves swaying under my forceful thrusts. Her nails biting into my shoulders as she rocks against me. The sultry onslaught rebounds my arousal. I glare at my dick, already hard and aching again.

With a deprecating groan, I wrap my length in a punishing grip and begin again.

I'm coming for you, Angel. In every possible way.

chapter twenty

Clea

THE LUSH SCENERY WHIZZES BY WHILE I GLANCE OUT MY WINDOW. Natural beauty stretches in every direction. Leafy forests and glittering lakes. Sprawling fields. A tumbleweed or two. Miles and miles of stunning landscape to gape at. If only that were appealing enough to hold my attention for longer than five seconds.

Nolan is driving and looking too sexy. Again. I'm in the passenger seat trying not to squirm. He gets me too flustered. But it's not only the sight of him reclined in comfort with a sculpted forearm propped on the wheel while he steers us to some undisclosed destination that gets me antsy. Memories of our mutual self-love session from last night are constantly fanning the flames.

My clit still hums in satisfaction. Just the thought of his eyes on me was plenty to stoke the embers primed to scorch. I could've reached the peak with a few swipes, but I delayed to make the experience last. His biceps bulging as he stroked himself will forever be seared into my brain. The fantasy playing out was hotter than any visual I could've whipped up. It's left me starving for more. From him, and us. His enthusiasm served to stir up my own. I'm realizing just how lacking the possibilities I've conjured up have been. Nothing will compare to the real deal.

How long until we take our relationship to the next intimate level? He seems content to let me lead in that regard, which is considerate but unnecessary. I've been ready for him to make me his—in the most physical sense—for six years. A girl doesn't need more time. Countless conversations with Vannah pop up in my mind. I release a soundless laugh.

Nolan peers over at me. "What's funny?"

I return his quick look. "Just thinking."

"About?"

"Stuff in general?" Prickles attack my hairline from being put under the spotlight. I'm not prepared to discuss the filthy route my thoughts continue wandering in.

"It's not nice to keep secrets, Patra." He squeezes my hand.

I stare at our linked fingers. We've been content to sit in relative silence, palms clutched together, for large portions of the trek. It's such a normal setting for established couples. How fast things can change. It's still surreal that he's beside me as more than my unrequited crush.

"You're really gonna go there?" I raise an eyebrow and turn to face him more fully. "Ready to tell me where you're taking us?"

His lips twitch with the threat of a smile "Nope. You'll see soon."

In thirty minutes, according to the directions displayed on Nolan's phone. Not much longer to wait in the overall scheme of our trip so far. We've been heading north for hours.

"But it's a cabin," I prod.

Nolan's grin surfaces. "Secluded and on the water."

That first detail gives me chills of the fiery variety. "Sounds cozy, and very romantic."

"I'm hoping so. My goal is to woo you with all this charm I apparently possess. I want to be in your good graces, Patra." He lifts our clasped hands and peppers my knuckles with kisses. His mouth lingers to add gentle suction. I wiggle as molten heat tingles in my core.

"You're already there."

"Oh?"

"Well, yeah. It should be obvious. You've pulled out all the stops to ensure my happiness." I lean over and brush my fingertips against the side of his neck.

"Oh," he moans.

"Exactly."

We approach a small town, the speed limit decreasing to a crawl. The meager buildings break apart the long stretches of trees and barren terrain. I bounce my leg as the navigation system mocks me. Nolan either isn't aware of my inner turmoil, or—more likely, now that I think about it—is choosing to ignore the jittery mess I'm becoming. It's his damn fault I'm so freaking horny.

"We should probably stop." He juts his chin at a gas station.

I clench my teeth to stave off the deep throb inside my belly. "Is that necessary?"

His brow furrows. "The rental doesn't come stocked with anything. We need food and basic supplies at the very least. This is the last place to buy stuff. From here on out, we'll be exiting civilization. Are you interested in grabbing lunch at the restaurant? That would save us the trouble of preparing something right away."

"Is there a bed?" My blurted question sends a flush to sting my cheeks.

He falters at my pitchy volume. "What?"

I fan my face, pressing a palm to the burn. "Does the cabin have a bed?"

"Yeah, of course." His wary tone doesn't deter me.

I'm aiming straight for the gutter and the brakes are cut. "I can't handle this anymore."

"The fuck?" Nolan's startled gaze snaps between mine and the road.

"It's too much. I'm burning up inside." I tug at my shirt for emphasis.

"Wait, what?"

I tuck a strand of hair behind my ear. "You're being so sweet and patient. Almost to a fault. Aren't you going crazy with lust? Or is it just me?"

"You're not alone. Trust me. I can barely think of much else." His confession reinforces the demand raging through my body.

"Then why are you trying to find more detours to delay us?"

"That's not what I'm doing." He waves a hand at the stores through the windshield. "We need shit for our stay. I was too preoccupied with the party and our little performance afterward to shop beforehand."

"Okay," I huff. This misunderstanding is doing nothing to calm the desire in my veins. If anything, the fever in my blood is only ratcheting higher. "Fine. Let's run errands."

"Fuck the groceries," he grunts.

"But that's a priority for you."

"The fuck it is, Patra. You're my priority. The only one, considering Tally is in very good hands with your parents." He expels a harsh breath. His excessive cursing is a major tell of how he truly feels. A giddy twist tickles my chest. "I wasn't sure if you were ready for that between us. The last thing I want is to rush you."

I cross my arms and gape at him. "You have no freaking clue."

"That's becoming more apparent the longer this conversation goes on. Why don't you fill me in?" The look he shoots back at me is brimming with barely-restrained control. This is a man nearing the edge of his rope where composure is concerned. It's about damn time—he was starting to make me feel like a hussy.

A slow exhale fills me with the ability to explain without jumping onto his lap. Safety first and all that. "Please don't think I'm not appreciative of everything you've done these past several weeks. It's been a legit fairy tale. That's what I needed to get over the hurt. I was upset and frustrated and had reached my bullshit tolerance where you were involved. But now I'm frustrated for an entirely different reason."

He rolls his eyes to glare at the roof for a pregnant pause. "All those wasted years."

"That was before. We've moved past the pain. This is now. We have nothing standing in our way anymore." I rest a palm on his straining forearm. "I'm crazy about you, Nolan. Like legit insane, saved myself on the off chance one day you'd finally come around and see me waiting here."

A loud screech precedes the stench of burning rubber. He swerves onto the shoulder, slamming the truck into park. I jerk in my seat from the abrupt shift. "You can't just admit that while I'm trying to concentrate on driving in a straight line."

I bite back a smile. "Well, excuse me for wanting to sleep with you."

"But you saved yourself for me?" The awe in his voice makes my eyes water.

My nod is a jerky bob. "Didn't seem like a choice."

A strangled noise chokes from his pressed lips. "What you do to me, Angel... The visions running through my head would scare you. It's indescribable. I want everything with you."

"Likewise," I murmur.

The fire in his gaze beckons me in. "I'm gonna be so good to you."

"You already are." I cup his jaw, my thumb cutting a line along the dark stubble there.

Nolan tilts into my touch. "I have so much more to give."

"Just more to look forward to."

"Do you think this town has a hotel?" He drags rough fingers through his hair, leaving the strands upright in disarray. The sight is similar to the fluttering jumble in my stomach.

I point at his phone. "We can survive that long. Consider it an exercise in delayed gratification."

His hand snatches mine from where I dropped it on my thigh. "We could write a book on the topic."

My laugh is sharp. "Not sure about you, but I certainly could."

He nips at my fingertip. "I haven't been with a woman since Tally was born. Hell, even months before that. Once I found out Rachel was pregnant, my playboy days were behind me."

I blink at him. The air in his truck is suddenly too dense. It must be the country atmosphere warping reality. I press my free palm to his forehead. "You're just talking nonsense at this point."

"No, I'm seeing quite clearly, Patra. You're the one I've been holding out for. It didn't feel like a choice for me either."

My inhale is garbled. His admission makes my wait worth it, even on the loneliest of days. My first time will be a memory to cherish. "Oh my gosh, Nolan. Seriously?"

He presses a kiss to my inner wrist. "Yes. I have no desire unless you're involved. That means I'm meant to be with you."

"This is incredible." And beyond my wildest dreams. The urge to swoon battles against my percolating lust. One way or another, I'm going to explode.

"I want to kiss you so fucking bad, but I won't be able to stop." Yet he still edges toward me, his control seeming to stretch without permission.

"Maybe we should get going, or I can't be held accountable for what happens next."

He adjusts the stiff ridge threatening to bust open his zipper. "Fuck, Patra. All you had to tell me was you're ready."

I flutter my lashes at him. "I'm ready. Please take me to bed."

"What the lady wants she gets." He slams on the gas, sending gravel in a spitting fit behind the tires.

"Finally," I moan.

Nolan isn't joking about that last line. He tests the limits with traffic laws for the remaining miles of our journey. By some miracle, it only takes fifteen minutes before we're making the final turn onto a narrow path. The man shaved off extra time thanks to his newfound motivation to hurry.

I've considered touching him on several occasions, since my dirty thoughts can't seem to mind their manners or control themselves. Nolan is strung tighter than a hunter's bow. One pluck and he's bound to unleash the beast. Watching the untamed version is intriguing. But the result could be dangerous. The threat of bodily harm staves my hunger. I have enough sense remaining to wait until we arrive unharmed.

The road is bumpy and overgrown. My teeth chatter from the rough ground, even though we're crawling at a turtle's pace. I distract myself by appreciating the wilderness surround us. There's nothing out here except trees and the lake. It's the definition of a rustic escape. I'm already in love with this area and we haven't caught sight of our humble abode yet.

A small structure comes into view after we pass a steep curve. The single-story cabin is nestled within thick evergreens. I can almost smell the sweet sap. Nolan whips his truck into what counts as a driveway. I barely have a moment to blink before he's hopping out.

He rounds the hood to my side and yanks open the door. With fumbling hands, he rips off my seatbelt. Then he's hoisting me into his arms. I struggle against him once my brain catches up with his hurried movements.

"What are you doing? I'm too heavy."

"Hush." His grumble puffs against my temple while he stomps up the porch steps.

The command has me clamping my lips and squeezing my legs together. Bossy Nolan is sexy beyond reason. I have to get control of these extreme reactions. Or maybe not.

For the moment, I choose to relax in his grip. He wants to snuggle me against him. I'm surely not going to complain. The massive pine feet from the porch casts a shadow over us. It's so tall that I have to crane my neck back in an attempt to see the top. Strangely—or not—the tree next to it looks like a maple. This area seems to have quite a variety, now that I'm searching.

My perusing is interrupted when Nolan tips me too far to the left. I overcorrect by banding an arm around his neck. He jostles me while fighting to punch a code into the keypad lock.

With renewed effort, I begin squirming in his hold. "Just put me down. You're making this more difficult than it needs to be."

He relents with a grunt, setting me on my feet. "I was trying to be honorable and carry you across the threshold."

I pat his chest. "Save that for another day."

His nose traces the shell of my ear. "I can hardly wait for that one to arrive."

Good grief. He's suddenly going full speed ahead. Not that I mind. It's just an abrupt whirlwind. Give a girl an anchor to hold onto with all this rapid change. I grip onto his belt loop for stability. The look he gives me has me going weak in the knees.

"It gets me so fucking hard that you love touching me. Gives me a reason to finally wrap myself around you all I want." Nolan demonstrates looping his muscular arms across my front, cinching me tight to him. He nuzzles his face into the crook of my shoulder.

An embarrassingly loud giggle squeaks from me. "That tickles."

"How about here?" His fingers drift to my ribs.

I gasp and attempt to wrestle free. "No, not there. Please quit."

He smooths his palms down my sides to rest at my hips. "We're gonna have so much fun."

"When?" I bump my ass into the hardness prodding at me.

Nolan successfully enters the code and shoves the door open. "After you."

I shuffle inside without further delay. The air is stale, but not unpleasant. An earthy undertone mixes with faint cinnamon. Wood and plaid decorate the small area.

The interior is plain with minimal decorations. Country swank with simple accents seems to be the theme. The walls are made of stacked logs. Each one is unique—actually harvested from a forest, not primly shaved by machines. The floorboards contain a similar quality. If I had to guess, this cabin is old and extremely special.

It's an open concept space. Only one section in the corner is closed off, which I assume is the bathroom. Two chairs near a fireplace. A threadbare rug that's seen finer afternoons. The large bed against the far wall. It's perfectly imperfect. Just right for us. It's no-frills, yet picturesque. I don't need lavish details to enjoy myself. All I need is him. The location—and breathtaking view—is more than enough to make me fall in love.

I stare out the huge bay window that takes up the top half of the north-facing side. The lake stretches from left to right. There are no technological intrusions. No traces of civilization hindering the natural experience. I can imagine sitting on the shore and being completely at peace.

"Secluded takes on a whole new meaning," I sigh.

"I can't wait to find out." The remark is quiet, mumbled under his breath.

"What's that?"

"If you're vocal during sex." His intrusive pondering has a fresh blush heating me from the inside out.

I guess this is my fault. There's no shying away. "Why don't you find out for yourself?"

The gentle pad of footsteps is all I hear before his hands meet my body. He bends to touch my bare skin below the hem of my dress. His palms skirt up along my thighs, moving higher until the fabric bunches at my waist. "Your curves were made to tempt me."

I spin to face him, locking my arms around his neck. "Show me how much."

chapter twenty-one

Nolan

CLEA SLAMS DOWN THE GAUNTLET WITH THOSE WORDS. I fist a hand in her hair and slam my mouth against hers. The fever spikes instantly as she glides her tongue out to meet mine. She has the power to decimate me with a single flick.

Our flames clash and blend, building into an inferno that will only rage hotter. I'm already losing my grip on reality. Just being this close to her has that effect on me. And her desire added into the equation is an unexpected punch that I didn't brace for.

I palm her ass and center myself. These curves will always send me toppling over the edge. With careful steps, I guide her toward the wall. She clings on tightly, like she never wants to let me go. I never want her to. I nip at her bottom lip and release a growl. In return, she claws at my shirt with a muffled mewl.

My girl is wanting, and bordering on desperate. I can't believe what a fool I've been. Again. But I'll reward her patience with me.

Starting with several orgasms.

Clea's dress is still lifted, the slinky fabric resting on her voluptuous hips. I crash to my knees, tug her panties to the floor, and drool over the decadence spread before me. The amount of salvia pooling in my mouth is obscene, but not at all surprising. She's seduction personified and inches from my filthy intentions. The sight should be a sin. Nothing this erotic can lead me to salvation. Except her. She's pure and honest and everything good. My heart pounds a ferocious beat as I prepare to worship this woman.

I part her lower lips between two fingers. Another flood fills my mouth while I reveal the supple flesh hidden within. Nothing obscures my view of her smooth center. She's slick and pink, ready for my tongue. My abstinence was more than worth constant blue balls if only for a glance at the innocence Clea has kept sacred for me. Her folds are petal-soft as I drag my thumbs up in a teasing stroke. She's so fucking wet and I've barely touched her.

"Wow, you're really getting up close and personal with my lady bits." Clea shifts slightly but is mostly immobile from the scrap of lace around her ankles.

"Has a man ever seen you here?" I trace a soft line across her core.

She shakes her head, a sputter feathering from that delectable pout. "Just you."

"That's right, Patra. Just me." The fact that I'm the first and only one does wicked things to me.

I'm fucking fascinated, frozen on the spot. Her modesty must come knocking as she once again attempts to snap her thighs closed. My palms keep her spread for me. She probably doesn't appreciate me leering at her for extended moments without explanation. But what is there to say? This woman casts me under a hypnotic spell as she waits for my pleasurable assault. She's splayed open and on display for me alone. That knowledge would make my legs buckle if I wasn't already crouching.

Clea gives another impatient shuffle. "What're you doing?"

"Enjoying the view."

Clea rubs her legs together. "Isn't that weird?"

"It's all part of the process."

She presses her ass into the wall, tilting her pelvis toward me. It doesn't seem as though she's even aware of her not-so-subtle offering. "I wouldn't know."

"Me either."

"How—"

I blow on her exposed center. Goosebumps immediately rise on her skin, a shiver following close behind. "Don't doubt me."

"But you're teasing me."

I lean in, drifting my nose along her naked mound. Sweet musk invades my nostrils. The aroma is delicate, yet intoxicating. "No, I'm savoring you."

Her nails scrape against my scalp. "I need more."

"Delayed gratification, remember?"

Clea retorts with a noncommittal sound. "Haven't we waited enough?"

"Don't rush me with this, Patra." But the temptation is too strong. I'm drawn in like a collared hound on a chain.

Just for the sake of calming our restlessness, I drag my tongue upward from her core to clit. Sweet nectar bursts on my tongue. Her flavor has a tangy kick chased with honey. That initial hit detonates a trigger inside me. I barely manage to wrench away.

She tosses her head back. "Please do that again. It feels fantastic."

"I've never savored a woman. You better believe you'll be my first." I hover my lips over her molten center. "And last."

"Yes, I'm ready."

"Almost."

"Why are you toying with me?"

"It's a slow burn. Trust me."

"I'm not sure what you mean." The last word breaks off on a whine when I exhale another fiery breath across her bared center. "Holy shit, you're gonna make me explode just from that."

Lust thrums through me. "I'm making you mine, Patra. One lick at a time."

"Just keep doing it," she begs. "What do I do?"

"Your only job is to come on my tongue."

She falters and loses her grip on me. It only takes a beat for her fingers to tunnel through my hair again. "Better be careful,

Nolan. You're going to make me"—she cuts off in a shuddering breath as I tease my lips up to hers—"explode!"

"I'll pick up your scattered pieces. Then I'll make you unravel all over again."

Any further protest fades from her lips with a whoosh. "Well, when you put it that way."

But her hips buck forward regardless.

My chuckle washes over her fiery core. "I'm famished, Angel. Are you gonna feed me?"

A knot bobs in her throat as she gulps. "I'd never stand in the way of you devouring a meal."

Fuck, she undoes me. Clea doesn't fit the profile of a typical shy virgin. She may be inexperienced, but she's not clueless. She's not afraid to let her kink out with me. That's the existing comfort and sexual attraction between us talking. Far from prying eyes and judgmental ears, we're free to revel in our combined dirtiness. It drives me wild.

I press a soft kiss to her heat. "There's so much I have planned for you. I'm not sure where to begin."

"What you're doing now is great. Excellent. I'm already so close. Just a little more. Please." The choppy whine in her voice is my undoing.

"No need to beg," I murmur before burying my mouth between her legs.

Clea's answering moan is erotic decadence. I want to bottle that sound for lonely nights when she's not near me. She releases another throaty purr, gripping my hair in an unrelenting hold.

"Oh, oh. It's too good." Yet she yanks me closer.

She isn't exaggerating about being on edge. I've only taken a few passes from front to back and she's already trembling. That doesn't mean I'm going to ease up. Quite the opposite. I spear through her slit with a swipe of my finger, gathering her slick excitement to her clit. Her body sags against the wall, providing me with easier access. The advantage is appreciated—and quickly repaid. I bat at her sensitive bundle with the tip of my tongue. Such a small button to strike, but her cries clue me in.

"There, yes. Keep going... right there."

I groan in response, earning me a pitchy squeal. Wet silk glides along my lips. The caress is a mere taunt. There's so much left to come undone. I grope and paw and demand. My control is fraying with every swipe, and I lash at her faster. I'm insatiable. The animalistic growl that tears from me is further proof. Nothing I eat after her will satisfy me. There's no competition against her salty sweetness. Another vibration rumbles up my throat. I binge on her like the exquisite course she is. Her arousal is the only taste to appease my palate after years of bland slop.

An ache spreads from my bent legs, but I don't pay the pain any mind. I will gladly kneel at her alter until my entire body is numb. Then a telltale quiver begins in her muscles. Clea flexes while thrusting forward. The sensations flood into me all at once and I double my efforts.

"Oh, oh, Nolan!" she cries. She shatters under my tongue, going rigid against me. Her climax gets me harder than a titanium rod. The tension flowing from her only serves to feed me more. I tongue her with swirling flicks until she begins pushing at me.

"Ah, too sensitive," she yelps.

I relent after a final swipe. "You're delicious."

"And you're very talented." Clea shudders and combs at her disheveled hair. She looks well-loved, but I'm just getting started.

"Would you believe I've never done that before?"

"No." She scoffs, then sobers at the honesty wafting from my expression.

"Just for you." I can feel her wetness coating my face. The claiming brand has my chest expanding.

Clea licks her lips while searing those fuck-hot baby blues into me. "What is it with you kneeling on the floor in front of me?"

I smooth a palm up her calf. "Are you complaining?"

"Not even a little bit."

"Good." I struggle to stand after that cramped position. "I'm ready for more."

"Me too." She reaches for my belt.

I circle her wrist, halting the thoughtful consideration before she can touch me. "More of you."

"Huh?" Her voice holds a raspy tone. Must be from all that screaming.

"That"—I gesture to her bared lower half—"was just a fast one to take the edge off."

Clea shakes her head. "I can't—"

"You can." I cup her blushing cheek.

"But—"

"Trust me." The assurance is murmured against her forehead as I press a gentle kiss there.

She nods against me. "Okay."

That's all the permission I require. I haul her wobbly form into my arms and rush to the mattress. Laundered sheets are the least of my worries, but the owners did ensure we'd have clean bedding. I place her in the middle with more grace than the snapping jaws of my lust suggest.

The panties still holding her ankles hostage vanish with a tug. I motion to her dress with a twirling finger. "Off with it."

She follows my demand without hesitation. The material pools on the floor a moment later. Clea bends an arm behind her back to unclasp the last garment concealing her naked glory. I let my jaw go slack as her breasts spill free. Her hands begin moving as if to shield my view.

I hover my palms over hers. "Please don't hide from me."

After a brief pause, Clea rests her arms on the bed. The unrestricted sight of her sultry curves makes me stumble. I move to the mattress and crawl between her parted legs. With an upward sweep from my palms, I encourage her to spread wider. I wedge my shoulders against the tension still twitching through her. She relaxes, framing my torso with her thighs. I kiss her lower belly.

She squeaks, the noise blending into a moan when I nuzzle her there. I make a downward trail leading to her pleasure. Once she's splayed for me again, I lower my mouth to her wanton slit.

I savor a lazy swipe. Her nudity only fuels the flames chasing me. I become the hunger that's shredding my gut. "Have you thought about this?"

Clea shifts closer. "Yes."

"How often?"

She claps a hand over her eyes. "Gosh, you're a talker."

"Does that bother you?"

"Only when it makes me wait." The petulance in her voice makes me chuckle.

I pepper kisses to her inner thigh. "Let me indulge. This is all new for me, Patra. I want to hear more fantasies."

Her nails scratch across my nape. "One wasn't enough?"

I scoff. "That's not a question."

Clea peers down at me with a quirked brow. "Daily."

My eyes bulge at the admission. "Damn. That'll stroke my ego."

"I'm hoping to stroke something with more girth," she jests.

"Naughty girl. Where do you want me?" I flick my tongue on her clit. "How about here?" I move my fingers to her pussy. "Or maybe here?"

Her puckered hole tempts me, but that's uncharted territory of a completely different variety. I'm not in the habit of pushing my luck. There's always someday.

"Both," she murmurs.

I start with a languid lick through her sex. That euphoric boom finds me, and I instantly dive in for more. While my tongue is busy on her clit, I trace a finger along her folds. Then I find her entrance and circle the edge. Clea clenches when I nudge inside. At first, I think she's trying to block me. The unforgiving clamp loosens in the next beat. She's tight but slippery. Her untried walls seem to suck me in.

"Holy wow, yes. More, more," she chants.

I can feel her arousal on my skin while rushing to follow the order. Her hesitancy from earlier melts away as she begins rocking against me. The visual of her fucking my face drags me to a point I might not come back from. I begin humping the bed while tonguing her slit. My finger pumps in and out, matching the steady rhythm. Sounds erupt from my mouth that I can barely hear over the pounding in my ears.

When I glance up the enticing shape of her body, she's palming her breasts. Peaked nipples appear between pinching fingertips. The sight has me salivating, and I gulp at the excess. Desperation urges me on. I need more of her.

My lips add suction with that promise driving me. I push my finger deeper, and she arches her back. Her resistance stretches and accepts a second digit. Both are sunk to the last knuckle. The pace is slow but increases with each inward slide. Heat spreads across my lower back, the muscles bunching there. I won't be able to avoid the embarrassment of soaking my jeans.

Just as I'm certain the mess is unavoidable, her muscles seize. There's a spasm against my fingers as her limbs go stiff. A scream cracks the silence while she topples over the edge.

"Fuck, fuck, holy shit. I can't—"

She cuts herself off with another wail. The walls might be vibrating. It's a good thing there's no one within miles. Not that I'd care. Even if we were smack in the middle of a city, I'd be all too willing to continue eating her. My appetite isn't sated. It never will be.

Clea pulls away with a muffled sob. "Stop, please. I'm on freaking fire."

I do, but not without a grumble. This isn't a surrender. I'm just preparing for the main course. There's always room for dessert—and additional servings.

"Okay, no more of that." Her breathing is labored, matching my own. She grabs at my arms and wrenches me upward. "I want you inside me. Now."

chapter twenty-two

Clea

M Y COMMAND DOES THE TRICK. NOLAN STRIPS LIKE IT'S A timed event, and his speed will somehow earn extra credit. A giggle tickles my throat as his clothes fly off in chaotic disarray. The noise morphs into a strangled choke once his dick bobs free from the elastic waistband. Any attempt at speech dies while my jaw goes slack. Shock and awe whistle from my lungs in a faint hiss.

Nolan wraps a palm around that girthy length and gives a few trial strokes. That's probably more for my benefit than his. I'm mesmerized by the unobstructed view, my eyes latched on his lazy motions. He just stands there—butt naked and on display—more than comfortable to let me get my fill.

I swipe at my mouth, certain there's drool escaping. "Umm, wow."

He straightens and squares his shoulders. "Do you approve?"

"Yep." I smack my lips. "Well done."

Well done? I almost smack my forehead. If anything, he's a premium cut from top-quality stock meant to be ordered rare. So much juicy goodness to slurp. All red-blooded and extra tender. Charred on the outside, heated just enough to warm the center. Another wave of salvia pools on my tongue.

"Patra?"

I twirl a strand of platinum blond around my finger while ogling his sculpted abs. "Hmmm?"

A dry chuckle shakes from him. "You okay?"

My gaze trails to the tattoos that are usually hidden from sight. Scrawled in a fancy script across his right side is the name Tallulah. A scene of a stormy night with angry clouds and lightning stretches across his left upper arm. Two figures appear to be emerging from the thunderous scene. I squint, but can't quite see the images clearly. That's a discussion topic for later. What matters in this moment is that Nolan is bared—and all mine. Finally.

"Oh, I'm about to be fabulous." I crook a finger at him. "C'mere."

Without pause, Nolan kneels on the bed and crawls forward. He blankets my body with his, aligning us in a way that guarantees we're touching at every possible point. I automatically lift my legs to cinch around him. My ankles cross against his lower back, tightening the hold ever so slightly. Our skin touches everywhere. That sensation sets me on fire, the flames blazing through my veins.

I rub my palms along his sides to share the heat. He's smooth, yet jagged and scarred. My fingers bump over the ridges at his ribs. He nips at my chin, allowing me to explore. Sunny warmth envelops me like a familiar embrace. His woodsy scent seems even stronger in this moment as he infiltrates my senses. I press my nose to his chest and breathe deep. Freaking yum. My toes curl against his ass. A rumble answers me while Nolan buries his face in my hair.

His much larger form makes me feel delicate. I can feel him hard and eager against my most intimate softness. That's a heady sensation, serving to further feed my desire churning in my belly. But a dark inkling casts a shadow over the blinding glow.

I've never been naked with a man. My hands automatically shift to cover those less-than-toned squishy spots.

"What're you doing?" The reprimand is similar to his chiding earlier.

A cringe pinches my features. I return my palms to his tempting flesh. "It's just… habit? A bad one, I know. Standing in the mirror, trying to find what angles work best. Sucking my belly in. Pressing down on certain areas and imagining how much better I'd look if I lost twenty pounds."

"Are you fucking with me?"

Revealing these unflattering toxins shows how close we've become, whether he realizes that or not. "No, but I'm more confident than ever. With one look from you, I feel really sexy."

"Damn right, Patra. Your body is lush and beautiful and designed to make me lose all good sense." He drifts a path of soft kisses to my ear. "Never doubt my attraction for you."

The buzz he gives me chases off the poison. "I don't. Truly. Thank you for that."

"I'm the one who should be giving thanks." Nolan props on a bent elbow to avoid crushing me. Our noses are close enough to touch, but he tilts ever so slightly to seal his mouth over mine.

The kiss is sweet and sensual, such a contrast to the vulgar banter we exchanged moments ago. The pressure of this situation settles on me. With that force comes a noticeable switch in mood. Gone are our raunchy comments and salacious gestures. This space is reserved for sweet sentiments and acknowledging the bond that's always been there. It was just waiting for us to drag our heads out of our own butts and commit.

Now that I'm noticing, his entire demeanor seems softer. I lift a palm to cup his scruffy jaw. "Is this real?"

Those damn dimples could cure chronic unhappiness. "It's a little late to assume otherwise."

"Surreal," I breathe.

He ghosts his lips across my forehead. "Destiny."

I shift under him, spreading my hands across the expanse of his back. "Then let's make it true."

Nolan goes rigid beneath my wandering fingers. I peek at him from under my lashes. His jaw is clenched to the point of grinding molars.

"Shit," he spits with a glare at the door. "I need to grab a condom."

Blistering indecision rushes up my neck, centering on my face. There's little doubt I look redder than a tomato. "Or not."

He goes still. "What?"

I gnaw on my inner cheek. "Well, I'm on birth control. Obviously, I haven't been with anyone else."

His chest heaves with a thick inhale. "Me either. None that are relevant for mentioning anyway."

I lift my brows. "So?"

"You're really okay going without?"

Flutters attack my core at just the idea of him sliding in bare. "Why wouldn't I be? That's how I've always imagined us. No barriers."

"Fuck, Patra." His muscles go taut, only to release and flex again in rapid succession. "Another fantasy?"

The ripple gives me chills and I shiver underneath him. "Coming true."

Nolan moves his hips. Steely insistence bumps my center and I gasp. That rigid shaft is somehow going to fit inside me. Nerves creep in, but I scare them off with a mental shove. He pushes my arms to rest over my head, drifting his palms along the stretched limbs. I moan and arch into him.

"Tease," is a murmured complaint against his neck.

He entwines our fingers. "You have no idea how long I've been waiting. We're taking our time."

I allow my lashes to flutter shut as his tip finds my entrance. Then he's gone. I blink and find him staring at me. "Um, hi?"

Nolan kisses my shoulder. "Keep your eyes open for me. I want to watch as you feel us joining as one."

It could be awkward looking at him while he's hovering naked above me. The flames scorch anything other than giddy anticipation. This is the man I've loved in not-so-secret since I was eighteen. I couldn't be more prepared. Especially after the two orgasms that left sparks that still trickle through me.

His cock glides along my slit, erasing any stray thoughts except for what this man is about to do. I want him to see me come undone. My head settles deeper into the pillow with a nod. "Yes, I'm ready."

There's a pregnant pause while Nolan lines up. I try not to flitch or clench or do anything else that would delay his entry. His arousal finds me slick and open. He edges in with a smooth glide. My breath hitches when the pinch intensifies into a roaring burn. The initial stretch isn't a completely foreign sensation. I've used toys—what girl hasn't?—but I've never experienced anything comparable to his caliber. He will take some adjusting to accommodate. Just when I believe the worst is cresting, a painful stab spreads through my core.

Nolan rips through the last remaining shred separating us. It's a searing blow, like cramps on steroids. The urge to curl in a fetal position twitches my legs. My body resists his intrusion with stabbing agony. A muffled cry betrays the brave face I tried putting forward. I'm stretched too far. There's no use pretending now. I lurch upward, my fingers still threaded through his. My exhale sputters to a hitch.

I sag into the mattress in an attempt to relax. Heat springs to my eyes, streaking in a fiery trail down my temple. He freezes as my breathing goes shallow.

"Shit, Angel. I'm hurting you."

"It's okay," I vow with conviction. "Just keep going."

"No." His blunt argument is followed by a measured retreat.

My thighs grip onto him. "I'm fine, baby."

The endearment registers and stops his hasty withdrawal. He dips his forehead to rest on mine. "But I want this to be good for you too."

"It's part of the process, right?"

"That's different." But he remains unmoving.

My smile is a tad wobbly at the edges. I nuzzle against the furrow between his brows. "It was always meant to be you."

The assurance seems to spur him on, and he begins pushing in again. "I promise it'll get better."

"It already is." And that's not a total lie.

The discomfort ebbs and a wave of numbness flows over me. Maybe that's my body's attempt at a defense. But I don't need protection against him. I want to feel it all. With a hiss, I push my hips into his. Nolan startles, wide eyes pinning me into place.

"I want this." I lean in for a kiss. "You inside me. Us finally being together."

When his lips brush mine in return, nothing else matters. Him pressing against me is heaven. The pain will fade, leaving only pleasure and passion behind.

His thrusts are slow, pushing in and out at an even pace. The sting is becoming more tolerable, easing into a dull throb. That gives me the confidence to lift my legs higher. Nolan sinks deeper from the change in angle. His motions almost feel pleasant. The hint of soothing relief reinforces my clarity.

Earlier, when Nolan's face was between my legs, I felt like we were doing the dirty. It was filthy and kinky and exactly what I needed to get loose. My nerves about sex had been properly settled. I went in assuming all would be just fine. But this?

It's a completely different—and unexpected—experience. We're making love. Nolan's ability to flip a switch and turn on the compassion brings emotion to the surface. I twist my wrists until his hands release me. In the next beat, I'm tunneling my fingers into his hair just to feel that much closer. He's tender and gentle and giving much more care than I could imagine for my first time.

Nolan licks a fiery trail across my jaw, down my throat, and nibbles along my collarbone. A sizzle zips through me at the added sensations. His mouth wanders lower yet, his tongue swirling around my breast. I shove my chest up for his taking. He takes the hint and latches on with strong suction. A need to move pummels through me. I begin grinding against him. That feeds the growing hunger I didn't realize was lying dormant in my stomach. The rush that follows almost makes me dizzy, sending a frantic pulse through my bloodstream.

We rock together in unison, searching for that promise of

euphoric release. I'm not certain I'll reach that peak, but there's always next time. He wedges a palm beneath my ass, tilting just enough to hit a spot that makes me clench for an entirely different reason. A familiar warmth blooms in my lower belly. My reaction fuels him to keep striking there—over and over—until I'm clutching to his shoulders. A chant for more spills from my lips. Maybe a third orgasm is in the stars after all.

"What do you need?"

I wiggle a bit more until his rolling strokes nudge my clit. A moan shortly follows. "There."

He speeds up at my encouraging sounds. Tingles form in the pit of my core, splaying outwards in a fiery wave. His teeth nip at my pebbled nipple. I shudder from the onslaught.

"Are you close?" His muffled question comes from my cleavage, where he's busy lavishing my breasts with attention.

My nod is frantic as I lunge for the edge. "So, so close."

Nolan's grip tightens as his speed kicks up another notch. "My pleasure comes from yours. Take us to the stars, Angel."

Then he surges inside with a powerful thrust. With a soundless shout, I dive into the unknown abyss. A cascade of blistering pleasure catches me. My muscles go taut as I hold on for the ride. I let my eyelids slide shut when spots dance in front of me. Nolan's motions turn erratic seconds before he jerks on top of me.

It seems like we're drifting in a thrumming vacuum. As aftershocks zap through my system, leaving me a quivering mess. His bulky frame collapses with a groan. Nolan slides slightly to the side so he doesn't crush me. My chest rises and falls from the exertion. His labored breath caresses my ear. The bubble surrounding us doesn't recede as we gather our bearings. That intimate enclosure stays, keeping us in its warmth.

He nuzzles into the crook of my shoulder. "I love you, Clea. I'll spend forever showing you how much. You agreeing to be mine is a gift I can never repay. I'll have to find creative ways to express my gratitude."

I sniffle when the impact of his words hits me. "You love me?"

Nolan's chuckle ghosts across my throat as he props onto a bent elbow. His bottomless gaze reflects the honesty behind his confession. "Of course. I've been in love with you for six years."

I loop my arms around his neck and tug until we're plastered together. "I love you so much it hurts."

A grunt escapes him while he straightens above me again. "That might be a lingering side effect from the sex."

"Are you really making jokes?"

A wince tightens his expression. "Too soon for comedic relief?"

"You're still semi-hard inside me. What do you think?"

He lowers to dust our noses together. "I wanted to lighten the mood."

"For?" I drag my nails along his scalp, earning a pleased rumble from him.

"The shower we're about to take."

"I'm listening."

"And I'll be doing the eating. It's time for my dessert."

chapter twenty-three

Nolan

STIR FROM THE SOUNDEST SLEEP I'VE HAD SINCE MY YOUTH. A pleasant soreness spreads through me as awareness filters in. Other than the subtle twinge, my body feels well-rested. That reset is exactly what I've needed for over six years.

When I crack my eyes open, the aged wood ceiling greets me. The rising sun splashes the room with a reflective glow and rich promises for a productive day. Vanilla and a floral aroma infuse the air. Sated passion lingers, too. A fresh burst will soon perfume the space if I have any stake in the game. I inhale until my lungs burn. Then I realize what roused me.

Clea is absently trailing a finger along my abs. The motion is a soft sweep as she stares out the window. Her blond hair is more tangled than not. I'll take full responsibility for that mussed style.

It appears she's lost in thought, and I won't be the one to disrupt her musings. I'm more than content to lie in this exact position until the sun goes down. The slight weight of her snuggled against me does crazy things to my libido. Not that I wasn't already pitching a tent with the sheets.

I let my mind wander while we're still drowsy and drifting. Yesterday was a chapter from the filthiest fantasy I could conjure. My tongue coated in her desire. Silky curves under my palms. Her succulent body was pliant and mine for the taking. Pitchy moans echo in my ears. Bubbles cascading down soapy skin while I washed her, only to get us dirty moments later. That tiny shower was a snug fit, but I didn't mind being crammed in with her rubbing against me one bit. Then I scooped her against me and hauled ass to town. It was the fastest trip known to man, and anyone in my position would do the same if they had a well-fucked Clea beside them. But that honor is mine. Only mine.

We ate, fell back into bed, explored each other's pleasure, and eventually let sleep take us. Here we are—recharged and ready for what's next.

I skate a hand along the smooth expanse of Clea's back. Her lower half is tucked away under the covers. That doesn't mean I can't feel every sinful inch. My cock twitches in agreement. I'll be even more possessive now, which she doesn't seem to mind.

"What's on your mind, Angel?" My voice is gritty from disuse.

Clea stretches with a groan. The blanket dips even lower, showing off her perky ass. She tilts her face to look up at me. Her eyes are heavy-lidded and glittering with a sultry hue. "Good morning, love."

"I might prefer that over your other nickname for me."

She snuggles closer, her cheek plastered to my pec. "Figured you would, considering Tally's aversion to being called baby."

The palm I have firmly planted on her ass clenches. "Let's not talk about my daughter while I'm groping you."

Clea wiggles her hips, earning a guttural groan from me. "Insatiable."

"Thanks to you." I trace a path across her supple flesh. "Are you sore?"

She shrugs. "A little."

I roll to the side for better access. "We won't have sex, but I can still make you feel good."

Her delicate hand shoves me back into the pillow. "It's my turn. You've done plenty. How does breakfast in bed sound?"

"Isn't that what I just suggested?"

She clucks her tongue. "Dirty boy. I mean actual food."

"That can wait." I drape her thigh over my waist.

She presses a finger over my lips. "No, nympho. My vajay-jay can use a breather."

My mouth droops against her bent knuckle. "Why didn't you tell me?"

"I just did. What difference would it make earlier? We've been snoozing." Her touch drifts to my upper arm, circling the ink there. "There are two people emerging from the dark clouds. I'm guessing the smaller one is Tally."

It was only a matter of time before the truth revealed itself. I go still beneath her wandering curiosity. "The other is you."

Clea's attention snaps to my eyes with a gasp. "What?"

I tuck some wild snarls behind her ear. "Of course, Patra. I couldn't escape the storm without you."

"When did you get this done?" The awe in her voice might as well be a fist around my dick.

The pulsing throb distracts me. I have to take a moment to pause and shake off the blood loss in my brain. "Um, four years ago."

"You permanently marked me into your skin before this?" She motions between our naked forms.

"Well, to be fair, you can't really tell who it is. That's all up here." I tap my temple.

She swats my chest. "Such an ass."

I grip her chin, tugging until our lips connect. "I love you. Now, later, and back then."

"Gosh, you're good with the charm. I should probably return the favor." Then she whips off the sheet and stares at my cock like it's a continental breakfast buffet. She can have all of me. "I'll be feasting on you in a bit. After we explore the woods and scenery a bit."

"But I've erected a monument in your honor." I gesture at the standing ovation my dick is giving her. A thrust from my hips further accentuates the point.

Clea rolls her eyes with a laugh. "I don't want to spend the entire weekend in bed."

I snag her wrist and press a gentle kiss to the soft area. "You've turned me into a fiend."

"That's the six years going without talking."

"Wrong. I only want you, Patra. Now that I've had you, I'll be craving more. Constantly," I tack on with conviction.

She huffs, but there's a smile brightening her features. "You're incorrigible."

"It's pronounced finally being satisfied and eager for another round. Can you blame me? You're so damn sexy."

"And you're determined." She chews on her thumbnail while edging off the mattress. "Let's get dressed and eat. Then we can take a hike."

"Don't forget about the boat."

"You were serious?" She grabs my discarded shirt and slips it over her head. The faded fabric swallows her shape, hanging down at mid-thigh. An empty pang ricochets in my gut over losing my view of her incredible rack. The fact she's wearing my clothes makes up for the loss, though.

I told her yesterday that I rented a pontoon for us. "You didn't believe me?"

"More like preoccupied with other activities." Clea roots through her bag and whips out clean panties. "Less walking might be better for my nether region situation."

"How about a calm cruise on the lake to appreciate our surroundings?"

"Sounds delightful. We can take the scenic tour. Scout the area. Snap some photos. Oh, I brought my camera!" she remembers. "We can document our trip."

"I'm good with that." Especially if Clea packed a bikini. Shit, maybe I am turning into a deviant. The thought is laughable. I've always been addicted to this woman.

A low vibration steals my focus. Clea's phone is buzzing

on the nightstand. I roll across the bed to reach the humming device.

"It's your mom. She wants to FaceTime." I show her the screen while grabbing my boxers from the floor. Exposing my naked ass to my future mother-in-law seems like a horrible idea.

Clea furrows her brow. "She doesn't know how to use that."

I shrug. "Tally does. She probably showed her how."

"Answer," she urges. "It might be important."

I tap the green circle and wait a beat while the call connects. Tally's beaming face appears and spans across the entire display. The gap from her missing teeth is front and center.

"Hi, Daddy! Where's Clea?" Her head swivels as she searches high and low, trying to look past me.

My chest shakes with roaring amusement. "Hello to you, Lou."

Clea shares my humor while sitting down beside me. "Hey, Lulah."

"Lele!" Tally narrows her eyes. "Why is your hair so messy? You're always telling me to brush mine. Did you forget?"

She combs through the tangled locks with her fingers. "Um, yep. This is from all the nature."

That's one way of explaining what we've been doing. I hide a snort by coughing into my fist. "How's your weekend going, Princess?"

My daughter bounces in place, shaking the phone with her erratic movements. "So super great! Brenda is like an older Clea. Isn't that fun? She's gonna make me cookies today. I'm gonna help. She said I can lick the spoon and beater things. Oh, and Chuck is taking the dogs for a walk with Uncle Kody. They're not home."

Clea and I share another laugh over Tally's rambling. My stomach is ready to cramp at this point. I clear my throat in an attempt to temper the hysterics. "Thanks for the update, kiddo. Are you having fun?"

"Uh-huh, lots. I've been a good listener. Hardly any burps and toots. But I always excuse myself after it happens. Sometimes it's not in my control. You said it's bad to hold the gas bubbles in. That's why you always fart so much at home."

Clea quirks a brow at me, her lips smashed in a firm line to stem an outburst at my expense. "Sounds stinky to me."

"They're super gross. I usually have to leave the room," Tally admits.

Heat rushes up my neck in a fiery wave. "Very funny, Lou. It's not nice to share private stuff about your dad."

She rolls her eyes. "Okay, whatever. I have a super import-ant question for Clea."

The woman beside me leans in. "What's up, Lulah?"

"Is it okay if I have a spa day with Rory and Rufus?"

"Sure?"

"Brenda!" Tally screams directly into the speaker.

I cringe, but the damage is done. A static ringing pounds into my ears.

Clea's mom appears in the background while Tally waves frantically. "Guess what? Clea said I can paint their nails. Neon pink, okay? Then we can put bows on their ears."

Meanwhile, Clea's bout of laughter returns. "Wait, what?"

"I'm gonna make 'em look so pretty. You'll see soon. When are you coming home again?"

"Tomorrow," I reply.

My daughter pouts. "Okay, fine. But hurry. I gotta go now."

"Well, good luck with all that. Take pictures," Clea's re-quest is a blurt.

I watch Tally's finger hover over the screen. "Wait, Lou. I bet Clea wants to chat with her mom. Can you give the phone to Brenda?"

"Uh, I guess." Then she disappears from view.

Clea takes her cell from me while I press a quick kiss to her cheek. Then I scoot off the bed to remove myself from the frame. "I'll get started on breakfast. We can eat on the boat."

She wiggles her brows. "Oh, I love that idea."

I slide on a pair of sweats. "Keep your expectations low. This is me preparing a meal that we're talking about."

Her hand bats the air. "It's all about the effort."

"In that case, prepare to be blown away." I catch her ogling my ass as I saunter toward the kitchen.

"I'm already there, lover."

"Clea? Can you hear me? I don't hear you." Brenda's voice echoes through the space.

A loud sigh comes from the corner. "Mom, we're on video. You need to pull the phone away from your face."

"What?"

"All I see is your squished cheek. Hold the screen in front of you."

There's some rustling. "I don't understand you, sweetie. Can you speak louder?"

"Is Tally nearby? She can explain."

That six-year-old understands more about technology than both of us put together. I hoot toward the ceiling before peeking at her over my shoulder. "Please record this conversation for demonstration purposes."

Clea makes a shooing motion. "Oh, hush."

"Are you talking to me, Clea? I still can't hear you very well." Brenda's huff crackles down the line.

I'm doubled over at this point. "Maybe you should call her back."

My girl gnashes her teeth. "You worry about feeding me."

The bossy demands really do something to me. "I hope you're in the mood for sausage."

Red splotches bloom across her face. "I'm really glad my mother can't hear you."

"What did I say wrong? I'm just whipping up an innocent breakfast."

"There's nothing innocent about that innuendo."

I pop my tongue into my cheek. Messing with her is becoming a favorite hobby. "If I just so happen to get personal enjoyment from watching you eat, that's a different story."

"Behave," she chides.

"Unlikely." I snap the elastic at my waist.

Clea licks her lower lip. "Then at least wait until I hang up."

"I'll see what I can do, but no promises." The odds are already stiff enough.

chapter twenty-four

Clea

BLOND WISPS DANCE ACROSS THE LENS WHILE I ATTEMPT TO capture an eagle perched high in a tree. I tuck the damp strands behind my ear, only for the tangles to whip free seconds later. More shots than not have been distorted by my hair. One downside to my chopped style is no longer having the option of a ponytail. With a sigh, I lower the camera to my lap. I could switch seats again, or just enjoy the view. The latter wins.

Nolan is sprawled in the captain's chair like the king he appears to be. His shaggy locks ruffle in a cool tousle, giving him a roguish charm. He guides the boat across the glassy lake with an ease that seems to naturally fit him. The flip in my belly approves. Every mannerism exudes a calm confidence that seems totally unlike Nolan—and yet completely natural. This is a side to him I never thought I'd be fortunate enough to see. The fact that I might have played a role in this change is unfathomable.

Yet here we are.

The wind howls in my ears as Nolan presses harder on the throttle. I turn fully to face him, allowing my rat's nest to do what it will. His booming laugh finds me even among the deafening noise. He slows down before cutting the engine. Moments later, the roaring gusts recede to a tame breeze.

"I was afraid you'd be swept away from me." Nolan's smile sends those wicked dimples out to play.

I try, in vain, to smooth the snarls. "I'm not going anywhere."

He pats the chair beside him. "Come here."

I do without hesitation, plopping down with a sigh. "What's the plan, captain?"

"Does that make you my first mate?"

"The one and only."

"I love the sound of that." He leans over to grant me a kiss. A few stray droplets cling to his skin from the errant splashing.

"Are we going to swim again?" I tug at my bikini strap.

"That depends." Nolan's gaze is rapt on my movements as I toy with the pink string dangling from my nape. "Are you getting hungry for lunch?"

"Not even a little bit. Your breakfast filled me up." He did in fact cook sausage. That scored a full-on cackle from me. I'm on track to getting a six-pack from all this laughing. "Plus, I packed that small cooler with drinks and snacks."

He lifts the soda can from his cup holder. "Thinking ahead."

"I didn't want to cut our cruise short on account of empty stomachs or parched throats."

The sun glitters across his naked chest when he settles deeper against the vinyl. That golden shimmer draws my eye, itching to snap a picture. "We can stay on the water for hours."

"Just the two of us." My voice is breathless. I accused him of being insatiable, but I'm just as guilty. Maybe more so.

"You're going to get me in trouble with that look." His intense smolder is flames lapping at my sensitive flesh.

I lift my camera to freeze the moment. The shutter offers a soft click as I store his desire to memory. "That's just for me."

Nolan's tongue makes a slow drag along his lower lip. "On lonely nights?"

My upper half bends toward him without permission. "I'm hoping there won't be many more of those in my future."

His finger skates across the line of my cleavage. Despite the heat, goosebumps prickle in his wake. "Not if my plans go accordingly."

A pair of jet skis zip by, yanking me from the lustful stupor. The pontoon rocks slightly from the resulting waves. I inhale the crisp wonder swirling around me while wafting more at my face. "Wow, that's nice. It just smells… clean. Is that weird?"

He chuckles at my deflection. "The air is really fresh."

My head bobs in beat with the lingering tide. "I love this area. How did you find it?"

Nolan's focus drifts to the shore we're coasting along. "A buddy from college owns property not far from here. We spent a few weekends at his cabin. The memories are hazy, but I was always struck at how peaceful it was. Seemed like the perfect spot for a getaway."

"We've never talked about your college days."

A long exhale slouches his posture. "It seems like a different life. It's bizarre to think about those frivolous years. All I had to worry about was getting my ass to class and finding a job after graduation. Beer money helped too. How naïve I was."

"Did you meet Tally's mom on campus?" The question escapes before I can trap it. I manage to mask my wince, though.

His expression remains slack, and I breathe a little easier. "Yeah, senior year at a party. I didn't know her before that. Our paths only crossed because she happened to be visiting a friend. She was wild and carefree, just looking for her next adventure. Turns out that she got more than she bargained for with me."

I rub at a sore spot blooming in my chest. "You gave her the greatest gift. I'm only sad she isn't here to see Tally grow."

Nolan's smile is crooked, halfway dipped in sorrow. "So am I. Rachel never wanted kids. Not sure I told you that before. I remember the night she made that confession. She was eight months pregnant, and the cold feet had started kicking in. The doctors assured us that her reaction was perfectly normal. New mom jitters seemed legit. But she wasn't convinced. Those typical instincts never clicked, even after Tally was born."

My inhale is hitched. "Really? I thought she wanted to be a family."

He shrugs, sharing my perplexity. "I'm not sure Tally ever had a place in her grand scheme."

"How is that possible? I can't imagine being anything less than enamored by that little girl."

"Welcome to the fucked-up chaos in my head." Nolan taps his temple for emphasis.

Now I do flinch. "Shit, I'm sorry. I never should've—"

"No, it's okay. I don't want to hide her as some secret. It's good to talk about her. We can't be afraid of the ghosts from our past, right?"

"I suppose." But my tone betrays the doubt stabbing at me.

"This is therapeutic for me." He motions between us. "I don't like thinking bad about Rachel, especially when she isn't able to defend herself, but that woman made poor choices. Her driving goal was to find love. Little did she realize how pure the love from a child is. You've helped me realize that I could only do so much. I couldn't be more thankful that our crushed duo found you that stormy night."

Oh, he's striking me straight in the feels. I pinch the sting attacking my nose. If only my sunglasses weren't on the opposite side of the boat. "Gah, you always have the right thing to say."

Nolan scoots forward until our knees touch. "Are you all right?"

"Yep." I stare off into the distance, trying to rein in the freaking waterworks. "I should be the one asking you that."

He scoffs. "I just told you I'm fine."

"You should know that word has a very different meaning to a woman," I hedge.

"Why are you upset?"

I flail my hands in erratic spirals just to keep them occupied. "All these emotions. You've helped me so much too. And Tally… don't even get me going on her. I'd be lost without you two. You've filled me with so much confidence over the years. Even when you were being an ass. I overcame countless mental battles thanks to your silent support."

His palm lands on my nape, hauling me in until our foreheads meet. "I love you, Patra. You rejuvenate me, remember?"

I get lost in the conviction sparking in his eyes. "I do recall something along those lines."

He loops his other arm around my waist and yanks me onto his lap. "If I do even a tiny fraction of that for you, I'll consider myself extremely accomplished. You've healed me, Angel."

"That's rather lofty," I murmur.

"Doesn't make it less true."

We're close enough that our noses bump. I breathe him in while he pulls me impossibly closer. A sizzling energy connects us, bringing forth a shiver. He tightens his embrace, as if there's a chance I could be cold with his arms around me. Quite the opposite.

The heat traveling between us is far more potent than simple lust or yearning. This is our souls entwining, solidifying an already unbreakable bond. The shift resonates deep within my bones. That probably sounds cheesy, but this man reaches me on a spiritual level. He turned me into a hopeless romantic years ago with one look. And now in the short span of a few weeks, he's taken 'hopeless' out of the equation and restored my faith for so much more.

My exhale puffs across his lips. "I love you, by the way. Even if your stupid sexy face drives me to distraction every day. You make me lose control."

He scrubs a hand over his stubbled jaw. "How much?"

I wiggle in his lap. "I'd say your estimate is pretty spot on. Are you always hard?"

His thumb traces my cheekbone. "When you're sitting on me, wearing next to nothing? Abso-fucking-lutely."

"That's fair. Maybe you need some relief after the weight of that discission."

"What do you have in mind?" His foot taps the cooler. "A beer?"

"That form of refreshment can wait." I glance over my shoulder, studying the lake's glassy surface. Other than the jet skis, I haven't seen anyone motoring around. That semblance of privacy spurs me on. I slink off his lap and settle on the floor between his knees. "I've been meaning to try this."

Nolan doesn't move a muscle as I reach for his waistband. "Holy shit, is this really happening?"

"Well, not yet." I'm emboldened by this salacious act—and thrilled at the thought of doing it out in the open. That's why I lick my lips with a soft hum. The physical pleasure might be all his, but there's a noticeable buzz in my lower belly. I smile as the exhilaration spikes hotter. "Do you want me to stop?"

"I'm not insane, so no. Please continue." He lifts his ass off the seat, making the chore of yanking his wet trunks down much easier.

I peek to my left, but the boat wall blocks my view. That's a decent sign no one will spot me unless they're cruising right next to us. I drag his shorts down and off, tossing them to the side. My ass is firmly parked on my folded ankles while I appreciate this man in all his erect glory. It's quite a sight to behold.

Then I'm wrapping a palm around his hard shaft. He twitches as I give him a cursory stroke and hisses between his clenched teeth.

"Fuck, Patra. Keep going. Please," he begs while thrusting into my grip.

"Have you thought about this?" I'm more than capable of returning his teasing chatter while in a precarious position.

"Yes." He nudges his hips forward.

"How often?"

His gaze collides with mine. The green is swirling with unbridled need. "It feels like every second, especially now."

"Are you aching?"

"Dammit, Patra. You're teasing me." There's no hostility in his tone. Just mounting frustration.

"How does it feel, lover? Or should I call you baby?"

His Adam's apple bounces with a thick swallow. "I need your mouth. Should I beg?"

"That won't be necessary." I give him a gentle tug. "You better warn me if someone is coming."

His grunt is a strangled sound. "I'll be the only one coming."

"Don't get your hopes up," I repeat his caution from this morning. "I've never done this before."

"The sight of your lips wrapped around me is plenty."

My gaze is latched onto the impressive girth I'm holding. I can barely get my fingers to touch. How this bad boy fit inside me is a mystery. It's no freaking wonder I'm sore. "You're just saying that."

"I guess we'll find out." His fingers curl into the chair cushion, knuckles white and trembling.

"Indeed," I purr.

Then I rise into a kneel and treat myself to a taste. Nolan spits out a curse while I lick his tip. When that initial salty burst hits my tongue, I realize why he seems very inclined to go down on me. Having his flavor in my mouth is a heady stimulation. I'll be needing to experience it regularly. And I can't wait.

chapter twenty-five

Nolan

THUMP MY FINGERS AGAINST THE WHEEL AS THE PLUNKED PIANO AND saccharine singing of a classic rock ballad bleeds from the speakers. The open road stretches in front of us while my mind wanders. A belated realization strikes me in this moment. I've driven more during these past few months than I have in years.

The avoidance wasn't intentional. Not really, anyway. After Tally's mother died, I became more cautious in general. To a fault. It's strange how such routine motions can become crippling. I didn't grasp just how long I'd been captive in the shadows until Clea chased off those shackles.

In addition to her other healing abilities, the woman beside me has smoothed this discomfort as well. I haven't hesitated before settling into the driver's seat lately. The seemingly mundane task has returned to just that—a standard mode of transportation.

It doesn't hurt that we've been traveling all over the damn state. I'm getting accustomed to chauffeuring my girl around. There's just something about having her within reach, nestled in my truck, that spreads a comforting warmth through me. A glance to my right, and there she is. My palm is clutching her bare thigh. Her nails are tracing the veins in my forearm.

Clea swivels to face me. "Did you think I wouldn't notice?"

The shrewd awareness is another story, but I love her incessant curiosity. She's not afraid to question me, regardless of the subject. I find that brazen confidence extremely refreshing. Not to mention sexy as fuck.

"Not sure what you mean," I mumble while avoiding her pointed stare.

"You're taking a detour."

"Maybe I'm avoiding traffic."

She quirks a brow. "Are you?"

"It's more than likely."

"You're being evasive. I thought we were going home."

Home. That simple word sends a shiver down my spine. How long until we share the same one? "We have a quick stop to make on the way."

"And let me guess, you're not going to tell me where we're going."

"I'm glad you understand the rules," I reply with a wink.

She twists her lips to one side. "Maybe I should be more spontaneous too."

My gaze latches onto her mouth. "You have nothing to worry about in that department."

"There's always room for improvement." Seduction gravitates toward me from her raspy tone.

I find myself contemplating an unexpected break in our route. But the clock is ticking. "We can practice later. You might discover some newfound motivation to… deliver."

Not that I truly expect anything from her in return.

Clea huffs, scattering blond strands across her forehead. "Now you're just being ominous."

"Patience." I emphasize the word with a stroke to her knee.

This is the final lap in my grand gesture tour. The final ace up my sleeve. It took extra effort to pull off, and I'm hoping every loose end is tied. Seven minutes until the big reveal. A surge enters my system and I shift against the onslaught.

I couldn't have predicted how rewarding Clea's shocked glee would be. Pretend as she might, these surprises spark a fire inside her. She's practically glowing while attempting to pout. That expression alone sends a fresh wave of ideas for future endeavors flooding me in a stream. But it's more than special outings and frivolous acts. Those are temporary. The desire to provide for her—period—pumps through my veins. I'll never give her cause to doubt me again.

"Is there a way I can convince you to tell me now?" Clea walks her fingers up my leg.

I peek over at her grinning features. "What're you doing, Patra?"

She props an elbow on the center console, giving me an eyeful of her cleavage. "Persuasion is an art," she purrs, running a finger slowly down my thigh. "And with you, it works every time."

She's got me there. My gulp is lined with sandpaper. "You want the surprise ruined?"

Her palm drifts upward. "How about just a hint?"

"Okay, how about this: we're almost there."

"That doesn't count!" She swats at me.

But the impact she's having on my dick certainly does. I'll be walking with a limp if she doesn't quit. After flicking on the blinker, I hang a left into the lot. "See?"

Clea flops down onto her ass with a whoosh, eyes scanning the scene for any clues. It's almost expected that she pushes her nose to the glass. "There are lots of cars."

That's the entire view thanks to the tall trees framing the grounds. "Must be a popular place."

She groans at the ceiling. "You're impossible."

I pull into an empty spot near the far corner. "This is the last surprise you'll get with that attitude."

That's a bold-faced lie, but it's fun to rile her up.

Let's not be hasty. Her hands move to unbuckle her seatbelt.

I move to step out. "Stay put."

Her beaming grin greets me when I open her door. "Such a gentleman. You're a dying breed."

"We'll just have to raise a few more."

She chokes on nothing but air. "What?"

"Too soon?"

"Between you and Tally, we'll be married and expecting by Christmas." Clea's laughter floats along the warm breeze.

I shrug and reach for her hand, linking our fingers together. "Maybe New Year's Eve."

"Oh my gosh, I was joking." Then she notices the sign in our path. "An art fair?"

"Yep. All local businesses showing off their goods."

"How thoughtful," she coos and snuggles against my side. "I love these events."

"I had a feeling." But that's just the foundation.

With the stealth of Tally trying to sneak cookies before dinner, I whip out my phone and search for the specific booth number. The organizers emailed me a map of the grounds and the layout. I squint at the sunny glare across the screen, tilting my cell for better clarity.

"What're you doing?" Clea has a palm shielding her eyes against the blinding rays.

"Tickets," I blurt.

"It's not free to enter?"

Fuck. I give my forehead an internal smack. "It's more like a... reservation."

Her brow knits. "Um, okay."

"I have no clue how this works. We'll just see how it goes." I guide her toward the entrance, which is framed by balloons and colorful pennant flags.

"Looks pretty standard to me," she muses as we stride along the main aisle.

The exhibitor booths are set up in a complicated maze formation. We're aiming for a rear stall on the outer edge. "Right this way."

"Wait, we're passing all these stands." She protests by digging her heels into the grass.

I give her a little tug. "We'll circle back."

"But—"

"Just trust me."

"Why—?"

"There's a suggested starting point at this end."

Clea grumbles under her breath but allows me to steer her in the direction of my choosing. "How do you know?"

"You'll find out."

A gasp trips off her lips the second she does. The stand directly in front of us captivates her attention more than the epic Black Friday deals at Target. "That's—that's—"

"That's…?"

"That's my logo."

I glance at the stand. A green rose surrounded by thorns is front and center on a large white banner at the top of the stand. Around the rim of the design circles the name Montague Imagery, and just below is her website. "Oh?"

"And those are my pictures." She stumbles forward, jaw slack and lashes fluttering to an erratic beat.

All around us, artfully displayed on easels, in frames, arranged out on a table, are photographs Clea has taken. Some are large, beautiful landscape shots, some are wildlife or still life photography. There's even a frame of Rory and Rufus looking perfectly posed like supermodel dogs in front of a display of other pet portraits she's taken.

"Surprise," I whisper against her temple, barely holding back my grin.

Clea turns her watery gaze to me. "What did you do, Nolan?"

"This is your booth."

Her hands fly up to cradle her head. "How?"

I offer a lazy shrug. "Kody knew where to find your galleries with images available for purchase. Tally and I chose our favorites. I sent them off to a buddy who does custom framing and displays."

"This is…" Her mouth opens and closes several times in rapid succession. "I've never had the guts to do this."

I scrub at my nape. "Is it okay that I made it happen?"

"Are you joking? Of course." She dusts her lips across my cheek. "I—you've—I'm speechless," she sputters. She leans forward and picks up a photo of the historic downtown of Greenbury. A slight dusting of snow covers the beautiful vintage brick buildings. Old lanterns strung up above the town square give a warm, comforting glow. The sidewalks are packed with people walking, couples holding hands, and families huddled together. It's a gorgeous photo of a winter wonderland. "I did this?"

"You did that, Clea. I may have put it together, but this is all you."

She places the photo down and wipes her eyes.

With a yank to her hip, I haul her against me. "You really love it?"

Clea's smile lifts along mine. "I love you. This is the most unexpected of the unexpected."

"Happy I kept it a surprise?"

"Yes, but don't let it go to your head."

"Too late." I bump the evidence into her upper thigh.

"Oh, hello. Down boy. I have an event to do." Her breath hitches. "How crazy does that sound? I'll be showing off my work to all these people. It makes me feel like a real photographer."

"Don't sell yourself short, Patra. You're the best I've seen. No contest." I wave a hand at the hanging frames on proud display.

Clea rolls her eyes. "You have to say that as my boyfriend."

A rumble rises from me. "Fuck, I like that claim."

"Well, it's true." She nibbles her bottom lip. "Right?"

"Without a doubt. Although, it's not quite serious enough for me."

She pats my chest. "We'll get there."

"In the meantime, I get to watch my girlfriend flaunt her talents." I wag my brows.

Clea strokes a palm against my scruff. "Your support is a beautiful thing."

"If I can encourage your dreams"—I dip to her ear—"and fulfill your fantasies, then I'm hitting my goals."

"Overachiever."

I swat her ass. "The fair opens to the public in twenty minutes. You still have time to finalize details and change the arrangement. A volunteer organized your listings."

"Surreal," she exhales while walking into the domain created for her.

My chest swells until breathing is a challenge. To distract myself from reveling in pride, I focus on the fruits of my labor. I study the assortment of landscapes, animals, and flowers. People aren't popular in her albums. Unless you count Tally and me. Blooming petals catch my gaze.

I hover near the table blocking the front of her booth. "I've been meaning to ask about something since collecting your images."

"This should be good." She giggles and adjusts a picture on its hook.

"What's with all the roses? They seem to be a popular subject for you."

Clea's complexion takes on a noticeable flush. "It's embarrassing."

"You can tell me anything."

"They remind me of you."

Of all the explanations, that certainly wasn't on the list. "What?"

She nods and dips her chin. "Roses are often seen as generic. A safe choice. That couldn't be further from the truth. They're complicated, layered, and resilient. Prickly with thorns for protection. Soft and silky to draw those willing to take a chance. I've just always found myself drawn to them. Plus, they're more appealing than onions."

I find my gaze drifting to an enlarged photograph of the flower in mention. "You've just turned me into a rose fan."

"Yeah?"

"Such passion, Angel. Ready to share it with the good people attending Hendrex Art Fair?"

Clea does a shimmy toward me. "You're so getting laid for this."

I loop my arms around her, drawing her in for a hug. "Yeah?"

Her chin nudges my shoulder when she confirms. "Multiple O's. I'm feeling extremely motivated by this spectacle."

"Allow me to provide more inspiration." I palm her ass, giving a squeeze.

"Of the kinky variety?"

"It's cute that you think there's another choice."

chapter twenty-six

Clea

TALLY TWIRLS IN A CIRCLE AS WE ENTER FANCY FOOT BOWLING & Eatery, her blond curls forming a golden cape from the quick movements. The smile she's wearing overshadows the wattage from every lightbulb in this joint. She doesn't hesitate before striding into the lobby, her luminous gaze doing a sweep from floor to ceiling. The booming crashes of balls striking pins reverberate in the distance like fireworks. Tally hops up and down in glee.

"Someone is excited." I rest my head against Nolan's shoulder.

He presses a kiss into my hair. "I'll try to rein it in. Maybe others won't notice my exuberance with Tally out front."

I stifle a snort. "The corny dad jokes are so…"

"Sexy," he finishes for me.

"Stole the words from my mouth."

"That's not all I want to take from you."

I give his bicep a squeeze. "You're relentless."

A disgruntled squeak pops our intimate bubble. Tally has her hands on her hips, not-so-patiently waiting for us to catch up. Her sandal taps faster for every second we delay. "Would you two step on the gas? I've been waiting my whole life for this."

I feel a tug at my brows. "Bowling?"

"No," she deadpans like the diva princess she is. "I already told you why it's im-por-ant. Were you listening? You always tell me to listen, Lele."

The sweep of her arm further indicates the aforementioned explanation. She dressed herself for this outing. A hot pink shirt to match the neon leggings with a tutu circling her waist. She opted to leave her crown headband at home. Something about going too far and not wanting to outshine us.

I trap a laugh behind my palm. "Oh, I heard you."

It's our first official date as a family. She's been giddy about celebrating and tucking me into their fold ever since Nolan pulled his truck into the driveway last weekend. I wasn't about to discredit the assumption, knocking her down a peg or five. It doesn't hurt that the title has a delightful charm to it.

But Tally rambles without pause as if I hadn't even answered. "But you're getting so distracted. Is it because you're in love? Love makes you float on sparkly hearts with extra glitter. It's like a fairy tale!"

Her wistful sigh gets a chuckle from Nolan. "You're quite the romantic, Lou."

"I learn from the best." She points between us.

My smile turns into sentimental mush. "Well, I certainly love you."

Tally parks her fist on a cocked hip. "But you love my daddy too. You can spill the beans. We're not keeping secrets anymore."

I peek over at Nolan to find him already looking at me. "Yes, I love him too."

He winks, both dimples proudly on display. "And I love her."

She slaps her palms together with a giggle. "Oh my gosh, I love you!" she squeals. "And now I can have a baby sister too!"

That snaps me from the dopey haze. My response is a hasty blurt. "Not yet."

Nolan answers in the same instant, which I almost miss over my choked gasp. "Well, maybe."

My shock whips to his face, finding impulsive certainty. "Definitely no."

He rubs a hand along my back, like that's going to soothe me. "Okay, fine. It's too soon."

"Thought so," Tally huffs. "Just wanted to double-check."

I tug at my shirt in an attempt to flow more oxygen into my lungs. "How about we quit loitering and... you know."

"Is someone flustered?" Nolan skates a finger down the fire scorching my cheek.

I scoff. "Hardly. I'm just ready to bowl."

"Not sure that statement belongs in your vocabulary."

"Oh, and wanting more babies in our very near future is expected in yours?"

"I want everything with you, Patra." The words are murmured close to my temple, away from prying eavesdroppers. "But patience is our third wheel. We'll go at your pace. I'm just along for the ride."

My pulse sputters into a sprint. We've barely been dating for two weeks. We may have made our commitment and claims to each other, but that doesn't mean we're cemented in forever. Yet.

Still, I find myself fantasizing about not too far down the road when we could legally be a family. Truthfully, I've wished I could call this little girl mine for a long, long time—a wish that could only be granted in my imagination. That strife no longer holds the imposing improbability.

Tally is just staring at us. The blinding smile has returned to her lips. "I'm so happy right now."

That reminds me of an earlier discussion—and a convenient distraction. "Just hanging out with us? You really didn't want to bring a friend? We could've picked up Ruby or Alexandra."

"Nah-uh. Then I might've missed some sparks." She curls her fingers to make fake binoculars, zooming in on us.

We need to watch our actions with this one within range. A companion would take the pressure off. "Or maybe that boy from the party."

Nolan cuts his gaze to me. "Let's not encourage that relationship."

"It's harmless."

"For now," he mutters.

"All right, fine." I motion us onward. "Let's get fit for shoes. That's still a thing, right?"

"Isn't that information you should know as an eager bowler?"

"You're being a smarty-pants," I retort from the side of my mouth.

Tally falls into stride beside me. "I'm gonna have a little sister super soon the way you two are talking."

Wedged between them is a dangerous position. I focus on the teenager behind the checkout counter. His eyes are barely visible under his unkempt hair. He jerks his chin in a flipping motion to send the strands flying.

"Hey, folks. Welcome to Fancy Foot."

Tally plops her palms flat on the glass surface. "Why is it called Fancy Foot?"

His slim shoulders lift to his ears. "Uh, I dunno? We give you sneaks that glow in the blacklight."

She sucks in a sharp breath while glancing at her feet. "Really? That's so cool."

"Yeah, what size are you?" He pauses to give our trio a slow perusal. "Unless you'd like to try our outdoor option."

"We can play outside?" The wonder in Tally's voice is answer enough.

"Sure can. We have lanes on the roof." He points at the ceiling.

"The roof?" Tally's eyes transform into exclamation points and her mouth drops open. She spins to us, hands already clasped with a plea. "Can we go up there?"

The guy clears his throat. "I should warn you that it's not regular bowling."

Tally returns her attention to him with a fast swivel. "That's okay. I wanna try it."

Nolan's eyes bounce to mine. I offer an easy shrug. "I'm good with whatever. This is Tally's date idea."

She nods on repeat. "Uh-huh, yep. And I wanna go up, up, up."

Her dad agrees with a soft smile that would melt my heart if it wasn't already toasty warm with his name scrawled across the center. "All right, kiddo. Rooftop bowling it is."

"Awesome," the kid drawls. He punches in our order, offers directions, and sends us off with a wave.

The elevator delivers us to the outdoor lanes within minutes. Half of the space is sectioned for lawn bowling, the other part reserved for a wide bar and surrounding tables. Large overhangs stretched on tall poles shade the area while still allowing the sun to speckle certain spots.

"Wow, this is nice." I complete my inspection with an impressed whistle.

"Told you so," Tally replies with a curtsey.

"Humble as always," Nolan snorts.

"Clea said I get that from you. I don't get it." She wrinkles her button nose. "Adults are weird."

I hold up my palms toward him. "Guilty as charged."

"Didn't hear many complaints about my mighty ego last night." He wags his brows.

Tally tips her head. "What's a ego?"

I tap my wrist while walking to lane five. "The clock is ticking. We better get going."

They follow in my shadow toward our designated turf. Three rows of balls are stacked by the wall. There are two of each color, similar to bocce. The wooden pins are already set in proper formation. I rub my hands together, bending in a stretch.

"Oh, it's going to be that kind of game?"

When I glance at Nolan, his eyes are firmly plastered on my ass. "You know I have a competitive nature."

He folds his arms across his solid chest. "Are we setting terms?"

Tally's focus bounces from me to him. "What are you two arguing about?"

"We're making a bet, Lou."

"To spice things up," I add.

"Ooooh, okay. That's super exciting." She taps her lips. "If I win, you have to get married."

I lift a brow at her. "That's a bit extreme, Lulah."

"Then you better beat me." She skips over to the ball rack. "I'm gonna be pink. That's my favorite."

"What are you playing for, Patra?" Nolan cinches my waist and pulls me in for a hug.

I dance my nails up his shirt. "Bragging rights."

A loud booing sound erupts from beside us. "That's lame, Lele. Pick something more funner. I think you should have a baby."

"But I'm not ready for that."

Her tongue pokes out. "Okay, whatever. How about a new puppy?"

"Rory and Rufus are plenty. Let's see." I take a moment for consideration, and dramatic effect. "I want to choose the movie we watch after dinner."

"It better have a princess." Tally squints at me.

"We'll see."

"Daddy?"

Nolan seems startled awake, preoccupied with watching us. "Just for this to continue."

Tally's expression screws tight. "Huh?"

"The three of us spending dates together."

She brightens with a wide grin. "Yes, I agree. Nice choice, Dad."

He bows. "Thank you."

"Pick your balls," Tally demands while preparing to throw her first.

Nolan hovers behind her. "Do you need help?"

She shoots him a glare. "I'm a big girl. I've totally got this."

It's a solid attempt. A pink blur whizzes down the narrow strip, bouncing against the dividers in a chaotic zigzag. She knocks over two pins. Her second toss earns another one. Tally frowns at those left standing like they've personally offended her.

"Great job, kiddo." I loop my arm around her shoulder for an encouraging squeeze.

"You'll never get married at this rate." She blindly gestures at the lane.

"It was your first try. We'll probably do worse." I hitch a thumb between her dad and my chest.

"Are we throwing the game on purpose?" Nolan murmurs under his breath so only I can hear.

"Not with these stakes," I whisper-shout.

"Right, of course." He almost sounds disappointed. With a forward sweep, he motions for me to go ahead. "Your turn."

I'm about to choose the purple set when an unpleasant gurgle ripples through my gut. I wince while resting a palm over the noise. My stomach isn't happy about something.

Nolan moves next to me, rubbing a comforting palm along my spine. "Are you okay?"

"Yeah, I'm sure it's just—"

"Do you need to toot? We don't mind. Just let it go, like Elsa." Tally shouts this from her squatted spot several feet away.

"Thanks, Lulah." But it's not gas. Could be something I ate, or my period. I'm confident confirming this isn't a pregnancy scare. Aunt Flow was kind enough to hold off on arriving until yesterday and not intrude on my sex-a-thon with Nolan at the cabin.

Nolan's forehead creases. "Maybe you should sit down?"

"It's passing, I think." I straighten as the sickening somersaults in my belly subside. "This doesn't mean anything. I'll still take you down, Jasper."

"Trash talk gets you nowhere," he retorts with a dry chuckle.

"We'll see," I sing-song while lining up. After a slow exhale, I swing my arm back and follow through to release. The ball rolls across the smooth ground in a straight line. Dead center for a strike. I jump in the air with a whoop, then immediately fold in half. "Ah, crap. Quite literally."

"You're not okay. Maybe we should leave," Nolan's suggestion gets a pout from Tally.

"But we've barely played." She stares longingly at the pins being reset by an attendant.

"No, don't stop on my account." I begin backing toward the elevator. "Keep going without me. I'm just going to use the bathroom."

Nolan parts his lips to argue, then must think better of going against me. "We'll be waiting right here."

"I'm counting on it." Then I beat cheeks for the shitter, the concern in their voices tailing my hasty retreat.

chapter twenty-seven

Nolan

THREE DAYS, TWELVE HOURS, AND TWENTY-SEVEN FUCKING minutes.

That's how long it's been since I've seen Clea. Held her in my arms. Had her within reach to ensure she's safe. Every single second—each breath—has been excruciating. The band cinching my ribs tightens another notch. If only I were exaggerating.

She's sick. Really fucking sick.

That's the extent of my knowledge. I don't have a damn clue about her current condition, or what she's been dealing with. She hasn't given me shit to go on.

According to Kody, Clea has extreme intestinal distress and has barely left the bathroom. I've tried to visit, but she pleaded with me to stay away. Ignoring her wishes doesn't bode well with the promises I've served. But sitting here and doing nothing goes against my gut instincts. The conflict has been nonstop, a relentless tugging across my chest. I have yet to determine which side will conquer the other.

Clea's communication has been shitty at best, not that I fault her under the current circumstances. When I'd told her we can go at her pace, I didn't mean leave me hanging out to dry while she suffers alone. My skin is crawling without word from her. I want—no, need—to be there for her. This desperation is ready to rip out of me.

She did assure me that pregnancy isn't the cause. That reason hadn't occurred to me. I realize now that she'd been trying to put my mind at ease. Even while fighting her own battle, she's thinking about my feelings. All I want is an update.

Between forcing Tally away from the window and heeding my own advice, every nerve I have is shot. My gaze pongs to the view of her house from where I sit. Still nothing.

Tally yanks at the gauzy dress she put on for playing fashion show. The shimmery monstrosity once belonged to Clea and is now handed down to the next generation. Her frown mirrors my own. "I miss her."

A slow exhale tempers my mounting frustration. "So do I, Lou."

"Why won't she answer?"

My spirits take another devastating hit. In the long haul, this separation is a mere blip. We've gone weeks, nearly a month, without seeing her in the past. But that's not our normal anymore. Clea belongs beside us. Period. There's an essential piece missing in our tripod. The loss is debilitating.

I flatten a palm to my chest that might as well have a hole carving into the flesh. "Clea isn't feeling well. I'm sure she's resting."

"But we could bring her soup." Optimism clangs from her voice. It pains me to disappoint her.

My posture deflates on its own accord. "Kody told us she isn't eating much. When she's ready, we'll make more."

That doesn't appease her based on the furrow in her brow. "Can we call her?"

"Lou—"

"Please?" Tally rises on her knees, hands clasped in desperation.

There's only so much I can take before giving in. "I'll send her a message."

"Okay." Her dejected tone resonates deep within my heart, a hollow pang crushing me from the force.

I grab my phone, which has been mocking me with silence.

The screen is blank. Not a single notification to break apart the clouds shrouding my bleak mood.

> **Me: Hey, Patra. We wanted to check on you. Tally misses you and won't quit until she sees you. I feel the same way. Is there anything we can do to make you feel better?**

After pushing send, the soundless vacuum resumes. There's no sign of the three dots indicating her typing a response. I expel the predicted disappointment, my shoulders hunching inward.

A shuffle across the carpet cracks the quiet. "Dad?"

I lift my gaze to Tally, who's staring at me with expectation glittering in her eyes. "Yeah, kiddo?"

Her small palm settles over my much bigger one. "Maybe Clea will answer this one. We should cross our fingers. And toes."

I clench my eyes shut against the stinging pressure. Texting her has been hit or miss, mostly the latter. If she does respond, it's one or two words. I have a feeling it's mostly to ensure I don't bust her door down. I've been more than tempted on several occasions. This moment is ramping to become another one.

My lungs protest from my deep inhale. "Good idea—"

"Daddy, look!" Tally points out our window facing Clea's house.

I snap my gaze in that direction. Even with the setting sun stealing visibility, I can see Kody escorting Clea to his car. She's wrapped in a blanket with a hat on her head despite the warm temperature.

"What the f—?" I cut off my own question at the last moment.

My feet are carrying me to the door before I've finished processing the full picture. Tally's footsteps follow close behind. We cover the distance between our yards in less than a minute. Kody is just about to assist Clea into the passenger's seat as we stride across their driveway.

"What's going on?"

Their heads whip toward our approach. My steps falter at Clea's ashen complexion. Her cheeks are sunken and splotched with angry red. That type of flush reveals the illness wreaking havoc on her system. Sweat dampens her skin while she shivers. My woman will always be gorgeous, but she's a bit rough around at the edges right now.

"Her fever spiked. She can't keep food or water down. It's getting worse," Kody explains.

I prowl forward, Tally scurrying to match my stride. "Why didn't you call me?"

"Kinda have my hands full." He nods at his sister.

"Where are you going?"

"Urgent care." He peers down at Clea when she trembles against him.

I'm flanking her other side in the next beat. "Let me take you."

Her resistance is a weak whimper. "No, it's—"

"Not an option, Patra. I'm taking you."

Her unfocused gaze lifts to the general vicinity of my face—glassy and heavy-lidded. "Okay."

That mere croak seems to cost her valuable energy. She collapses into my waiting embrace with a wheeze. I scoop her trembling form into my arms. She doesn't muster the strength to cling on while I cradle her to my chest. But it doesn't matter. I'll hold on for both of us.

Just as I'm ready to cut across the grass to my truck, a belated thought pierces the fog.

"Can you watch Tally—"

Her scoff interrupts me. "I'm coming with you, Dad."

"Just stay with Kody—"

She steps into my path, an imposing blockage dipped in grit and sass. "No! Clea is mine just as much as she's yours. I wanna make sure she gets better."

How can I argue with that? Simple—I don't. That doesn't mean someone else won't.

Clea cranes her neck to catch Tally's eye. "The hospital has too many germs for you, Lulah. It's safer for you to stay with Uncle Kody. I'm not even sure you'd be allowed beyond the waiting room. The doctor will probably send me right home anyway. Keep Rory and Rufus company for me, okay?"

My daughter wants to put up a fuss. That much is obvious in her pinched lips and rigid stance. "Are you sure?"

Clea's lashes flutter, her energy draining. "Positive."

"Can I at least help with the truck door?" She motions to my arms currently tied up with Clea.

"That would be very kind, Lou. Thank you."

With a sharp nod, I signal her to lead us. She rushes ahead and opens the passenger's side. I navigate the path with caution slowing my measured pace. Clea nuzzles my shoulder, mumbling incoherently under her breath. I tighten my grip for another moment and soak her in. There are so many things I want to say, but now's not the time. She needs a doctor.

I try not to jostle her too much while buckling her in. Clea cracks her eyes open for a moment before returning under the veil of unconscious bliss. Tally backpedals onto the yard while I round the hood and get behind the wheel.

I roll the window down. "Be on your best behavior for Uncle Kody, yeah?"

"Uh-huh. You need to hurry. My almost-mama has to get better." Her resolute claim on the woman beside me soothes the jagged strain chewing at my composure.

"She will." The conviction in my words leaves no room for another option.

"Then what are you waiting for?"

I shift into reverse and press on the gas. "That's a really good question." On our way, Lou.

chapter twenty-eight

Nolan

THE DRIVE PASSES IN A BLUR OF WHITE KNUCKLES AND VULGAR expletives. I'm convinced that every traffic light has a personal vendetta against me. The color red will hold a negative undertone from now on. Unless it's slicked across Clea's lips in gloss form.

Speaking of her, she hasn't made a peep since we left. Her body is curled into a shivering ball against the seat. The silence is giving me too much freedom to assume the worst and dwell on her recent preference to shove me from the loop. If the circumstances were different, I'd be worried.

Thankfully, the lot is mostly empty when I pull in and park near the front. After hauling ass to the passenger's side, I force my haste to calm and hoist Clea against me. She rouses from her silent stupor with a pitiful moan.

"Are we at the hospital?" Her scratchy voice grates against my steady pace.

"Yeah, Angel. I just need to get you registered."

She shifts in my arms. "You can let me down."

"I can carry you. Save your strength."

Further protest evaporates from her chapped lips, and she sags into me. "All right. Just a little longer."

The lobby doors open with a swish, announcing our arrival. A sterile aroma smacks me in the face as I scan our surroundings. I stride straight ahead to the urgent care wing. There's a lady watching our approach from behind the reception desk.

Her painted mouth knits into a judgmental pucker. "How can I help you, sir?"

"She needs a doctor." I signal to Clea with my chin.

The redhead blinks at me. "For?"

"A fever." I take a beat to determine what else to share. "And severe intestinal distress. Probably a stomach bug, if I had to guess."

"How long have her symptoms been present?"

"Almost four days."

She hums and types on her keyboard. "Did you call the emergency line before coming in?"

"Uh, no?"

"I have the flu," Clea chimes in weakly. A shudder wracks her limbs immediately after.

The lady releases her disapproval with a sigh. "There's not much we can do for that."

Clea brushes damp hair from her cheek. "My temperature is over one-oh-three."

The receptionist's jaw drops with a gasp. "Oh, that deserves a visit. We'll get you into an exam room and go from there. Can you walk?"

Damn, she certainly changed her perspective quick. I return the lady's startled gawk, then take a meaningful glance down at Clea shivering in my arms. "Not well."

But the woman in question wriggles against me. She doesn't move far. "I can walk."

A disbelieving grunt sounds from the other side of the desk. "The nurse can bring a wheelchair."

"I don't need one," Clea murmurs in a thin voice, betraying her stubborn pride.

"I can carry her." That's the best option, in my personal opinion.

"If the patient can't walk, a wheelchair will be provided." She quirks a brow, waiting for me to argue.

"If that's policy," I mutter.

She nods, victory curling her lips. Her shrewd gaze narrows on Clea's huddled form. "Sure is. There are a few forms you'll need to complete, but I'll send them along with your…"

"Fiancé," I finish. It's common knowledge that a family tag needs to be attached to me if I plan to go beyond the waiting room. Bated breath stalls in my lungs while waiting if to see Clea will reject me.

Clea wrinkles her nose but otherwise doesn't dispute my declaration. "He can take the clipboard."

I flip my gaze to the redhead. "Can you send the paperwork back with us? My hands are full."

"Absolutely. I just need her name and date of birth to get her in the system."

"Clea Renee Montague. March eighth, nineteen ninety-seven."

She lifts a shaky hand to cradle my cheek. "I love you."

The sentiment further soothes the ache in my chest. I kiss the tip of her nose. "Love you, Patra."

A dreamy exhale intrudes on our moment. The lady is beaming at us. Her attitude adjustment is more unstable than Clea's balance, even while clutched in my hold. "That's good for now. You take care of her."

Motion to our left has me twisting in that direction. Frosted glass doors glide open, revealing a man pushing Clea's chariot. The guy rolls the wheelchair toward us. He pats the seat and I ease Clea down. The blanket is still draped over her shoulders, hat firmly tucked over matted blond hair. She wheezes with a visible tremble. It's no secret she's suffering. The sooner we get her proper treatment and medication, the better for everyone.

The nurse glances between us. "I'm Marc. You'll be mostly dealing with me while under our care."

"Nolan," I reply with a jut of my chin. "That lovely lady on the wheels is Clea."

"It's nice to meet you both. Clea, you'll be cooped up in

room three." Then he grips the handles and begins pushing her away.

I move to follow them down the hall, but he halts my stride. "Are you family?"

"Yes," Clea states with authority.

"Got it." He motions me on. "Right this way."

Marc steers Clea into a small room with little more than a bed. Typical white walls and the stench of antiseptic. A few machines are clumped in the corner. No frills. For whatever reason, the space offers me a reprieve. Her road to recovery will start here.

I offer her a hand so she can climb onto the mattress. Her exhale is labored while we wait for instructions. The nurse washes his hands, then digs in a drawer.

"Let's get your temperature quick." He sticks the thermometer under her tongue. It beeps seconds later. His eyes bulge. "Wow, yep. One-oh-three point seven. This calls for fluids while we run a few more tests. How are you with needles?"

"We have an understanding of sorts." She attempts a smile, but the expression is brittle.

I grunt and rock on my heels. "Making jokes, Patra?"

Her glassy eyes lift to me. "Trying to lighten the mood."

"You're doing a great job." I link our fingers together just as my phone vibrates with a text alert. There's no chance I'm spending this moment staring at a screen.

She tugs the hat off her head and collapses against the pillow. "I appreciate the moral support."

The nurse glances between us. "I'll be right back with supplies. Would you like some ice chips?"

She rubs her throat. "Yes, please."

He leaves us alone, shutting the door behind him. I lean in and press a kiss to her balmy forehead. My lips feel singed upon contact. "Shit, you're burning up."

Clea bumps her nose along mine. "Yeah, that seems to be a trend as of late."

"And I had no idea how bad it was." With a muffled curse, I scrub over my face. Weariness clings to my bones and I slump into the folding chair. The rickety joints groan in protest.

"Are you okay?" The meek drawl is another reminder of just how sick she is. The desire for her to get well, for her spark to rekindle, surges in my gut.

I rest my elbow on the bed beside her hip. "You're asking me?"

"Is that all right?" She lowers her lashes. My willful girl is on a leave of absence for the time being.

"Of course." I lift the fingers threaded through mine, pressing her bent knuckles to my mouth. "Honestly, I'm not okay. I've been slowly losing my mind over the last few days."

She clenches her eyes shut and whimpers, as if a wave of pain is swooping in. "You and me both," she croaks. "I'm sorry. I didn't mean to keep you in the dark."

"I know. We can talk about that later." Another notification buzz pulses against my thigh. There's no remaining doubt as to who the insistent senders are.

Clea's gaze strays to my hair and a giggle breaks free. "You have a little sparkly something there."

I pat my head, coming up empty. "Where?"

She points to the spot. "I think it's a clip."

"Oh," I blindly grab at the area. "We were playing dress-up."

"Jeez," she yanks at her shirt and tosses the blanket aside. "I'm hot enough. No need to add to my fever."

Marc enters before I can respond. Ten minutes provides ample opportunity for Clea to get an IV line pumping hydration directly into her veins. Color has resurfaced to her skin. Her inhales don't sputter with effort. The dude has been bustling about in constant motion trying to get her comfortable. He finally stops moving long enough to stand by her side with a tablet in his hand.

"We need to run a few general diagnostics. Part of that is gathering a stool sample."

A vibrant blush washes over her face with a vengeance. "This is why I wanted Kody to bring me."

A crease dents his brow. "What are the chances you can collect one without medical intervention?"

"Please, no!" She gasps and slaps a palm to her stomach. "I mean, uh, the tank is kind of empty."

"Do you need some sustenance?"

"That's probably not a good idea. I'll try without first." She buries her flaming cheeks under her palms.

He taps on the tablet in his grip. "That's the much easier route. A scope is far less pleasant for everyone."

Clea gags. "That sounds horrific."

Marc's features lift in what I assume is meant to be encouragement. "Which is why we will try to avoid it."

In what I hope is a comforting motion, I reach over and rub her shoulder. "What's bothering you, aside from the obvious?"

"This isn't sexy," she mumbles.

A dry scoff reveals my feelings on the matter. "I can handle a little poop talk. I raised a baby."

"This is very different," she replies.

"How?" Shit is all the same.

"We aren't even in the honeymoon phase yet, *fiancé*." Clea injects a hint of warning into that last word that I should probably heed. "I don't want to ruin the allure and mystery."

But pleading my case to remain planted in this seat is more vital. "I know that you poop, Patra."

She lets out a mock sob. "This isn't happening."

"Why are you embarrassed?"

This is the point that our audience meets his threshold for delaying the systematic flow. "Do you want him to wait outside while we finish discussing this part?" he asks.

My gut clenches. I don't want to leave, but it's not my choice. "I'll give you privacy, Angel."

Clea chews on her bottom lip while searching my gaze.

For what, I'm not positive. I guarantee she'll only find sincerity. "You can stay."

"Thank you." That small allowance gives me the strength to sit that much straighter.

"Don't worry," the nurse offers with a kind smile. "You won't be required to pass the bowel movement on the bed."

"At least there's that tiny mercy." Uncertainty still resides in her shuttered gaze.

"Hey," I squeeze her hand. "I can wait in the lobby or outside. The last thing I want is to make you more uncomfortable."

"It's fine."

"That isn't reassuring." The thrum from my phone kicks in again, disrupting the path we're stumbling along. I rub at the pinch in my jaw, but it does little to alleviate the burn. That's when I realize my molars are clenched tighter than a vise. My features have been set in a perpetual scowl since who knows when.

Clea gives me a scowl of her own. "Don't make this more difficult. I want you here."

I bob my head in a sharp nod. "I want to be here."

"Glad that's taken care of," the nurse laughs. "Now for the fun. The bathroom is just down the hall. There are instructions on how to collect a clean specimen. The deposit station is against the wall. You can't miss it. Gloves and containers are in the bins. If you need assistance, I can call for a female practitioner to aid in the process."

"I'm sure that won't be needed." Clea's embarrassment is still reflecting across her ruddy hue. She moves to scoot off the mattress. "Can I take this with me?"

Marc's eyes shift to the IV stand. "We can disconnect it. The tubes can get tangled and make a mess."

"Yeah, that's what I'm worried about." Sarcasm coats the words. Her accompanying laughter is the sweetest relief.

He puts a clamp on the line and sets her free. "Take your time. Once that's done, we'll keep you hooked up for a few hours while the rapid results are spinning. That'll give the doctor time to check on you. As of now, you won't be admitted to the hospital."

Clea tucks some blond tangles behind her ear. "That's good, right?"

"Very. You want to avoid being stuck there if possible."

Her posture relaxes as she stands from the bed. To her credit, she barely wobbles. "I'm already feeling better, if that counts for anything."

The nurse glances at his tablet. "That's definitely a positive sign, but not surprising. Dehydration is extremely common and can cause a slew of other issues. Let's hope the fever isn't caused by something more serious than a mild infection."

She crosses her fingers. "Here's hoping."

He whips out a pink medical gown from the cabinet. "Put this on, if you don't mind. It will give the doctor easier access later."

I'll admit to despising the sound of that, but know better than to comment. "I won't move from this spot."

Clea bends to kiss my cheek. "Love you."

I turn to press our lips together. "I love you so fucking much."

The nurse coughs. "When's the wedding?"

We share a glance, the pause dragging on to become suspicious. "Next June."

"Well, congratulations. Feel free to change, then take care of the sample. I'll check back in a bit." He strides from the room without further instruction.

"I guess you're getting a free show." She begins stripping her clothes.

In an attempt to grant her a modicum of decency, and not leer at her nudity in this extremely inappropriate setting, I pull out my phone to find six waiting messages from Kody. I scan through the similar requests. "What are the chances your brother and Tally can call when you're done?"

"I'd say pretty decent." She shrugs on the loose fabric. "Do I actually have a choice?"

On impulse, I begin tying the strings down her back. "I could try appeasing her with a picture."

Clea holds up a thumb and smiles. "Cheese."

I snap the shot with a chuckle. "You're a good sport."

"More like if we don't, we'll never hear the end of it. You know how your daughter operates. I don't want her to worry."

Little does she realize just how concerned we've been on her behalf. That conversation is banging against my vocal cords, demanding an escape route. I gulp against the strain and search for a distraction.

She's shuffling to the door when I step behind her. "Need a hand?"

"Very funny." Clea rolls her eyes and points to the chair. "Sit down. I've got this under control."

I hold up my palms, retreating to my seat. "Let me know if you need backup."

Her vibrant spirit makes a glorious reappearance as she giggles. "Trust me, that's the least of my concerns."

chapter twenty-nine

Clea

I SWING MY GAZE TO THE CLOCK HANGING DIRECTLY IN FRONT OF ME. It's been two minutes since I last checked, and that's being generous. Each second that ticks by is another hanging in the balance while waiting for the doctor to deliver my results. Not that I can complain. The constant churning in my digestive system has calmed somewhat. That reprieve should be cause for celebration. If only this ball of pressure would quit growing in my chest.

The hours have trickled by agonizingly slowly since I turned in my stool sample. Just repeating that term sends an unpleasant prickle across my feverish skin. I've certainly met my poop quota for the year. Nolan is privy to that knowledge as well. If this isn't a trial for what our relationship can withstand, I'm not sure what is. Talk about a testament to our bond. Good grief.

Wandering along that rocky path makes my stomach cramp—as if it wasn't going through enough. In an effort to calm myself down, I search for a distraction. Maybe I could call Tally and Kody again. Or my parents. Vannah, Presley, and Audria are sure to get a laugh from my comedic retelling of this shitty experience. Pun most definitely intended.

My head thumps against the pillow as I release a drawn-out sigh. I got off the phone with Tally half an hour ago. It suddenly feels like days, with this silence dragging on. She was a chatterbox, as always. The total opposite from the man brooding beside me.

Nolan is staring at our clasped hands with a furrow denting his forehead. I can tell he has plenty to say. For whatever reason, he's choosing to sit idly by and let this soundless vacuum envelop us instead. The better my belly feels, the worse my heart aches. I fiddle with the blanket over my lap. *Why does it seem like there's a separation wedged between us?*

"Do you want me to buzz the nurse?"

My gaze whips to Nolan. "Huh?"

"You're fidgeting and puffing louder than a steam engine. Those are clear signs of distress or agitation. I don't want your treatment to go off the rails over something that could be easily fixed." His voice is too sympathetic considering the agitation brewing in my veins. The tension is growing into a thick wall we'll need a freaking ladder to climb.

"You're suddenly an expert." My tone is snide. The wince that follows is an apology on its own. "Sorry, that was rude."

The groove between his brows carves deeper lines. "What's bothering you?"

"Aside from lying in a hospital bed?"

"Obviously."

"Why don't you tell me what's wrong," I deflect with a smooth pivot.

His sigh is steeped in exasperation. "This isn't about me."

Frustration is mounting into a living entity between us. The hospital-grade gown becomes too restricting. I yank at the draped neckline, fanning cool air underneath. "I can't focus with your gloomy energy thundering all about."

Nolan's emotions are a tangible beast. A pungent cloud of misery intoxicates the air. I can hear his gears grinding while he tries—and fails—to maintain a neutral expression. It makes me jittery and is impossible to ignore. Any semblance of comfort is strained against this ballooning issue. The vibe and mood are tainted, but not permanently damaged.

His exhale is a booming rumble. "We can talk about it later."

"Why wait? We're not going anywhere."

"This shouldn't take much longer. The nurse said he'll be back with an update soon." His retort falls flat.

"Oh my gosh," I smack my lumpy mattress with my palm. "Just tell me why you're sulking, Nolan."

"Why didn't you call me, Patra?" The sorrow in his gaze is too reminiscent of the past. A withdrawn version I never want to witness again.

"What do you mean?"

"I hardly heard from you for days. This is serious." He motions at my prone form, hooked up to an IV, stuck until further notice.

"Not sure if you're aware, but I was barely able to move." That requires no further explanation considering he carried me inside.

But that's beside the point he's trying to make.

Nolan is staring at me, those green depths pleading for my understanding. "You were suffering to the extreme of needing medical attention and I had no idea. I should've been with you."

My inhale is cut short with a hitch. "We don't even know what I have yet. It's mostly likely contagious. I didn't want you to get sick."

"I don't care about getting sick," his gritty timbre lashes against the pristine walls with a resounding crack. "I care about being there for you. That option was stolen from me. You told me to stay away. Kody wouldn't let me in the front door. It's a helpless, horrible feeling knowing the woman I'm crazy about doesn't want me near her."

"What?" The slithering sensation crawling along my spine is extremely unpleasant. I shiver, but not from the fever still attacking me. "That has nothing to do with my love for you. If anything, I was trying to protect you."

His lips crook into a lopsided grin, but there's no joy in the expression. "I see it differently."

"How so?" Suspicion slows my tone.

"You still don't rely on me. Maybe I don't deserve your full trust after years of letting you down. I'll own that." He strokes a finger down my arm. "But it fucking hurts, Patra."

"It's not like that," I insist.

"No? Then tell me why you shut me out."

"It was not a pretty sight, Nolan. I was embarrassed enough that Kody was within earshot. I didn't want you to see me like that."

"You'd rather have me worrying nonstop and reaching the edge of sanity? I was close to losing my mind."

"Ouch," I wince with a hiss. "It wasn't my intention to ignore you. I really didn't want to bother you with this."

Hurt reflects in his drooping features. The guy looks beaten down. "You could never bother me. I want you to rely on me, in any capacity. It's not a chore or hindrance by any stretch. You're a privilege I take very seriously. I want to be responsible for taking care of your needs. All of them. Please come to me for anything and everything."

"I usually would. This was... different. Please don't take it personally."

"Too late." Nolan's frown sags lower. "It's too familiar. You rarely initiate contact, other than sex. I'm not complaining about that, trust me. It would just be nice to know you depend on me for more than my dick."

I rear backward, his words a harsh slap to my cheek. "Is that what you think?"

"No, not really. I'm just... frustrated." He lifts our joined hands to his mouth, kissing my inner wrist. "How long will you punish me for? I deserve it, but I can't handle you not depending on me."

"Baby," I force myself upright and cradle his scruffy jaw. "I love you. So freaking much that I waited for six years for you to finally figure your shit out. Never doubt my commitment to you."

"I don't, but—" He's cut off when my finger presses against his lips.

"But please understand that when I have explosive diarrhea, I might not want you anywhere near my ass. It's just a hard limit for me." That's not a secret. I might as well spell it out.

His chuckle is a muffled sputter. "Damn. I'm being stupid, huh?"

"I mean, maybe just a pinch. We wouldn't be us without acting ridiculous every now and then."

"Other than my brush with panic attacks." He groans at the ceiling. "I shouldn't be so fucking sensitive."

A scoff answers that nonsense. "I have no problem with you expressing yourself. It's much preferred to the alternative."

"It was bad then." The fact he can recognize and admit that there was a problem proves his healing.

"We've mended, and are growing in the right direction. I'm aware that my communication can be better in certain situations. It's okay to question where we stand. This is still new between us." I'm stable on solid ground and hoping he's right next to me.

Nolan shakes his head. "I would never doubt us. It's my own insecurity causing problems. I'm not used to being vulnerable, but there's not a moment I don't wonder where we're headed."

The breath I didn't realize I was holding whooshes from my lungs. "Me either."

He stands to dust a kiss against my forehead. "I apologize about losing my screws there for a minute."

I shrug against him. "At least we're not boring."

The door swings open in the following beat, popping our intimate display. Nolan returns to his seat while I slouch into the stiff pillow. Doctor Klein smiles at me as she approaches the bed.

"So, I have mostly good news, with some potentially not as great news."

I didn't hear the word bad, which has me doing an internal happy dance. "What's wrong with me?"

Her brown eyes sparkle with mirth. "Straight to the point. I like your style."

"No offense, but I'm ready to ditch this joint. The sterilized fumes are going to my brain."

Nolan chuckles. "I think you're dizzy from all the poo—"

I clap a hand over his mouth. "Nope. We're done discussing that subject."

The doctor laughs. "I'm glad you're in uplifted spirits. It shouldn't take much to get you on the mend completely. You have a mild gastrointestinal infection. The cause is uncertain, but probably from something you ate or drank. I'll prescribe an antibiotic as well as a recommended diet for the next several days. You should see improvement very quickly."

Relief floods from me with a heavy exhale. "That's fantastic. Am I free to go?"

She rests a hand on my shoulder. "Now for the not-so-great news. I'll agree to let you leave if there's someone at home who can keep an eye out. You need rest and plenty of fluids. No getting out of bed except for when duty calls and the other essentials."

Nolan raises his arm. "That's not a problem. She can stay at my house. I'll take really good care of her. My daughter will no doubt be her shadow too."

Doctor Klein types on the tablet in her grip. "Fantastic. You're all set then. Just give your pharmacy information to Marc when he comes to disconnect your IV. Then I'll get the script sent right over."

She ducks from the room with the fluid efficiency one would expect from a competent medical professional. I blink over at Nolan, who's already staring at me. The flutters that erupt in my belly are a much welcome change. A sigh pairs with the lazy grin stretching my lips.

"What's that look for?" He leans an elbow on the mattress by my hip.

"I'm getting upgraded from neighbor to roommate?"

Nolan twirls a lock of my hair around his finger, giving a gentle tug. "Let's be honest, it was only a matter of time."

"Oh?"

"You belong in my bed, Angel. From this day forward, that's where you'll be."

"Confident much?"

"When it comes to us? Without hesitation."

There's not much left to say. I wiggle my brows at him while pointing toward the corner. "Would you be so kind as to assist in putting my pants on?"

"Usually, that would go against every code in my rulebook. But in this case, abso-fucking-lutely. I can't wait to get you home, Patra."

A tremble skates through me. "Why does that have such a nice ring to it?"

His signature smolder framed by both dimples threatens to incinerate me. "I don't have a ring yet, but that's next on the list."

chapter thirty

Nolan

WALK TO THE FRIDGE AND GRAB THE ORANGE JUICE, POURING WHAT'S left in a short glass. That's the finishing touch for Clea's breakfast. A glance at the tray shows massive improvement, if I'm allowed to boast on my own behalf. I actually baked. The cinnamon rolls might have come from a canister, but they're not burnt. It still blows my mind that she makes these from scratch.

Tally appears beside me in her typical stealth mode. I'm almost convinced she's about to smile when an exaggerated huff sends stray hair flying off her forehead. The purposeful crossing of her arms while maintaining eye contact shortly follows. She's baiting me again. The line she's casting is practically begging for a nibble. My daughter has been pouting since I carried Clea into my room two nights ago.

"Problem, Lou?" I shouldn't encourage her, but she's too stinking cute.

Another haughty scoff. "It's not fair."

"Your bed isn't big enough to share." I pair the reminder with a boop to her wrinkling nose.

"Then I should get a new one," Tally states as though it's the only logical solution.

I lower myself into a crouch. "How about once Clea is feeling better, we have a slumber party in my bed?"

Her gasp reveals how appealing that option is. That unfiltered confession doesn't last more than five seconds. She reins in her excitement with a sniff, recalling the solemn vow to remain mad at me. "Or we can just put blankets on my floor and make a fort."

"Why not both?"

She squints at me. "Okay, deal."

I accept her outstretched palm. "It's a pleasure doing business with you, Princess."

That earns a genuine giggle. "You're silly, Daddy."

"Lead the way, but be quiet. I'm not sure if Clea is awake yet." I motion to the stairs.

Tally bolts without further instruction, bounding up the steps with the grace of an elephant. I grab the tray and follow at a pace that won't fling the dishes at our ceiling. When I reach the second-floor landing, my daughter already has the door cracked open. She gestures for me to hurry with a spin from her wrist.

""You're a slowpoke." She tacks on that comment for good measure.

"I'm carrying precious cargo." I nod at Clea's breakfast.

Tally stretches her arms out. "Want me to take a turn?"

"And steal all the credit? No way." I chuckle when she pouts. "How about you hold the fruit bowl?"

"Gimme, gimme!" Her grabby fingers move like lightning.

"What are you two not whispering about out there?" Clea's voice reaches us from her perched position on the bed. She sets her Kindle aside. Blue-light blocking glasses frame her sparkling gaze as she watches us enter.

"We made you breakfast!" Tally tiptoes into the room with the bowl clutched between her palms.

"It smells delicious."

"I'm the official taste tester. Dad did the cooking. You do the eating." Tally's disgruntled farce crumbles with a wide smile once we're in Clea's presence. Go figure. In her humble opinion, this mismatched living arrangement is entirely my fault. I can't correct her.

Our loyal customer shoots me a wink. "That's a winning

combo. This looks like another impressive spread. You're going through too much trouble for me."

"You better get used to it, Patra. This is your normal now. Never a bother, remember? It gives me an excuse to practice my skills in the kitchen." I set the tray on her covered lap.

"And I'm being super careful. See?" Tally passes her the heaping dish without a wobble.

"You're very talented," Clea agrees with a matching grin.

Rory and Rufus lift their heads in unison as Tally bends to give them a scratch around the ears. There wasn't a discussion regarding their relocation to my house. I told Kody to drop them off. He did so without hesitation. End of story.

Their massive cushion is situated in the corner, covering enough space to be mistaken for an area rug. One compromise that's left me somewhat in my daughter's good graces is allowing the dogs to sleep with her. They're all too pleased to share the twin mattress.

"Oh, this is yummy." Clea licks a glob of frosting from her bottom lip.

Pride puffs out my chest as I slide in beside her. No more sitting on a chair across the room for this guy. "Glad you approve."

"I already ate mine so my fingers wouldn't be sticky." Tally whips out a Go Fish deck from her pocket. What else she has stashed in there is anyone's guess.

Clea polishes off the gooey pastry, brushing crumbs onto her plate. "Are we playing?"

Tally climbs onto the bed, settling in front of us at the foot. She dumps the cards into a pile, tosses them like lettuce, and meticulously stacks one after another until each is accounted for. "There. All shuffled."

I nod at her thorough—albeit time-consuming—strategy. "Who's the dealer?"

She recites a rhyme I don't recognize while bouncing her pointer finger between us. Clea is the chosen one. After wiping any leftover residue from her hands, she gives us each five cards. Tally's focus doesn't waver from her movements.

"All right, who goes first?" Clea bites her lip and winks at me.

"Me, duh." Tally snorts, then goes utterly still. "Oh! I have a fun idea."

"This should be interesting," I murmur from the corner of my mouth.

"Since we didn't get to finish bowling, should we use the same bet thingy or whatever?" She crosses her fingers and whispers under her breath.

I glance at Clea, who shrugs in return. "Fine by me."

"You're totally getting married," Tally murmurs while picking up her cards.

"There's always someday," Clea sings.

Our little matchmaker's grin falters. "Wait, what? That's like saying maybe, but really meaning no."

The woman beside me rubs her arm against mine. "I mean, it will probably happen."

Without conscious thought, my gaze travels to hers. I get lost in those ocean depths. "If she'll have me."

Tally studies our exchange with narrowed eyes. "Yeah, you're totally getting married."

We don't dispute her assumption, which gets my blood pumping hotter than appropriate for this setting. Our conversation tapers off as we start playing. After several rounds, I'm wondering if Clea is throwing the game on purpose. Either that or Tally has suddenly gained psychic abilities. I catch my daughter staring at Clea's lenses. That's when I notice the reflection.

"Lou."

She snaps her attention to me. Guilt flushes her cheeks. "I didn't do it on purpose."

"Does that make it better?"

Clea glances between us. "What's happening?"

I lift my brows at Tally. "Maybe the princess should spill her secret."

Her slim shoulders slump after being properly reprimanded. "Okay, fine. I can see your cards in the mirror from your glasses."

"The reflection," I clarify with a chuckle.

Clea whips off her blue blockers as though they've personally offended her. "No wonder I was losing so bad."

I lift Clea's arm, adding a shrill whistle for victory. "You're the winner by default."

Tally tilts her head to the side. "What's that mean?"

"Since you were peeking, and I have zero matches, Clea automatically wins." I dip to whisper in the victor's ear. "Maybe I'll get to prove myself later."

"That seems like a consolation prize we can both enjoy." She taps her lips. "I accept."

Tally flops onto her back with a groan. "What movie are you gonna choose?"

Clea rubs her temples. "Oh, I don't know. I'll have to debate on it for a few hours."

"That doesn't make any sense." My daughter's complaint is muffled against the blankets. The dogs rise from their slumber to check on her with a dutiful sniff test. She giggles as their wet noses bump against her.

With her semi-distracted, I focus on the woman pressing her thigh against mine. "How are you feeling, Patra?"

"Much better, thanks for asking. I'm hoping to take another walk if the weather cooperates." It's been raining on and off for days.

The sun is streaking through the blinds, hinting at agreeable conditions. "That's doable."

"Much like you." She walks her fingers up my chest.

"Quit or I won't be able to stand without causing an indecent scene or mentally scarring my daughter."

Her gaze trickles down to my lap. "I'll gladly cause one with you later."

"Jesus, woman." I bite my fist. "You're going to get me in trouble."

"We wouldn't want that." Clea sobers with a cough, although the fire still crackles in her eyes.

She must be experiencing a similar longing that's ripping my control to shreds. The heat is ratcheting to uncomfortable levels. With feigned nonchalance, I shift to adjust the strain. I went years without, but this woman is a constant temptation.

"What are you two whispering about?" Tally's hands are parked on her hips.

Clea waves her hand. "Just boring adult stuff."

"Okay." She hops off the bed and opens the curtains. Just as predicted, there's not a cloud in the sky.

"Beautiful day." Clea's comment seems distant as she stares outside.

"Isn't this wonderful?" Tally's content sentiment reminds me of cotton candy blended with hot fudge and chocolate chips. Her smushed expression matches the sugary confection.

I can't stop a smile from spreading across my own features. Everything I need is in this room. "Which part?"

"All of it." She spreads her arms wide. "We're finally the family I always wanted."

Clea rests a flat palm to her chest. "That's so sweet, Lulah. I'm honored to fit in that picture with you two."

She scoffs. "You're a vital piece. Always have been."

"Oh, gosh." A sheen twinkles over her eyes. "It's too early for crying."

"Is it still morning?"

I squint at Tally. "Yeah, why?"

"Can we have ice cream? That never makes me cry. Well, except when I eat too fast and my brain hurts. I don't like when that happens. So, take little bites." She sucks in a long breath. "Why aren't you saying anything?"

"Just taking it all in. Savoring my present. Listening to my future." I press a kiss to Clea's forehead. "Giving thanks to the past for stepping aside and making this possible."

chapter thirty-one

Nolan

HOW QUICKLY OUR DAYS ARE SOLIDIFYING INTO A FAMILIAR routine. Not in the monotonous, predictable sense. More like finally settling into a relaxed comfort that was meant to be ours all along. That luxury deserves to be cherished. Not a moment will be taken for granted. I've been basking in it since Clea moved in last week.

Tally is slumped along my side after giving up the fight against sleep halfway through *The Little Mermaid*. The closing credits are scrolling on the screen when I glance over at Clea. Her hooded gaze is already locked on me, suggestion steeping in the sparkling blue hue.

"Just give me a minute," I whisper, scooping Tally in my arms.

Clea nibbles her bottom lip with a nod. "I'm not going anywhere."

And she's not. Never again, if I have any say in the matter. She's found her home with us and that's how we'll stay.

I climb the stairs and stride to Tally's room. Her dutiful bunkmates are hot on my heels as I tuck her in bed. Rory and Rufus don't bother pausing before hopping onto the mattress. Tally doesn't so much as flutter her lashes at their movements. I switch on her white noise machine for extra precaution.

After sweeping her hair aside, I press a gentle kiss to her forehead. "Love you, Princess."

Then I'm off to spend some much-needed alone time with

my woman. My steps are hurried as I return to the den. Clea is exactly where I left her, although she's sprawling a bit more across the couch. I slide in beside her on the cushion, lifting her legs to set on my lap.

"It seems this couch is destined to be our frequent hot spot." I drift a palm along the smooth skin of her inner thigh.

"The deep seat is very accommodating." Her hand makes an upward path along my arm, dipping under my t-shirt sleeve to rest over the tattoo hidden there.

A rumble thrums through my chest and I shift to cover her body with mine. Lust is pumping fire into my veins, steaming up the space with demand and desire. Clea cradles my hips between her bent knees. We click together with a snug fit. That's just us—locking into the intimate embrace with ease.

I dust my mouth over hers. "Can I do things to you?"

Her nails scratch along my scalp. "We can do things to each other. You've been doing me for a week without letting me return the favor."

Prickles shoot across my entire form, centering on my dick. "You're supposed to be resting."

"I'm all better. Can I show you?" Clea arcs to lick the shell of my ear.

A shiver wracks my limbs despite the smoldering heat enveloping us. "Please do."

She pushes my shoulders until I'm sitting again. Clea slinks onto the floor, propping in a crouch framed by my feet. The position sends a heady rush straight south until I'm dizzy with want. I'm not left questioning her intentions for long. Her deft fingers make quick work of the button on my jeans. She tugs at the denim, taking my boxer briefs in the same motion. My cock stands to greet her.

"Oh, you're ready for me." Clea wraps her fingers around my length. A slow, teasing stroke follows.

"Are you surprised?" My voice is already strained, just from this simple touch.

"I haven't even started yet." She tightens her grip. That clenching squeeze is a vise I never want to escape.

"Just looking at you gets me hard." My chest heaves from the effort of holding back.

"Charmer," she purrs while lowering her lips to my tip.

"I don't need charm when you're preparing to swallow me."

"True." Her tongue swirls around the crown to taste me. A moan bubbles from her mouth. "My man is salty and aching for me."

"Need you," I mumble.

She licks up and down my shaft, teasing while driving my desire to catastrophic levels. "This is all mine."

"Only yours," I agree with a jerky nod.

"You're so hard." Her wrist rolls with a downward glide while she opens wide to take me in. That velvet caress melts away my resolve to remain still.

I fist my hands into the cushions. "Fuck, Patra. What your mouth does to me."

She sucks more of me along her tongue with a shallow pull. That initial bob could send me over the edge. A streak of white explodes across my vision. I lower further onto the sofa, spreading my legs to give her more space. She takes advantage and wedges closer. Her lips form a tight ring around me as she adds more suction. Warmth blooms along every inch until she retreats, only to repeat the motions. I'm captivated by the sight. That's why I don't notice the tingles until it's almost too late.

I trace her jaw with my thumb. "Angel, you have to stop. I want to be inside you."

She pops off my length, her lips glistening in the dim light. "You already are."

"Don't make me wait." I swoop in to seal us in a scorching kiss. My tongue lashes out to swipe along her lower lip. She nips at me, groaning into my mouth. I tunnel my fingers into her hair and pull us apart. "Ride me."

There's no hesitation as she stands, bunches her dress, and

reaches under the hem. With a shimmy, she strips off her panties and kicks the silky scrap aside. Then she's straddling my lap, suspended right above my dick. "Is this what you want?"

"Fuck yes. Use me for your pleasure." My palms move to her exposed hips, guiding the connection with soft pressure.

Clea lowers until my cock is sliding into her slick heat. She doesn't stop until I'm buried to the hilt. I buck against her, driving that much deeper. A muffled cry escapes her, trapped behind sealed lips. She releases the fabric still clutched in her palm. The flowy skirt fans out to cover our joined union. No one would be the wiser if my pants weren't resting on my ankles.

"I've missed this." She leans in to rest her forehead on mine.

"Fuck, yes. If all goes according to plan, you'll never go without again."

She rocks against me. "That's a promise you better keep."

"It's a guarantee."

That conviction settles over us as we let our bodies do the talking. She stretches for me as I notch myself into her welcoming depths. Her nails spear into my skin as she anchors herself, then begins rocking on a steady track. Forward and back, the seductive cycle gaining momentum with each pass. She swivels for more friction while I use my grip on her to steer our frantic lust. The shield her dress creates hides our lower halves from view. That heightens the electric sensitivity skimming from her flesh against mine. Our arousal builds with each stroke, prodding at the promise of relief.

"Just like that," Clea moans.

"You feel so damn good." The room is spinning from how hard I'm falling.

"Faster." Her demand matches mine, and I'm all too happy to deliver.

I piston in and out while she rises and falls. Our rhythm fuels the carnal yearning that's chasing us. Even concealed from view, Clea's tits treat me to an erotic sight. She bounces with a desperate tempo. I bury my face in her breasts, those ample curves cushioning me. Saliva pools on my tongue. I'm ravenous for more. My hunger breathes fire along her flesh, releasing in a throaty growl.

Clea meets my desire with a raspy mewl. She thrusts her chest toward me, granting my mouth permission to explore. While my tongue traces her cleavage, she snaps her hips faster. Her desire is outlined in the faint glow from the television. I'm drawn in on a spinning reel, fascinated as she gyrates to the melody of our passion.

The clap of flesh bounces off the walls as we surrender. I'm consumed by her. Every piece that defines me is hers to dictate. She takes advantage of my weakness and increases her grinding to a blistering pace. Her skin sizzles under my hands. The babbling encouragements spilling from her lips block all other noise. That hypnotic melody entices me to be bold.

I trace my thumbs along the crack of her ass. She clenches on my cock—either in warning or spurring me on. When her gaze clashes with mine, unadulterated lust threatens to pummel me. I palm her lush bottom and use the leverage to speed our movements. There's only so much more I can handle before the climax will drag me under. I move one hand to the juncture where our bodies meet, searching for her clit. She gasps to the ceiling when my finger hits the spot.

"So close," she murmurs.

"What do you need?" I flick that tiny bundle while spasms begin twitching her limbs.

"More, more," she chants.

With a palm flattened to the base of her spine, I hammer our hips together while working her clit. The rush of euphoria builds in my cock just as Clea goes rigid in my arms. I let go with a muted shout, clutching her against me as we tumble into the endless abyss. She goes limp and collapses in a satisfied heap. Sweat coats me while I attempt to get my breathing under control.

She nuzzles into the crook of my shoulder. "We're totally doing that again."

"Already?"

Clea's nod bumps my chin. "Don't doubt me."

"Never."

"Good. Take me to bed and prove it." The mumbled command is a puff against my sticky skin.

"With pleasure, Patra."

chapter thirty-two

Clea

SWITCH THE PHONE TO MY LEFT EAR WHILE PAUSING AT THE HALL mirror. "How long have you been there?"

Vannah's slurp carries down the line. "However many minutes it takes for me to polish off a margarita."

"And that's her second one," a masculine voice chimes in from the background.

"Tell Landon I say hello."

She does. He responds with, "Hi, Clea. Get your ass moving or my wife will be white-girl wasted before happy hour is over."

"Eloquent as always," I mutter. "Why are you so thirsty, Van?"

"I'm stress drinking."

"Okay?"

Her sigh is drawn out to exaggerated measures. "Presley's ex is in town. He's making her antsy, which in turn is putting a big ol' sour grape in everyone else's mouth. It's awkward as fuck."

"Simon? I didn't realize she ever cared enough about him." I squint at my reflection, giving my glossy waves a final fluff.

Vannah snorts. "No, *the* ex. They dated in high school. I've never met him until now. Hell, I don't think she mentioned him more than once or twice."

Her emphasis on that one word snags my thoughts. "They were serious?"

"Apparently," she drawls. "Just hurry, okay? I'm not sure what's going to happen."

"I'm all set. Tally is packed for her sleepover. Nolan is… somewhere." I glance toward the kitchen but don't hear any traces of him. "We'll be right over after dropping the kiddo off at her friend's house."

"Look at you, being a mom." Her tone is cloying. Whimsical, even. It goes against everything she stands for.

I blanch at her uncharacteristic attitude. "What has gotten into you?"

She's quiet for a beat, only the idle chatter from those nearby crooning at me. "Love is thick in the atmosphere. You're lucky Lannie already shagged me dirty, or I'd probably be humping his leg."

A very unladylike snort shoots from me. "Okay, wow. Lay off the sauce, Van."

She huffs. "I'm painfully sober. The bartender barely put any tequila in these bad boys."

"Keep telling yourself that," Landon chuckles.

I share in his amusement with a laugh. "Okay, see you soon."

"Tootles," she sings and ends the call.

After slathering my lips with gloss and puckering at the mirror, I go in search of my purse. That's when I catch the view through the bay window. Furious gray clouds are clogging the sunny sky. My feet carry me forward without permission.

I press a hand to the glass. "Is it supposed to storm?"

Nolan's footsteps alert me to his approach. "Not that I'm aware of."

"The sky looks angry. That ruins our patio arrangement at the restaurant." The petulance in my mood is more appropriate for the six-year-old under this roof.

He begins massaging my shoulders, peppering the sensitive skin at my nape with kisses. "We'll just move our group inside. There aren't many of us."

"Presley might be adding a plus-one."

"Oh?" His exhale ghosts across my neck, eliciting a trail of goosebumps.

"That feels nice." I shiver against him. "We should get going, or I'll try convincing you to make a detour."

"They can wait a bit longer for us." Nolan's arms band around my waist from behind. He nudges his hard approval into my ass.

The elicit moment pops when Tally dashes into the room. Her backpack is strapped on, ready for an evening of slumber party fun. "Are we leaving yet?"

She's been asking that question incessantly since this morning. I turn toward her as Nolan takes a minute for himself to calm his raging libido. "Yep, I'm going to run next door quick and get my jacket."

"Oh, yay. That's a good idea. I'll wear one too." She twirls to the closet, showing off her boundless energy.

September is just beginning, but there's already a bite in the air. The rain will only intensify that chill. I rub my prickles still racing along my arms.

Nolan's warmth returns to my side. "You need to finish moving your stuff over here. This is your home now."

I cup his stubbled cheek in my palm. "It's all part of the process."

"Those words haunt me."

"Patience is difficult," I laugh. "I still have clothes at Presley's house. It will all make its way home eventually."

A rumble rises off his chest as he presses closer. "Love you calling this place home."

I fiddle with the buttons on his shirt, patting the spot over his heart. "That's because it is."

As a huddled trio, we walk outside into the unpredictable elements. Lightning flashes in the distance. The zapping streaks renew my haste and I stride across the dry lawn. Soon moisture will slick the trail.

"It's probably best if you just wait for me. This won't take more than thirty seconds." Only silence answers me. I pivot on my heel. "Did you hear me?"

Nolan lowers his gaze from the blustery sky, a crooked smile slanting his lips. Those freaking dimples wink at me as he pins me with a smoldering intensity I can't decipher. Then he lowers onto one knee.

My lashes flutter to an erratic beat while I just stare. "What are you doing?"

"Tying my shoe?" But his fingers aren't moving in that direction. Quite the opposite, in fact. He shoves a hand into his front pocket. The small velvet box he pulls out stalls my breath.

"Daddy!" Tally clasps a hand over her mouth. "You're ruining the surprise!"

His attention shifts to her. Confidence squares his broad frame while he remains kneeling in front of me. "It's okay, Princess. This will be even better."

Her blind faith in him shines from a wide grin. "I can't believe you're going to ask her—"

"Shh, Lou. Don't steal my thunder."

"Oh, right." A giggle squeaks past her lips. Then she peers up at the brewing system heading our way. "I dunno if it's me you gotta worry about."

Nolan hasn't announced his intentions to me, but a molten knot is already forming in my throat. Emotion crashes over me in a torrential wave. My vision blurs while I fight to suck oxygen into my lungs. "What are you doing?"

Repeating the question is all I can manage.

"Being spontaneous, and making you ours. Officially." He snaps the lid open, revealing a radiant ring meant for a solitary purpose.

It's absolutely gorgeous. The flawless diamond is flanked by two smaller ones on each side and mounted on a twisting platinum band, coming apart and together again like an endless infinity symbol. One glance and I already know the symbolism—two becoming one.

"Oh my gosh." The shock rushes from me as heat stings

my eyes. I blink and send a scalding droplet cascading down my cheek.

Nolan's torso expands with a deep inhale. "We were going to stop at the rose gardens for this since they're your favorite. I had a plan. It was sentimental and romantic and quite brilliant, if I do say so myself. We were going to do a whole speech surrounded by those colorful blooms. But that's not really our style. We stormed into your life unannounced and have created havoc ever since. Since then, it's been proven that some of the best decisions are made on impulse. You're always willing to take the plunge with me. With us," he corrects. "I'm sort of a package deal."

"This is it." The hushed murmur comes from the little girl who stole my heart all those years ago. Just like her father did. Tally is vibrating in place. I catch her focus bouncing between us from my periphery. She pokes her dad's arm, motioning for him to continue. Ever the instigator.

Nolan doesn't take his eyes from me. He reaches for my left hand, lacing our trembling fingers into an intimate embrace fit for this tender exchange. "Clea, you're the love of my life. You're our missing piece. I'm still getting over the shock that you agreed to give me a chance. One I didn't deserve. One that I'll forever be grateful to receive. That unconditional devotion feels incredible. I didn't have a clue what the future could hold before you showed me. We might've started as a fumbling disaster riddled with misunderstandings, but those mistakes were a necessary foundation to build our happily ever after on. That's just how we operate."

His throat bobs with a heavy gulp. "Tally is here as my witness. I won't promise to be perfect, but I'll treat you like the queen you are. Your dreams will thrive with endless encouragement. We'll live them with you while making our own together. We'll strive for more, but never take what we have for granted. From this day forward, our road is one we'll travel together. The way we always should've been."

I sniff against the burn in my nose. Nothing has ever been so right standing beside these two. Pure joy radiates from his smile, matching the giddy glee in Tally's expression. I soak it all in.

Nolan plucks the ring from the cushion and holds the dazzling band out to me. "The sanctity of marriage didn't register until you gave me a reason to believe. Will you do me the honor of becoming my wife?"

I'm nodding, tears tracing along my face. Forget the rain. I'll water the freaking grass with my sheer joy. "Yes. Definitely yes."

He slides the diamond onto my finger, solidifying the preliminary vow. When he stands, I launch myself into his open arms. He clutches me against him and seals our lips in a sizzling kiss. Affection and muffled declarations of love fuse our connection. We break apart after a few beats. There's another we need to share this occasion with.

I collapse to my knees and haul Tally in for a tight hug. She squeezes me in return. Nolan bends to wrap us in a protective cocoon reinforced with the special bond that's always existed.

"Love you both," I whisper into our cuddle.

Nolan presses his lips to my temple, spreading the affection to Tally next. "Love my girls with all I have to give."

"Oh, I almost forgot." She wiggles away from our hold.

"What could possibly be missing?" My gaze is still watery.

"I didn't wanna be left out." Tally digs in her pocket and whips out a handful of fuzz. There's something buried within the fluff, though. "This is for you to wear for me. I made it myself. It's pink with sparkles."

The beaded creation is stretchy and just how she described. I hold out my right hand, wiggling the third digit in particular as a hint. "Will you do the honors?"

She does without hesitation. Her gift balances this momentous promise, forming a circle fit for three. "I get my own side and everything. Wow. Can I call you Mama now?"

I look to Nolan for guidance, and he nods with automatic acceptance. "Yes, Lulah. I suppose you can."

epilogue

Clea

"MAMA?" TALLY'S CALL WARNS ME OF HER INCOMING intrusion about one second before the door crashes open.

The resulting bang sends my heart straight into an erratic gallop. I snap my legs together, but the toilet bowl hinders any major movement. The plastic stick is hidden from view behind my tucked knees. It's a miracle that I didn't drop the freaking thing. I whip my gaze to the sparkling princess with zero boundaries.

She skips forward without pause, not recognizing this is an infringement on my personal space. The veil she wore at our wedding is perched proudly on her crown. "Are you peeing on yourself?"

I trap a snort behind pinched lips. She's as curious—and hilarious—as ever. It requires immense control to gulp the amusement down. I really need to start locking the door—and enforcing the importance of privacy. I hang my head and focus on the bigger picture as a distraction.

"Tallulah." The scold hangs heavy in my voice. I can't recall how often we've had this discussion. It's become even more frequent since I moved in a year ago.

"Uh-oh." She halts her progress and immediately begins retreating toward the hall.

"Privacy is important," I remind her.

Tally bobs her head. "I'll wait for you right here."

Then she shuts the door with a satisfying click. I finish my business and put the capped test on the counter facing down. The result takes three minutes to appear. What are the chances she's going to wait that long? That gives me pause. Why should she? Nolan deserves to be a witness too. The three of us should be together for this. Unless it's negative. I chew on my bottom lip as indecision sloshes through me.

"Are you done?" A quiet knock accompanies her impatience.

I stare at the test for a pregnant beat. Pun potentially intended. I snatch the stick and tuck it in my back pocket away from prying eyes. "Yes, Lulah."

Tally returns to my side within seconds. "Sandwiches are ready. Daddy sent me to get you."

The chaotic flips in my stomach will make it impossible to eat. Not that she needs to hear that. I wash my hands quickly and steer her to the stairs with a palm. "Then we better go."

She rolls her eyes up to me. "What do you think I've been trying to do?"

I boop her nose. "Someone is wearing their sassy pants."

A renewed flurry kicks in my pulse as we descend the final step. What are the chances I can hold in the secret until after lunch? Highly unlikely. The unknown is already threatening to burn a hole through the denim against my butt.

The decision is made for me moments later.

"Mama was peeing on herself," Tally announces as we stride into the kitchen.

Nolan's gaze flings to mine. Those green depths swirl with comprehension of what's left unsaid. We just decided to start trying last month after returning from our honeymoon. It would be fast, but possible all the same. The somersaults in my belly are reminiscent of good news.

He stands on wobbling knees. "So?"

My bottom lip is trapped between my teeth as I shuffle from one foot to the other. "I haven't looked yet."

A disgruntled huff comes from Tally. "What adult stuff are you two whispering about now?"

Nolan's smile wobbles at the edges. "We want to have a baby."

"Really?" Her gasp echoes around the wide room. She stares at my stomach that's flat for the most part.

I comb my fingers through her curly tangles. "Yeah, are you okay with that?"

"Well, duh. It's only my biggest wish. I've been asking for a little sister for-ev-er." That's a slight exaggeration, but she does beg for a sibling at least once per week. "But I don't see anything."

I hold my hem steady as she tries to raise my shirt. "It's not that simple."

"We aren't sure yet, kiddo," Nolan adds and walks toward us. He strokes a finger along my arm once I'm within reach. The warmth radiating from his gaze heats me from top to toe.

Her intent focus hasn't left my torso. "Okay, so what happens now?"

"I took a test." The item in question remains out of sight. I pat my pocket for extra insurance. The plastic feels hot in my palm as I keep it hidden behind my back.

A dent creases the smooth skin between her brows. "How?"

"That's what I was doing in the bathroom."

"Peeing on yourself." It seems the clarification is as much for my benefit as it is for hers.

My shoulders bounce with the humor I'd previously corralled. "Not quite, Lulah. I have to pee on a little strip for the test to work. It's actually quite surprising that I didn't get any on my hands."

"Gross." She sticks her tongue out. Then her expression goes slack and morphs into open wonder. "How are babies made?"

I choke on my saliva, nearly hacking out a lung while coughing over the sensation. Nolan rubs my back while squeezing his nape. Tally crosses her arms during our dramatic reactions. She taps her foot for good measure, waiting not so patiently.

"Very carefully," I croak and wipe the moisture leaking down my cheeks.

"Uh, yeah," Nolan stammers. "It's like… magic."

But she isn't settling for fluffy non-answers. "Just tell me. I can handle boring adult stuff."

"Well," I look to Nolan.

His features are frozen solid in shock. I can almost see the fear reflecting in his wide eyes. "Want to take this one?"

I clutch my throat. "Me? But I'm—"

"Always more eloquent with the delicate subjects," he interjects. His hands fold together in a silent plea.

I pinch the bridge of my nose. "Okay, fine."

How in the heck do I explain this to a child? She's almost eight, but that's too young for the full birds and bees discussion. I wrack my brain for a glossed-over version that will appease her.

"So, uh, Mama and Daddy love each other very much." My gaze skitters off her unwavering interest. This girl could make a seasoned judge sweat.

Tally blinks at me. "I already know that."

"Great. I'm glad that's not up for debate." I wince as my pitchy tone grates at my ears. "There comes a point in our relationship when we decide to expand our family. We have more love to give than just to each other. Once we're ready to spread that love, a baby can be made."

The breath I'd been holding rushes out in a whoosh. Simple enough. I smile at Nolan. He looks to be biting back a laugh.

"Wow, that's so romantic." Tally's gaze is lost to some unseen point on the ceiling. "When I meet a man to marry, I'm gonna spread love with him every day so we can have lots of babies."

Okay, I'm already seeing the error in my explanation. Heaven forbid she shares this with her friends. I'll have irate parents blowing up my phone. "Um, well…"

"It doesn't always happen every day," Nolan cuts in unhelpfully.

Tally scoffs. "It will for me. I'm going to make sure to spread the love as often as I can. Then we will have so many babies. I'll need extra bottles. Oh, and diapers. Babies poop lots and lots. I've heard it smells super bad."

The color leeches from Nolan's face. He gags on his next swallow. "Can we please stop? This is traumatizing."

"Right, moving on." The perfect segue is literally tucked in my back pocket. I reach for the test and bring my curled fist forward. The result is still hidden from view, just waiting to be revealed.

"So, did it work?" Tally is bouncing on the balls of her feet.

I peek up at Nolan. He dips his head in soundless agreement. "Why don't you tell us, Lulah?"

Then I open my hand and angle the stick so the word in the little window is visible. She squints at the letters, her mouth forming the sounds.

"Positive? That's good, right?" She glances between us.

I slap my free palm over my mouth as heat instantly floods my eyes. Nolan wears a similar expression. He loops his arms around us to form a group hug, crushing us against his chest.

"We're going to have a baby," I blubber.

"Yes, I knew it! You two spread the love so good." Tally is beaming at us from the center of our huddle.

Nolan's forehead rests on mine while he places a palm flat on my stomach. "We sure did."

Tally copies his movement, her small hand drifting in a circle across my abdomen. "A baby is in there. That's so cool."

A memory strikes me in this moment. A distant, seemingly forgotten moment. It's one I never stopped wishing, though.

I settle my fingers over theirs, stilling Tally's wandering touch. "Do you remember when we were driving to the Belvine County Festival last summer?"

Nolan straightens to meet my gaze. "Of course. Why?"

"You forgot to ask me what I was thinking about. It's been over a year."

His jaw hangs loose. "I told you I wouldn't forget. How did I manage to do just that?"

I laugh at his stricken expression. "We've been busy."

"Tell me." The prod is whispered against my temple.

I sag into his embrace, our daughter still wedged in the middle. "I was thinking about this. The three of us together. Married and officially a family."

"With a baby on the way," Tally adds. Her blinding smile overflows the joy already flooding me.

"Yes," I sigh. "Our love will only continue to grow and spread from this day onward."

It may have taken a lot of waiting for our someday to arrive. The journey wasn't without struggle, but that someday is finally here. And I wouldn't change a single thing.

what to read next

Vannah and Landon have their own story to share with you. *Something Like Hate* is available to read now. Take a peek at this excerpt to get you in the snarky banter mood.

His dark gaze tracks my slinky approach. I add more sway to my hips under his intense focus. While I erase the distance separating us, my eyes have a feast of their own. His hair is a dark shade of blond, styled in that effortless way I want to tousle with my fingers. A slight shadow coats his jaw in stubble. Just enough to elicit a burn against sensitive flesh. Flammable tingles stir in my lower belly. All I need is a fuse to go off like a rocket. Yes, please. Is it too early to ask for seconds?

I shamelessly prop myself against the wall he's leaning on. With a quirked brow, I glance at his drink. Bourbon, maybe? The sophisticated choice wouldn't be a surprise. He smells like money. The ancient type that's seared into his DNA. He wasn't just born with a silver spoon in his mouth—it was already there before his parents had sex. An entitled kind of stench seeps from his pores. Luxury and privilege drape over his casual pose, fitting even better than his custom-tailored suit. He reeks of expensive liquor, fast cars, and bad decisions.

And I'm hooked on it.

He remains unmoving and imposing, much like a concrete pillar. Perhaps his emotions resemble a similar structure. Breaking this thick ice between us is also my responsibility, apparently, as he continues to wear a mask of indifference. The sneaking suspicion that he's a bad choice begins whispering in my ear. I mentally swat at that pesky voice, refusing to surrender without a proper attempt.

"Hey, handsome. I'm Vannah." I offer him my hand to shake—or kiss, if he's into that sort of thing.

The ass sneers at my outstretched palm as if I'm poisonous. To a man like him, I just might be. "I'd say it's nice to meet you, but I've never been a good liar."

"Wow, okay." I drop my arm. "That's how it is?"

His features return to a neutral state of disregard. "You interrupted me."

A glance over my shoulder lands on the packed dance floor. "Creeping on someone?"

He snorts into his crystal tumbler. "Hardly."

"Care to fill me in?" I straighten from my come-hither position.

"Just enjoying destruction in the making."

What an odd thing to say. "Vague much?"

"That's intentional."

It feels like my lashes are coated in concrete as I blink at him. "All right then."

Well, this is a bust. Pressure of my own making threatens to hunch my shoulders. Dignity rattles through my posture, keeping me poised and on guard. I almost startle when the silence ends between us.

"So… Savannah." His tone resembles a hiss. "How do you fit into this scenario?"

I ignore his question, still mulling over his audacity and the urge to set sights on prospects with actual potential. Then I process what he else he said. Why does he assume that's my full name? The fact that he's correct boils my blood a bit hotter. "Everyone calls me Vannah."

"I'm not everyone," he drawls.

"No, you're clearly not." I wrinkle my nose and re-appraise him with a lazy perusal. Such a pity to discover his appearance is hiding an ugly spirit.

He swirls the remaining alcohol in his glass. "Are you going to answer my question?"

"Do you actually care about my response?"

"No." His blunt retort should be expected at this point, but the bite still burns.

I could walk away, as any logical woman would. But this is becoming a matter of stubborn nature and principle. Who has the bigger balls? Metaphorical or not, this guy isn't getting the final word.

With a haughty tilt of my chin, I stare him down and prepare for battle. "Ashlee is my cousin, but we might as well be sisters."

"How nice. I suppose that explains your dress," he says with a curl of his upper lip.

I roll my eyes. "Yes, I'm a bridesmaid. The maid of honor, actually."

He grunts, polishing off the rest of his beverage. "What an idiotic tradition. This spectacle is all for show. Not to mention a horrific waste of money."

A storm cloud seems to be thundering above his head. I get a chill from that stony look. Not that I'd ever expose my reaction. On the outside, I appear calm and detached to a fault. That's how I got the reputation as a snarky diva, defense mechanism or not. My resting bitch face could win a gold medal at the Olympics. This dickhead has nothing on me.

I press my lips into a firm line to keep an expletive shower from pouring out. "Then why did you bother attending?"

"Josh is an old friend. I felt the need to watch him go down in flames." His wrist flicks in that dismissive way cocky men overuse.

"How kind."

"I aim to please."

It's my turn to huff. "Okay. Mr. Grey."

A furrow creases his harsh brow. "What?"

No shock that the similar phrase and reference are lost on him, although it would be funny if he'd read the popular books. "Never mind. You don't believe in the sanctity of marriage?"

He shoves a fist into his trouser pocket. "Only if the

arrangement financially benefits both parties and there's a bulletproof prenup."

Bile churns in my stomach. I gulp to avoid chucking filet mignon over his loafers. "Like a business transaction?"

He nods, the movement sharper than his sculpted jawline. "Precisely. A merger of sorts."

"Wow," I stretch the word with feigned enthusiasm. "You're a real piece of work."

"Thank you." The douche tips an imaginary hat.

"That wasn't meant to be a compliment."

"Could've fooled me."

Read *Something Like Hate* now!

Audria (and Reeve) are from *Leave Him Loved*, which is available to read now! Enjoy this excerpt from their meet cute.

A laundry list of yummy goodness forms in my mind as I wander to the cart corral. It's never wise to go shopping on an empty stomach. The meal plans stack up faster than I can track ingredients. I absently tug at a cart sticking out on the end. Nothing happens. That gets my attention, knocking me from my food stupor. I put in more effort but struggle to remove one from the bunch. They're all wedged together in tight formation. Kudos to the attendant for shoving them in with such precision. I giggle to myself, thinking about Vannah cackling over that last comment.

I shake my head and get back on track. With more force than I probably needed, I yank backward. Not even a single squeak of metal. The damn things don't budge. I exhale harshly, blowing stray hair off my forehead. Next comes a little mental stretch to prepare for war. I grip the handle and wrench with all my might. There's barely a wiggle.

On my next futile attempt, I ram an elbow into an unforgiving surface. Since I don't have a wall behind me, it's safe to assume someone just got jabbed in the gut. My innocent victim releases a muffled grunt, confirming the worst. I hang my head as a wash of humiliation singes my cheeks. My hopes of making a good impression are dashing off faster than the power-walking supermoms in aisle four.

"Whoa, easy there."

I spin on my heel at the gritty timbre, feeling like a spooked horse. *Is he trying to soothe me? Make sure I don't trigger a stampede?* Those thoughts vanish as I take my first decent glance at the man.

When I picture a hunk of farm-raised hotness, Scott Eastwood from *The Longest Ride* pops into my brain. This guy couldn't be farther from that stereotype. He's dark and broody without leather chaps or a Western shirt in sight. Broad shoulders, toned muscles, and a trim waist fill my vision. His white T-shirt is tight enough to hint at a set of defined abs. It's no wonder my arm is still vibrating from the impact. Without shame, I admit my mouth waters at the idea of tracing those washboard lines. I would gladly volunteer to scale him faster than a hayloft ladder.

The logo on his hat is familiar. Carhartt has a recognizable enough stamp, even to someone detached from country style. I'm pretty sure their apparel is made with heavy-duty labor in mind. Back home, the brand is popular with the hipster crowd. I have a feeling this guy didn't choose the label to be trendy. Maybe he's more purposeful about his fashion statements than I'm giving him credit for. He makes a ball cap look ultra-sexy, regardless of his purpose. As if hearing my thoughts, his stare bores into me from the shadows under the curled brim.

The chance to offer a polite apology and salvage my manners is vanishing with each stilted breath. I nearly choke on the buckets of sand lodged in my throat. "Shit... I mean, shoot. I'm really sorry. Are you okay?"

Painful silence is all that greets me. It seems the stranger is too busy giving my body a full scan. I shift my weight from the blatant perusal. The need to fidget needles at me. *Is he sizing me up because I'm seriously lacking in the height department?* A tiny nudge from me certainly wouldn't result in serious damage—to his flexing physique or otherwise. To be fair, anyone over six feet makes me look like a shrimp. I wait several seconds for a response, but he remains disturbingly quiet.

Taking the hint, I creep toward a stack of small baskets and prepare to sulk off without causing further injury. "Um, okay then. I'll just be moving along."

He blinks at me, drawing attention to his alluring gaze.

"Wow, are you wearing contacts?" I squint at him like some sort of stage-five creeper.

If possible, his frown dips lower. "No."

"I'm aware that it's super weird for a stranger to randomly ask. Your eyes are just really blue."

"And yours are brown," he deadpans.

Speaking of, I'm not scoring any brownie points with this guy. "Solid observation. Isn't it rare to have light eyes with dark hair?"

"Can I question the same for your blond hair and dark eyes? Unless you use dye."

I gasp, twirling a loose strand around my finger, holding it out for inspection. "This color is natural, thank you very much. And I'm really leaving now. Sorry again for the bang."

There goes the remainder of my dignity. I press my lips together to trap more nonsense from spewing out, futile as it might seem. The damage is already wreaking havoc on my pride.

The man's harsh mask cracks, a slice of amusement twitching his lips. I catch a twinkle in his eyes while that slight humor grows into a crooked grin. My earlier assessment is no longer valid. He isn't the hardcore, surly sort, other than his resting dick face—also known as RDF, for future reference. It's almost a relief to see the expression I came across so often in high school and college. Without having to mutter a word, these guys would receive a wide berth from most. That skill is essential in chasing off unwanted attention, for themselves and others.

A dimple dents his cheek as he graces me with a full smile. The oxygen meant for my brain fizzles into a puff of smoke. As if this fella needs more ammunition to reel in the ladies.

"You're not from here."

I slap on a grin of my own to cover the undeniable scent of lust wafting off me. "Why is that so obvious?"

"Any lifer could sniff you out in an instant," he drawls. "We don't get a lot of visitors in our small section of paradise."

"No?"

"Not that look like you."

I almost recoil. "That's not very gentlemanly. Do you

make a habit of being rude to women in the entryway of the supermarket?"

My word vomit erases any progress I managed to make, not that he doesn't deserve it. But the stranger surprises me with a raspy chuckle.

"Nah, you're proving to be a special case."

"Should I be offended?"

"Not in the slightest, darling. I meant that as a compliment. You're so... shiny."

I glance down at my outfit, noticing an obvious lack of sparkle. "Like a new toy?"

He scrubs a hand over his mouth, hiding a smirk. "Not sure I'm bold enough to cross that line just yet."

"I'm not following."

He smooths a thumb over the bill of his hat. "You have a certain something that we don't see too often. We usually get truckers, farmers, and the occasional business suit eager to make deals. Crops of ladies looking to let loose pass through every now and then, but that's fairly rare."

I drop my gaze, taking a sudden interest in the checkered floor. "Well, all right."

"So, what brings you to Bam?"

"Bam?"

He motions around us. "The great Bampton Valley."

I track his gesture, still regaining my footing after receiving the heat of his focus aiming at me. "It definitely has some luster to enjoy."

"Only some? You wound me, woman." He clutches his chest, showing off the outline of an impressive pec.

"I take it you're a lifer?"

"Born and raised."

"Well." I offer him an outstretched hand. "It's nice to meet you. I'm Audria."

His loud whistle turns more than a few heads. "I should've

known the fancy lady has a name to match. Reeve Colton, at your service."

I raise a brow at that. "It's a pleasure."

A low sound rumbles from the depths of him. "I would hope so after you rammed into me."

"Oh, please. It was a light tap at worst."

Read their story today!

more titles from
HARLOE RAE

Ask Me Why: **A single dad, enemies-to-lovers romance**
One deep breath. Two slow blinks. Three hollow beats.
I'm still here.
After three years, that reminder isn't as necessary. But
everyone has their bad days. This is definitely one of
them. Until an adorable little boy dashes into my store.
His zest for life makes me smile in a way that's been
long lost. Then I meet his father.
Well, confront is more like it.

Brance Stone is volatile.
Offensive.
Harsh.
And can't be bothered to care.
Not that I want him to. I get frostbite just looking
into Brance's glacial stare. But there's something
undeniable about him.

My misery suddenly craves company. The suffocating
numbness lifts whenever Brance is near. That alone
should have me running in the opposite direction. Try
as I might, there's no avoiding him. If only I could
understand why. As if he'd let me.

I don't ask. He doesn't tell. A silent, bitter truce
settles between us.
That was our first mistake.
It's certainly not the last.

***Left for Wild*: A stranded/strangers to lovers romance**
Arrested. Wrongfully accused. Sentenced to ten years.
But the steel bars release me early.
After serving half of my time for a crime I didn't commit,
they grant me parole—with a very short leash. My second
chance at freedom begins now, and I won't waste it. I
should've been paying more attention.

Ambushed. Captured. Stranded.
When I wake in the depths of a snowy forest, all seems lost.
I've been left alone in the wilderness with zero means of
escape. Until someone rouses beside me.

I recognize Blakely Cross instantly, yet she's barely more than
a stranger. Now she's stuck with me in the worst possible
place, as collateral damage.

Blakely blames me, and rightfully so. This entire situation is
my fault. Our destinies are inadvertently twisted together by
forces far larger than us. Whether she hates me or not, we
need each other to stay alive.

Cope. Adapt. Persevere.
They tossed us out to be buried, but underestimated our
determination.
The bond we're building will overcome the harshest
conditions.
And we're not willing to surrender.

Breaker: a brother's best friend romance
"Tell me a happy something, Sutton."

I was only seven the first time Grady Bowen whispered those words to me. Cloaked by the black sky under a blanket of stars, it was easy to get lost. He didn't have any good memories of his own and needed to borrow mine. I would willingly give him anything.

Being infatuated with that boy was a beautiful curse. What could have been special didn't get the chance to bloom. He'd never see me as more than his best friend's kid sister. That was a hard lesson to learn, but not the most difficult.

Grady had always been struggling against the odds. Eventually he quit fighting and let his family's reputation own him. Try as I might, those influences were beyond my reach.

He didn't mean to break my heart. Or maybe he did. I shouldn't have made it so easy for him. Either way, our wrongs against each other carved new lines between us.

I went four years without seeing Grady—each one more painful than the last. That distance did nothing to dull my feelings toward him. But things are different now. Most noticeably is Grady. I barely recognize this man he's become. And that's the way he intends to keep it. Not that it really matters.

Grady Bowen stopped being my happy something long ago.

***Loner*: a single parent/enemies to lovers romance**
"Everyone deserves a chance to be rescued."

That's the mantra I'm repeating when a well-equipped biker pulls over to save me. One glance at the scowl Crawford Doxe is wearing proves he isn't impressed with the task. My efforts to change his mind deflate faster than the shredded tire at our feet. But disgruntled or not, my so-called hero still agrees to fix my flat.

I don't expect to see Crawford again, but he's suddenly very visible in our small town. Avoiding him would be my preference. That's not how this story goes. For whatever reason, my daughter finds an ally in the broody mechanic. Denying her is something I do my best to avoid. I can only hope Crawford's shine wears off before he tarnishes what little trust still exists.

As if the odds are ever on my side.

Commitments are a foreign concept to him. He doesn't make any promises to try. That should've been enough for me to steer clear. It most certainly isn't.

What follows can only be described as a disastrous clash of epic proportions.

But one indisputable fact remains. That lone soul has no plans of opening his heart.

GENT: An enemies to lovers standalone
Raven Elliot blasts into town like a wrecking ball—striking and devastating.
With a few simple words, my reliable routine crumbles to dust.

"Is this seat taken?"

I could close my eyes and let her voice wrap around me like a lover's caress.
But this isn't that type of story.
And I'm sure as hell not that kind of man.

She hovers in my space, batting her lashes and smiling shyly.
The glimmer in her sapphire eyes is a promise of peace.
But I'm not falling for it.
And Raven doesn't take the hint.

What starts as a battle of wills, explodes into a turf war.
She stands directly in my path everywhere I turn.
No matter how hard I shove, she won't budge.
Raven seems dead set on driving me insane.
But I was here first.
And I'm not going down easy.

After all, no one ever taught me how to treat a lady.

Watch Me Follow
A stalker, double virgin romance.

Creep. Freak. Crazy Eyes.
I've heard it all.
Over the years, they've slammed me with every demeaning
name in the book.
Their taunts warped me like a steady stream of poison.
Anger replaced anxiety as I started believing the
cruelty spat my way.
Until she showed up and changed everything.

Lennon Bennett is pure innocence—warm sunshine breaking
apart my stormy existence.
She's everything good and maybe I can be too.
For her. With her. Because of her.
Lennon doesn't know I'm beckoned closer with each breath.
She isn't aware that I'm completely consumed with her.
It's become my sole purpose to protect her,
by any means necessary.
But if she discovers the depth of my
obsession, it will be the end of me.
So, I remain in the shadows.
Waiting. Watching. Wanting.
She'll be my first. My last. My only.

Redefining Us
A standalone friends to lovers, military romance.

In order to truly save him, I need to redefine us.

Xander Dixon was my best friend.
Loyal and dependable.
A brave warrior.
A permanent presence in my life until that fateful day he
boarded a plane headed overseas.

Xander's unwelcome silence haunted me for three years...
Until he suddenly resurfaces.
Blinded by misplaced fury.
Trapped in a pool of darkness.
Unable to escape the perpetual pain.

Though it would be easy to walk away,
I refuse to give up on him.
I want to know his misery and torment, so I can rescue him.
Then Xander will finally be mine.

acknowledgements

This one hit me in the feels from the very start. The title alone fills me with such whimsy. I wanted to give Clea, Nolan, and little Tally a story full of hope—even where it didn't seem like there was much to find. There's Always Someday is a sentiment we can all hold close. Never give up on your dreams and fantasies. I'm hoping this story gave you a good boost in the positive.

I need to start by thanking my son, for he gave me all the inspiration for Tally's ridiculous humor. Her goofy phrases and silly mannerisms are all him. He helped me bring her character is life. A huge thanks to my husband for always supporting me and my baby girl for pushing me to strive for more.

To my readers… to YOU. Thank you SO MUCH for picking up my book to read. That alone never ceases to boggle my mind. I greatly appreciate your support.

Renee, I'd be lost without you. Not only do you keep me sane and manage my disorganization, but you're a very close friend. I'm so thankful to call you mine.

Kk and Heather—my bestest beeches. I love you both something fierce, enough to wake up at 3 am to catch a flight. Your friendship means everything to me. Thank you for being the greatest.

A big thanks, as always, to Talia with Book Cover Kingdom. My covers are always stunning thanks to you. Book after book, you manage to up the standard. I can't wait to see what we create next!

To Kate for always lending me an ear to ramble on about random nonsense. I'm so grateful for our friendship. Thank you for the daily doses of encouragement to get this book done.

I have been extremely fortunate to find genuine friendships in this crazy-amazing book world. Whenever I need a shoulder to lean on or a kind word or a quick boost, these ladies are there for me. I know I can turn to you, no matter what, and that kind of supportive comfort is priceless. Thank you to KL, Tia, Annie, Leigh, Ava, Michelle, Keri, Nicole, TJ, MPP, Lacie, BB, Ace, Suzie, Kandi, and many more. Your friendship is irreplaceable. Thank you, thank you.

An extra loud shoutout to my reader group—Harloe's Hotties—and my review crew. Because of you, my cup is always overflowing. If I'm ever having a bad day, I know I can turn to our special place on social media for a smile. That means more to me than words can describe. You're my people and I love you dearly!

Thank you to Candi Kane and her team at Candi Kane PR. She's such an unstoppable force and works tirelessly to ensure each release goes off without a hitch. I'm forever grateful. Also, a big thanks to the wonderful ladies at Give Me Books. Once again, your help for this release is invaluable and very much appreciated.

Thanks to Rafa, the very talented photographer who shot the sultry image of Alex to become the muse for Nolan. Isn't he the best?

Sending a huge thanks to Alex with Infinite Well for editing and polishing There's Always Someday until the story sparkled. It was great working with you to make this book even better!

Stacey from Champagne Book Design once again created the most stunning interior for my book baby. I cannot recommend her formatting services enough!

I can't end without sending out another massive round of thanks to all the readers, reviewers, bloggers, bookstagrammers, BookTokers, and romance lovers out there. Because of you, authors like me get to continue writing and doing what we love. You're who we strive to reach and aim to be better for. Thank you to infinity for continuing to be there for all of us!

And last but definitely not least, if you enjoyed There's Always Someday and want to do me a huge favor, please consider leaving a review. It really helps others find my books. Thank you for reading!

about the author

Harloe Rae is a *USA Today* & Amazon Top 10 best-selling author. Her passion for writing and reading has taken on a whole new meaning. Each day is an unforgettable adventure.

She's a Minnesota gal with a serious addiction to romance. There's nothing quite like an epic happily ever after. When she's not buried in the writing cave, Harloe can be found hanging with her hubby and kiddos. If the weather permits, she loves being lakeside or out in the country with her horses.

Harloe is the author of the Reclusive series, *Watch Me Follow*, the #BitterSweetHeat series, *Ask Me Why*, the Silo Springs series, *Left for Wild, Leave Him Loved*, and *Something Like Hate*. These titles are available on Amazon.

Stay in the know by subscribing to her newsletter at bit.ly/HarloesList

Join her reader group, Harloe's Hotties, at www.facebook.com/groups/harloehotties

Check out her site at www.harloe-rae.blog